TOMORROW,

AND TOMORROW,

AND TOMORROW

TOMORROW,

AND TOMORROW,

AND TOMORROW

GABRIELLE ZEVIN

ALFRED A. KNOPF   NEW YORK   2023

THIS IS A BORZOI BOOK
PUBLISHED BY ALFRED A. KNOPF

www.aaknopf.com

Knopf, Borzoi Books, and the colophon are registered
trademarks of Penguin Random House LLC.

Grateful acknowledgment is made to Harvard University Press
for permission to reprint "That Love is all there is" J 1765/F 1747 Source:
The Poems of Emily Dickinson: Reading Edition, edited by Ralph W. Franklin,
Cambridge, Mass.: The Belknap Press of Harvard University Press,
Copyright © 1998, 1999 by the President and Fellows of Harvard
College. Copyright © 1951, 1955, 1979, 1983 by the President and
Fellows of Harvard College.

Library of Congress Cataloging-in-Publication Data
Names: Zevin, Gabrielle, author.
Title: Tomorrow, and tomorrow, and tomorrow: a novel / Gabrielle Zevin.
Description: New York: Alfred A. Knopf, [2022]
Identifiers: LCCN 2021032441 (print) | LCCN 2021032442 (ebook) | ISBN 9780593321201
(hardcover) | ISBN 9780593466490 (trade paperback) | ISBN 9780593321218 (ebook) |
ISBN 9781524712228 (export edition)
Classification: LCC PS3626.E95 T66 2022 (print) | LCC PS3626.E95 (ebook) |
DDC 813/.6—dc23
LC record available at https://lccn.loc.gov/2021032441
LC ebook record available at https://lccn.loc.gov/2021032442

Jacket image: *The Great Wave* (detail) by Katsushika Hokusai.
The Metropolitan Museum of Art, New York
Jacket design by John Gall

Printed in the United States of America
Reprinted Fourteen Times
Sixteenth Printing, February 2023

Again, for H.C.—in work and in play

That Love is all there is,
Is all we know of Love;
It is enough, the freight should be
Proportioned to the groove.

—EMILY DICKINSON

CONTENTS

I

SICK KIDS

1

Before Mazer invented himself as Mazer, he was Samson Mazer, and before he was Samson Mazer, he was Samson Masur—a change of two letters that transformed him from a nice, ostensibly Jewish boy to a Professional Builder of Worlds—and for most of his youth, he was Sam, S.A.M. on the hall of fame of his grandfather's *Donkey Kong* machine, but mainly Sam.

On a late December afternoon, in the waning twentieth century, Sam exited a subway car and found the artery to the escalator clogged by an inert mass of people, who were gaping at a station advertisement. Sam was late. He had a meeting with his academic adviser that he had been postponing for over a month, but that everyone agreed absolutely needed to happen before winter break. Sam didn't care for crowds—being in them, or whatever foolishness they tended to enjoy en masse. But this crowd would not be avoided. He would have to force his way through it if he were to be delivered to the aboveground world.

Sam wore an elephantine navy wool peacoat that he had inherited from his roommate, Marx, who had bought it freshman year from the Army Navy Surplus Store in town. Marx had left it moldering in its plastic shopping bag just short of an entire semester before Sam asked if he might borrow it. That winter had been unrelenting, and it was an April nor'easter (April! What madness, these Massachusetts winters!) that finally wore Sam's pride down enough to ask Marx for the forgotten coat. Sam pretended that he liked the style of it, and Marx said that Sam might as well take it, which is what Sam knew he would say.

Like most things purchased from the Army Navy Surplus Store, the coat emanated mold, dust, and the perspiration of dead boys, and Sam tried not to speculate why the garment had been surplussed. But the coat was far warmer than the windbreaker he had brought from California his freshman year. He also believed that the large coat worked to conceal his size. The coat, its ridiculous scale, only made him look smaller and more childlike.

That is to say, Sam Masur at age twenty-one did not have a build for pushing and shoving and so, as much as possible, he weaved through the crowd, feeling somewhat like the doomed amphibian from the video game *Frogger*. He found himself uttering a series of "excuse mes" that he did not mean. A truly magnificent thing about the way the brain was coded, Sam thought, was that it could say "Excuse me" while meaning "Screw you." Unless they were unreliable or clearly established as lunatics or scoundrels, characters in novels, movies, and games were meant to be taken at face value—the totality of what they did or what they said. But people—the ordinary, the decent and basically honest—couldn't get through the day without that one indispensable bit of programming that allowed you to say one thing and mean, feel, even do, another.

"Can't you go around?" a man in a black and green macramé hat yelled at Sam.

"Excuse me," Sam said.

"Dammit, I almost had it," a woman with a baby in a sling muttered as Sam passed in front of her.

"Excuse me," Sam said.

Occasionally, someone would hastily leave, creating gaps in the crowd. The gaps should have been opportunities of escape for Sam, but somehow, they immediately filled with new humans, hungry for diversion.

He was nearly to the subway's escalator when he turned back to see what the crowd had been looking at. Sam could imagine reporting the congestion in the train station, and Marx saying, "Weren't you even curious what it was? There's a world of people and things, if you can manage to stop being a misanthrope for a second." Sam didn't like Marx thinking of him as a misanthrope, even if he was one, and so, he turned. That was when he espied his old comrade, Sadie Green.

It wasn't as if he hadn't seen her at all in the intervening years.

4

They had been habitués of science fairs, the Academic Games league, and numerous other competitions (oratory, robotics, creative writing, programming). Because whether you went to a mediocre public high school in the east (Sam), or a fancy private school in the west (Sadie), the Los Angeles smart-kid circuit was the same. They would exchange glances across a room of nerds—sometimes, she'd even smile at him, as if to corroborate their détente—and then she would be swept up in the vulturine circle of attractive, smart kids that always surrounded her. Boys and girls like himself, but wealthier, whiter, and with better glasses and teeth. And he did not want to be one more ugly, nerdy person hovering around Sadie Green. Sometimes, he would make a villain of her and imagine ways that she had slighted him: that time she had turned away from him; that time she had avoided his eyes. But she hadn't done those things—it would have been almost better if she had.

He had known that she had gone to MIT and had wondered if he might run into her when he got into Harvard. For two and a half years, he had done nothing to force such an occasion. Neither had she.

But there she was: Sadie Green, in the flesh. And to see her almost made him want to cry. It was as if she were a mathematical proof that had eluded him for many years, but all at once, with fresh, well-rested eyes, the proof had a completely obvious solution. *There's Sadie,* he thought. *Yes.*

He was about to call her name, but then he didn't. He felt overwhelmed by how much time had passed since he and Sadie had last been alone together. How could a person still be as young as he objectively knew himself to be and have had so much time pass? And why was it suddenly so easy to forget that he despised her? Time, Sam thought, was a mystery. But with a second's reflection, he thought better of such sentiment. Time was mathematically explicable; it was the heart—the part of the brain represented by the heart—that was the mystery.

Sadie finished staring at whatever the crowd was staring at, and now she was walking toward the inbound Red Line train.

Sam called her name, "SADIE!" In addition to the rumble of the incoming train, the station was roaring with the usual humanity. A teenage girl played Penguin Cafe Orchestra on a cello for tips. A man with a clipboard asked passersby if they could spare a moment for

Muslim refugees in Srebrenica. Adjacent to Sadie was a stand selling six-dollar fruit shakes. The blender had begun to whir, diffusing the scent of citrus and strawberries through the musty, subterranean air, just as Sam had first called her name. "Sadie Green!" he called out again. Still she didn't hear him. He quickened his pace, as much as he could. When he walked quickly, he counterintuitively felt like a person in a three-legged race.

"Sadie! SADIE!" He felt foolish. "SADIE MIRANDA GREEN! YOU HAVE DIED OF DYSENTERY!"

Finally, she turned. She scanned the crowd slowly and when she spotted Sam, the smile spread over her face like a time-lapse video he had once seen in a high school physics class of a rose in bloom. It was beautiful, Sam thought, and perhaps, he worried, a tad ersatz. She walked over to him, still smiling—one dimple on her right cheek, an almost imperceptibly wider gap between the two middle teeth on the top—and he thought that the crowd seemed to part for her, in a way that the world never moved for him.

"It's my sister who died of dysentery, Sam Masur," Sadie said. "I died of exhaustion, following a snakebite."

"And of not wanting to shoot the bison," Sam said.

"It's wasteful. All that meat just rots."

Sadie threw her arms around him. "Sam Masur! I kept hoping I'd run into you."

"I'm in the directory," Sam said.

"Well, maybe I hoped it would be organic," Sadie said. "And now it is."

"What brings you to Harvard Square?" Sam asked.

"Why, the Magic Eye, of course," she said playfully. She gestured in front of her, toward the advertisement. For the first time, Sam registered the 60-by-40-inch poster that had transformed commuters into a zombie horde.

SEE THE WORLD IN A WHOLE NEW WAY.
THIS CHRISTMAS, THE GIFT EVERYONE WANTS IS THE
MAGIC EYE.

The imagery on the poster was a psychedelic pattern in Christmas tones of emerald, ruby, and gold. If you stared at the pattern long enough, your brain would trick itself into seeing a hidden 3D image. It was called an autostereogram, and it was easy to make one if you were a modestly skilled programmer. *This?* Sam thought. *The things people find amusing.* He groaned.

"You disapprove?" Sadie said.

"This can be found in any dorm common room on campus."

"Not this particular one, Sam. This one's unique to—"

"Every train station in Boston."

"Maybe the U.S.?" Sadie laughed. "So, Sam, don't you want to see the world with magic eyes?"

"I'm always seeing the world with magic eyes," he said. "I'm exploding with childish wonder."

Sadie pointed toward a boy of about six: "Look how happy he is! He's got it now! Well done!"

"Have you seen it?" Sam asked.

"I didn't see it yet," Sadie admitted. "And now, I really do have to catch this next train, or I'll be late for class."

"Surely, you have another five minutes so that you can see the world with magic eyes," Sam said.

"Maybe next time."

"Come on, Sadie. There'll always be another class. How many times can you look at something and know that everyone around you is seeing the same thing or at the very least that their brains and eyes are responding to the same phenomenon? How much proof do you ever have that we're all in the same world?"

Sadie smiled ruefully and punched Sam lightly on the shoulder. "That was about the most Sam thing you could have said."

"Sam I am."

She sighed as she heard the rumble of her train leaving the station. "If I fail Advanced Topics in Computer Graphics, it's your fault." She repositioned herself so that she was looking at the poster again. "You do it with me, Sam."

"Yes, ma'am." Sam squared his shoulders, and he stared straight ahead. He had not stood this near to Sadie in years.

Directions on the poster said to relax one's eyes and to concentrate on a single point until a secret image emerged. If that didn't work, they suggested coming closer to the poster and then slowly backing up, but there wasn't room for that in the train station. In any case, Sam didn't care what the secret image was. He could guess that it was a Christmas tree, an angel, a star, though probably not a Star of David, something seasonal, trite, and broadly appealing, something meant to sell more Magic Eye products. Autostereograms had never worked for Sam. He theorized it was something to do with his glasses. The glasses, which corrected a significant myopia, wouldn't let his eyes relax enough for his brain to perceive the illusion. And so, after a respectable amount of time (fifteen seconds), Sam stopped trying to see the secret image and studied Sadie instead.

Her hair was shorter and more fashionable, he guessed, but it was the same mahogany waves that she'd always had. The light freckling on her nose was the same, and her skin was still olive, though she was much paler than when they were kids in California, and her lips were chapped. Her eyes were the same brown, with golden flecks. Anna, his mother, had had similar eyes, and she'd told Sam that coloration like this was called heterochromia. At the time, he had thought it sounded like a disease, something for his mother to potentially die from. Beneath Sadie's eyes were barely perceptible crescents, but then, she'd had these as a kid too. Still, he felt she seemed tired. Sam looked at Sadie, and he thought, *This is what time travel is.* It's looking at a person, and seeing them in the present and the past, concurrently. And that mode of transport only worked with those one had known a significant time.

"I saw it!" she said. Her eyes were bright, and she wore an expression he remembered from when she was eleven.

Sam quickly turned his gaze back to the poster.

"Did you see it?" she asked.

"Yes," he said. "I saw it."

Sadie looked at him. "What did you see?"

"It," Sam said. "It was amazingly great. Terribly festive."

"Did you actually see it?" Sadie's lips were twitching upward. Those heterochromic eyes looked at him with mirth.

"Yes, but I don't want to spoil it for anyone else who hasn't." He gestured toward the horde.

"Okay, Sam," Sadie said. "That's thoughtful of you."

He knew she knew that he hadn't seen it. He smiled at her, and she smiled at him.

"Isn't it strange?" Sadie said. "I feel like I never stopped seeing you.

I feel like we come down to this T station to stare at this poster every day."

"We grok," Sam said.

"We do grok. And I take back what I said before. That is the Sammest thing you could have said."

"Sammest I Ammest. You're—" As he was speaking, the blender began to whir again.

"What?" she said.

"You're in the wrong square," he repeated.

"What's the 'wrong square'?"

"You're in Harvard Square, when you should be in Central Square or Kendall Square. I think I heard you'd gone to MIT."

"My boyfriend lives around here," Sadie said, in a way that indicated she had no more she wished to say on that subject. "I wonder why they're called squares. They're not really squares, are they?" Another inbound train was approaching. "That's my train. Again."

"That's how trains work," Sam said.

"It's true. There's a train, and a train, and a train."

"In which case, the only proper thing for us to do right now is have coffee," Sam said. "Or whatever you drink, if coffee's too much of a cliché for you. Chai tea. Matcha. Snapple. Champagne. There's a world with infinite beverage possibilities, right over our heads, you know? All we have to do is ride that escalator and it's ours for the partaking."

"I wish I could, but I have to get to class. I've done maybe half the reading. The only thing I have going for me is my punctuality and attendance."

"I doubt that," Sam said. Sadie was one of the most brilliant people he knew.

She gave Sam another quick hug. "Good running into you."

She started walking toward the train, and Sam tried to figure out a way to make her stop. If this were a game, he could hit pause. He could restart, say different things, the right ones this time. He could search his inventory for the item that would make Sadie not leave.

They hadn't even exchanged phone numbers, he thought desperately. His mind cycled through the ways a person could find a person in 1995. In the old days, when Sam was a child, people could be lost forever, but people were not as easily lost as they once were. Increasingly, all you needed was the desire to convert a person from a digital conjecture to the unruly flesh. So, he comforted himself that even though the figure of his old friend was growing smaller and smaller in the train station, the world was trending in the same direction—what, with globalization, the information superhighway, and the like. It would be easy to find Sadie Green. He could guess her email—MIT emails followed the same pattern. He could search the MIT directory online. He could call the Computer Science Department—he was assuming computer science. He could call her parents, Steven Green and Sharyn Friedman-Green, in California.

And yet, he knew himself and he knew he was the type of person that never called anyone, unless he was absolutely certain the advance would be welcomed. His brain was treacherously negative. He would invent that she had been cold toward him, that she hadn't even had a class that day, that she had simply wanted to get away from Sam. His brain would insist that if she'd wanted to see him, she would have given him a way to contact her. He would conclude that, to Sadie, Sam represented a painful period of her life, and so, of course, she didn't want to see him again. Or, maybe, as he'd often suspected, he meant nothing to her—he had been a rich girl's good deed. He would dwell on the mention of a boyfriend in Harvard Square. He would track down her number, her email address, her physical address, and he would never use any of them. And so, with a phenomenological heaviness, he realized that this very well could be the last time he ever saw Sadie Green, and he tried to memorize the details of what she looked like, walking away, in a train station, on a bitter cold day in December. Beige cashmere hat, mittens, and scarf. Camel-colored three-quarter-length peacoat, most definitely not from the Army Navy Surplus Store. Blue jeans, quite worn, irregularly fraying boot-cut at the bottom. Black sneakers with a white stripe. Cognac leather crossbody messenger bag that was as wide as she was, and overstuffed, the arm of an ecru sweater sticking out the side. Her hair—shiny, lightly damp, just past her shoulder blades. There was no echt Sadie in this view, he decided. She looked indistinguishable from any number of smart, well-maintained college girls in the train station.

On the verge of disappearing, she turned, and she ran back to him. "Sam!" she said. "Do you still game?"

"Yes," Sam answered with too much enthusiasm. "Definitely. All the time."

"Here." She pressed a 3.25-inch disk into his hands. "This is my game. You're probably super busy but give it a play if you have the time. I'd love to know what you think."

She ran back into the train, and Sam trailed after her. "Wait! Sadie! How do I get in touch with you?"

"My email's on the disk," Sadie said. "In the Readme."

The train doors closed, returning Sadie to her square. Sam looked down at the disk: the title of the game was *Solution*. She had hand-written the label. He would know her handwriting anywhere.

When he got back to the apartment later that night, he didn't immediately install *Solution*, though he did set it next to the disk drive of his computer. He found *not playing* Sadie's game to be a great motivator, though, and he worked on his junior paper proposal, which was already a month overdue, and which would have, at that point, waited until after the holidays. His topic, after much wringing of hands, was "Alternative Approaches to the Banach-Tarski Paradox in the Absence of the Axiom of Choice," and as he was quite bored writing the proposal, he actively feared the drudgery that writing the paper would entail. He had begun to suspect that while he had an obvious aptitude for math, he was not particularly inspired by it. His adviser in the Mathematics Department, Anders Larsson, who would go on to win a Fields Medal, had said as much in that afternoon's meeting. His parting words: "You're incredibly gifted, Sam. But it is worth noting that to be good at something is not quite the same as loving it."

Sam ate takeout Italian food with Marx—Marx over-ordered so that Sam would have leftovers to eat while Marx was out of town. Marx re-extended an invitation to come skiing with him in Telluride over the holidays: "You really should come, and if it's the skiing you're worried about, everyone mostly hangs out in the lodge anyway." Sam rarely had enough money to go home for the holidays, and so these invitations were extended and rejected at regular intervals. After dinner, Sam started the reading for his Moral Reasoning class (the class was studying the philosophy of the young Wittgenstein, the era before he'd decided he was wrong about everything), and Marx organized himself to go away for the break. When Marx was finished packing, he wrote out a holiday card to Sam and left it on his desk, along with a fifty-dollar gift certificate to the brew house. That was when Marx came across the disk.

"What's *Solution*?" Marx asked. He picked up the green disk and held it out to Sam.

"It's my friend's game," Sam said.

"What friend?" Marx said. They had lived together for going on three years, and Marx had rarely known Sam to mention any friends.

"My friend from California."

"Are you going to play it?"

"Eventually. It'll probably suck. I'm only looking at it, as a favor." Sam felt like he was betraying Sadie saying that, but it probably would suck.

"What's it about?" Marx said.

"No idea."

"Cool title, though." Marx sat down at Sam's computer. "I've got a couple of minutes. Should we boot it up?"

"Why not?" Though Sam had been planning to play alone, Marx and he gamed together with some regularity. They favored martial arts video games: *Mortal Kombat, Tekken, Street Fighter*. They also had a Dungeons & Dragons campaign that they picked up from time to time. The campaign, for which Sam was dungeon master, had been going on for over two years. Playing Dungeons & Dragons in a group of two people is a peculiar, intimate experience, and the existence of the campaign was kept a secret from everyone they knew.

Marx put the disk in the machine, and Sam installed it on his hard drive.

Several hours later, Sam and Marx were done with their first play-through of *Solution*.

"What the hell *was* that?" Marx said. "I'm so late getting to Ajda's place. She's going to kill me." Ajda was Marx's latest paramour—a five-eleven squash player and occasional model from Turkey, an average résumé for one of Marx's love interests. "I honestly thought we'd play for five minutes."

Marx put on his coat—camel colored, like Sadie's. "Your friend is sick as hell. And maybe, a genius. How do you know him again?"

12

2

On the day Sadie first met Sam, she had been banished from her older sister Alice's hospital room. Alice was moody in the way of thirteen-year-olds, but she was also moody in the way of people who might be dying of cancer. Their mother, Sharyn, said that Alice should be given a great deal of latitude, that the dual storm fronts of puberty and illness were a lot for one body to grapple with. *A great deal of latitude* meant Sadie should go into the waiting area until Alice was no longer angry with her.

Sadie was not entirely sure what she had done to provoke Alice this time. She had shown Alice a picture in *Teen* magazine of a girl in a red beret and said something to the effect of *You would look good in this hat.* Sadie barely remembered what she had said, but whatever it was, Alice hadn't taken it well, screaming absurdly, *No one wears hats like that in Los Angeles! This is why you don't have any friends, Sadie Green!* Alice had gone into the bathroom and started crying, which sounded like choking, because her nose was congested and her throat was coated in sores. Sharyn, who had been sleeping in the bedside chair, told Alice to calm down, that she would make herself sick. *I'm already sick,* Alice said. At this point, Sadie started crying, too—she knew she didn't have any friends, but it was still mean of Alice to point it out. Sharyn told Sadie to go to the waiting area.

"It's not fair," Sadie had said to her mother. "I didn't *do* anything. She's being completely unreasonable."

"It isn't fair," Sharyn agreed.

In exile, Sadie tried to puzzle out what had happened—she honestly had thought Alice *would* look good in a red hat. But upon reflection, she determined that, by mentioning the hat, Alice must have thought Sadie was saying something about Alice's hair, which had grown thin from the chemotherapy. And if that's what Alice thought, Sadie felt sorry that she had ever mentioned the stupid hat in the first place. She went to knock on Alice's hospital door to apologize. Through the glass panel on her window, Sharyn mouthed, "Come back later. Alice is sleeping."

Around lunchtime, Sadie felt hungry and, thus, somewhat less sorry for Alice and sorrier for herself. It was irritating the way Alice acted like an asshole and Sadie was the one who was punished. As Sadie had repeatedly been told, Alice was sick, but she was not dying. Alice's variety of leukemia had a particularly high remission rate. She had been responding well to treatment, and she'd probably even be able to start high school, on schedule, in the fall. Alice would only have to be in the hospital for two nights this time, and it was only out of, according to her mother, "an abundance of caution." Sadie liked the phrase "an abundance of caution." It reminded her of a murder of crows, a flock of seagulls, a pack of wolves. She imagined that "caution" was a creature of some kind—maybe, a cross between a Saint Bernard and an elephant. A large, intelligent, friendly animal that could be counted on to defend the Green sisters from threats, existential and otherwise.

A nurse, noticing the unattended, conspicuously healthy eleven-year-old in the waiting room, gave Sadie a vanilla pudding cup. He recognized Sadie as one of the many neglected siblings of sick kids and suggested that she might like to use the game room. There was a Nintendo console, he promised, which was rarely used on weekday afternoons. Sadie and Alice already had a Nintendo, but Sadie had nothing else to do for the next five hours until Sharyn could drive her back home. It was summer, and she had already finished reading *The Phantom Tollbooth* for the second time, which was the only book she'd brought with her that day. If Alice hadn't gotten pissed off, the day would have been filled with their usual activities: watching their favorite morning game shows, *Press That Button!* and *The Price Is Right*; reading *Seventeen* magazine and giving each other personality quizzes; playing *Oregon Trail* or any of the other educational games that had come preloaded on the twenty-pound laptop computer Alice had been given to do her makeup school work; and the myriad casual ways the girls had always found to pass time together. Sadie might not have many friends, but she'd never felt that she needed them: Alice was ne plus ultra. No one was cleverer, more daring, more beautiful, more athletic, more hilarious, more fill-in-the-adjective-of-your-choice than Alice. Even though they insisted Alice would recover, Sadie often found herself imagining a world that didn't have Alice in it. A world that lacked shared jokes and music and sweaters and par-baked brownies and sister skin casually against sister skin, under the blankets, in the darkness, and most of all, lacking Alice, the keeper of the innermost secrets and shames of Sadie's innocent heart. There was no one Sadie loved more than Alice, not her parents, not her grandmother. The world sans Alice was bleak, like a grainy photograph of Neil Armstrong on the moon, and it kept the eleven-year-old up late at night. It would be a relief to escape into the world of Nintendo for a while.

But the game room was not empty. A boy was playing *Super Mario Bros.* Sadie determined he was a sick kid, and not a sibling or a visitor like herself: he was wearing pajamas in the middle of the day, a pair of crutches rested on the floor beside his chair, and his left foot was surrounded by a medieval-looking cage-like contraption. She estimated the boy was her age, eleven, or a little older. He had tangled curly black hair, a puggish nose, glasses, a cartoonishly round head. In Sadie's art class at school, she had been taught to draw by breaking things down into basic shapes. To depict this boy, she would have needed mainly circles.

She sat on the floor next to him and watched him play. He was skilled—at the end of the level, he could make Mario land at the top of the flagpole, something Sadie had never mastered. Although Sadie liked to be the player, there was a pleasure to watching someone who was a dexterous player—it was like watching a dance. He never looked over at her. Indeed, he didn't seem to notice she was there. He cleared the first boss battle, and the words BUT OUR PRINCESS IS IN ANOTHER CASTLE appeared on the screen. Without looking over at her, he said, "You want to play the rest of this life?"

Sadie shook her head. "No. You're doing really well. I can wait until you're dead."

The boy nodded. He continued to play, and Sadie continued to watch.

"Before. I shouldn't have said that," Sadie apologized. "I mean, in case you are actually dying. This being a children's hospital."

The boy, piloting Mario, climbed up a vine that led to a cloudy, coin-filled area. "This being the world, everyone's dying," he said.

"True," Sadie said.

"But I'm not currently dying."

"That's good."

"Are you dying?" the boy asked.

"No," Sadie said. "Not currently."

"What's wrong with you, then?"

"It's my sister. She's sick."

"What's wrong with her?"

"Dysentery." Sadie didn't feel like invoking cancer, the destroyer of natural conversation.

The boy looked at Sadie as if he were going to ask a follow-up question. But instead, he handed the controller to her. "Here. My thumbs are tired anyway."

Sadie acquitted herself well through the level, powering up Mario and adding another life.

"You're not that bad," the boy said.

"We have a Nintendo at home, but I'm only allowed to play it an hour a week," Sadie said. "But no one pays attention to me anymore, since my sister Al got sick . . ."

"Dysentery," the boy filled in.

"Yeah. I was supposed to go to Space Camp in Florida this summer, but my parents decided I should stay home to keep Al company." Sadie ground pounded a Goomba, one of the mushroom-like creatures that were abundant in Super Mario. "I feel bad for the Goombas."

"They're just henchmen," the boy said.

"But it feels like they've gotten mixed up in something that has nothing to do with them."

"That's the life of a henchman. Go down that pipe," the boy instructed. "There's a bunch of coins down there."

"I know! I'm getting to it," Sadie said. "Al seems annoyed with me most of the time, so I don't know why I couldn't go to Space Camp.

It would have been my first time at overnight camp and my first time flying alone on a plane. It was only going to be for two weeks anyway." Sadie was nearing the end of the level. "What's the secret to landing high on the flagpole?"

"Hold down the run button as long as you can, then crouch down and jump just before you're about to fall," the boy said.

Sadie/Mario landed on the top of the flagpole. "Hey, it worked. I'm Sadie, by the way."

"Sam."

"Your turn." She returned the controller to him. "What's wrong with you?" she asked.

"I was in a car accident," Sam said. "My foot is broken in twenty-seven places."

"That's a lot of places," Sadie said. "Are you exaggerating, or is that the number?"

"It's the number. I'm very particular about numbers."

"Me too."

"But sometimes the number goes up slightly because they have to break other parts of it to reset it," Sam said. "They might have to cut it off. I can't stand on it at all. I've already had three surgeries and it's not even a foot. It's a flesh bag, with bone chips in it."

"Sounds delicious," Sadie said. "Sorry, if that was gross. Your description made me think of potato chips. We skip a lot of meals since my sister got sick, and I don't think anyone would even notice if I starved to death. All I've had today is a pudding cup."

"You're weird, Sadie," Sam said, with interest in his voice.

"I know," Sadie said. "I really hope they don't have to amputate your foot, Sam. My sister has cancer, by the way."

"I thought she had dysentery."

"Well, the cancer treatment gives her dysentery. The dysentery thing's kind of a joke between us. Do you know that computer game *Oregon Trail*?"

"Possibly." Sam avoided a direct admission of ignorance.

"It's probably in the computer lab at your school. It's, maybe, my favorite game, even though it's a little boring. It's about these people in the 1800s, and they're trying to get from the East Coast to the West Coast, in a wagon, with a couple of oxen, and the goal is to make it so everyone in your party doesn't die. You have to feed them enough, not go too fast, buy the right supplies, stuff like that. But sometimes, someone, or even you, still dies, like of a rattlesnake bite, or starvation, or—"

"Dysentery."

"Yes! Exactly. And this always makes me and Al laugh."

"What *is* dysentery?" Sam asked.

"It's diarrhea," Sadie whispered. "We didn't know at first either."

Sam laughed, but just as abruptly, he stopped laughing. "I'm still laughing," he said. "But it hurts when I laugh."

"I promise not to say anything funny ever again, then," Sadie said, in an odd, emotionless voice.

"Stop! That voice is going to make me laugh even more. What are you even trying to be?"

"A robot."

"A robot sounds like this." Sam did his impression of a robot, which cracked them up all over again.

"You're not supposed to laugh!" Sadie said.

"You're not supposed to *make me* laugh. Do people truly die of dysentery?" Sam asked.

"In the olden days, I guess they did."

"Do you think they put it on people's tombstones?"

"I don't think they put cause of death on tombstones, Sam."

"At the Haunted Mansion at Disneyland, they do. I kind of hope I die of dysentery now. Shall we switch to playing *Duck Hunt*?"

Sadie nodded.

"You'll have to set up the guns. They're right up there." Sadie retrieved the light guns and plugged them into the console. She let Sam shoot first.

"You're fantastically good," she said. "Do you have a Nintendo at home?"

"No," Sam said, "but my grandfather has a *Donkey Kong* machine in his restaurant. He lets me play as much as I want for free. And the thing about games is, if you get good at one game, you can be good at any game. That's what I think. They're all hand-eye coordination and observing patterns."

"I agree. And *what*? Your grandfather owns a *Donkey Kong* machine? That is so cool! I love those old machines. What kind of restaurant is it?"

"It's a pizza place," Sam said.

"*What?* I love pizza! It's my favorite food on earth. Can you eat all the pizza you want for free?"

Sam nodded while expertly annihilating two ducks.

"That's, like, my dream. You're living my actual dream. You have to let me go with you, Sam. What's the name of the restaurant? Maybe I've already been to it."

"Dong and Bong's New York Style House of Pizza. Dong and Bong are my grandparents' names. It's not even funny in Korean. It's like being called Jack and Jill," Sam said. "The restaurant is on Wilshire in K-town."

"What's K-town?"

"Lady, are you even from Los Angeles? K-town is Koreatown. How do you not know that?" Sam said. "Everyone knows K-town."

"I know what Koreatown is. I didn't know people called it K-town."

"Where do you live anyway?" Sam asked.

"The flats."

"What are the flats?"

"It's the flat part of Beverly Hills," Sadie said. "It's pretty close to K-town. See, you didn't know what the flats were! People in L.A. only ever know about the part of town that they live in."

"I guess you're right."

For the rest of the afternoon, Sam and Sadie chatted amiably while slaughtering several generations of virtual ducks. "What did the ducks ever do to us?" Sadie commented.

"Maybe we're shooting them for digital food. The digital usses will starve without the virtual ducks."

"Still, I feel bad for the ducks."

"You feel bad for the Goombas. You basically feel bad for everyone," Sam said.

"I do," Sadie said. "I also feel bad for the bison in *Oregon Trail.*"

"Why?" Sam asked.

Sadie's mother poked her head into the game room: Alice had something she wanted to tell Sadie, which was code for Sadie having been forgiven. "I'll tell you next time," Sadie said to Sam, though she didn't know if there would ever be a next time.

"See you around," Sam said.

"Who's your little friend?" Sharyn asked as they were leaving.

"Some boy." Sadie looked back at Sam, who had already returned his attention to the game. "He was nice."

On the way to Alice's room, Sadie thanked the nurse who had told her to use the game room. The nurse smiled at Sadie's mother—manners were honestly somewhat rare in kids these days. "Was it empty like I said?"

"No, a boy was in there. Sam . . ." She didn't know his last name yet.

"You met Sam?" The nurse's sudden interest made Sadie wonder if she had broken a secret hospital rule by occupying the game room when a sick kid had wanted to use it. There were so many rules since Alice had gotten cancer.

"Yes," Sadie tried to explain. "We talked and played Nintendo. He didn't seem to mind that I was there."

"Sam, with the curly hair and glasses. That Sam?"

Sadie nodded.

The nurse asked to speak to Sharyn alone, and Sharyn told Sadie to go on ahead to Alice.

When Sadie opened the door to Alice's room, she felt uneasy. "I think I'm in trouble," she announced.

"What did you do now?" Alice said. Sadie explained her theoretical crime. "They *told* you to use it," Alice reasoned, "so, you can't have done anything wrong."

Sadie sat on Alice's bed, and Alice started braiding her hair.

"I bet that's not even why the nurse wanted to speak to Mom," Alice continued. "It could have been about me. Which nurse was it?"

"I don't know."

"Don't worry, kid. If it turns out you *are* in trouble, cry and say your sister has cancer."

"Sorry about the whole hat thing," Sadie said.

"What hat thing? Oh, right. My fault. I don't know what's wrong with me."

"Leukemia, probably," Sadie said.

"Dysentery," Alice corrected.

By the time they were on the drive back home, Sharyn had still not mentioned the game room, and Sadie was reasonably confident that the incident had been forgotten. They were listening to an NPR story about the centenary of the Statue of Liberty, and Sadie was thinking how awful it would be if the Statue of Liberty were an actual woman. How strange it would be to have people inside you. The people would feel like invaders, like a disease, like head lice or cancer. The thought disturbed her, and Sadie was relieved when her mother turned off the radio. "You know that boy you were talking to today?"

Here it is, Sadie thought. "Yes," Sadie said quietly. She noted that they were passing through K-town and she tried to spot Dong and Bong's New York Style House of Pizza. "I'm not in trouble, am I?"

"No. Why would you be in trouble?"

Because lately, Sadie was almost always in trouble. It was impossible to be eleven, with a sick sister, and for people to find your conduct beyond reproach. She was always saying the wrong thing, or being too loud, or demanding too much (time, love, food), even though she had not demanded more than what had been freely given before. "No reason."

"The nurse told me he was in a horrific car accident," Sharyn continued. "He hasn't said more than two words to anyone in the six weeks since he was injured. He's been in terrible pain, and he'll probably have to be in and out of the hospital for a very long time. It was a big deal that he talked to you."

"Really? Sam seemed pretty normal to me."

"They've been trying everything to make him open up. Therapists, friends, family. What did you two talk about?"

"I don't know. Nothing much." She tried to remember their conversation. "Games, I guess?"

"Well, this is entirely up to you," Sharyn said. "But the nurse wondered if you might come back tomorrow to talk to Sam again." Before Sadie had time to respond, Sharyn added, "I know you have to do community service for your Bat Mitzvah next year, and I'm sure this would probably count."

To allow yourself to play with another person is no small risk. It means allowing yourself to be open, to be exposed, to be hurt. It is the human equivalent of the dog rolling on its back—*I know you won't hurt me, even though you can.* It is the dog putting its mouth around your hand and never biting down. To play requires trust and love. Many years later, as Sam would controversially say in an interview with the gaming website *Kotaku,* "There is no more intimate act than play, even sex." The internet responded: no one who had had good sex

21

would ever say that, and there must be something seriously wrong with Sam.

Sadie went to the hospital the next day, and the next day, and the next day, and then whatever days Sam was well enough to play but sick enough to be in the hospital. They would become great playmates. They competed sometimes, but they took their greatest pleasure from copiloting a single player character, passing a keyboard or a controller back and forth between them while discussing the ways they could ease this virtual person's journey through an inevitably perilous game world. While they gamed, they told each other the stories of their relatively short lives. Eventually, Sadie knew everything about Sam, and Sam, about Sadie. They thought they did, at least. She taught him the programming she'd picked up at school (BASIC, a little Pascal) and he expanded her drawing technique beyond circles and squares (crosshatching, perspective, chiaroscuro). Even at twelve, he was an excellent draftsman.

Since the accident, Sam had begun making intricate, M. C. Escher–style mazes. His psychologist encouraged him, believing that mazes could help Sam deal with his significant physical and emotional pain. She interpreted the mazes as a hopeful indication that Sam was plotting a way beyond his current situation. But the doctor was wrong. Sam's mazes were always for Sadie. He would slip one into her pocket before she left. "I made this for you," he'd say. "It's nothing much. Bring it back next time so I can see the solution."

Sam would later tell people that these mazes were his first attempts at writing games. "A maze," he would say, "is a video game distilled to its purest form." Maybe so, but this was revisionist and self-aggrandizing. The mazes were for Sadie. To design a game is to imagine the person who will eventually play it.

At the end of each visit, Sadie would stealthily present a timesheet to one of the nurses to sign. Most friendships cannot be quantified, but the form provided a log of the exact number of hours Sadie had spent being friends with Sam.

It was several months into Sam and Sadie's friendship when Sadie's grandmother, Freda, first broached the subject of whether Sadie was truly doing community service or not. Freda Green often chauffeured Sadie to the hospital to see Sam. She drove a red, American-made convertible, with the top down if weather permitted (in Los Angeles, it usually did) and a silk printed scarf in her hair. She was barely five feet, only an inch taller than the eleven-year-old Sadie, but she was always dressed impeccably in the bespoke clothes she bought in Paris once a year: crisp white blouses, soft gray wool pants, bouclé or cashmere sweaters. She was never without her hexagonal weapon of a leather handbag, her scarlet lipstick, her delicate gold wristwatch, her tuberose-scented perfume, her pearls. Sadie thought she was the most stylish woman in the world. In addition to being Sadie's grandmother, Freda was also a Los Angeles real estate tycoon, with a reputation for being terrifying and unfailingly scrupulous in business negotiations.

"Mine Sadie," she said as they drove from the west to the east. "You know I am overjoyed to drive you to the hospital."

"Thanks, Bubbe. I appreciate it."

"But, I think, based on what you have told me, that the boy might be more of a friend."

The waterlogged community service form had been sticking out of her math book, and Sadie tucked it inside. "It was Mom's idea," Sadie defended herself. "The nurses and doctors say I'm helping. Last week, his grandfather gave me a hug *and* a slice of mushroom pizza. I don't see what's wrong with it."

"Yes, but the boy doesn't know about the arrangement, am I right?"

"No," Sadie said. "It never came up."

"And do you think there might be a reason you haven't brought it up?"

"When I'm with Sam, we're busy," Sadie said lamely.

"Darling, it may come out later, and it could hurt your friend's feelings, if he thinks he is a charity to you, and not a genuine friendship."

"Can't something be both?" Sadie said.

"Friendship is friendship, and charity is charity," Freda said. "You know very well that I was in Germany as a child, and you have heard the stories, so I won't tell them to you again. But I can tell you that the people who give you charity are never your friends. It is not possible to receive charity *from* a friend."

"I hadn't thought of it that way," Sadie said.

Freda stroked Sadie's hand. "Mine Sadie. This life is filled with inescapable moral compromises. We should do what we can to avoid the easy ones."

Sadie knew that Freda was right. Still, she continued to present the timesheet for signature. She liked the ritual of it, and she liked the praise she received—from the nurses and sometimes the doctors, but also from her parents and the people at her temple. There was even a minor pleasure to filling out the log itself. It was a game to her, and she didn't think the game had much to do with Sam himself. It wasn't a deception, per se. She wasn't hiding the fact of her community service from Sam, but the longer it went on, the less she felt that she could ever tell him. She knew that the presence of the timesheet made it seem as if she had an ulterior motive, though the truth was obvious to her: Sadie Green liked being praised, and Sam Masur was the best friend she had ever had.

Sadie's community service project went on for fourteen months. Predictably, it ended the day Sam discovered its existence. Their friendship amounted to 609 hours, plus the 4 hours of the first day, which had not been part of the tally. A Bat Mitzvah at Temple Beth El required only 20 hours of community service, and Sadie was given an award by the fine women of Hadassah for her exceptional record of good works.

3

The Advanced Games seminar met once a week, Thursday afternoons from two to four. There were only ten spots, and students were accepted by application. The seminar was led by twenty-eight-year-old Dov Mizrah, surname in the course catalog, but known only by his given name in gaming circles. It was said of Dov that he was like the two Johns (Carmack, Romero), the American boy wonders who'd programmed and designed *Commander Keen* and *Doom*, rolled into one. Dov was famous for his mane of dark, curly hair, wearing tight leather pants to gaming conventions, and yes, a game called *Dead Sea*, an underwater zombie adventure, originally for PC, for which he had invented a groundbreaking graphics engine, Ulysses, to render photorealistic light and shadow in water. Sadie, and about five hundred thousand other nerds, had played *Dead Sea* the prior summer. Dov was the first professor she'd ever had whose work she had enjoyed *before* she'd taken the class, not *because* she'd taken the class. Gamers, like herself, were avidly awaiting a sequel to *Dead Sea*, and when she saw his name in the course catalog, she had wondered why someone like him had wanted to interrupt a brilliant career designing games to teach.

"Look," Dov said on the first day of the seminar, "I'm not here to teach you how to program. This is an advanced games seminar at MIT. You already know how to program, and if you don't . . ." He gestured toward the door.

The format for the class was not unlike a creative writing class. Each week, two of the students would bring in a game, a simple game or a part of a longer game, whatever could be feasibly programmed given the time constraints. The others would play the games, and then they'd critique them. The students were responsible for making two games during the semester.

Hannah Levin, the only girl in the seminar besides Sadie (though this was an ordinary male-to-female class ratio at MIT), asked if Dov cared which programming language they used.

"Why would I care? They're all identical. They all can suck my dick. And I mean that literally. You have to make whatever programming language you use suck your dick. It needs to serve you." Dov looked over at Hannah. "You don't have a dick, so clit, whatever. Pick the programming language that is going to make you come."

Hannah laughed nervously and avoided Dov's eyes. "So, Java is good?" Hannah said quietly. "Some people I know don't, like, respect Java, but—"

"*Respect* Java? Seriously, fuck whoever said that. Whatever. Pick the programming language that is going to make *me* come," Dov added.

"Yes, but if there's one you prefer."

"Dude, what's your name?"

"Hannah Levin."

"Dude, Hannah Levin. You have to chill out. I'm not interested in telling you *how* to make your game. Use three programming languages for all I care. That's how I do it. I write some, and if I'm blocked, I'll sometimes work in another language for a while. That's what compilers are for. Does anyone else have any questions?"

Sadie found Dov vulgar, repellent, and a little sexy.

"The idea is to blow each other's minds," Dov said. "I don't want to see versions of my games, or any other games I've already played. I don't want to see pretty pictures without any thought behind them. I don't want to see coding that is seamless in service of worlds that are uninteresting. I hate hate hate hate hate being bored. Astonish me. Disturb me. Offend me. It's not possible to offend me."

After class, Sadie went up to Hannah. "Hey, Hannah, I'm Sadie. Kind of rough in there, right?"

"It was fine," Hannah said.

"Have you played *Dead Sea*? It's amazing."

"What's *Dead Sea*?"

26

"It's his game. It's, you know, the whole reason I'm in this class. The main POV is this little girl, who is the lone survivor of—"

Hannah interrupted. "I guess I should check it out."

"You should. What kind of games do you play?" Sadie said.

Hannah frowned. "Yeah, sorry, I have to run. Nice meeting you!"

Sadie didn't know why she bothered. You would think women would want to stick together when there weren't that many of them, but they never did. It was as if being a woman was a disease that you didn't wish to catch. As long as you didn't associate with the other women, you could imply to the majority, the men: *I'm not like those other ones.* Sadie was, by nature, a loner, but even she found going to MIT in a female body to be an isolating experience. The year Sadie was admitted to MIT, women were slightly over a third of her class, but somehow, it felt like even less than that. Sadie sometimes felt as if she could go weeks without seeing a woman. It might have been that the men, most of them at least, assumed you were stupid if you were a woman. Or, if not stupid, less smart than they were. They were operating under the assumption that it was easier to get into MIT if you were a woman, and statistically, it was—women had a 10 percent higher admittance rate over men. But there could have been many reasons for that statistic. A likely one was self-elimination: female applicants to MIT might have held themselves to higher standards than male applicants. The conclusion should not have been that the women who got into MIT were less gifted, less worthy of their places, and yet, that seemed to be what it was.

Sadie had the fortune or the misfortune of being the seventh student to present a game that semester. She had struggled with what to program. She had wanted to make a statement about the kind of designer she was going to be. She didn't want to present something that seemed cliché, or too genre, or too simplistic, graphically or in a ludic sense. But after seeing her fellow seminarians be eviscerated by Dov, she knew that it barely mattered what she presented. Dov hated everything. He hated variations on *Dungeons & Dragons* and turn-based RPGs. He hated platformers, other than *Super Mario,* though he loathed gaming consoles. He hated sports. He hated cute animals. He hated games based on intellectual property. He hated the fact that so many games were based on the idea that one was either chasing or being chased. But above all, he despised shooters, which meant he hated most of the games that were made by professionals or students, and a significant portion of the games that were successful. "Guys," Dov said. "You know I've served in the army, right? Guns are so fucking romantic to you Americans, because you don't know what it is to be at war and to be constantly under siege. It's truly pathetic."

Florian, the skinny engineering major whose game was currently on the chopping block, said, "Dov, I'm not even from America." Florian's game wasn't a shooter either: it was an archery game that had been inspired by competing as a youth archer in Poland.

"Right, but you've absorbed its values."

"But you've got shooting in *Dead Sea*."

Dov insisted that there wasn't any shooting in *Dead Sea*.

"What are you talking about?" Florian said. "The girl beats a guy with a log."

"That's not shooting," Dov said. "That's violence. A little girl hitting a violent predator with a log is hand-to-hand combat and that's *honest*. A man, who is represented by a hand, shooting a series of unknown henchmen is *dishonest*. It's not violence that I hate anyway. It's lazy games that act as if the only thing you can possibly do in life is shoot at something. It's lazy, Florian. And the problem with your game is not that it's a shooter, but that your game isn't any fun to play. Let me ask you a question: Did you play it?"

"Yes, of course I played it."

"Did you think it was fun?"

"I don't think of archery as fun," Florian said.

"Okay, fuck that, who cares if it's fun? Did it feel like archery to you?"

Florian shrugged.

"Because it didn't feel like archery to me."

"I don't know what that means."

"I'll tell you. The shooting mechanic has a lag. I can't tell where the sights are aimed. And it doesn't at all simulate the feeling of pulling back on a bow, as I'm sure you know. There's no tension, and the heads-up display obscures more than it helps. It's just a game with some pictures of a bow and a bullseye. It could be a game about anything, by anyone. And also, you haven't created any kind of story. The problem with your game is not that it's a shooter, but that it's a bad shooter and it has no character."

"This is bullshit, Dov," Florian said. He was very pale, and his skin flushed a psychedelic pink.

"Dude, dude." Dov smacked Florian affectionately on the shoulder, and then he pulled him into an aggressive bear hug. "Next time, we fail better."

When Sadie went to make her first game, she had no idea what Dov would like. And she started to wonder if this was the point. There was no pleasing Dov, so you might as well make something that amused you, at least. Out of desperation and with almost no time left, Sadie made a game about the poetry of Emily Dickinson. She titled it *EmilyBlaster*. Poetic fragments fell from the top of the screen and, using a quill that shot ink as it tracked along the bottom of the screen, the player had to shoot the fragments that added up to one of Emily Dickinson's poems. And then once the player had successfully cleared the level by shooting several of Emily's verses, you earned points to decorate a room in Emily's Amherst house.

```
Because
SHOOT
I could not
SHOOT
stop for
SHOOT
Death
```

The class hated it. Hannah Levin was the first to offer feedback. "So . . . I thought some of the graphics were nice, but the thing is, the game kind of sucked. It was weirdly violent, and also weirdly bucolic at the same time. And Dov told us not to make shooters, but a pen that shoots ink, is still a gun, right?" The rest of the feedback would continue along the same line.

Florian had one mildly positive comment: "I like when you shoot the words, it turns into a little black spot of ink, and I like the plosive sound you added, when the ink hits the screen."

Hannah Levin countered, "I thought it sounded like a—excuse me if this is rude—I thought it sounded like a fart." Hannah Levin covered her mouth as if she herself had just farted.

Nigel from England added, "But I think it technically sounded more like a queef."

The class hooted.

"Wait," Hannah said, "what's a *queef*?"

The class laughed even more, and Sadie laughed, too.

"I wanted to work on the sound some more, but I ran out of time," Sadie apologized, though no one seemed to hear her.

"Guys, calm down. I hate this, too," Dov said, "but actually, I don't hate it as much as some of the other ones." Dov looked at Sadie as if seeing her for the first time. (It was the fourth week of class.) He glanced at his roster and Sadie could tell that he was learning her name, and she felt flattered, even if it was the FOURTH week of class. "It's a rip-off of *Space Invaders*, but with a pen instead of a gun. At the very least, I can say I haven't played this exact rip-off before, Sadie Green."

Dov played another round of *EmilyBlaster*, and Sadie knew she was being paid another compliment. "Fun," he said quietly, but loud enough so that everyone heard.

For her second game, Sadie felt she could and should be more ambitious. This time, she did not struggle with a concept.

Sadie's game was set in a nondescript black-and-white factory that made unspecified widgets. Points were given for each of the widgets you assembled. Sadie had designed the mechanic of the game to be like *Tetris*, a game for which Dov had often expressed admiration. (He loved *Tetris* because it was fundamentally creative—a game about building and figuring out how to make pieces fit.) With each of the game's levels, you assembled widgets that had more pieces and greater complexity, and you had less and less time to accomplish the assemblies. At various times in the game, a text bubble came up, asking if you wanted to exchange points for information about the factory and the kind of products it produced. The game warned that if you received information about the factory, it would result in a minor reduction of your high score. The player had the option to skip as much or as little of this information as they wanted.

As was the procedure, Sadie distributed the 3.25-inch disks at the class before which she was to present, so that the group could play her game over the next week. By way of description, she said, "Well, um, my game is called *Solution*. It was inspired by my grandmother. You guys can play it, and I'm sure you'll tell me what you think."

Sadie got an email from Hannah Levin at the end of the weekend. *Dear Sadie, I played your "game," and I honestly don't know what to say. It is disgusting and offensive, and you are a sick person. I'm cc'ing Dov on this email. I'm not sure if I will be able to attend class, because I'm too disturbed. This class is no longer a safe space for me.—Hannah*

Sadie smiled when she read this email. She took her time crafting a reply: *Dear Hannah, I'm not entirely sorry that you were disturbed by my game. The game is meant to be disturbing, and as I mentioned in class, it was inspired by my grandmother.*

Hannah replied, *Fuck you, Sadie.*

Dov replied a couple of hours later, just to Sadie: *Sadie, Haven't played yet. Looking forward, Dov.*

Dov called Sadie the next day. "So, we both know Hannah Levin is an impossible idiot, right?"

Dov had spent the last hour on the phone with Hannah, who wanted Dov to report Sadie to MIT's Committee on Discipline. Hannah felt that *Solution* violated the student code of conduct, which prohibited hate speech. "I think I talked her off the ledge," Dov said. "She is an incredibly tedious person. Who has time for people like this? But congratulations, Sadie Green, your game offended her deeply."

"That's crazy," Sadie said.

"I guess she didn't like being told she was a Nazi," Dov said.

"You played the game?"

"Of course," Dov said. "I had to."

"Did you win?"

"Everyone wins," Dov said. "That's the genius of it, right?"

"Everyone loses," Sadie said. "The game's about being complicit." *Genius.* Dov had said *genius.*

The idea of *Solution* was that if you asked questions and didn't keep mindlessly building widgets, your score would be lower, but you would find out you were working in a factory that supplied machine parts to the Third Reich. Once you had this information, you could potentially slow your output. You could make the bare number of parts required not to be detected by the Reich, or you could stop producing parts entirely. The player who did not ask questions, the Good German, would blithely get the highest score possible, but in the end, they'd find out what their factory was doing. Fraktur-style script blazed across the screen: *Congratulations, Nazi! You have helped lead the Third Reich to Victory! You are a true Master of Efficiency.* Cue MIDI Wagner. The idea of *Solution* was that if you won the game on points, you lost it morally.

"Listen, I loved the game. I thought it was hilarious."

"Hilarious?" Sadie had meant it to be soul crushing, disturbing.

"My sense of humor is very dark," Dov said. "Screw it. Do you want to get coffee?"

They went to a coffee place in Harvard Square, near Dov's apartment. Sadie hadn't known if the meeting would be about Hannah's complaint, but in fact, they didn't speak of her. Sadie told him how much she loved *Dead Sea,* and she was able to ask him quite technical questions about rendering light with the Ulysses engine. Dov answered her questions and told her about designing *Dead Sea,* and how it had been inspired by his fear of drowning. Sadie spoke of her grandmother, growing up in Los Angeles, her sister's illness. They discussed their favorite games, as children and now. Dov spoke to her as if they were colleagues, and this was thrilling for Sadie. She didn't care if she got called in front of the Committee on Discipline for making *Solution.* For this moment, with someone like Dov, it was worth it.

Dov reached across the table and wiped a bit of coffee foam from her lip.

"I think I'm in serious trouble," Dov said.

"Because of Hannah?" Sadie said.

"Who's Hannah?" Dov said. "Oh, right. *Her.* I think I'm in trouble because I want you to come back to my apartment, and I know I shouldn't do that."

"Why shouldn't you?" Sadie said. "I'd like to see where you live."

It was the first adult relationship Sadie had ever had, though he was also very much her teacher. But as her lover, he was a much better teacher than when he'd just been her teacher. She learned so much from him. It was like having seminar all the time. He encouraged her to improve *Solution.* He showed her techniques he had for building game engines. "Never use someone else's engine, if you can help it," Dov warned. "You cede too much power to them." She loved playing games with him, and having sex with him, and telling her ideas to him. She loved him.

She didn't find out he was married until about four months in, as her sophomore year was ending. He said he needed to tell her something before this got any more serious. They had been planning for Sadie to spend the summer in his apartment.

He said that his wife was back in Israel. They were separated. That's why he'd come to MIT. They both needed a break from the marriage.

"So, she knows about me?" Sadie asked.

"Not in so many words, but she knows about the possibility of someone like you," Dov said. "Don't worry. There's nothing shady about it."

And yet, Sadie did feel shady about it. She did not entirely believe Dov, and Sadie felt as if she had been tricked into behaving amorally. She had inadvertently ended up having an affair with a married man and even though she hadn't known that at the beginning, she knew it now. And maybe, if she were honest with herself, she had known. Maybe she had been like the player in *Solution*. Maybe she hadn't asked the right or enough questions because she hadn't wanted to know the answers.

Still, she spent the summer with Dov. She loved him and was, at this point, a bit addicted to being with him. She did an internship at Cellar Door Games in Boston and she never told anyone at the company who her boyfriend was. Among game designers, Dov was famous, and she didn't want it to get back to Dov's wife. She was so busy concealing (and having) the affair with Dov that she didn't feel like she made much of an impression at Cellar Door. She didn't feel creative, and she was always the first one to leave.

It perhaps goes without saying that Sadie hadn't only been protecting Dov when she didn't reveal to her colleagues at Cellar Door who her boyfriend was. She had also been protecting herself. There were even fewer women in professional games than there were at MIT, and Sadie didn't want to hobble herself before she'd begun her career. It was unfair, but attractive young women who had reputations for sleeping with powerful men acquired professional baggage. They sometimes found they had a difficult time being taken seriously when they moved on from those men. She did not want her unofficial résumé in gaming to begin with the words "Dov Mizrah's teenage mistress." As much in love as she was with Dov, Sadie was already imagining a future that didn't have him in it.

In the fall of her junior year, she took Artificial Intelligence, and Hannah Levin, who she had not seen since Dov's seminar, was in the same breakout recitation session as her. "I hope there aren't any hard feelings," Sadie said at the end of class. "I never intended to offend you."

"Please. The only reason you make a game like that is to offend," Hannah replied. "I didn't pursue it because *your boyfriend* talked me out of it and I didn't want it to come back and bite me in the ass someday."

"He wasn't my boyfriend when I was in the class," Sadie said, but Hannah was already walking out the door.

Sadie hadn't worked on a game of her own since she'd been with Dov, though she did occasionally help him with his. It was easier, in some ways, to work with and for Dov than it was to do her own work. Her work seemed basic and uninteresting compared to the kind of work Dov was doing. Her work *was* basic and uninteresting. She had just turned twenty. Everyone's work is basic and uninteresting at twenty. But being around Dov made her feel impatient with her twenty-year-old brain and the quality of its ideas.

She had been with Dov ten months when she ran into Sam in the train station. She saw him long before he saw her. There he was: his coat too big over his boyish frame, his gait lurching but determined, his eyes focused ahead—she was quite sure he would never look back and notice her, and she was glad of it. He was unchanged, pure. He had not done the things she had done. Compared to him, she felt aged and withered, and she thought, if they spoke, he would be able to sense her decay. But for whatever reason, he turned back. And when he called her name, she kept walking.

But then, he called out one more time, "SADIE MIRANDA GREEN, YOU HAVE DIED OF DYSENTERY!"

Sam could be ignored, but the childish shared reference could not be. It was an invitation to play.

She turned.

Before returning to Israel for the winter break, Dov had warned Sadie that he wouldn't be in contact much. "Family things," he said. "You know how it is." Sadie said she was cool, though even as she said it, she wasn't sure if she *was* cool. She knew she had no choice but to be cool. And cool girls definitely didn't ask their lovers if they were planning to see their supposedly estranged wives over winter break. If she wasn't cool, Dov might end the relationship, and Sadie couldn't bear that. She had come to depend on Dov. She realized, in retrospect, that the one and a half years she'd spent at MIT before she met Dov had been incredibly lonely. She hadn't made any real friends. And to go from having no friends to having Dov as your friend was an intense experience. He was like a bright, warm light over everything in her life. She felt lit up, turned on. There was no one better to talk to about games. There was no one better to run ideas by. Yes, she loved him, but she also liked him. She liked herself when she was with him.

Recently, she had suspected he was losing interest in her. So, she had attempted to make herself more interesting. She had tried to dress better, and she'd gotten a haircut and she bought lacy underwear. She had read a book about wine, so she could be knowledgeable at dinner, the way she imagined an older lover would be. He once said, in passing, that it was amazing how little American Jews knew about Israel, and she read a book about the founding of Israel, so she'd be conversant. But it didn't seem to matter.

She sometimes felt as if he was trying to find fault with her. If Sadie spent the day reading a novel, he'd say, "When I was your age, I was constantly programming." Or if Sadie was too slow to complete a task Dov had assigned to her, he would say, "You're brilliant, but you're lazy." In addition to working on Dov's games, Sadie had a full course load. If Sadie mentioned this to Dov, he would say, "Never ever ever complain." Or he'd say, "This is why I don't work with students." If she told him about a game she admired that he didn't think much of, he would tell her the reasons the game was terrible. And that didn't just go for games—it was movies, books, and art, too. It got to the point where she would never outright say her opinion of anything. She trained herself to begin conversations, "What did you think, Dov?"

And so she'd be cool, because that's what mistresses were. *Mistress,* Sadie thought. Sadie laughed a bit to herself, thinking this was what it was like to play someone else's game: to have the illusion of choice, without actual choice.

"Why does the brilliant one laugh so very ruefully?" Dov asked.

"No reason. Call me when you get back," she said.

Sadie was moody and quiet the entire time she was in California for the holidays. She felt flu-ish, permanently jet-lagged, worn out. She spent most of the holidays sleeping in her childhood bed, under faded rose-print sheets, reading the dog-eared paperbacks of her youth. "What's wrong with you?" Alice asked. "Everyone's worried." Alice was in her first year of medical school at UCLA.

"I'm fine," Sadie said. "I think I might have caught something on the plane."

"Well, don't get me sick. I can't afford it." Alice refused to lose even one more day of her life to malady.

Sadie didn't feel like she could tell anyone in her family about Dov, even Alice or perhaps, especially Alice. Alice, like their grandmother, had a strong distaste for life's inevitable gray areas.

Alice studied Sadie. She put her hand on her forehead and then she looked into Sadie's eyes. "You don't feel hot, but I don't think you *are* fine," Alice said.

Sadie changed the subject. "You'll never guess who I ran into in Harvard Square."

In the end, Alice had been the one who told Sam about Sadie's community service project. Alice always claimed that jealousy hadn't been a motivator, and Sadie came to believe that it hadn't been. But it was no secret that Alice had never liked the idea of Sadie doing community service at the hospital, and Alice had been disgusted when Sadie received the community service award from the temple.

About three months before Sadie's Bat Mitzvah, Alice had run into Sam at the hospital. Alice had been there for a routine follow-up blood test—she had been in remission for about a year; Sam had been there for yet another surgery revision on his foot. They did not know each other well, and what Alice did know of Sam, she did not particularly like. She found Sadie's relationship with Sam to be strange. Part of this was Sadie's fault. When Alice expressed interest in meeting her new friend, Sadie had claimed that Sam wasn't really her friend. She had emphasized the volunteerism aspects of the relationship and had described Sam as "pretty pathetic." There was a part of Sadie that hadn't wanted Alice to *know* Sam, to offer her opinions about him as candidly as Alice offered opinions of Sadie's other friends and classmates. Alice was clever, but she had the kind of cleverness that verged on the unkind, and this had only gotten worse in the years since she had been diagnosed with leukemia. Sadie didn't want Sam viewed through her sister's acute and often unforgiving lens.

And so, when Alice saw Sam at the hospital, Alice's first instinct was to ignore him.

"You're Sadie's sister, right?" Sam said. "I'm Sam."

"I know who you are," Alice said.

One of Sam's many doctors, a pediatric orthopedist, spotted the two kids together and mistook Alice for Sadie, who was always at the hospital. "Hi, Sam! Hi, Sadie!"

"Dr. Tybalt," Sam said, "this isn't Sadie; it's her sister, Alice."

"Of course!" the doctor said. "You two do look alike."

"Yes," Alice said. "But I'm two years older, and my hair is straighter. But the easiest way to tell my sister from me is that I don't have a timesheet with me."

The conversation ended when the nurse called Alice's name. They were ready to take her blood.

"See you around, Sam," Alice called.

Sam called Sadie at home that night. "I ran into your sister at the hospital," Sam reported.

"Yeah, Alice was there," Sadie said. "Sorry, I was going to try to go, but I had Bat Mitzvah class. Guess what game I'm looking at right now?"

"What?"

"*King's Quest IV*. I got Bubbe to take me to Babbage's, and it was on the shelf a whole month early. I screamed when I saw it. Sam, the graphics are so much better than the last one. They're maybe better than *Zelda* even."

"You said you'd wait for me to start."

"I didn't really start. I installed it, that's all. Listen, the music's gotten better, too."

Sadie held the phone up to the computer so that he could hear the MIDI track.

"It's not coming through very well," Sam said. "Sadie, Alice said this weird thing . . ."

"Ignore her, that's just Alice. She's THE RUDEST PERSON I KNOW." Sadie yelled this loud enough for Alice to overhear. "Do you think if your foot isn't hurting too much and you're out of the hospital,

Dong Hyun can drive you over to my house on Sunday so we can play through *KQIV*? If Dong Hyun drives you, I'm pretty sure I can get my dad to drive you back."

"I don't know. I think I'll be here at least a week, maybe longer, this time."

"That's cool. Maybe I can bring the disks and we'll install it on—"

"Sadie, she said this thing about you having a timesheet, or something like that."

Sadie paused for a second. Though she had known this day would come, she had not prepared what she would say.

"Sadie?"

"It's not a big thing," Sadie said. "It's this form I get filled out when I'm at the hospital. I think everyone has them."

"Sure," Sam said. "Right . . . But my grandparents don't have them."

"Oh, that's weird. Maybe they do have them, and you never noticed? Or maybe . . . *Maybe* it's so kids can visit other kids at the hospital."

"That makes sense."

"For security," Sadie improvised. "Sharyn's calling me to dinner. Can I call you back?" Sadie did not call him back. Five minutes before nine, the latest time he was allowed to call her house, he phoned her again. For a moment, she considered telling her dad to say she wasn't home.

"But Sadie, Alice called it a timesheet," Sam said.

"Sure, it's also a timesheet. It says how many hours I was at the hospital. Why are you fixating on this? Did you ask Dong Hyun about this weekend?"

"But why would you need to know that?"

"I . . ." Sadie said. "To keep track of things, I guess."

Long pause. "Are you some sort of a candy striper?"

"If I was a candy striper, I'd have to wear that dress, and I'd never wear that dress."

"Other than the dress?"

"Samson, you're being incredibly tedious. Can we talk about something else?"

"Was I some sort of community service project to you?" Sam asked.

"No, Sam."

"Were we friends, or did you just feel bad for me, or was I a homework assignment, or what, Sadie? What was it? I need to know."

"Friends. How can you think otherwise? You're my best friend." Sadie was near tears.

"I don't believe you," Sam said. "*You* were never my friend. You're some rich asshole volunteer from Beverly Hills, and I'm a mentally ill poor kid, with a screwed-up leg. Well, I don't require your patronage anymore."

"Sam, it's hard to explain, but it had nothing to do with you. The form was a game to me. I . . . Well, I guess I liked seeing the hours add up." She suddenly had an insight that she thought Sam would respond to. "I was going for the high score. I got up to six hundred nine, but I think it's more than—"

"You're a liar and a really bad person and . . ." None of this seemed strong enough. "You're a . . . a . . ." He searched his mind for the worst word he had ever heard. "Cunt," he whispered. He had never said that word before, and the word felt exotic, as if he were speaking a foreign language.

"What?" Sadie said.

Sam knew "cunt" to be a Rubicon. He had once overheard his mother's boyfriend call her this word during an argument, and Anna had transformed from a woman into an obelisk. After that night, he had never seen this boyfriend again, and so he knew those four letters possessed profound, magical properties. "Cunt" could make a person disappear from your life forever, and he decided that indeed, this was what he wanted: to forget he had ever met Sadie Green and that he had ever been so pathetic and cretinous as to imagine *she* was his friend. "You're a *cunt*," he repeated. "I never want to see you again." Sam hung up the phone.

Sadie sat on her rose-print comforter, holding the telephone by her burning cheek. "Cunt" wasn't Sam's typical diction, and when he said it, his reedy voice had sounded comical to Sadie. Her impulse had been to laugh. She was not popular at her school, but she was a sturdy, weatherproof individual, and most insults didn't feel like anything. Ugly, annoying, nerd, bitch, stuck-up, whatever. But Sam's words, she felt. The phone began to chirp adamantly, but she could not bring herself to hang it up. She wasn't even entirely sure what a cunt was. She only knew that she had hurt Sam, and she probably was a cunt.

The next day, Sadie's father drove Sadie to the hospital. She went to the desk, and the nurse went to get Sam, but he refused to see her. "I'm sorry, Sadie," the nurse said. "He's in a mood." Sadie sat in the waiting area and waited until her mother would pick her up two hours later. She wrote Sam a note, using a couple lines of BASIC, the rudimentary programming language she and Sam were both learning:

```
10 READY
20 FOR X = 1 to 100
30 PRINT "I'M SORRY, SAM ACHILLES MASUR"
40 NEXT X
50 PRINT "PLEASE PLEASE PLEASE FORGIVE ME.
LOVE, YOUR FRIEND SADIE MIRANDA GREEN"
60 NEXT X
70 PRINT "DO YOU FORGIVE ME?"
80 NEXT X
90 PRINT "Y OR N"
100 NEXT X
110 LET A = GET CHAR ()
120 IF A = "Y" OR A = "N" THEN GOTO 130
130 IF A = "N" THEN 20
140 IF A = "Y" THEN 150
150 END PROGRAM
```

She folded the note in half and wrote README on the outside of the paper. If he put the program in a computer, the screen would fill up with I'M SORRY, SAMs. If he accepted her apology, the program ended. But if he didn't accept her apology, the program would repeat until he did.

The nurse brought the note to Sam's room, then came back several minutes later: Sam had refused the note. And that night, when Sadie inputted the program into her own computer, she realized she'd made a syntactical error anyway.

A week later, it was Freda's turn to drive Sadie to the hospital. Sadie did not want to confess to her grandmother what had happened. She did not want to admit that Freda had been right. She let Freda drive her all the way to Children's Hospital, but when they arrived there, Sadie did not get out of the car.

"What is it, mine Sadie?" Freda asked.

"I messed up," Sadie said miserably. "I'm a terrible person." She worried that Freda would yell at her, say I told you so, insist that Sadie go in and try to apologize to Sam, which Sadie knew would be pointless. Adults always thought they could fix children's problems.

Freda simply nodded and took Sadie in her arms. "Oh, my love, this must be a very great loss." She got on her enormous cell phone, and she canceled her afternoon, and she took Sadie to lunch at her favorite restaurant, a divey Italian place in Beverly Hills, where all the waiters flirted with Freda. They ordered chicken parmigiana, Sadie's favorite, and ice cream sundaes. The only mention Freda made of the whole situation was when she was paying the bill. "There are people like you and like me. We have bad things happen to us, and we survive them. We are sturdy. But with people like your friend, you must be exceptionally gentle, or they may break."

"What have I ever survived, Bubbe?"

"Your sister's cancer. You were very strong during that, even if your mother and father didn't mention it as much as they should have. But I noticed, and I am proud of you."

Sadie felt embarrassed. "That's nothing like what you survived."

"It is no easy matter being the little sister, this I know. And I am also proud of you for befriending that boy. Even if things ended badly, it was a good thing you did for him and for yourself. That boy was utterly friendless, injured, alone. You were not a perfect friend, but you were his friend, and he needed a friend."

"You told me what would happen."

"Meh," Freda said. "Bubbe-meise. An old woman's guess."

"The thing is, I'll really miss him." Sadie held back tears.

"Maybe you'll see him again."

"I don't think so. He hates me now, Bubbe."

"Always remember, mine Sadie: life is very long, unless it is not." Sadie knew this to be a tautology, but it also happened to be true.

.   .
.

Dov did not call when he returned to Cambridge. The day of his scheduled arrival had come and gone, and it was almost the middle of January, and classes were about to begin. She hadn't wanted to call him, and she thought it would be rude to go over to his apartment. She decided to send him an email, which she revised extensively. In the end, the revisions did not lead to a sparkling result: *Hi Dov, Started playing Chrono Trigger. Some interesting elements there.*

He didn't reply for an entire day: *I've already played it. We should talk, though. Do you want to come over tonight?*

Sadie knew she was dressing for her funeral, so she wore black: dress, tights, Doc Martens. She wanted to look sexy. She wanted him to feel bad about what he would be missing, but she didn't want to be obvious about it. She took the train to Harvard Square, and when she arrived, she found that the Magic Eye advertisement was still up, though lightly graffiti-covered and peeling on the sides. The rest of the world had apparently lost interest in it since Christmas. She decided to delay her arrival to Dov's place by looking at it again: *Walk up close, and back away. Let your eyes relax.*

She went to the magic place, and she felt her mind go clear. She told herself that no matter what Dov said, she wouldn't argue, cry, or complain.

When she arrived at Dov's apartment, she didn't let herself in, even though she had the key. She rang the bell, and he came down to get her. He kissed her on the cheek, and he started to help her off with her coat. But she didn't want to take off her coat. She wanted to have the armor of the cashmere wool blend Freda had bought her at Filene's Basement in the fall of her freshman year. At the time, Sadie had worried that the coat was too bulky, but Freda had advised, "Winter will be colder than you think, mine Sadie. This I promise you."

"Let me have it," Sadie said. She looked him in the eye and she crossed her arms over her breasts. *I'm brave,* she thought.

"Batia and I are going to try to make it work," Dov said. "I'm so sorry." He was taking a leave from MIT, packing up—suddenly, she became aware of the boxes—and subletting his apartment; he would need the key. He was going back to Israel to work on *Dead Sea II*.

Sadie would not cry. "When I didn't hear from you, I thought it was something like that," she said in an easy, practiced voice. *Be cool,* she thought. Her brain furiously ran through all the reasons to *be cool.* She might want a recommendation letter from him some day, if she decided to go to grad school. She might want to work at a company that he worked for. She might want to design a game with him. She might end up on a panel with him, or he might be the judge for a gaming award. Sadie, like Sam, had a gift for imagining herself in the future. She saw a future in which she would not be Dov's lover, but she still might be his colleague, his employee, his friend. If she was cool, this time won't have been a waste. *Life is very long,* she thought, *unless it is not.*

"You're being very good about this," Dov said. "It's making me feel awful. I think I'd prefer if you screamed and yelled."

Sadie shrugged. "I knew you were married." *Had she?* Yes, she had known even if she had tried to pretend to herself and to Dov that she hadn't. She had seen his biography on a nascent gaming website, long before she had taken the class. She had looked him up on the internet after she'd played *Dead Sea* the summer before her sophomore year. A wife had been mentioned, as had a son. They didn't have names, and so they weren't characters to her, but that didn't mean they didn't exist. He had never told her about them himself, and so she rationalized her involvement with him by thinking, *Until he tells me, it's not my business.* "It's my fault," she said.

"Come here," he said.

Sadie shook her head. She didn't want him to touch her. "Please, Dov."

Now that Dov knew Sadie wouldn't make things difficult for him, she could see his eyes soften. She could see them fill with love and regret for her. Sadie wanted to remember Dov's face like this. She began to edge toward the door.

"Sadie, you don't have to go. Let me order some Thai for us. A colleague sent me a press copy of the new Hideo Kojima. It won't be out here for at least a year, maybe longer."

"*Metal Gear III?*"

"They're not calling it *Metal Gear III.* They're calling it *Metal Gear Solid.* Kojima is disappointed with the sales of the previous *Metal Gears* in the States, so he doesn't want it to be a sequel."

"But those games were great," Sadie said.

"He's being smart actually, if he thinks he has a hit on his hands," Dov said. "It's not only being a good programmer or a good designer, Sadie. You have to be a marketeer and a showman. You'll learn that eventually."

Though she was not in the mood to be taught, Sadie found herself taking off her coat.

"I like the dress," Dov said.

She had forgotten she was wearing a dress, and now she felt sorry for the Sadie she had been an hour ago who had decided to objectify herself by wearing a dress. She sat down at Dov's desk. He loaded the game, and then he handed her the controller.

Metal Gear Solid was a stealth game, which meant it was strategically advantageous to avoid being seen more than it was to engage someone in combat. The player spent a great deal of the game bored—hiding and waiting. Sadie found the relative boredom of *Metal Gear Solid* comforting. As Sadie made her character crouch and hide behind boxes or walls or doorways, she realized *stealth* would be a good strategy for her, in this particular moment. She would be here, in this room with Dov, but she would not provoke him or engage him unless she absolutely had to.

Sadie had reached a part in *Metal Gear Solid* where the player character was spying on a female non-player character exercising in her underwear. The NPC's name was Meryl Silverburgh, which also struck Sadie as ridiculous.

"Come on," Sadie said. "Meryl fricking Silverburgh in her underwear."

"Maybe Kojima's into Jewesses?"

Sadie wondered if most gamers would be turned on by this. She often had to put herself into a male point of view to even understand a game at all. As Dov was fond of saying to her, "You aren't just a gamer when you play anymore. You're a builder of worlds, and if you're a builder of worlds, your feelings are not as important as what your gamers are feeling. You must imagine them at all times. There is no artist more empathetic than the game designer." Sadie the gamer found this scene sexist and strange. At the same time, Sadie the world builder accepted that the game was made by one of the most creative minds in gaming. And in those days, girls like Sadie were conditioned to ignore the sexist generally, not just in gaming—it wasn't *cool* to point such things out. If you wanted to play with the boys, they couldn't be afraid of saying things around you. If someone said the sound effect in your game sounded like a queef, it was your job to laugh. But on this evening, Sadie wasn't in the mood to laugh.

44

"I don't want to play a game that's a collection of some guy's fetishes," Sadie said.

"Dude, Sadie, you described ninety-nine percent of all games. But the boobs are a bit much, I'll give you that. How does she not topple over?" Dov said. "Kojima's brilliant, though."

"Yes," Sadie said, wedging her character into an air vent.

The Thai food arrived. Dov made conversation as if it were a normal night, and not their last supper. She didn't have much of an appetite. She drank a bit of the wine he poured her—she would never be much of a drinker—and she felt light-headed, distantly nauseous, but not drunk. She felt too light-headed to make any of the clever comments about wine she'd learned.

"You look beautiful," Dov said. He leaned across the table and he kissed her, and she felt too tired to insist that if he was breaking up with her, the least he could do was let her go without a final fuck. Because she was cool, but she wasn't sure she was *that cool*. But it was hard for Sadie to talk without being angry or sad, and she'd come this far without being either of those things.

"Dov," she said. She wanted to say no. But her mouth didn't make the words, and in the end, she decided, what was the difference? She had had sex with him many times before. And she had liked having sex with Dov.

He took off her tights and her dress and her underwear, and he ran his hand up and down her body, in an appraising way, like a farmer inspecting land he was about to sell. "I am going to miss you," he said. "I am going to miss this." She imagined she was not in her body, but back in the world of *Metal Gear Solid*. The character you play in *Metal Gear Solid* is called Solid Snake, whose main antagonist is Liquid Snake, who is constructed from the same genetic material as you. The profundity of this struck Sadie in this moment—yes, what greater enemy does one have than oneself? And wasn't she to blame for all of this more than Dov? He had said it would be trouble if she came to his apartment, and still she had gone. If someone tells you there will be trouble, believe them.

When the cab arrived, he walked her down to the street.

"Friends?" he said.

"Of course," Sadie said. She handed him his key, without waiting for him to ask for it.

He hugged her, deposited her in the cab, and closed the door.

As the cab headed down Massachusetts Avenue, she felt hot in her winter coat and like she couldn't breathe, so she asked the driver if she could roll down the window. From the window, she could see the water tower of the New England Confectionery Company's factory, which had recently been painted to resemble a roll of Necco wafers, those barely flavored, pastel-colored, vaguely religious-looking chalky disks. As they approached the factory, the air increasingly smelled of sugar, and the scent made Sadie nostalgic for a candy she had never even tasted.

4

The day after Christmas, Sam sent Sadie an email: *Hello Stranger, I've played your game twice now, and I want to talk to you about it! Let's get together when you're back from the holidays. Say Hi to our old friend California for me.—S.A.M. P.S. I'm glad we ran into each other.*

She did not immediately reply, the fact of which did not trouble Sam. In those days, a person might not be able to check her email when she was away from school.

By the middle of January, she still hadn't replied, and he began to worry that his email hadn't been received. He decided to send another.

While he waited for her response, he played *Solution* again. At that point, he had played through the game, alone, three times. The first time he played, he didn't get any of the information, just went for points, and he received the rank of Grand Nazi Collaborator. The second time he played, he took all the information but still solved the levels as quickly as possible. He was given the rank of Facilitator. The last time he played, he received all the information and played the levels as slowly as he could while still leveling up. He received the rank of Conscientious Objector. Sam believed that Conscientious Objector was the best possible rank you could obtain in *Solution,* though he hadn't gone into the code to confirm it.

As Sam played, he began to take notes on the game. He thought the game was clever, but he also thought there were small things she might improve. At the same time, there were other small things that had been done so well, he wanted to make sure she knew that he, at one time her best friend, had noticed her labors. He organized the micro feedback into a spreadsheet, with categories like *sounds, delays, mechanics, prose, graphics, pacing, HUD, controls, general ludic thoughts.* He hadn't decided if he would give her this file.

The thing he most wanted to talk to her about was the game on a macro level. His biggest note was that the game should have greater complexity. *Solution,* he felt, was fantastic as an academic exercise. But wouldn't it be even better if you could open another part of the game if you chose the moral path. After a while, if you used your points for *any* of the information, the mystery was obvious and the game became repetitive. Wouldn't it be better if those who played well enough and morally enough could figure out how to reroute the factory's output? The simulation, Sam felt, was incomplete, and thus, not fully satisfying. The simulation was incomplete because it didn't have a call to action. The only feeling a player could have at the end of Sadie's game was nihilism. Sam fully got what she was trying to do, but he also believed that she would have to do more if she were to make games that people loved, not just games that people admired.

He felt excited when he was coming up with these thoughts for Sadie. He felt excited in a way he didn't feel when he worked on "Alternative Approaches to the Banach-Tarski Paradox . . ." The words of Anders Larsson came back to him: "To be good at something is not quite the same as loving it." After playing *Solution,* he knew what he would love (and what he thought he would be good at): he would love to make a game with Sadie Green. And as soon as she wrote back, he would convince her that this was what they should do.

Another week passed, and she still hadn't replied. Harvard's reading period was over; Sam had finished all his exams, and the new term was about to begin. Normally, Sam would have taken the hint and forgotten that he had ever encountered Sadie Green in the subway station. But *Solution* wouldn't let him. She had given him the game for a reason, he felt, and he had to talk to her, even if it was for the last time. The Readme file contained her email address, but also a physical address (no phone number), which appeared to be an apartment on Columbia Street, equidistant between Kendall and Central Squares. This is to say, there was no easy way to get to Sadie's apartment from the closest T stop. Sam would have to walk about a quarter of a mile from the station, and that was difficult for him, with his cobbled-together left foot, on the icy, irregular streets of Cambridge, in the middle of winter. He considered taking a cab, but he couldn't afford one. The weather was cold but fine, and he had no obligations, so he decided to brave the walk. He rarely used his cane—even though it was medically necessary, he felt it made him look affected, like a twenty-one-year-old Mr. Monopoly—but on this occasion he used it. This, he felt, was business.

He arrived at Sadie's apartment, and he rang the bell. At the last second, he worried that it was an old address on Sadie's Readme, and that he would have come all this way for nothing.

After about five minutes, a roommate answered. Sam said he was looking for Sadie, and the roommate looked suspiciously at Sam for a beat, before deciding he was harmless. "Sadie!" the roommate called. "There's a kid out here to see you."

Sadie emerged from her bedroom. It was two in the afternoon, and Sam could tell that he had woken her.

"Sam," she said drowsily. "Hey."

She looked un-showered. Her MIT sweatshirt had reddish and whitish stains on it. And even though the sweatshirt was baggy, he could tell that she was unusually thin underneath it. Her hair was matted and dirty, like an animal who had been in the wild a long time. She had—it must be said—an odor. Sam surmised that this wasn't the result of one day of sleeping in.

"Are you okay?" Sam asked. Six weeks ago, she had appeared fine.

"Sure," Sadie said. "Why are you here?"

"I . . ." He was so momentarily disturbed by this Sadie, he forgot why he had come. "I tried to email you. I wanted to talk about *Solution*. Do you remember? You gave me the disk—"

Sadie interrupted him with a heavy sigh. "Listen, Sam, it's not a good time."

He was about to leave, but then he didn't. "Could I—? I walked all this way from Central Square, and it would be great if I could sit down a minute."

She looked at his cane and at his foot. "Come in," she said wearily.

Sam followed Sadie into her bedroom. The curtains were drawn, and there were clothes and other detritus everywhere. This wasn't like the Sadie he had known. He asked if something had happened.

"Why would you care? We aren't *real* friends, remember?" Sadie met Sam's gaze. "And it's rude to not call before you show up at someone's apartment."

"I'm sorry. I didn't have your number. And you weren't emailing me back," Sam said.

"I suppose I've fallen behind on my email correspondence, Samson." Sadie got back into bed and put her head under the covers. "I need to get some sleep." Her voice was muffled by the sheets. "Show yourself out."

Sam moved some clothes off her desk chair, and he sat down on it.

Without emerging from the blankets, she said, "That coat is ridiculous." A few seconds later, Sam could hear the regular sound of Sadie's somnolent breathing.

Sam looked around Sadie's room. There was a Duane Hanson "Tourists" poster above the bed, and a Hokusai wave over her dresser. Above the desk, he noticed a small, framed drawing. It was a maze, depicting the city of Los Angeles. The frame, a delicate carved bamboo, was listing to the left, so he straightened it. On the desk, he noticed a disk, with Sadie's handwriting on it: *EmilyBlaster*. Sam put the disk in his coat pocket, and then he left.

The invitation had arrived in September, a month or so after Sam had found out about Sadie's community service project and called her a cunt. *Mr. Samson A. Masur,* in calligraphy on the envelope. *Sharyn Friedman-Green and Steven Green invite you to the Bat Mitzvah of their daughter, Sadie Miranda . . . Service at 10, followed by lunch . . . Your response requested . . .*

The invitation was quite plain, which is to say, it was not obviously fancy. Heavy cream card stock, raised text, vellum-lined envelope. But Sam was old enough to have noticed that simple things were often the most expensive. He held the invitation to his nose and he took a certain pleasure in the scent of fine paper. Sam didn't think it smelled like money, because money was dirty. It smelled rich and clean, like a hardcover from a bookstore, like Sadie herself.

Sam set the invitation on the back of his desk and considered the envelope separately. The paper proved an irresistible temptation. He loosened its seams with steam from the tap and turned the envelope into a flat sheet of paper. He took out his favorite Staedtler Mars Lumograph pencil and began to draw a maze on the rescued paper. Sam did not always know what he was drawing when he began a maze, but this time, he found himself drawing a series of circles and curves, and these circles somehow became Los Angeles. The maze started on the Eastside, in Echo Park, where Sam lived, and ended on the Westside, in the Beverly Hills flats, where Sadie lived. It wound through West Hollywood, up the Hollywood hills to Studio City, back down the hills to East Hollywood, Los Feliz, and Silver Lake, before finally circling around to Koreatown and Mid-City. He grew so absorbed in drawing the maze that he didn't even notice when Dong Hyun came into the room. It was late, and Dong Hyun smelled of pizza, as he usually did.

"That's a good one," Dong Hyun said. His hand reached toward the invitation on Sam's desk: "May I?" Unlike Sam's grandmother, Bong Cha, Dong Hyun always asked permission before touching Sam's possessions.

Sam sighed. "If you must."

"It is nice to be invited places," Dong Hyun pronounced upon reading the invitation. He and Sam's grandmother were worried about Sam's mood since he'd stopped seeing Sadie. Sam wouldn't tell them what had happened, aside from saying that she hadn't been the person he thought she was.

Sam set down his pencil and looked at Dong Hyun. "I honestly don't want to go. I don't know any of Sadie's friends."

"You're Sadie's friend," Dong Hyun said.

Sam shook his head, no. "She wasn't. She was just being nice."

Several weeks later, Sadie called Sam on the phone. They hadn't spoken for two months, and her voice sounded high-pitched and strange. "My dad needs to know if you're coming. You didn't send back the response card."

"I don't know," Sam said. "I might have something that day."

"Well, could you let me know when you know? We need to plan the number of meals, or whatever," Sadie said.

"Fine."

"Sam, you can't be mad at me forever."

Sam hung up the phone.

Bong Cha had spied on Sam's phone call from the phone in the kitchen, and she returned the response card the next day in the affirmative. She bought Sam a new pair of khaki pants, a blue oxford shirt, a cotton necktie with flowers on it, and Bass loafers. She had been told by her other grandson, Albert, that this was what fourteen-year-old boys wore to fancy parties. The morning of the party, she presented Sam with the new clothes and informed him that he should get ready to go to the Bat Mitzvah.

"You shouldn't have done that!" Sam yelled. "I'm not going!"

"But look, Sam, I made a present for Sadie." Bong Cha opened a gift bag. She had had the maze that Sam had drawn from Sadie's house to theirs framed and matted.

Sam banged his hand on the wall. "You had no right to do that! These are my private things! And Sadie doesn't want a piece of crap like that!"

"But you were drawing it for her, weren't you? It's a very nice picture, Sam," Bong Cha said. "I'm sure Sadie will like it so much."

Sam picked up the frame and lifted it up high in the air. He was about to slam it on the floor when he changed his mind and set it down on the table instead.

Sam stalked up the stairs to his bedroom—he could not yet manage to run up stairs. He slammed the door.

After a bit, Dong Hyun knocked. "Your grandmother only wants to help," he said. "She's worried about you."

"I don't want to go," Sam said. "Please don't make me go." He could feel that he might cry, and he was determined not to.

"Why?" Dong Hyun asked.

"I don't know." Sam was embarrassed to tell Dong Hyun that his only friend hadn't been a friend at all.

"I don't think your grandmother was right to do what she did," Dong Hyun said. "But it is done now, and it may hurt Sadie's feelings if you don't go."

"I don't care if I hurt her feelings, and it won't hurt them anyway. It's a huge party. All her rich friends will be there, and her parents' rich friends. She won't even notice if I'm not there."

"I think she will notice," Dong Hyun said.

Sam shook his head. What did Dong Hyun know about life? "My foot hurts." Sam never complained about his pain, and he knew that if he did, Dong Hyun wouldn't pressure him to do anything. "It hurts all the time. I just can't."

Dong Hyun nodded. "If it's okay with you, I'll drop off the gift at the party. I think she will like the present you and your grandmother made."

"Her parents can buy her anything she wants. Why would she want some dumb thing I drew on the back of an envelope?" Sam said.

"I suppose," Dong Hyun said, "because her parents can buy her anything she wants."

. .
.

```
That Love is
SHOOT
all there is
SHOOT
is all we know of
```

Sam was about to shoot *Love* when Marx came into his room to ask him if he wanted to go to dinner. "What's that?" Marx asked.

"It's another one of my friend's games. It's not as good as *Solution*, but it's still somewhat fun," Sam reported.

Marx sat down next to Sam, and Sam handed him the keyboard so that he could play a round.

```
Because
SHOOT
I could not
SHOOT
stop for
SHOOT
kindly
```

An ink pot combusted on the screen, indicating that Marx, having shot the wrong phrase, had lost a life. "This is the most violent poetry game I've ever played," Marx said.

"You've played other poetry games?"

"Well, technically, no," Marx said. "Your friend's talented. And odd."

Marx Watanabe and Sam were both born in 1974, making them a

year older than most of the class of 1997. Marx had taken a gap year, working for his father's investment firm; Sam, of course, had fallen back because of the time he'd spent in the hospital. They did not, at first glance, have a great deal in common, and in all likelihood, their shared birth year was the reason they had both been assigned to be freshman-year roommates.

The layout of Wigglesworth doubles was such that the room could either be set up as two singles, with one being a walk-through, or as a shared single, with a common area. Marx was quite social, and before he met Sam, he had been hoping to convince him to set up the room with the common area, which would be optimal for having company.

Sam had gotten to the room before Marx, and so Marx met Sam's possessions before he met Sam: an aging desktop computer with a Doctor Who sticker on one side and a Dungeons & Dragons sticker on the other; one large, travel-beaten, hard-sided, baby blue American Tourister suitcase (which would turn out to be filled with impractical lightweight clothes); a black cane; a small bamboo in a pot shaped like an elephant. The vibe Marx got was *single*.

When Sam finally returned to the room, Marx couldn't help but smile. With his sweet, roundish face, light-colored eyes, and mix of white and Asian features, Sam looked almost exactly like an anime character. Astro Boy, or one of the many wisecracking little brothers of manga. As for his personal style: Sam looked like Oliver Twist, during the Artful Dodger years, if Oliver Twist had been from Southern California and a low-level pot dealer instead of a pickpocket. Sam had dark curly hair that he wore parted in the middle and bluntly cut, just above his shoulders. He wore cheap John Lennon–style wire-rimmed glasses and one of those rough hemp striped parkas that are sold in Mexico. His blue jeans were holey and faded to almost white, and he paired his Teva sandals with thick white athletic socks. "I'm Sam," he said, his voice a bit reedy, as if he weren't quite getting enough air. "You must be Marx? You wouldn't happen to know the best place to buy sheets and towels for cheap?"

"Don't worry about it," Marx said, smiling at the cartoon boy come to life. "I've got extras of everything."

"Seriously? Are you sure?" Sam said. "I don't want to impose."

"We're roommates. What's mine is yours," Marx said.

And so it went. Marx helped Sam with everything while never appearing to be helping Sam at all. And so, coats miraculously materialized in plastic bags, just waiting for Sam to ask about them. And gift certificates for restaurants were always left before the holidays when Sam couldn't travel home. And when it became clear that Sam struggled to take the stairs in the dormitory they'd been assigned to, and that the elevator was only intermittently functional, Marx announced his intention to live off campus. Almost no undergraduates at Harvard lived off campus, and Marx said he understood if Sam didn't want to join him. And when the rent on the new place with the elevator was significantly more than what the dorm would have cost, Marx said he'd take the bigger bedroom (which, by the way, wasn't much bigger)—Sam could continue to pay what he'd been paying for the dorm. (The smaller bedroom had a view of the Charles.) And when Sam didn't call home often enough, it was Marx who took the time to call the Lees, back in Los Angeles. "Halmeoni and Halabeoji," he'd greet them in Korean. "Our boy is doing fine." (Marx's father was Japanese, and his mother was Korean American.)

Why did Marx do this for this strange boy, who most people found vaguely unpleasant? He *liked* Sam. He had spent his childhood among rich and supposedly interesting people, and he knew that truly unusual minds were rare. He felt that when Harvard had assigned them to be roommates, Sam had become his responsibility. So, he protected Sam, and he made the world a little easier for Sam, and it cost him next to nothing to do so. Marx's life had been filled with such abundance that he was one of those people who found it natural to care for those around him. In this case, what Marx received in return was the pleasure of Sam's company.

Sam had grown so accustomed to Marx's assistance that it probably went unacknowledged more than it should have, and it was rare, possibly unprecedented, for Sam to ask Marx for anything, least of all his advice.

"You always know the right things to do," Sam said while he watched Marx murdering the poetry of Emily Dickinson. "When it comes to people, I mean."

"Are you saying I don't know the right thing to do when it comes to other things?" Marx joked.

Sam described what he had seen at Sadie's apartment.

Marx said what Sam already knew: "It sounds like your friend is depressed."

"So, what do you do for that?"

Marx paused the game, looked at his friend with a mix of gravity and amusement. Sometimes, Sam seemed so much younger than his twenty-one years. "You can call her parents or tell someone at her college."

Sam took the keyboard from Marx and resumed the game. He positioned his reticle over Hope. "I'm not sure if it's as bad as that, and I feel like that would be an invasion of her privacy."

Marx considered this information. "This is your good friend, right?"

"She used to be my best friend, but we had a falling-out."

"Then, my advice to you is to keep coming around to her apartment," Marx said. "That's what I would do, if it were my friend."

"I don't think she wants me there." Sam paused. "I'm not good at going places where I'm not wanted."

"That doesn't matter," Marx said. "It isn't about you. Just show up every day to check in with her."

"What if she won't talk to me?"

"Let her know you're there. And if you can manage it, bring her a cookie, a book, a movie to watch. Friendship," Marx said, "is kind of like having a Tamagotchi." Tamagotchis, the digital pet keychains, were everywhere that year. Marx had recently killed one that he had received as a holiday gift from a girlfriend. The girlfriend had taken it to be a sign of deeper flaws in Marx's character. "Get her to take a shower, talk a little, go for a walk. Open the windows, if you can. And if things don't improve, see if you can get her to see a professional. And if things *still* don't improve, then you do have to call her parents."

The idea of doing any of these things made Sam supremely uncomfortable, but the next day, after class, he trudged back to Sadie's place, his foot aching by the time he arrived. He went up the stairs, knocked on the door. "Sadie, it's that kid again," the roommate called.

Sadie yelled back, "Tell him I'm not here."

The roommate, who was worried about Sadie as well, swung the door open for Sam, and Sam went back to Sadie's bedroom. She looked the same as yesterday, though she was wearing a different sweatshirt.

Sadie briefly looked up at him. "Sam, honestly, go away," she said. "I'll be fine. I just need to sleep this off." She put her head under the covers.

Sam sat down in Sadie's desk chair. He took out his reading for the core history class he was taking on the history of Asians in America.

Several hours later, he had finished the reading, which had been about Chinese immigration to America in the nineteenth and twentieth centuries, and how Chinese immigrants had only been allowed to do certain kinds of work, like food or cleaning, and that's why there were so many Chinese restaurants and Chinese laundries, i.e., systemic racism. It made him think of his own Korean grandparents, back in K-town, and how proud they'd been when he'd gotten into Harvard. They'd put Harvard merchandise everywhere: bumper stickers on both their aging cars; a CONGRATULATIONS TO OUR GRANDSON, SAMSON, HARVARD, CLASS OF 1997 banner that Bong Cha had hand-quilted, had hung in the pizza place that entire summer; Dong Hyun wore his Harvard T-shirt to work so often, there were holes in it—it had been Marx who had finally sent Sam's grandfather a replacement. Sam felt guilty that he hadn't called them, and then he felt guilty that he was failing to distinguish himself in the Math Department, or in any other way, since he'd gotten to Harvard.

"Are you still here?" Sadie asked.

"I am," Sam said.

He took a bagel in a paper bag out of his backpack and set it on her desk, under his maze, and then he left. If he was honest with himself, it was the presence of the maze that kept him coming back. She had kept it all these years, and then taken it across the country with her, and moved it from dorm room to apartment. The next time he called home, he would tell his grandparents, *Yes, you were right. Sadie had liked the gift.*

On the third day, he brought a library copy of the novel *Galatea 2.2,* which he had recently enjoyed.

On the fourth day, he brought her a handheld version of the original *Donkey Kong* that Marx had once given him as a holiday present.

"Why do you keep coming?" she asked.

"Because," he said. *Click on this word,* he thought, *and you will find links to everything it means. Because you are my oldest friend. Because once, when I was at my lowest, you saved me. Because I might have died without you or ended up in a children's psychiatric hospital. Because I owe you.*

Because, selfishly, I see a future where we make fantastic games together, if you can manage to get out of bed. "Because," he repeated.

On the fifth day, she wasn't in. Sam asked the roommate where she was. "She went to Medical," the roommate reported. The roommate gave Sam a hug. "She seemed a little better, though."

Except for the day he worked his shift at Lamont Library, he went to see her every afternoon for the next week. He would leave her a small offering, per Marx's suggestion, and then he would stay a while before heading back to his apartment.

On the twelfth day, she asked him, "Did you steal *EmilyBlaster?*"

"I borrowed it," Sam said.

"You can have it," she said. "I've got other copies."

On the thirteenth day, he sat at her desk. It had been many years since he had drawn a maze, but he had decided to make her a new one. He had become a better draftsman in the years since he'd drawn that last one, and he wanted her to have a sample of his more recent work. The new maze would show the route from Sam's apartment, by the Charles River, to Sadie's apartment, by the Necco factory.

Sadie got up from the bed, and she looked over Sam's shoulder, at his drawing. "It took a long time for you to get here, didn't it?"

"The average amount of time," he said.

"I might be out tomorrow," she said. "If I start going to my classes and doing the work this week, the dean says I can still salvage the semester."

Sam stood, carefully slipping the maze and his drawing pencils into his backpack. "Are you saying you don't want me to come and see you anymore?"

Sadie laughed. It had been a long time since Sam had heard Sadie laugh genuinely. Many things had changed about her, but he was pleased to discover that her basic laugh was untouched, aside from an inevitable, slight change of key. She had, he thought, one of the world's great laughs. The kind of laugh where a person didn't feel that he was being laughed at. The kind of laugh that was an invitation: *I cordially invite you to join in this matter that I find amusing.* "No, you idiot, I want to schedule a time for us to see each other. I didn't want you to show up and not find me here.

"Promise me, we won't ever do this again," Sadie said. "Promise me, that no matter what happens, no matter what dumb thing we supposedly perpetrate on each other, we won't ever go six years without talking to each other. Promise me you'll always forgive me, and I promise I'll always forgive you." These, of course, are the kinds of vows young people feel comfortable making when they have no idea what life has in store for them.

Sadie offered Sam her hand to shake. Sadie's voice was strong, but Sam thought her eyes looked vulnerable and tired. He took her hand, which was freezing and sweaty at the same time. Whatever her sickness had been, Sam could tell it had not entirely passed.

"You kept my maze," he said.

"I did. Now, let's hear what you thought of *Solution*," Sadie said. She stood up and opened the window of her room, and the fresh air that came in was so crisp and cool, it almost felt like a drug. "Go easy on me, Sammy. You may have noticed that I've been a little depressed."

II

———

INFLUENCES

1

Ichigo, though it was not yet called *Ichigo,* was supposed to be easy. Something that Sam and Sadie could accomplish during the summer between their junior and senior years.

Although the idea that the two of them should make a game together had been foremost in his thoughts since playing *Solution* in December, Sam did not broach the subject with her until March. It was unlike Sam to show such restraint, but he intuited that he needed to proceed slowly. She had been occupied with schoolwork, having fallen behind in her classes because of that dark month, the cause of which was still a mystery to Sam. The terse explanation she'd given for her depression was a "bad breakup." Sam felt it had to be more than that, but out of respect for her, he did not push her to elaborate. They had the rare kind of friendship that allowed for a great deal of privacy within it. One of the reasons they had become such good friends originally was because she had not insisted he tell his sad stories to satisfy her own curiosity. The least he could do was return the favor.

The other thing stopping him was how much he was enjoying having Sadie's fellowship again. The two of them had easily slipped back into the rhythms of their friendship, and they saw each other several times a week for movies, meals, games. He felt fortified in her presence. His arguments and observations were sharper. He was less aware of the brutal New England cold than he had been in the two winters he'd spent without Sadie, and the constant, low-level pain in his foot was less central to his thoughts. When he walked with her, he even dreaded the cobblestones less. Most of the time, Sam did not experience himself as disabled, but the cobblestones, the ice, and the glacial pace at which he had to negotiate them suggested otherwise. If it had snowed, and depending on where the class was located, Sam would sometimes have to leave for class forty-five minutes early, hobbling across campus like an emeritus professor. As he had not considered himself to be disabled, the California boy had not factored in any of this when he'd decided to go to school in the Northeast.

Retrospectively, he realized that he had made a grave miscalculation when he had ended the friendship with Sadie. His mistake had been in thinking the world would be filled with Sadie Greens, people like her. It was not. His high school certainly hadn't been. He had held out some hope that Harvard might be, but the college had proven especially disappointing on this front. There were smart people, yes. There were people with whom you might have a decent conversation for twenty minutes. But to find someone who you wanted to talk to for 609 hours—that was rare. Even Marx—Marx was devoted, creative, and bright, but he was not Sadie.

Sam decided that March was the cutoff point to convince Sadie to make a game. The high achievers who went to Harvard and MIT had usually settled their summer plans by March, if not earlier. On a personal level, Sam felt an urgency to that summer. In a year, give or take, student loans would come due—Harvard was need-blind (that was significantly why he had chosen it), but even his generous financial aid package didn't cover everything. He didn't owe much, but he couldn't conceive of asking Dong Hyun and Bong Cha to help with his loans, and he had not gone to Harvard to be a poor person. He had slowly begun to accept the truth of what Anders Larsson had said to him. Sam did not *love* higher math, there was no Fields Medal in his future, and there was no way it made sense for Sam to take on more debt to get a graduate degree in mathematics. Most likely, he would have to take a job working in tech, finance, or related consultancies—this was what most of his peers did. The way he put it to Marx: "This summer is my last chance to do something truly grand."

One of Sam's eventual strengths as an artist and as a businessman was that he knew the importance of drama, of setting the scene. He wanted to ask her to work with him at a special place—the occasion of their prospective creative union should be memorable. Even then, he felt that if they made a game, and if the game became what he knew it could be, he would want there to be a story about the day Sam Masur and Sadie Green had decided to work together. He was already imagining Sam-and-Sadie lore, and he didn't even have a definitive idea for a game yet. But this was classic Sam—he had learned to tolerate the sometimes-painful present by living in the future.

The way he saw it, he would be proposing to Sadie. He would be getting down on one knee and saying, "Will you work with me? Will you give me your time, and will you trust my hunch that this time will be well spent? Will you believe that we could make great things together?" For all his natural arrogance, he did not assume that she would say yes.

It was Marx who suggested the Glass Flowers. Sam had asked Marx for the most interesting place at Harvard. Marx had been a Harvard Yard tour guide, but even if he hadn't been, he was the kind of well-traveled cicerone who always knew the best parts of any city.

The Ware Collection of Blaschka Glass Models of Plants consists of around four thousand painstakingly accurate fire-blown glass and hand-painted specimens. A German father-and-son team had made them, around the turn of the nineteenth century, as a commission from the university. They were the answer to a problem: How do you preserve the impossible to preserve? Or, in other words, how do you stop time and death? Could there have been a more propitious place to begin the company that would become Unfair Games? What, after all, is a video game's subtextual preoccupation if not the erasure of mortality?

As Sadie described it, in a 2011 interview with the *Descendants of Lovelace* blog:

s.g.: Mazer knew I had made a couple of games at MIT, nothing much more than mini-games at that point. This one called *Solution* got me a little attention.

d.l.: That's the Holocaust one, right? It almost got you thrown out of school.

s.g.: [Rolls eyes.] That's how Sam likes to tell the story. He likes it to have drama, but honestly one person complained, it wasn't that big of a thing ... But Sam—sorry I know I'm supposed to call Sam Mazer, but I always forget. Mazer loved *Solution*. Mazer felt like it was a breakthrough for me. To be honest, I wasn't sure if I'd ever make another game after *Solution*. I felt pretty burnt out. But toward the end of my junior year, Sam says, "You want to go to the Glass Flowers?" And the truth is, I really didn't! It didn't at all sound like something I'd want to do, and it's fairly inconvenient to get to the Harvard Museum of Natural History from where I was living at MIT. But I went up there, because Sam—Mazer!—can be a little persistent when Mazer wants something. And as you probably know, Mazer always wants something. [Laughs.]

So, we trudge up to the exhibit and it's *closed*. It's, like, museum inventory day, or cleaning, or something. There's a poster out front for the Glass Flowers, and I'm not the first person to make this observation, but it's fairly pointless to put up a picture of the Glass Flowers, because the models are so good, they look like *actual* flowers.

And I'm kind of irritated, because now I've gotten all the way here, and I'm not going to see the Glass Flowers, which I didn't want to see in the first place, and I'm annoyed with Sam for not calling the museum first. Sam sits down on a bench and he's kind of out of breath from the walk and he says, "What are you doing this summer?"

And I'm, like, "What are you talking about?"

And he goes, "Stay here, take three months, and make a game with me. Carmack and Romero were the same age as us when they made *Wolfenstein 3D* and *Commander Keen*. We can use Marx's [Watanabe, producer, *Ichigo*] apartment for free. I already asked."

From the time we were kids, we had always gamed together, but until he said that, I had no idea he even wanted to make games. Sam always kept things pretty close to the vest. But, well, I was at a crossroads with my own designing career, and Sam is a brilliant guy and my oldest friend, so I thought, Why not? If it works out, great. If not, I'll spend the summer with my friend. And Marx's apartment was pretty damn sweet—panoramic windows with views of the Charles, on Kennedy Street, just west of Harvard Square.

So, I told him I'd think about it, but I could tell he knew I was going to do it.

We walk back to town, and he looks at me seriously and he says, "Sadie, when you tell this story, say I asked you at the glass flower exhibit. Don't say it was closed." The myth, the narrative, whatever you want to call it, was always of supreme importance to Sam. So, I guess, by even telling this story, I'm betraying him.

When Sadie was in her mid-thirties and what had felt like many lifetimes had passed, she would finally visit the Glass Flowers and find them unexpectedly moving. The flowers were magnificent, of course, but what struck her even more were the models the Blaschkas had made of decomposing fruits, their bruises and discolorations, in medias res, preserved for eternity. *What a world*, Sadie thought. *People once made glass sculptures of decay, and they put these sculptures in museums. How strange and beautiful human beings are. And how fragile.* An elegant older woman, who reminded her of Freda, two years gone, had been the only other person in the gallery that morning. The woman (cashmere cardigan; redolent of Fracas, with its distinctive tuberose notes) had trailed slightly behind Sadie the entire time. When they were done, the woman asked Sadie, "Those were lovely, but where are the *glass* flowers?" The models' verisimilitude was so convincing, the woman had thought they were real.

Sadie's instinct had been to tell Sam, but they weren't speaking at the time.

2

When we first meet Ichigo in a cutscene at the beginning of *Ichigo: A Child of the Sea,* they—for Sadie and Sam conceived of Ichigo as having no gender—are a small child who knows few words and cannot read. Ichigo is sitting on the beach, by their parents' modest seaside house, in what looks like a remote fishing village. They have a shiny black bowl haircut of the kind that an Asian child of any gender might have, and they are wearing only their favorite sports jersey (number 15), which goes to their knees like a dress, and wooden flip-flops. Ichigo is playing with a small bucket and a shovel when the tsunami hits.

Ichigo is swept out to sea, and that is where the game begins. With a limited vocabulary, their only tools that bucket and shovel, Ichigo must find their way home.

A bromide about the creative process is that an artist's first idea is usually the best one. *Ichigo* was not Sam and Sadie's first idea. It was, perhaps, their thousandth.

Herein, the difficulty. Sam and Sadie both knew what they liked in a game, and they could easily tell a good game from a bad game. For Sadie, that knowledge was not necessarily helpful. Her time with Dov and her years studying games in general had made her critical of everything. She could tell you exactly what was *wrong* with any game, but she didn't necessarily know how to make a great game herself. There is a time for any fledgling artist where one's taste exceeds one's abilities. The only way to get through this period is to make things anyway. And it is possible that, without Sam (or someone like him) pushing her through this period, Sadie might not have become the game designer she became. She might not have become a designer at all.

Sadie knew she didn't want to make a shooter, though, again, that was what tended to be popular. (She would *never* want to make a shooter—she, Dov's student to her core, found them disgusting, immoral, and the disease of an immature society; Sam, for his part, enjoyed shooters.) And, in a summer, with only a team of two, there were limitations to what she felt they could accomplish. They weren't trying to go for consoles, and they didn't have the resources to make a fully 3D action game like an N64-era *Zelda* or a *Mario* anyway. The game would be for PC, and it would be 2D or 2½D, if she could swing it. For a long time, that was the extent of what she knew about their game.

In the weeks leading up to the end of the school year, Sadie and Sam brainstormed a long list of ideas on a whiteboard that Sam had stolen from the Science Center. Even with his bad foot, Sam was an accomplished thief, and he enjoyed a petty theft from time to time. He had walked into the Science Center for a goodbye meeting with Larsson. On the way out, he had seen the whiteboard unattended in a hallway, and he rolled it right out of the building, and then kept rolling it—across Harvard Yard, waving at a tour of prospective students as he passed, through Harvard Square, straight down Kennedy Street, and right up into the elevator of their building. The key to being a good thief, Sam always felt, was utter brazenness. Later in the week, he stole a pack of multicolor dry-erase markers from the Harvard Coop. He slipped them into the enormous pocket of the enormous coat that Marx had given him, and he walked right out the door.

For a long time, nothing they wrote on the whiteboard felt essential to them. They might have never made a game before. Their office might be in Sam's rich roommate's apartment, but they were young enough to believe that whatever they made, it could very well become a classic. As Sam often said to Sadie, "Why make anything if you don't believe it could be great?"

It is worth noting that greatness for Sam and Sadie meant different things. To oversimplify: For Sam, greatness meant *popular*. For Sadie, *art*.

By May, with Sam's purloined dry-erase markers already squeaky and parched, Sadie was worried that they would never settle on an idea, and that they'd run out of time to make the game. From her point of view, they were already on an incredibly, indeed impossibly, tight schedule.

They stood in front of the whiteboard, which was covered with their rainbow of brainstorms. "There's something here, I know it," Sam said.

"What if there's not?" Sadie said.

"Then we'll come up with something else," Sam said. He grinned at Sadie.

"You have no right to be this happy," Sadie said.

While Sadie experienced this period of indecision as stressful, Sam didn't feel that way at all. *The best part of this moment,* he thought, *is that everything is still possible.* But then, Sam could feel that way. Sam was a decent artist and he would come to be a decent programmer and level designer, but remember, he had never made a single game before. It was Sadie who knew what it took to make a game—even a bad game—and it was Sadie who would do most of the heavy lifting when it came to the programming, the engine building, and everything else.

Sam was not a physically affectionate person—something to do with having been touched too much during his years in the hospital. But he took Sadie's shoulders in his hands—she was a full inch taller than him—and he looked into her eyes. "Sadie," he said. "Do you know why I want to make a game?"

"Of course. Because you foolishly think it will make you rich and famous."

"No. It's very simple. I want to make something that will make people happy."

"That seems trite," Sadie remarked.

"I don't think it is. Do you remember when we were kids, and how much fun it used to be to spend the whole afternoon in some game world?"

"Of course," Sadie said.

"Sometimes, I would be in so much pain. The only thing that kept me from wanting to die was the fact that I could leave my body and be in a body that worked perfectly for a while—better than perfectly, actually—with a set of problems that were not my own."

"You couldn't land at the top of a pole, but Mario could."

"Exactly. I could save the princess, even when I could barely get out of bed. So, I do want to be rich and famous. I am, as you know, a bottomless pit of ambition and need. But I also want to make something sweet. Something kids like us would have wanted to play to forget their troubles for a while."

Sadie was moved by Sam's words—in the years she had known him, he so rarely mentioned his own pain. "Okay," she said. "Okay."

"Good," Sam said, as if they had settled something. "We should leave for the theater now."

They were taking the night off to go see Marx in a student production of *Twelfth Night* at the mainstage of the American Repertory Theater. It was something of a big deal to be cast in the mainstage show. Since Marx was lending them the apartment for the summer, Sam had thought it would be a good idea for both of them to go.

Without knowing why, Sam had tried to keep Sadie and Marx apart. It wasn't about either of them as individuals. But Sam could be private, verging on paranoid, and he liked to control the flow of information. He feared them comparing notes and somehow ganging up on him. There was another secret part of him that feared they would *prefer* each other to him—everyone, in Sam's estimation, loved Sadie and Marx. No one, Sam felt, had ever loved him except those who had been obligated to love him: his mother (before she had died), his grandparents, Sadie (disputed hospital volunteer), Marx (his assigned roommate). But now, with Marx lending them the apartment, Sadie and Marx would inevitably know each other. Marx, who was playing the lead role of Orsino, had suggested that Sam bring Sadie to the show, and then they could all have dinner at the Charles Hotel afterward, with Marx's dad, who was in town to see the play. "She's moving in next week," Marx said. "I'd like to break bread with her before I leave." Marx was planning to spend the greater part of the summer interning for an investment banking firm in London.

Although Marx participated in college theater for three of his four years, he did not want to be an actor. He had the looks of an actor— six feet tall, wide shoulders, slim waist and hips that looked elegant in clothes, strong jaw and voice, good posture and skin, a glorious pompadour of thick, black hair. If he had a complaint about his college theater career, it was that he was always being cast as wooden strongmen or priggish dukes. In life, Marx wasn't at all wooden or priggish.

He was quick to laugh, warm and energetic, verging on goofy, and so it was strange to him that he was cast this way, that people saw him this way. He wondered what it was about himself. At a cast party for *Hamlet,* having smoked a couple of joints, he once asked a director friend, "What is it about me? Why am I a Laertes and not a Hamlet?"

The friend had seemed uncomfortable when Marx had posed the question. "It's your quality," he had said.

"What about my quality?" Marx had insisted.

"Like, your charisma or something."

"What about my charisma?"

The friend had giggled. "Brother, don't ask me about this now. I'm so wasted."

"Seriously," Marx said. "I want to know."

The friend put his index fingers up to the side corners of his eyes and pulled them wide. He was making Asian eyes. The friend struck that pose for barely a second, and then it was gone. The friend giggled, apologetic. "Forgive me, Marx. I'm so fucking high. I don't know what I'm doing."

"Hey," Marx said. "That is not cool."

"You're so goddamn beautiful," the director said, kissing Marx on the lips.

But in a way, Marx was grateful that the friend had made that racist gesture. It was clarifying to him. The inscrutable, inaccessible, mysterious, exotic thing about him was—*duh*—his Asianness, and it was permanent. And even in *college* theater, there were only so many parts that an Asian actor could play.

Marx's mother was an American-born Korean, and his father was Japanese. At his mother's insistence, he'd gone to an international school in Tokyo, with kids from all over the world in it. It had sheltered him, for the most part, from the racism in his own country. Still, he was aware of a certain amount of racism that the Japanese felt against Koreans, in particular, and foreigners, in general. For example, his Korean American mother, who had taught textile design at Tokyo University, had made very few friends in all the years they had lived in Tokyo—but he could not say whether that was the result of xenophobia, his mother's reserved nature, or her imperfect Japanese. But because he had been mostly raised in Asia, he had been completely sheltered from the kind of racism that Asians experienced in America.

Until Harvard, he had not realized that in America—and not just in its college theaters—there were only so many roles an Asian could play.

The week after that party, Marx changed his major from English (this was as close as Harvard came to a theater major) to economics.

But as much as Sam did not love math, Marx loved college theater. It wasn't so much being on stage that he loved, but the productions themselves. He loved the intimacy of being in a tight group of people who had come together, miraculously, for a brief period in time, for the purpose of making art. He mourned every time a production was over, and he rejoiced when he was cast in a new one. The brief seasons of his college life were marked by the plays in which he performed. Freshman year: *Macbeth*, *The Marriage of Bette and Boo*. Sophomore year: *The Mikado*, *Hamlet*. Junior year: *King Lear*, *Twelfth Night*.

Twelfth Night begins with a shipwreck, though textually this happens offstage. But the director, who was a professional and not a student, had decided to elaborately stage the shipwreck, using much of the ample budget the college had given her to entice her to work with students in the first place. Undulating layers of programmed laser light and smoke; the sounds of waves crashing, thunder, and rain; and even a gentle misting of cold water that made the audience gasp and applaud like delighted children. The cast had sniped that the only thing Jules cared about was the shipwreck, and that it was clear she wished she was directing *The Tempest* instead of *Twelfth Night*.

Sadie, who knew nothing of this scuttlebutt, found the shipwreck mesmerizing. She whispered in Sam's ear, "Our game should start with a shipwreck. Or maybe, a storm." Even as she was saying it, she knew that "shipwreck," and all the elements that a shipwreck could entail, meant that the game might not be finished by September.

"*Yes,*" Sam whispered back. "A child is lost at sea."

Sadie nodded and whispered back, "A little girl—she's maybe two or three years old—is lost at sea and she has to get back to her family, even though she doesn't even know her last name or her phone number or many words or numbers past ten."

"Why is it a little girl?" Sam asked. "Why isn't it a little boy?"

"I don't know. Because in *Twelfth Night* it's a girl?" Sadie said.

Someone sitting nearby shushed them.

"Let's design the character so they don't have a gender," Sam said in a softer whisper. "At that age, gender barely matters. And that way, every gamer will be able to see themselves in him/her."

Sadie nodded. "Cool," Sadie said. "I can live with that."

Marx came onstage as Orsino, to deliver the opening speech of the play: "If music be the food of love, play on." But, by then, Sadie wasn't paying attention to Marx, their benefactor, or the play. She was dreaming about the storm she would make.

After the show, they went to dinner with Marx's father at the restaurant in his hotel. "You already know Sam, and this is Sam's partner, Sadie Green," Marx introduced them. "They're the ones whose video game I'm producing."

Sam had never mentioned to Sadie that Marx would be a producer on the game, which, of course, didn't yet have either a title or a single line of code to its credit. Sadie intuited Sam's reasoning—Marx was giving them the apartment, and the apartment was certainly a kind of equity investment. Still, she felt resentful that she and Sam had never discussed it, and for the next several minutes, she found herself unable to concentrate on the conversation.

Ryu Watanabe would turn out to be far more interested in the nascent game than he was in the play his son had been in. Around the time of Marx's birth, Watanabe-san, a Princeton-educated economist, had left the academic world to get rich. He had succeeded. His portfolio included a chain of convenience stores, a medium-sized cell phone company, and a variety of other international investments. He told them he regretted that he had missed an early opportunity to invest in Nintendo in the 1970s. "They were just a playing-card company," Watanabe-san said, with a self-deprecating laugh. "Hanafuda. For aunties and little children, you know?" Nintendo's most successful product before they made *Donkey Kong* was, indeed, a deck of hanafuda playing cards.

"What's hanafuda?" Sam asked.

"Plastic cards. Quite small and thick, with flowers and scenes of nature," Watanabe-san said.

"Oh!" Sam said. "I know these! I used to play them with my grandmother, but we didn't call them hanafuda. I think the game we played was called Stop-Go?"

"Yes," Watanabe-san said. "In Japan, the game most people play with hanafuda is called Koi Koi, which means . . ."

"Come come," Marx filled in.

"Good boy," Watanabe-san said. "You haven't forgotten all your Japanese."

"It's funny," Sam said. "I always assumed the game was Korean." He turned to Sadie. "Do you remember those little flower cards Bong Cha used to bring to the hospital?"

"Yes," she said, distracted. She was still thinking about Marx and the producer credit, so she didn't even know what she was saying yes to. She decided to change the subject. She turned to Marx's father. "Mr. Watanabe, what did you think of the play?"

"The storm," Watanabe-san said, "was terrific."

"Much better than the duke," Marx said.

"I loved it, too," Sadie said.

"It reminded me of my childhood," Watanabe-san said. "I'm not like Marx here. I'm not a city boy. I was born in a small town on the west coast of Japan, and every year, we waited for the great rains, which always came in the summer. As a child, my greatest fear was that I, or my father, who owned a small fleet of fishing boats, would be washed away to sea."

Sadie nodded and exchanged a look with Sam.

"What conspiracy is this?" Watanabe-san said, smiling.

"Well," Sam said. "That's how our game begins, actually."

"A child is washed out to sea," Sadie said. Once she said it, she knew she would have to do it. "And the rest of the game is how the child gets back home."

"Yes." Watanabe-san nodded. "This is a classic story."

When Sam had described the relationship between Marx and his father, he had said it was fraught, that Watanabe-san was demanding and sometimes even demeaning to Marx. Sadie saw no evidence of that. She found Marx's father to be bright, interesting, and engaged.

Other people's parents are often a delight.

The next day, Sam helped Sadie pack. To save money, Sadie would live in Marx's room and sublet her apartment. "Are you going to put the art in storage?" Sam asked. Whenever he was in her room, he found

Sadie's art comforting, an extension of Sadie herself: the Hokusai wave, the Duane Hanson "Tourists," the Sam Masur maze.

Sadie stopped packing and stood in front of the Hokusai wave, hands on her hips. In the three hours since they'd been at it, Sam had come to realize that, while she was a wonderful person, she was a terrible packer. Each decision required extensive deliberation—which clothes? Which cords? Which computer hardware? It had taken ninety minutes to go through her relatively small bookshelf: Did Sam think she would finally have time to read *Chaos* this summer? Did Sam want to read it? Oh, he had already read it. Well then, she should probably take it, unless he had a copy, in which case she could read his and store hers. And then she would pick up *A Brief History of Time*, and fondly pat its cover. *Maybe I'll read it again this summer?* And then, *Hackers. Have you read this, Sam? It's so good.* Hackers *has a whole section on the Williamses. You know, Sierra games?* King's Quest. Leisure Suit Larry. *We used to love those games.* Sam was beginning to think it would have been easier if she'd taken everything.

"Sadie," Sam said gently. "You can take the art, you know? Marx won't mind if you hang it."

Sadie continued to stare at the Hokusai wave.

"Sadie," Sam repeated.

"Sam, look at this." She pushed him a little so that he had the same vantage point she did. "This is what the game should look like."

The Hokusai print on Sadie's wall was an exhibition poster from the Metropolitan Museum of Art, where it was identified as *The Great Wave at Kanagawa*. (In Japanese, the title is far more ominous, something like, *Under the Wave off Kanagawa*.) *The Great Wave* is arguably the most famous Japanese artwork in the world, and in the 1990s, it was absolutely an MIT student housing staple, only slightly less ubiquitous than those Magic Eye prints that always left Sam so cold. *The Great Wave* depicts an enormous wave that dwarfs the other elements in the frame, three fishing boats and a mountain. The style is clean and graphic, befitting the fact that it was designed to be carved into a cherrywood block and infinitely reproduced.

Sadie knew that the key to making a video game on limited resources was to make the limitations part of the style. (That was why she had made *Solution* black-and-white.) For the same reason that the print would have been reproducible in the 1830s (its limited palette and the deceptive simplicity of its form language), Sadie knew she would be able to re-create this look in computer graphics as well.

Sam considered the Hokusai wave. He backed up, cleaned his glasses, and then considered it some more. "I see it," he said. They were at that rare moment in a collaboration where they were consistently grokking, where consensus was reached quickly on almost everything. "Is the child Japanese like Marx's father?"

"No," Sadie said. "Not explicitly. Or maybe that's not the right word. Not obviously. Not like we're making a point of it. But, in a way, it doesn't matter where the child is from—they aren't verbal, right? They can't speak much or read. Their own language is a foreign language. So, the gamer won't know anyway."

The decision to style the world after the Hokusai pushed everything in a Japanese direction, though. And as they were coming up with the character design for their "child," they found themselves drawn to Japanese references over and over: the deceptively innocent paintings of Yoshitomo Nara; Miyazaki anime like *Kiki's Delivery Service* and *Princess Mononoke;* other, more adult anime like *Akira* and *Ghost in the Shell,* both of which Sam had loved; and of course, Hokusai's *Thirty-Six Views of Mount Fuji* series, the first of which is *The Great Wave.*

It was 1996, and the word "appropriation" never occurred to either of them. They were drawn to these references because they loved them, and they found them inspiring. They weren't trying to steal from another culture, though that is probably what they did.

Consider Mazer in a 2017 interview with *Kotaku,* celebrating the twentieth-anniversary Nintendo Switch port of the original *Ichigo:*

KOTAKU: It is said that the original *Ichigo* is one of the most graphically beautiful low-budget games ever made, but its critics also accuse it of appropriation. How do you respond to that?

MAZER: I do not respond to that.

KOTAKU: Okay . . . But would you make the same game if you were making it now?

MAZER: No, because I am a different person than I was then.

KOTAKU: In terms of its obvious Japanese references, I mean. Ichigo looks like a character Yoshitomo Nara could have painted. The world design looks like Hokusai, except for the

Undead level, which looks like Murakami. The soundtrack sounds like Toshiro Mayuzumi . . .

MAZER: I won't apologize for the game Sadie and I made. [Long pause.] We had many references—Dickens, Shakespeare, Homer, the Bible, Philip Glass, Chuck Close, Escher. [Another long pause.] And what is the alternative to appropriation?

KOTAKU: I don't know.

MAZER: The alternative to appropriation is a world in which artists only reference their own cultures.

KOTAKU: That's an oversimplification of the issue.

MAZER: The alternative to appropriation is a world where white European people make art about white European people, with only white European references in it. Swap African or Asian or Latin or whatever culture you want for European. A world where everyone is blind and deaf to any culture or experience that is not their own. I hate that world, don't you? I'm terrified of that world, and I don't want to live in that world, and as a mixed-race person, I literally don't exist in it. My dad, who I barely knew, was Jewish. My mom was an American-born Korean. I was raised by Korean immigrant grandparents in Koreatown, Los Angeles. And as any mixed-race person will tell you—to be half of two things is to be whole of nothing. And, by the way, I don't own or have a particularly rich understanding of the references of Jewishness or Koreanness because I happen to be those things. But if Ichigo had been fucking Korean, it wouldn't be a problem for you, I guess?

Sam and his mother, Anna Lee, arrived in Los Angeles in July of 1984. It was the summer of the Olympics, the first Summer Olympics to be held in the United States in fifty years. The mood was hopeful and manic. Los Angeles, especially when taken from a distance, was not a beautiful city, but she could will herself to be beautiful, if only for two weeks. Beauty, after all, is almost always a matter of angles and resolve. Urban renewal projects were accomplished so frantically it seemed like time-lapse photography. Stadiums built, hotels refurbished, decrepit buildings detonated, flora planted, less appealing native flora removed, roads paved, bus routes added, uniforms created, musicians recruited, dancers hired, corporate sponsors slapped on any surface that would receive a logo, graffiti painted over, homeless discreetly relocated, coyotes euthanized, bribes paid; deeper schisms around race and class momentarily tabled because company was coming! L.A. reinvented herself as a bright, modern city of the future who knew how to throw a party. With the narcissism of childhood, Sam would feel as if the "improvements" were being enacted for his and Anna's benefit, and he would always feel a tenderness when he thought of those first months in Los Angeles and the way the city had rolled out its red carpet just for him.

They stayed with Anna's parents, Dong Hyun and Bong Cha Lee, in their yellow Craftsman-style house in sleepy Echo Park, which was still twenty years away from being a hipster enclave. Dong Hyun and Bong Cha spent most of their waking hours at their eponymous pizzeria in nearby Koreatown, and that was where Sam would pass most of that summer. Anna had told Sam about K-town, but he had no sense of how large K-town would actually be. He thought it would be like Chinatown in New York, a couple of blocks of apothecaries, gift shops, and restaurants, or like Thirty-Second Street, Manhattan's Korean restaurant row, where he and his mom would sometimes go after a show for bulgogi and banchan. K-town in Los Angeles was massive. It was miles and miles of Korean people and things, right in the center of town. There were Korean faces on the billboards, and these Korean faces were celebrities, and even if Sam didn't know who these celebrities were, he hadn't known that there *could be* Korean celebrities. There was bubbly Korean writing on all the storefronts, more Korean writing than English. If you didn't read hangul, you were basically a K-town illiterate. There were Korean bookstores and bridal salons and grocery stores as big as white-people grocery stores that sold enormous, individually wrapped Asian pears and family-sized jars of kimchi and thousands of Korean beauty products promising textureless skin, and thick paperback volumes of fluorescent and pastel-colored manhwa. There were enough Korean barbecues to eat at a different one every day for a year. There were even two Korean television channels that came in on Bong Cha's antenna. And yes, there were people. Sam had never seen so many Asian people in one place before. And seeing them made him wonder if he had completely mis-understood the world and who the people in it were. Maybe the whole world was Asian?

What was amazing to Sam—and what became a theme of the games he would go on to make with Sadie—was how quickly the world could shift. How your sense of self could change depending on your location. As Sadie would put it in an interview with *Wired*, "The game character, like the self, is contextual." In Koreatown, no one ever thought Sam was Korean. In Manhattan, no one had ever thought he was white. In Los Angeles, he was the "white cousin." In New York, he was that "little Chinese kid." And yet, in K-town, he felt more Korean than he ever had before. Or to put a finer point on it, he felt more aware of the fact that he was a Korean and that that was not neces-sarily a negative or even a neutral fact about him. The awareness gave him pause: perhaps a funny-looking mixed-race kid could exist at the center of the world, not just on its periphery.

In Los Angeles, Sam suddenly had grandparents, aunts, uncles, cousins, all of them invested in the drama of his and Anna's lives. Where would Anna and Sam live? Where would they go to church? Would Sam enroll in Korean school? Would Anna star in a television show? Why had she left New York? All of these issues weighed plea-surably on the family. His mother was treated like a celebrity. She was the Korean girl who had made it among white people. She had been in *A Chorus Line*. On Broadway! His grandmother, Bong Cha, doted on him, and they played the Korean card game Stop-Go, and she fed him mandu and pleaded with his mother to take him to church. "But he will grow up without God, Anna. He will grow up lost," Bong Cha said.

"Sam's very spiritual," Anna said. "We talk about the universe all the time."

"Oh, Anna," Bong Cha said.

That summer, Sam's greatest spiritual experience was with the *Donkey Kong* machine in his grandparents' pizza place. The machine had been a promotional idea of Dong Hyun's during the early-'80s height of arcade game mania. When the machine had arrived, he had sent out postcards: DONG & BONG'S GETS DONKEY KONG. FAMI-LIES, COME EAT AND PLAY! BUY ONE OF OUR FAMOUS, NEW YORK STYLE PIZZAS! ONE GAME FREE ON US! The postcard had a non-

Nintendo-licensed illustration of Donkey Kong tossing pizza dough in the air that Bong Cha had drawn. When he named the restaurant in 1972, Dong Hyun knew that if you removed the Hyun and the Cha from his and his wife's perfectly ordinary, respectable Korean names, Dong and Bong became hilarious-sounding to white people. He hoped the *Donkey Kong* promotion would further capitalize on the comic properties of their names, drawing in customers from beyond K-town even—that is to say, nice white people. For a time, it did.

By the time Sam arrived in Los Angeles, arcade mania had passed, and almost no one ever competed with him to play Dong Hyun's machine. Dong Hyun would turn the machine's release key so Sam could play as long as he wanted. Sam felt a peacefulness come over him when he was playing *Donkey Kong* in his grandparents' pizza parlor. When he could time the little Japanese Italian plumber's jumps and ascend the staircases at the right pace, it felt as if the universe was capable of being ordered. It felt as if it were possible to achieve a perfect timing. It felt like synchronicity. It felt like the opposite of a frigid winter night when a woman had jumped from an apartment building on Amsterdam Avenue and landed at his and his mother's feet. That woman, her face, the gruesome angle of her neck like the handle of an umbrella, the earthy, copper scent of her blood mixed with his mother's familiar tuberose perfume—she appeared to him almost every night in his dreams. He wondered what had happened to her after she'd been taken away in an ambulance. He wondered what her name was. He never mentioned her to Anna. He knew that woman was the reason they had left New York. "In California," his mother had promised, "nothing bad will ever happen to us again."

Sam turned ten the day Mary Lou Retton won the women's all-around gold medal. At the party his grandparents threw for him, the television was left on, but muted, so that people could celebrate Sam while still watching Mary Lou. It didn't matter to Sam that everyone's eyes were on the television; he, too, wanted to know if she would win. Sam blew out ten candles, and in the distance, Mary Lou Retton received a perfect 10 on her floor routine. And he almost felt like he, by blowing out the ten candles at the precise moment that he had, had been what caused her to get the perfect 10. He fantasized that the universe was a Rube Goldberg machine. If he had blown out only nine candles, maybe the Romanian girl would have won instead.

That next day, Sam and Anna went to lunch by themselves. To Sam, it seemed like years since it had just been them, and even at barely ten years old, he felt a palpable nostalgia for the railroad flat in derelict Manhattan Valley and the takeout Chinese and the life they had left behind. At a nearby table, two men in suits were discussing the gymnastics final in booming voices.

"She never would have won if the Russians hadn't boycotted," the man insisted. "It's not a victory if the best players aren't there."

Sam asked his mother whether she thought the man with the loud voice was right.

"Hmm." Anna sipped at her iced tea and then she rested her chin in her hands, which Sam had learned to recognize as her philosophizing gesture. Anna was a great talker, and it was one of the most profound pleasures of young Sam's life to discuss the world and its mysteries with his mother. No one took him, and his queries, more seriously than she did. "Even if what he says is true, I think it's still a victory," she said. "Because she won on this day, with this particular set of people. We can never know what else might have happened had other competitors been there. The Russian girls could have won, or they could have gotten jet-lagged and choked." Anna shrugged. "And this is the truth of any game—it can only exist at the moment that it is being played. It's the same with being an actor. In the end, all we can ever know is the game that was played, in the only world that we know."

Sam considered his French fries. "Are there other worlds?"

"I think there probably are," Anna said. "But I don't have any hard proof."

"In some other world, maybe Mary Lou doesn't win the gold medal. Maybe she doesn't even place?"

"Maybe."

"I like Mary Lou," Sam said. "She seems like a hard worker."

"Yes, but I imagine all those girls work hard. Even the ones that didn't win."

"Did you know she's only four foot nine inches tall? That's only two inches taller than me."

"Sam, do you have a crush on Mary Lou Retton?"

"No," Sam said. "I was stating a fact."

"She's only six years older than you."

"Mom, don't be gross."

"It seems like a big age gap now, but it won't in a couple of years."

At that moment, one of the men in suits approached their table. "Anna?" It was the man with the loud voice.

Anna turned. "Oh hello," she said.

"I thought that was you," the man with the loud voice said. "You're looking well."

"George, how are you?" Anna said.

The man with the loud voice turned toward Sam. "Hello there, Sam."

Sam knew the man was familiar, but for half a second, he couldn't quite place him. It had been three years since he had last seen him, a lifetime when one is ten. And then he remembered who George was. "Hi, George," Sam said. George shook Sam's hand in a casual, professional way.

"I didn't know you were in L.A.," George said.

"We just got here," Anna said. "I was planning to call you when we'd gotten settled."

"So, this is a permanent thing?" George said.

"Yes, I think so," Anna said. "My agent has been begging me to come out for pilot season for years."

"Pilot season is in the spring," George said.

"Yes," Anna said. "Of course, I know that. But I had to wait until Sam's school year ended, so we're here now, and I'll be ready for next year."

George nodded. "Well. Good to see you, Anna." George began to walk away and then he turned and walked back to the table. "Sam," George said, "if you have the time, I would very much like us to have lunch. You name the day, and my assistant, Miss Elliot, will set it up."

Sam met his father, George Masur, at La Scala, one of those pleasantly decaying Los Angeles establishments that sounded fancier than they actually were. He had only met George a half-dozen times before, usually when George had been in New York City on business. On these occasions, they did New York City–tourist or divorced-dad things together: FAO Schwarz, afternoon tea at the Plaza, the Bronx Zoo, the Children's Museum of Manhattan, the Rockettes, etc. These activities had not bonded them, and Sam felt no meaningful connection to George. He did not, for instance, call him Dad; he called him

George. When he thought of George, he thought of him as a person that his mother had once had sex with, though Sam, at age ten, was not entirely clear on the mechanics of sex.

Sam knew that George was an agent for the William Morris Agency, and that the William Morris Agency was not the agency that represented his mother. He knew that George had come backstage after a revival performance of *Flower Drum Song* to tell his mother that her rendition of "I Enjoy Being a Girl" had been the best thing in it. He knew that George and his mother had dated for about six weeks and that his mother had ended it for ambiguous reasons. He knew that six weeks after that, she had determined that she was pregnant. He knew that she had considered having an abortion, and he knew what an abortion was. He knew that she had never wanted to marry George. He knew that George had written her a check for $10,000 when she told him about the pregnancy, but that she had never asked for it. He knew that the money had been deposited in a trust fund for Sam's college, and that George had not made any contributions to the fund since. Sam knew these things mainly from Anna's acting class friend, Gary. He sometimes babysat for Anna when she had to work, and he was chatty to a fault.

George was wearing a suit of fine, summer-weight wool—Sam would think of him as always wearing a suit. He offered Sam his hand to shake. "Hello, Sam. Thanks for making the time for this meeting," George said.

"You're welcome," Sam said.

"I'm glad we were able to make this happen."

Sam asked George what he should order, and George suggested the "famous chopped salad," which Sam would end up finding watery. They spoke of the Olympics, the family in K-town, the differences between living in New York City and Los Angeles.

"You know," George said, "I'm Jewish, which means that you are partially Jewish as well."

"Does it?" Sam said.

"I know it probably doesn't seem like it, but you're half of what I am."

Sam nodded.

"It wasn't my choice that we should see each other so little, you know."

Sam nodded again.

"I'm not saying it's Anna's fault, but your mother doesn't always make things easy. Did you know that I asked her to move here when she was pregnant? She refused. She said she couldn't see herself raising a child in Los Angeles. And now she's here." George shrugged. "What's funnier than people, right?" He looked at Sam expectantly.

"People," Sam said, sounding like a sixty-year-old man. It seemed like the response George was seeking.

"People is right. I have a place in Malibu," George said. "Do you think you'd like to come to the Bu sometime?"

"Yes," Sam said politely, though he felt no particular desire to go to Malibu. "It takes a long time to drive to . . . the Bu."

"Not that long. Maybe you'd like to meet my girlfriend? She's a very nice-looking woman. I'm not saying this to brag, but to paint a picture for you. It is important to make things visual for people. If you can do that, you'll be ahead of the game, Sam my boy. But yes, my girlfriend is a very attractive woman. Do you know the James Bond movies? She was Bond's second secretary in the last one. Some people say that playing the secretary in a Bond movie is not the same as being a Bond girl, but I think it is." He looked at Sam. "What do you think?"

"Hmm," Sam said. "I don't really have an opinion about that."

George gestured a checkmark, and a waiter brought the bill. He paid the check and shook Sam's hand again. George handed Sam a business card: GEORGE MASUR, MOTION PICTURE TALENT AGENT, WILLIAM MORRIS AGENCY.

"You can call this number if you ever need anything. Miss Elliot will answer, but she always knows where to find me, and if she can't find me, she will give me the message."

They went outside. They were a few minutes shy of the time Bong Cha was supposed to pick Sam up.

George looked at his watch.

"You don't have to wait," Sam said.

"No, it's fine."

"I'm by myself all the time." Sam realized that there might have been an implied insult to his mother in this disclosure. "I mean, not all the time."

At precisely one o'clock, Bong Cha drove up to the curb, neatly wedging her burgundy MG into a space barely half a foot longer than the length of the car. Bong Cha was a spectacular, aggressive driver. She had driven for a local moving company when she and Dong Hyun had first arrived in L.A., and she was known in the family for her epic parallel parking abilities. Sam said she drove like she was playing *Tetris*.

Sam waved to George as he got into the car. "Goodbye, George."

"Goodbye, Sam."

Sam closed the door. Bong Cha wore a head kerchief and professional driving gloves that had been a gift from her husband, and her car's interior was, as always, immaculate. The driver's seat had a wooden bead overlay that supposedly gave a massage or did something for circulation; maneki neko, the zaftig hospitality cat, waved from the back window; an air freshener in the shape of the Virgin Mary hung from the rearview mirror. The scent had long faded, but a label indicated that it had once been pine. As Sam often put it, "To be in a car with my grandmother was to know everything you needed to know about her."

"Your mother says not to say. But I do not like him," Bong Cha said.

"He said I could come visit him in Malibu."

"Malibu," Bong Cha said, as if the word was disgusting to her. "Your mother is so beautiful and talented. But she has terrible taste in men."

"But," Sam said, "George said I was half-him. And if I'm half-him . . ."

Bong Cha caught her mistake. "You are one-hundred-percent perfect, good Korean boy I love."

At the stoplight, Bong Cha patted Sam on the head, and then she kissed him on his forehead and then both of his delicious, round, shtetl Buddha cheeks, and Sam accepted her lie without argument.

3

The first week of July, Marx emailed Sam to say he was returning from the internship early: *Dungeon Master Masur, Coming back from London this Saturday. The internship was a bust—will explain later. I'd like to crash on the couch, if it's copacetic with you and Miss Green. I can also run any errands you guys need and generally smooth the way in my role as "producer," ha ha. Dad was quite impressed with the two of you. Can't wait to see how the game is going. Does it have a title yet? Marx, Level 9 Paladin*

When Sam reported to Sadie that Marx would be back on Saturday, she was not pleased. "Can't you ask him not to come?" Sadie said.

"I can't," Sam said. "It's *his* apartment."

"I know," Sadie said. "That's why he's getting a producer credit. If he stays with us, does that mean we *don't* have to give him a credit anymore?"

"No," Sam said.

"We're finally getting into a good work rhythm," Sadie said.

"Marx is awesome," Sam said. "He can help us if he's here."

"With what?" Sadie said. As far as Sadie knew, Marx was a good-looking rich kid with a wide range of interests and very few skills. At Crossroads, where she'd gone to high school, half of her male classmates had been Marxes.

"With everything that we're not doing. You'll see," Sam said. "He's a resource, if we choose to employ him that way."

As the matter had already been decided, Sadie went back to work.

They had made a great deal of progress on the design of their still nameless child. Sam had come up with the child's wardrobe: the father's sports jersey worn long, like a dress; the wooden flip-flops. They had settled on the slick bowl haircut, which they both liked aesthetically and practically. A helmet-like hairstyle would have the cleanest look when layered into the complicated Hokusai-inspired backgrounds.

With the child's design squared away, Sadie was perfecting the child's movements. She wanted the walk to feel buoyant and slightly out of control, like a baby duck trailing after its mother. In the design document that she and Sam had written: "The child's body moves the way a body can move before it has felt or even encountered the idea of pain." Oh, the ambitions of design documents!

Sadie devoted several days to the problem of the child's walk. She gave the character a tiny stride length, with fast steps that would leave bird-like, fading footprints. This was better, but what finally cracked it for her was to make the child not just move linearly, but to always have a few awkward accelerating steps to the side even when the player was piloting the character forward.

She showed her work to Sam. "It's good," Sam said. He moved the child around the screen. "But that's me," he said. "That's how I walk."

"No, it isn't," Sadie said.

"I'm a lot slower. But when I want to go forward, I end up going to the side," Sam said. "At my high school, this one asshole used to call it the Sam shuffle."

"I hate kids," Sadie said. "I'm never having them." Sadie took the keyboard back from Sam. She moved their child around the screen. "Okay, it might be a little bit you," Sadie conceded. "But I honestly wasn't thinking of you when I was doing it."

Suddenly, Sadie became aware of the sound of explosions. "What's that?" She crouched down, and Sam went to the window. Distantly, they could see fireworks. They had both forgotten it was the Fourth of July.

When Marx arrived in town, they showed him a demo of the first level. "This isn't at all finished," Sadie said. "There's no lighting or sound, but it'll give you a sense of the look we're going for, and what the basic gameplay will feel like. I haven't started making the storm yet either."

Sam handed Marx the controller. The screen showed the child in the middle of the water, debris floating around them. Marx was an experienced gamer, but it took him a bit to get the hang of it, and the child perished several times under his command. "Jesus, this is hard," Marx said.

The challenge of *Ichigo*'s first level was to make your way to shore without drowning while managing to grab your bucket and shovel. It was part rhythm game—you must figure out the controls that make the child swim—part action-adventure. The world was completely immersive: there were few clues, and no text. Eventually, Marx made it to the beach. When he saw the child walk, he exclaimed, delighted, "It's Little Sam!"

"Please don't call them that," Sadie begged.

"I told you so," Sam said to Sadie.

Marx manipulated the character around the beach.

"There's no level two yet," Sadie warned.

"No, I just wanted to see what Little Sam looked like from behind."

"Please stop calling them that," Sadie said.

"What's the fourteen on the back of Little Sam's jersey mean?" Marx asked.

"Nothing," Sam said. "The number of the kid's father's favorite sports star or something. We haven't decided yet."

"Juu-yon," Marx said.

"What's Juu-yon?" Sam asked.

"It's fourteen in Japanese," Marx said. "You said the kid doesn't have a name, right? Maybe someone calls him Juu-yon for the number on the back of the jersey."

"Interesting," Sam said.

"They're not a he, and I don't like the *Jew* part," Sadie said. "For obvious reasons, that will sound weird to American audiences."

"How about Ichi Yon. That means one, four. Maybe the kid can't count above ten, so they don't know the word for fourteen yet," Marx said.

Sadie nodded. "I almost like that. But it's maybe not dynamic enough."

"You know what might be better than one, four? How about one, five? Ichi, Go. The kid's name is Ichigo," Marx said. "You could call the game that, too. Ichigo also means strawberry."

"Ichigo," Sam tried out the word. "Go is dynamic. Go, go, Ichigo, go."

"Reminds me of the theme from *Speed Racer*," Sadie said dismissively.

"Right. That's a good thing," Sam said.

"It's totally up to you guys, obviously," Marx said. "I'm not the designer."

Sadie thought about it. She didn't love that Marx, whom she already resented, had just named their game. "Ichigo," she said slowly. *Dammit*, she thought, *it's fun to say*. "I can live with that."

Though it took Sadie years to admit this to Sam, Marx did prove incredibly useful that summer. No, Marx wasn't a game designer. He wasn't an ace programmer, like Sadie, and he couldn't draw, like Sam. But he did almost everything else for them, and his contributions ranged from the pedestrian, but necessary, to the creatively essential. Marx organized workflow, so Sadie and Sam were more aware of what the other was doing and what they needed to be doing. He made long lists of supplies they would need. He was more than liberal with his credit card—they always needed more memory and storage, and they were regularly burning out graphics cards—and he must have made fifty trips to the large computer store in Central Square that summer. He opened a bank account, and an LLC, Go, Ichigo, Go. He arranged for them to pay taxes (which saved them money in the short term by making their business purchases tax-free), and if, at some point, they needed to hire people, which he knew they would, he set them up for that, too. He made sure everyone ate, hydrated, and slept (at least a little), and he kept their workspaces clean and free of chaos. He was an experienced gamer, and as such, made an excellent level tester and bug spotter. Beyond all that, Marx also had taste and a sense of story. It was Marx who suggested the famous "underworld" sequence in Ichigo ("Ichigo needs to be as low as possible," he said), and it was Marx who turned them on to Takashi Murakami and Tsuguharu Foujita. It was Marx, with his love of avant-garde instrumental music, who played Brian Eno, John Cage, Terry Riley, Miles Davis, and Philip Glass on his CD player while Sadie and Sam worked. It was Marx who suggested they reread *The Odyssey* and *The Call of the Wild* and *Call It Courage*. He also had them read the story structure book *The Hero's Journey*, and a book about children and verbal development, *The Language Instinct*. He wanted the pre-verbal Ichigo to feel authentic, to have details that came from life. Marx saw Ichigo as a homecoming story, but also a language story. How do we communicate in a world when we don't have language? This story compelled Marx, in part, because his mother had never fully spoken Japanese, and he believed that was why she had spent most of her adult life lonely and sometimes depressed. It was Marx who began to understand the game on a sales level, too. It is one thing to have made a great game, but there will inevitably come a time when someone needs to be able to articulate to other people *why* it's a great game.

By the middle of August, Sadie and Sam had rough versions of six of Ichigo's eventual fifteen levels, and this was, in large part, a result of Marx's organization. In a way, Marx found producing for Sadie and Sam to be not entirely different from just being Sam's roommate. Without calling a great deal of attention to himself, he made things easy for them. He fought fires. He anticipated needs and obstacles before they arose. That is what a producer does, and Marx would turn out to be a very fine producer.

But the best thing Marx did for them was this: He believed in them. He loved Ichigo. He loved Sam. He was growing to love Sadie, too.

"So, what's the deal with you and Sadie?" Marx asked Sam on a sweltering night in early August. The air-conditioning had gone out in the apartment, which was already hot from the computer equipment they were running. To try to keep cool, Marx and Sam were wearing nothing but their boxer shorts and pressing cold bottles to their foreheads. It was rare that the three of them weren't together, but on this night, Sadie had left the house to meet with a friend from high school who was in town and, possibly, to escape the heat of the computers for a while.

"She's my best friend," Sam said.

"Sure," Marx said, "I get that. But is it, you know—I hope this isn't weird that I'm asking this—is it romantic? Or has it ever been romantic?"

"No," Sam said. "We've never . . . It's more than romantic. It's better than romance. It's friendship." Sam laughed. "Who cares about romance anyway?"

"Some people do," Marx said. "I guess I'm asking because . . . well, would you mind if I ever asked her out?"

Sam laughed again. "Ask *Sadie Green* out? Go for it. I doubt she would say yes."

"Why?" Marx said.

"Because . . ." *She hates you,* Sam wanted to say. *Because she thinks you're an idiot and she resents that you're even here.* "Because she knows you date a lot," Sam said.

"How?"

"I mean, it's not exactly a state secret. You're always with someone, and never for more than two weeks. Actually, now that I'm thinking about it, I don't think it's a good idea if you ask Sadie out. Not because I feel *that way* toward her, but because we're all colleagues, aren't we? I don't want anything to get in *Ichigo*'s way."

"No, you're right," Marx said. "Forget I mentioned it."

The "two weeks" figure Sam had given was an exaggeration—Marx's usual relationship lasted around six. Marx was great at being in love, for a bit, and certainly, no one ever left a relationship with Marx feeling abused or hurt. He had the gift of letting people think it was their idea to end the relationship, thereby converting most of his ex-lovers into friends. It was only weeks, months, sometimes years later that Marx's ex would think, "Hmm, I think Marx may have broken up with *me.*" That said, Marx could not set foot in Harvard Square without running into an ex, and usually, that person was happy to see him.

If Marx at twenty-two had a problem, it was that he was attracted to too many things and people. Marx's favorite adjective was "interesting." The world seemed filled with interesting books to read, interesting plays and movies to see, interesting games to play, interesting food to taste, and interesting people to have sex with and sometimes even to fall in love with. To Marx, it seemed foolish not to love as many things as you could. In the first months she knew him, Sadie disparaged Marx to Sam by calling him "the romantic dilettante."

But for Marx, the world was like a breakfast at a five-star hotel in an Asian country—the abundance of it was almost overwhelming. Who wouldn't want a pineapple smoothie, a roast pork bun, an omelet, pickled vegetables, sushi, and a green-tea-flavored croissant? They were all there for the taking and delicious, in their own way.

Among the many people who had dated Marx since he'd been at Harvard, it was said, sometimes bitterly, that the only real relationship Marx had was with Sam. Marx did love Sam, but he did not want to have sex with Sam. Sam felt like his baby brother. He would protect him to the death.

Sadie, however . . . Marx felt that she was another story. Sadie was *like* Sam, but she was not Sam, and this was deeply attractive to him. To Marx, there was something richer and more *interesting* and complicated about her than the people he typically dated. He was not foolish—he knew that she didn't seem to like him—this was rare for Marx; everyone liked Marx!—but still, he wanted to know what it would be like if she did like him. He wanted her to talk to him the way she talked to Sam. Marx was a prodigious reader, and he felt like Sadie might be the kind of book that one could read many times, and always come away with something new. But Marx was attracted to so many people that when Sam told him not to pursue her, he didn't take it especially hard.

4

Sadie didn't begin work on the storm until the middle of August. She knew the storm would be the gamer's first experience of *Ichigo*, and she felt pressure to make it spectacular. She also knew it would, in all likelihood, be the last thing she had a chance of completing before she and Sam both had to return to their respective schools in the fall.

Sam and Sadie hadn't said it to each other yet, but they both knew they weren't going to finish the game by September. They knew the work they were doing was good—better than good even. They may have felt that if they articulated the fact that the game would not be completed in the summer—which after all, had been Sam's arbitrary deadline—they would somehow break the magic of their collaboration. Marx, ever the good producer, had tried to gently broach the subject with them. He had suggested they come up with a school year work schedule, but neither had wanted to discuss it. Sam and Sadie would ignore the realities of their lives and crunch for as long as they could.

Like most twenty-year-olds, Sadie had never built a complicated graphics and physics engine before, and it was to be expected that she struggled with building one for *Ichigo*. Sam and Sadie wanted the graphics to have the lightness of transparent watercolors, but Sadie could not achieve this lightness, no matter what she tried. When Ichigo ran, for instance, she wanted the look to be less solid, almost watery. The aspirational design document she and Sam had written described Ichigo's run (in contrast to their walk) as having "the speed, beauty, and danger of water in motion. When the child runs, they resemble nothing so much as a wave. When they jump, they are a typhoon." In her initial attempts, Ichigo only looked blurry and invisible—nothing like "water in motion." When she approached the look she wanted, the game would, more often than not, abruptly crash. But the real weaknesses of Sadie's engine did not become apparent until she was forced to make the storm.

What is a storm? Sadie thought. *It is water, and it is light, and it is wind. And it is how these three elements act on the surfaces they touch. How hard can that be?*

Sadie showed her first attempt at the cutscene storm to Sam. He watched it twice before he weighed in.

"Sadie," he said, "I don't want to hurt your feelings, but this isn't that good yet."

Sadie knew it wasn't good, but it still pissed her off. "What isn't good about it?" she demanded.

"Nothing feels real."

"How can anything feel real when our landscapes look like wood-block prints?"

"Maybe 'real' is the wrong word. I don't feel anything when I look at it. I don't feel scared. I don't feel . . ." Sam played the scene again. "It's the lighting," Sam said. "I think the lighting is off. And the texture. The water . . . The water doesn't feel, like, *wet.*"

"If it's so easy, you try building a fucking storm!" Sadie went into her room and she slammed the door, and then once she was alone, she effortlessly made a storm with her eyes.

Sadie was exhausted, and she felt that she was failing *Ichigo.* The ideas in their design document were beautiful, and the work Sam was creating was beautiful, and it was her job to render this work in game form. Sadie loathed games where the box art was spectacular but when you went to play the actual game, it looked nothing like the concept art.

And it wasn't only that Sam hadn't liked her storm, or that his criticisms potentially suggested larger issues in the game's graphics overall. It was that she had barely slept or showered for three months, and they still weren't going to finish this game! They had done so much work—they had mapped out all the levels and they had written the entire story and they had designed the backgrounds and the characters, and yet . . . there was still SO MUCH WORK to do. She felt herself begin to panic. She went into Marx's nightstand where she knew he had left a passel of neatly rolled joints, and she smoked one.

Sam knocked on the door. "May I come in?"

"Sure," Sadie said. She was beginning to be pleasantly high.

Sam sat on the bed next to her, and she offered him the joint, which he refused. He hated when Sadie or Marx smoked, and he opened the window. At twenty-two, Sam was a complete teetotaler. He never drank, didn't even like taking aspirin. The only drugs he'd ever taken were whatever painkillers he'd been given in the hospital, and he hadn't liked the way they had clouded his ability to think. The body part that worked consistently well for Sam was his brain, and he was not going to compromise it. Because of this experience, Sam often suffered through pain that probably should have and could have been somewhat ameliorated.

"It's the engine," Sadie said without emotion. "It's my lighting and texture engine. It's no good."

"What's wrong with it?" Sam asked.

"It's . . ." Sadie said. "It's me . . . I'm not good enough at making one yet."

"You can do anything," Sam said. "I completely believe in you."

Sam's belief weighed heavily on her. She got into bed and pulled the covers over her head. "I need a nap."

While Sadie rested, Sam went to work researching game engines. He knew it was possible to borrow game engines from other companies. If you found one that was like the work you wanted, using another designer's game engine might save you a lot of work and even, in the long run, expense. He and Sadie had discussed this once before, and he knew she was against using another designer's engine. From the beginning, she had insisted all the programming be theirs. Because if it wasn't, their game would be less original, and they'd cede power (and often, profit) to the maker of the engine. Of course, she was parroting Dov's teachings.

Still, Sam spent the rest of the afternoon looking through all the games that he, Sadie, and Marx owned. As a largely self-taught programmer, Sam learned to do things by taking games apart. Although reverse engineering is a common practice in tech, Sam had learned this technique from his grandfather. When something broke in the restaurant—from the cash register to the outdoor floodlights to the pizza oven to the pay phone to the dishwasher—Dong Hyun would painstakingly disassemble the broken thing, meticulously laying out all the parts, in order, on an old tablecloth. Most of the time, he would be able to fix whatever it was. He'd hold up a corroded gasket in triumph and say, "Ah ha! Here's the culprit! I can get a new one of these for ninety-nine cents at the hardware store!" And then Dong Hyun would replace the part and put everything back together again. Sam's grandfather had two core beliefs: (1) all things were knowable by anyone, and (2) anything was fixable if you took the time to figure out what was broken. Sam believed these things as well.

Sam decided he would study other games to find anything close to the lighting and texture effects they wanted. He would dismantle the game, if it was possible to dismantle, and see what he could learn/steal, and then he would report his findings to Sadie.

At the bottom of Sadie's pile, he found a copy of *Dead Sea*. Sam had heard about *Dead Sea*, but he'd never taken the time to play it.

When Sadie woke up, Marx and Sam were gathered in front of Sam's computer. "Look at this," Sam said. "This is sort of what the storm should look like, right?"

Sadie had never spoken to Sam about Dov, and she had never asked him if he had played *Dead Sea*. She casually sidled up to the PC to look at her ex-lover's game, as if she hadn't seen it a hundred times before. "It's a bit moodier than what I thought we were going for," Sadie said.

"Of course," Sam said. "I don't mean it literally looks like this. But the quality he gives to light. Do you see the refraction through the water? Do you see the airiness? The atmosphere?"

"I do," Sadie said. She sat down next to Sam. "You're going to need to pick up that log," Sadie said to Marx, who was playing the game. "You're going to need it to brain that zombie."

"Thanks," Marx said.

"His engine is called Ulysses, by the way," Sadie said. "And he designed it himself."

"Who's *he*?" Sam asked.

"The designer and programmer. His name is Dov Mizrah. I used to know him a bit."

"How?" Sam said.

"He was my professor," Sadie said.

"Well, why don't you call him up?" Sam said. "If you're still struggling with building the engine, I mean . . ."

"Right," Sadie said. "I probably should."

"Maybe he'd have tips?" Sam added. "Or maybe we could even use his graphics engine?"

"I don't know, Sam."

"If I can ease your mind. We're doing so many things with this game already. I don't think that every last bit of the programming has to be original. You have this purity thing, but seriously, no one will care. There is no purity in art. The process of how you arrive at something doesn't matter at all. The game is going to be completely original because *we* made it. If you have access to a tool that will help, there is no reason not to use that tool. Our game isn't going to be anything like *Dead Sea,* so what difference does it make in the end?"

In the morning, Sadie emailed Dov, and it turned out he was back in Cambridge, teaching the games seminar in the fall and completing work on *Dead Sea II.* He invited her to come down to his studio, and so she went.

When she arrived at Dov's studio, she held out her hand for him to shake, and he pulled her into an embrace. "I'm so glad you emailed me, Sadie Green! I was planning to email you, but things got too crazy. I'm almost done with *Dead Sea II.* Last time I ever do a sequel. How are *you?*" he said.

She told him about *Ichigo.*

"Good title. This is what you should be doing," he said, maybe a dash of condescension in his voice. "You should be making your own games."

Sadie took some of Sam's concept art out of her messenger bag and she showed it to him. "Whoa, trippy," Dov said. Then she took out her laptop so that he could play the first level. "This is fucking fantastic work," Dov said. He never gave compliments that he didn't mean, and Sadie almost felt like crying. It was frankly embarrassing how much his approval still meant to her. "I like this." Dov looked at Sadie. He set the concept art on the desk. He looked in her eyes, and then he nodded. "You're here for Ulysses, aren't you?"

At first, Sadie was going to deny it, claim she wanted some tips about building her own engine. "Yes," she said. "I want Ulysses."

"You know what I always say about making your own engines."

She nodded.

"But I can see how Ulysses would be a perfect fit for what you and your colleague—what's his name?"

"Sam Masur."

"What you and Mr. Masur are trying to accomplish. And how can I deny my Sadie when she comes to me in need?"

It was that simple. Dov gave her the engine, and in exchange, he became a producer and equity partner on *Ichigo*, bonding him to her professional life forever.

When Dov came down to the apartment to help Sadie set up Ulysses, Marx hated him immediately: the leather pants, the tight black T-shirt, the heavy silver jewelry, the immaculate goatee, the eyebrows permanently in the shape of circumflexes, the topknot. "The poor man's Chris Cornell," Marx whispered, referencing the lead singer of the grunge band Soundgarden.

"Chris Cornell?" Sam said. "I think he looks like a satyr."

But it was Dov's cologne that Marx loathed. It wasn't a cheap cologne, but as soon as he came into the room, his scent was everywhere, and even after he left, and they opened every window in the apartment, Marx could still smell him. The room felt murky and musky, oppressive with pine, patchouli, and cedar. It was, he felt, an aggressively male cologne, a roofie of a cologne.

Marx also felt that Dov was too physically intimate with Sadie. When Dov had been at Sadie's workstation, his hand kept drifting over to touch her and invade her space. The hand rested on her shoulder, the hand drifted onto her thigh, the hand on her keyboard, the hand on her mouse. Sadie, laughing with a strange, brittle tone. Dov, brushing strands of hair out of her eyes. Marx recognized it as the intimacy of ex-lovers.

Marx pulled Sam into the bedroom. "You didn't say that Sadie used to be Dov's girlfriend," Marx said to Sam.

Sam shrugged. "I didn't know."

"How could you *not* know?"

"We don't talk about those kinds of things," Sam said.

"I mean, he was her professor, too, right? That's an abuse of power. Don't you think that's relevant if he's going to be a producer with us?"

"I don't actually," Sam said. "Sadie's a grown-up."

"Barely," Marx said.

Marx poked his head out of the room, so he could continue to spy on Sadie and Dov.

Dov was doing most of the talking. "If I were you," Dov said, "I would take the next semester off."

Sadie was listening, nodding.

"You and your crew. You've got something here," Dov said. "I really believe that."

"But school . . ." Sadie's voice was barely audible. "My parents . . ."

"Who cares about any of that? No one cares if you're a good girl anymore, Sadie. I want to empower you to shed your conventional notions, once and for all. The point of your education has been to do exactly the thing that you're currently doing. Get the bulk of the programming done while you're in the flow, and then you can finish school in the spring and the summer, while you finish the sound and debug."

More listening, more nodding.

"Do you need me, your former professor, to order you?"

"Maybe," she said.

"I'll help you," Dov said.

"Thank you, Dov."

"I'm always here for you, brilliant one."

He took her in his hirsute arms and he pressed her face deep into his chest. Marx wondered how she could bear the stench.

Two weeks later, on the day she finished work on the storm, Sadie informed Marx and Sam that she was taking off the semester to finish the game. Implementing Ulysses meant redoing a significant portion of the work she'd already done, and she didn't want to lose momentum. "You don't have to take the semester off," she said to them, "but I'm going to."

"I was hoping you'd say that," Sam said. "Because that's what I want to do, too. Marx?"

"Sam, are you sure?"

Sam nodded. "I'm sure. But the big question is: Might we keep using the apartment?"

"You can have your room back, of course," Sadie said to Marx. "I'll find somewhere else to stay, but it would be great if we could keep working here."

"Where will you stay?" Sam asked.

"At Dov's," she said. There was no drama in her voice. "He's producing with us now, and he said he had an extra room that I could use." Everyone knew this was a lie.

That fall, Marx was the only one of them who returned to school. Due to his producing obligations, it was also the lone year that he wasn't in any plays. In truth, theater, far more than classes, had always taken up the bulk of Marx's time.

5

Almost a year to the day Sam had run into Sadie in the train station, *Ichigo* was completed. The game took three and a half months longer than Sam had promised it would.

With a major assist from Dov's Ulysses engine, Sadie and Sam had programmed *Ichigo,* nonstop, until their fingers bled. Literally, in Sam's case. His fingertips grew so dry and blistered that he had to put Band-Aids on them to stop blood from getting on his keyboard. But when the Band-Aids slowed down his typing, he removed them. He was accustomed to discomforts far greater.

But those were not the only injuries they sustained. By Halloween, Sadie had stared at her computer screen so long she burst a blood vessel in her right eye. She didn't even go to the doctor; she just sent Marx to the drugstore for eyedrops and Advil, and soldiered on. A week before Thanksgiving, Sam had passed out while walking to the Coop to buy a new power six-pack. Usually, Marx did their purchasing, but Marx was in class, and Sam could not wait. He literally passed out on the street, in front of the gourmet shop. With his big coat, people must have assumed he was homeless, and so he was barely noticed. When he awoke, his former adviser, Anders Larsson, was standing over him, looking like a blond Jesus in North Face. It made sense that Anders should find him. Anders, born in Sweden, was exactly the kind of decent, guileless person who did not look away when presented with the scourge of homelessness. "Samson Masur, are you all right?"

"Oh God, Anders, why are you here?"

"Why are you *there?*" Anders said.

Despite Sam's protests, Anders walked him over to University Health Services, where they determined Sam was malnourished. Sam was given an IV.

"So, what have you been up to?" Anders asked. He insisted on keeping Sam company while he received the fluids.

"I'm making a game!" Sam rambled on about *Ichigo* and Sadie, and Anders, who was not a gamer, looked at him blankly, but kindly. "It seems, my friend, you have found love?"

"Anders, you talk about love more than any mathematician I know."

In November, Marx hired a composer—Zoe Cadogan, one of Marx's many spectacular exes—to write a score inspired by the avant-garde composers they had listened to all summer. Zoe was a genius, Marx promised. As Sam would often tease him, "Marx never met a genius he didn't want to sleep with." A decade later, Zoe would win a Pulitzer Prize for an operatic adaptation of *Antigone* she had written using only female voices. But *Ichigo* would be the first time she was ever paid for her music, and the credit always appeared on her résumé.

They had just finished recording the score, and Marx had gone back to Zoe's dorm room in Adams House. They ate in the dining hall, and then they had sex. Marx usually enjoyed the experience of making love to an ex, and this evening was no exception. It was interesting to note the way your body had changed and how their body had changed in the time since you'd last been intimate. There was a pleasant Weltschmerz that came over him. It was the nostalgia one experienced when visiting an old school and finding that the desks were so much smaller than in one's memory.

"Why did we ever break up?" Zoe asked.

"You broke up with me, remember?" Marx said.

"Did I? Well, I must have had a good reason, but I can't remember it anymore." Zoe kissed Marx's chest. "I love your game," she said. "What I've seen and been told of it."

It was the first time anyone had ever called *Ichigo* Marx's game. "It's not really my game," Marx demurred. "It's Sadie's and Sam's."

"The scene at the end," she said. "It's very moving. When Ichigo is so much older, and the parents can't recognize her." She paused. "Or, I'm sorry, is Ichigo a him?"

"Sam and Sadie say *them*."

"Cool. When the parents can't recognize them. That moment is straight out of *The Odyssey*."

One of the most difficult challenges of *Ichigo*'s design had been Sadie and Sam's decision to make the Ichigo character age during the course of the story. Typically, a game character stays the same age and has the same basic design for the length of the story, if not the length of the series—think Mario or Lara Croft. The reasons for this are simple: branding, and it is *much less work*. But Sadie and Sam wanted Ichigo's journey to be reflected in their character. Ichigo ages and takes the damage inflicted by the narrative and time itself, and by the end of the story, when they finally make it home, after about seven years away, they are unrecognizable to their family. Ichigo returns home an exhausted, weary ten-year-old who has battled the ocean, the city, the tundra, and even the underworld. They stand on the doorstep of their home, and they hold their quivering hand over the door, afraid to knock. Eventually, Ichigo's mother lets them in, but the mother doesn't recognize them. But still, she thinks the child looks hungry and in need of love, and because she once lost her own child, she invites them inside. "What's your name?" she asks.

"Ichigo," they say.

"That's a strange name," she says.

At this point, Ichigo's father walks into the room. "Fifteen," he says. "That's Max Matsumoto. He's my favorite footballer. I used to have a jersey like that, but I lost it long ago."

With the score layered in and additional contributions by a sound designer friend of Zoe's to improve the aural landscape, the feeling at Kennedy Street was that the game had leveled up. "I feel like," Sadie said to Marx, "this might be something."

"I *know* it is," Marx said, with an evangelical fervor.

Sadie kissed Marx on both his cheeks, in a campy European way. He was such a fan. Every collaboration needs one.

When they finally got to the end of writing the game, the debugging period began. As they found bugs—and there were many—they'd write them on the stolen whiteboard, along with any other improvements they wanted to make. After each task was completed, it was erased. About a week before the winter break—they were still young enough to understand time in semesters—the board was empty aside from a hazy pastel palimpsest to remind them of the work they had done.

"Are we finished?" Sadie asked Sam. She opened the curtains. It was five a.m., and it was lightly snowing.

"I think we are," Sam said.

"I'm so tired." Sadie yawned. "For tonight, we're done. If we look at it tomorrow, and we still think we're done, then we'll say we're done. I'm heading over to Dov's."

"I'll walk you," Sam said.

"You sure? It'll be slippery out there." She worried about his foot, which she knew had been bothering him lately.

"It's not a very long walk," he said. "It'll be good for me."

No one was on the streets, and it was so quiet they could hear the snow as it hit the ground. The shortest way to Dov's apartment was through Harvard Yard, so they cut through it—the term was almost over, and the freshmen were sleeping. The combination of the predawn light and the snow was magical, like being inside a snow globe, a discrete world of their own. Sadie put her arm through Sam's, and he leaned into her a little. They were tired, but it was an honest tiredness, the kind that comes when you know you have put everything you have into a project. Of course, they would finish other games together, and the offices and the staffs on those games would be unimaginably larger. But Sam and Sadie would always remember this morning.

"Sam," she said, "tell me something and be honest."

He felt a bit panicked by her tone of voice. "Of course."

"Did you *truly* see the Magic Eye last December?"

"Sadie, how dare you!" he exclaimed with mock outrage.

"Well, if you saw it, tell me what it was."

"No," Sam said. "I won't dignify that."

Sadie nodded. They had reached the exterior door to Dov's apartment. She put her key in the lock, and then she turned.

"No matter what happens, thank you for making me do this. I love you, Sam. You don't have to say you love me, too. I know that kind of thing makes you terribly uncomfortable."

"Terribly," he said. "Terribly." Sam smiled, too wide, showing the huge mouth of crooked teeth that he was so self-conscious about, and he bowed awkwardly. Before he could tell her that he loved her, she was already inside. But he didn't feel bad that he hadn't said it. Sam knew that Sadie knew that he loved her. Sadie knew that Sam loved her in the same way she knew that Sam had not seen the Magic Eye.

The sun was coming up, and the snowfall had mostly stopped, and Sam walked home, feeling warm, despite the cold, and filled with gratitude that he was alive, and that Sadie Green had come into that game room that day. The universe, he felt, was just—or if not just, fair enough. It might take your mother, but it might give you someone else in return. As he rounded Kennedy Street, he began to chant to himself a poem that he had heard once, he wasn't sure where. "That love is all there is; is all we know of love. It is enough; the freight should be proportioned to the groove." What is the "freight"? he wondered. What is the "groove"? The mysteries of the poem entertained him, and the poem was so jaunty in its meter (almost, he thought, like the sound of a train barreling down the tracks), and he felt so uncharacteristically light and happy that he found himself skipping a little—Sam Masur! skipping!—which is why he took a less than careful step off the curb. His foot slipped out from under him.

Sam was so used to pain. He barely felt it, really. He passed out, for the second time that winter. "We should stop running into each other like this," he said to no one.

As he lay on the street, his bruised cheek on an icy cobblestone pillow, he had a vision of his mother, standing over him in the ice, wearing a huge white parka that went down to her ankles. Anna is the size of Godzilla, and under the tent of her parka, Sam knows he is safe. His Korean American mother is speaking Japanese. "Daijoubu, Samu-chan," she says.

Sam's mother decided to go west in the winter of 1984. Sam was nine; Anna, thirty-five. Anna had been contemplating leaving New York for twelve years—that is to say, as long as she had lived there. But the longing had only intensified in the years since Sam's birth. She felt plagued by bourgeois fantasies of a cheaper, cleaner, healthier, happier life for them in an unnamed, distant city. She imagined a backyard for Sam, and a yellow dog of indeterminate lineage from the shelter, and walk-in closets, and laundry done sans quarters and in the privacy of her own home, and no one living above them or below them. She imagined palm trees and warm weather and the scent of plumeria, and their ill-fitting, puffy coats unceremoniously tossed in garbage bags for donation to the Salvation Army. With equal intensity, she feared her New York life was the best of all possible worlds, and that once she left New York, the gates would come down and lock, and she'd be too feeble and parochial to ever be allowed to return. She might have continued in this speculative ouroboros forever, if another Anna Lee had not fallen from the sky.

On the night they encountered the other Anna Lee, Anna and Sam were walking back from the theater to their railroad flat in unstylish Manhattan Valley. An acting class friend, with whom she had had pleasant, perfunctory sex years earlier, was in the ensemble of *The Rink,* the Chita Rivera/Liza Minelli roller-skating musical, and had comped them two tickets to a preview performance. The friend had said, "I'm almost certain this is going to flop, but it might be perfect for a nine-year-old boy of mildly artistic temperament." Anna had laughed at this description of her son—it was interesting and occasionally appalling to see how other people viewed your child—but the friend had been right: Sam had loved the musical, and Anna had felt like a good mother for being able to provide Sam with the rich cultural experiences that only New York City could offer. Like magic, she was in love with New York again and felt certain that she could never leave it. She was having these cozy thoughts as she and Sam made their way down a Stygian stretch of Amsterdam Avenue. Sam tugged at Anna's coat sleeve. "Hey Mom? What's that up there?"

In the streetlight, Anna could see a vaguely organic silhouette perched atop the metal railing of a balcony about six stories up. "Maybe a large bird?" she said. "Or . . . a gargoyle? A statue?"

The statue leaped to the ground, improbably landing faceup, with a percussive splat and an explosion of red blood that suggested a Jackson Pollock painting, in process, more than it did a suicide. The woman's legs and arms were supernaturally akimbo. Both mother and son screamed, but it was New York City, so no one noticed or cared.

Once the statue had alighted, they could see it was most definitely a woman, and the woman was Asian, maybe even Korean, like Anna. The woman would die that night, but she was not dead yet. Sam laughed, not because he was cruel, but because the woman reminded him of his mother, and he could not figure out what else to do with himself when faced with such a gruesome spectacle less than ten steps in front of him. He had never seen anything die before and so, he could not be certain that she was dying. And yet, somewhere deep inside himself, he felt a recognition and then a reckoning: this was death, and he would die, and his mother would die, and everyone you ever met and ever loved would die, and maybe it would happen when you or they were old, but maybe not. To know this was unbearable: it was a fact too large for a nine-year-old avatar to contain. Anna punched him quite hard on the arm to get him to stop laughing. "I'm sorry," Sam whimpered. "I don't even know why I was laughing."

"It's okay," Anna said. She pointed to the bodega across the street. "Go in there and tell them to call 911."

Sam hesitated. "I don't want to," he said. "I can't move. My feet are stuck. They're stuck in the ice."

"They aren't stuck, Sam. There isn't any ice, and they aren't stuck. Go! Go now!" Anna pushed him toward the store, and Sam began to run.

Anna kneeled down by the woman's side. "Don't worry. Help is coming," Anna tried to reassure her. "I'm Anna, by the way. I'll stay with you until the ambulance gets here." Anna took the woman's hand.

"I'm Anna, too," the woman said.

"I'm Anna Lee," Anna said.

"I'm Anna Lee, too," the woman said. The woman inhaled raggedly and coughed in a peculiar, delicate way. Anna was certain the woman's neck was broken. Copious amounts of blood were flowing from some hole or series of holes in the woman's body, but Anna could not see an obvious way to stop the bleeding. Anna was getting blood on her white tennis shoes, which she was fastidious about keeping white. And the other Anna Lee was getting blood everywhere, but noticeably, to Anna, on the large, floppy, pink lace bow she wore, Madonna-style, in her shiny black hair.

"Oh, that makes sense," Anna said lightly. "There're a lot of us. Isn't Lee the most popular Asian surname in the world? In my union, I had to change my name to Anna Q. Lee, because you can't have more than one person with the same name. I'm the seventh Anna Lee in Equity."

"What's Equity?"

"It's the stage actor's union."

"You're an actor?" the woman said. "Would I have seen you in anything?"

"Well," Anna said. "I've played almost every Asian part an actress can play, but my biggest role was Connie Wong in *A Chorus Line*."

"I saw that the year it opened," the woman said. "You were good."

"I was the third Connie Wong on Broadway, and I was the second Connie Wong in the national touring company, too. So, you didn't see me. You probably saw Baayork Lee. Another Lee." Anna laughed. "So many of us."

"What does the Q. stand for?"

"Nothing," Anna said. "It was for the union. You probably don't want to talk about this." Anna looked in the other Anna Lee's eyes, which were the same golden brown, heterochromic color as her own. "Why did you . . . Do you mind my asking? I apologize if this is rude."

"I didn't know how else to leave," the other Anna Lee said. She tried to shrug, but then her body began to spasm, and ninety long seconds later, she died. Anna stood up. She stood over the other Anna Lee's body and began to feel giddily, vertiginously untethered from her own body. She felt as if she were seeing herself dead on that sidewalk. She knew she should stay with the other Anna's body until the ambulance got there, but it was frigid, and she feared spending more time with the other Anna would provoke some irreversible existential crisis, and she desperately wanted to be with Sam.

She went into the bodega to find her son. She quickly scanned the aisles, but she couldn't find him anywhere.

"Did my son come in here?" Anna said. She tried to ignore the paranoid fantasy that was forming in her mind: What if the other Anna Lee's death had merely been a distraction so that some evil party could kidnap Sam?

"You're the mother," the shopkeeper said. "What a world. What a thing for a boy to see."

"He didn't leave, did he?"

"No, but he was quite distraught, so I gave him quarters to play the machine in the back of my store. Children love games, though the machine doesn't make as much money for me as it once did."

"That was very kind of you," Anna said. "What do I owe you?"

The man waved his hand. "Please. It is hard enough to be a child in this world without women throwing themselves from buildings. How is she?"

Anna shook her head.

"What a world," the shopkeeper said, shaking his head, too.

She walked to the back of the store, where Sam was concealed by the mammoth, cheerful shell of the *Ms. Pac-Man* machine. From what Anna could tell, Ms. Pac-Man was no different than Pac-Man, except that she had a bow and was a Ms., which in 1984 was an honorific that usually signified a feminist.

"Hi," Anna said.

"Hi," Sam said, without looking at her. "You can watch if you want. I'm going to play until the end of this life."

"That's a good philosophy," Anna said. She concentrated on the game and tried not to hear the nearby sirens that meant the ambulance had come for the body of the other Anna Lee.

"If you eat the fruit," Sam said, "you can kill the ghosts, but only for a little while. And if you don't time it right, the ghosts can turn back and kill you."

"Amazing," Anna said. She decided that they couldn't leave the bodega until the sidewalk had been cleared of the body of the other Anna Lee.

"And sometimes, you get an extra life. But you might kill yourself trying to get the extra life, so it's not always worth it."

"You're good at this," Anna said. Once they were able to leave the bodega, she'd splurge on a taxi, even though they were only a dozen blocks from home.

"Not yet," Sam said. "If I had more time to practice, I could be. Darn it!" The descending chromatic wail of Ms. Pac-Man's death. "That was my last life." Sam looked at Anna cautiously. "What happened to her?"

"The ambulance is out there right now. They're taking her to the hospital."

"Will she be okay?" Sam said.

"I think so," Anna said. It wasn't exactly a lie. She *would* be okay. Dead was okay.

Sam nodded, but he had seen Anna in enough plays to know when she was lying, and he knew her well enough to know why she lied. When he lied, it was for the same reason: to protect her from that which she could not handle. "Why did she do that?" Sam asked.

"I think . . ." Anna said. "I think she must have been terribly blue. I think she must have had troubles in her life."

"Do you ever get blue?"

"Yes, everyone gets blue. But I don't think I could ever get melancholy like that, because I have you."

Sam nodded. "If the body had landed on us, do you think we could have saved her?"

"I don't know."

"Do you think we could have died?"

"I don't know."

"Because if we had walked a little faster, or if we hadn't stopped to buy bananas, we could have been directly under her, and we could have died."

"I don't think we would have died," Anna said.

"But if you drop a penny from the Empire State Building and it hits someone, they'll die, right?"

"I think that's an old wives' tale," Anna said. "Besides, the building she jumped from was only six stories."

"But a body is much heavier than a penny."

"Why don't you play again?" Anna dug through her purse and put a quarter in the machine. For Ms. Pac-Man, Anna thought, life was cheap and filled with second chances.

Sam played, and Anna watched, thinking about her next move.

The obvious place for them to go was Los Angeles, the city of her birth. She had resisted returning there because to return to one's hometown felt like surrender. And professionally, Los Angeles had no theater to speak of, which is to say, there would likely be even less work for Anna in L.A. than there had been for her in New York (and work in New York had always been intermittent at best). If she was lucky, she'd end up playing Asian hookers in cop shows and movies. She'd have to polish up her various "Asian" accents, because she'd never play an "American" again. Maybe some commercials or voice-overs or a bit of modeling here or there, though she might already be too old for that. Or maybe she'd stop acting entirely—learn to program computers, or sell real estate, or style hair, or become an interior decorator, or teach aerobics, or write screenplays, or find a rich husband—whatever it was ex-actors in Los Angeles did. But it would be nice to see her parents, and it would be nice for Sam to know his grandparents, and actually, Sam's father lived out there, too, and it would be nice for Sam to have a relationship with him, though Sam's father certainly could not be relied upon, and it would be nice to be in a city where Anna Lees didn't fall from the sky. Aside from a few scattered blocks, what part of Los Angeles was more than two stories high? And *this* Anna Lee, Anna Q. Lee, the seventh Anna Lee in Equity, wouldn't let herself be like that other Anna Lee. This Anna Lee would know how to leave.

"You're getting so good at killing ghosts," Anna said.

"I'm okay," Sam said. He turned to look at her. "Hey Mom, do you want a turn?"

6

It was startling how fast a person could go dark in 1996.

Sadie got to Marx's a little after ten and she found the apartment empty and, aside from the occasional chirp of a hard drive, silent. Maybe Sam and Marx were together, having breakfast? Since they were both gone, she didn't feel worried—Marx always took care of Sam. She didn't feel worried until Marx got home around one and reported he hadn't seen Sam all day. "I thought he was with you," Marx said. "He's always with you."

Sam didn't have a cell phone, but no one did then. (The only people Sadie knew with cell phones were Dov and her grandmother.) The best they could do was check to see the last time he'd logged in to his Harvard email, and from where: 3:03 this morning, from the apartment's IP address.

Sadie and Marx sat in the living room of the apartment, calmly suggesting places Sam might have gone. Maybe he went to the library and fell asleep? Maybe shopping for the new drive they had discussed needing? Maybe a pilgrimage to see the Glass Flowers? Maybe lunch with Anders? Maybe he'd finally been arrested for shoplifting?

They'd been at this for a while when Marx noticed the whiteboard. "There's nothing on it," he remarked.

"We're done," Sadie said. "We thought we were, at least."

"Congratulations," Marx said. He paused before he said, "Should I play it? We can't do anything about Sam yet. He's an adult, and it hasn't been that long."

Sadie considered this. "Yes, you should play it. Why not? I'm going to go look for him."

"Do you want me to come with you?"

"No. You should stay here in case he calls."

She went to all of their usual Harvard Square haunts: the movie theater, the library, the Coop, the Mexican place, the video store in the Garage, the bookstore, the other bookstore, the other other bookstore, the bagel store. And when she didn't find him in those places, she did the Central Square ones: the comic book store, the computer store, her old apartment, the Indian place. She went back to Harvard Square, walking up toward the Radcliffe Quad, to the university police station, and finally, defeated, she went to University Health. She didn't even have a photograph of Sam to show, so she kept having to describe him. Enormous coat, badly cut curly hair, glasses, limp. A collection of flaws and infirmities. She was glad Sam didn't have to hear her. No one had been seen who matched that description anyway. She walked back through Harvard Yard, calling out his name until her voice was ragged. A woman stopped her, and asked, "What does the dog look like? I'll keep an eye out." She retraced the same route she and Sam had taken just that morning when the world seemed soft-focused and filled with possibility. The path now seemed dismal and dangerous to her. And she thought to herself that it was strange how quickly the world could shift. She let her mind go to the dark place. What if Sam had been kidnapped or beaten? He was small and slow, and he would be easy to overpower. What if Sam were dead? She didn't truly believe that he was dead, but what if he was? She couldn't entirely articulate who he was to her. He was not Alice or Freda or Dov. Those relationships had easy names: sister, grandmother, boyfriend. Sam was her friend, but "friend" was a broad category, wasn't it? "Friend" was a word that was overused to the point that it had no meaning at all.

She came back to the apartment around midnight. Marx was about halfway through his first official play of *Ichigo: A Child of the Sea*.

"Any luck?" Marx asked, without looking away from the screen.

"No," Sadie said glumly. She flopped onto the sofa. "I feel like something terrible has happened to him."

Marx got up and put his arm around her. "He'll come back. It hasn't been that long yet."

"But it's not like him. Where could he have gone? They say I can't file a missing person report for another day, but it isn't right. We've spent almost every hour of the last six months together. I've barely gone ten minutes without speaking to him. Why would he disappear on the morning we finish the game?"

Marx shook his head. "I honestly don't know. But I've lived with Sam for three and a half years now, and I know that he's both private and tough as hell. We lived together for two years before I knew he'd been in a car accident. For years, I had no idea what was wrong with him. It could have been anything. I'd hint around it, and I'd notice him struggling and I'd do what I could to help, not that he'd ever ask for any. But I was curious, so I'd give him openings to talk. A normal person would probably have some desire to, like, *explain* to the person they lived with what was going on with them, but not Sam. Sam loves his secrets. My point is, I'm worried, but I'm not *that* worried."

"What made him finally tell you about the car accident?" Sadie asked.

"He never told me. Bong Cha did."

Sadie laughed. "He once went six years without speaking to me," she said.

"What did you do?" Marx said.

"I mean, it was bad, but it was basically a misunderstanding. It's so boring and nerdy I can't even explain it. And I was twelve!"

"He can hold a grudge like no one's business."

Sadie shook her head. "I shouldn't have let him walk me up to Dov's."

"Sadie, listen to me. Sam is going to be fine. There's going to be a story, and we're all going to laugh, I promise you." Marx stood up. "I'm in the middle of this very exciting game, and I'd like to finish it now if that's acceptable to you."

Sadie nodded. She went into Sam's room, and then she got into Sam's bed. She called Dov to let him know she wasn't coming back that night.

"Why?" Dov said. "You have no information. There's nothing you can do. The worry is pointless. Come home."

"I'm going to wait here in case he calls," she said.

Dov laughed. "I forget how young you are. You're still at the age where you mistake your friends and your colleagues for family."

"Yes, Dov," she said, trying to hide her irritation.

"When you have children, you'll never be able to worry about a friend as much again," Dov said.

"I'm tired," Sadie said. "I should go."

Sadie hung up the phone. She pulled Sam's blanket over her head, and then she went to sleep.

By the time Sadie woke up, it was eight o'clock the next night, and she'd slept so long that Marx had finished the first playthrough of *Ichigo*. She went out to the living room to ask if Sam had called yet, and she found Marx gazing at the dark monitor and gently smiling to himself, as if in possession of a great secret.

"Marx?"

When he saw Sadie, he ran over to her, and he lifted her up in his arms, and he spun her around the room.

"Marx!" Sadie protested.

"I love it," Marx said. "There's nothing more to say." And then in a booming actor voice, "I LOVE THIS WOMAN AND I LOVE THIS GAME! WHERE THE HELL IS SAM?"

As if in direct response to Marx's appeal to the universe, the phone rang. Sadie and Marx both jumped for it, but Sadie was closer, and she got to it first.

"It's him," Sadie reported to Marx. "Where the hell have you been?"

Sam had broken his ankle, the one above his damaged foot, and because of the poor condition of that entire extremity, he'd had to have emergency surgery on it. He was at Mass General in Boston, and he had to stay in the hospital for another night, but could they come and get him in the morning?

"Why didn't you call?" Sadie asked.

"I didn't want you to worry," Sam said.

"We worried *because* you didn't call." Sadie began to cry from the release of built-up tension. "I thought you were dead, Sam. *Dead*. That we'd finished the game and . . . I don't know what."

"Sadie, Sadie, it's all right." Sam said. "I'm fine. You'll see."

"If you ever do that again, I'm going to murder you," Sadie said.

"I know now. I should call. Sadie? Are you there?"

Sadie was blowing her nose, so Marx took the phone from her.

"For the record, I knew you were okay. I played the game," Marx said. "You're both geniuses. And I love you both so much. And that's it."

Sadie reclaimed the phone from Marx.

"Our first playthrough," Sam said. "So, we're done?"

"I think we are," Sadie said. "Mostly. I have a few things."

"I have a few things, too."

"I want to see you," Sadie said.

"I think visiting hours end at nine," Sam said. It was already 8:15. "I doubt that leaves you enough time to get here and get a community service timesheet together."

"Very funny."

"Seriously, there probably isn't enough time for you to get here."

"Okay, Sammy," she said. "I love you."

"Terribly," he said.

"We'll see you first thing in the morning." Sadie hung up the phone.

In yet another hospital bed (but his first with a view of the Charles River), Sam felt incredibly lonely and slightly sorry for himself. He had nausea from the anesthesia and from not having eaten enough in the last two days. Although he'd been given a goodly amount of drugs, he could still feel his foot enough to know that when he fully felt it, the pain was going to be terrifying. He was worried about what this latest mishap would end up costing (his bank account was near zero) and feared sorting out the related health insurance issues. The specialist had said that the condition of his foot was so poor it was now compromising his ankle. "There are only so many times a foot can be put back together before you have to start considering other options," the doctor said. The other options were medieval. At the very least, he knew he'd be on crutches for a couple of months, and he was dreading the rest of the winter and having to rely on Marx and Sadie more than he already did. The reason he hadn't called them when he'd first woken up in the hospital was because he was embarrassed. He had hoped the fall wouldn't have been as bad as it had ended up being. He had hoped he would be patched up and easily sent home, with an overpriced bottle of aspirin, and that neither of them would have had to be involved at all. He didn't want them to see him as weak, even though that was how he felt. Weak, frail, alone, exhausted. He was tired of his body, of his unreliable foot, which couldn't even handle the slightest expression of joy. He was tired of having to move so carefully, of having to be so careful. He wanted to be able to skip, for God's sake. He wanted to be Ichigo. He wanted to surf, and ski, and parasail, and fly, and scale mountains and buildings. He wanted to die a million deaths like Ichigo, and no matter what damage was inflicted on his body during the day, he'd wake up tomorrow, new and whole. He wanted Ichigo's life, a lifetime of endless, immaculate tomorrows, free of mistakes and the evidence of having lived. Or if he couldn't be Ichigo, at least he could be back at the apartment, with Sadie and Marx, making *Ichigo*.

Just when Sam had made himself feel as wretched as possible, he saw Sadie and Marx through the glass panel in the door. It was almost like they were a mirage. They were goddamn gorgeous, those two.

Even though they would only get fifteen minutes with him, Sadie and Marx had decided to take a cab down to the hospital anyway. "How many times do you get to toast your first game?" Marx had said. They had stopped at a liquor store to buy champagne and plastic flutes.

Sam was both embarrassed and pleased to see them. He knew he looked awful. His foot and ankle were in a bulky cast, about the hundredth cast of his life. And there was a multicolor bruise on his cheek and forehead. His friends were beautiful and strong, with their rosy outdoor cheeks, their cashmere coats, their shiny hair. If anyone saw them together, he was sure they would think he belonged to a different and feebler species. But then he reminded himself: *They are not only my friends. They are my colleagues.* He had turned them into his colleagues, and in a strange way, that was comforting to Sam. *Ichigo* bonded them to him for life.

Marx poured Sam a small glass of champagne. "Hope this doesn't interfere with whatever else they've given you."

"What happened anyway?" Sadie asked.

Sam tried to make an amusing anecdote of it. He talked about the skipping and the poem and the general happiness and well-being he had felt upon completing the game. He omitted the hallucination he'd had of his mother. "Do you know this poem? Something about love being all there is."

"That's the Beatles," Marx said. *"All you need is love, love . . ."*

"No, there was another part. Something about 'a freight and a groove'?"

"That's Emily Dickinson," Sadie said. "*The freight must be proportioned to the groove.* I used it in *EmilyBlaster.*"

Sam laughed. "*EmilyBlaster!* Of course!"

"Yes, I was thinking of how strange those lines were when I must have tripped over the curb."

"So, what you're saying is that you were Emily Blasted?" Marx said.

"You know, my whole class *hated* that game," Sadie said.

"Marx, what was the thing you said when you played *EmilyBlaster*?" Sam said.

"I said it was the most violent poetry game I'd ever played, and the person who made it must be incredibly peculiar," Marx said.

"I accept that compliment," Sadie said.

"So, what's next for *Ichigo* now that we're done?" Marx said.

"We show it to Dov, and we wait to hear what he thinks," Sam said.

The attending nurse, who was in her sixties and approaching retirement, let them stay until midnight. She was enjoying the sound of their laughter, their banter, and their gentle teasing. A game she often played with herself to pass the time was to try to figure out the relationships between patients and visitors. She liked to name the people, as she imagined what their lives and connections were. The hurt boy, she called Tiny Tim. The Asian boy, who looked like a fashion model or a soap opera heartthrob, was Keanu. The petite, pretty brunette with the thick eyebrows and the whimsically crooked nose, was Audrey. Tiny Tim looked slightly younger than the other two. Audrey and Keanu didn't seem to be a couple, though it seemed like Keanu wouldn't have minded if they were. In a strange way, Tiny Tim looked as if he could have been their son, though the ages didn't make sense for that. Maybe Tiny Tim was one of their little brothers? Maybe Audrey and Tiny Tim were a couple? Or maybe the two boys were the couple? Keanu had been so gentle when the boy had asked for water. And yet, the sense of ease between Audrey and Tiny Tim was palpable. While Keanu sat in the chair, Audrey lay in the bed next to Tiny Tim, their fingertips casually touching, in the way of people who were entirely comfortable around each other. She almost seemed to be an extension of him, and he, of her. There is love here, she thought. In the end, she decided, with some amount of disappointment, that none of them were involved romantically.

Despite Sam's injuries, Sam and Sadie continued to tweak the game through the rest of the month, and by the end of January, they were ready to show the game to Dov. He had seen and advised a significant amount of the work in progress, but he hadn't experienced it from front to back, and he didn't know how it would all come together. Sadie brought the drive with the finished game to his apartment. As he began his first playthrough, she hovered around him, enthusiastically offering him tips and insights into every moment of the game. She was nervous about Dov's reaction, but she was also incredibly proud of her work. She didn't want him to miss a single detail of their labors.

"Sadie, back off. I can't concentrate with you all over me. I want to play this," Dov said.

"Okay," Sadie said. "I'll be quiet."

Dov had reached level seven, the world of ice and snow, where Ichigo first encounters Gomibako, the ghost-monster who enslaves lost children. "I can feel you watching me. I can hear you breathing." He took her hand and he escorted her into his bedroom.

"Now be a good girl," he said.

"But . . ."

"You aren't disobeying me, are you?"

"No, Dov."

"I didn't think so." He looked at her. "Take off your clothes."

"I don't want to," she said. "Dov, it's freezing in here."

"Take. Off. Your. Clothes. You know what happens when you disobey."

Sadie took off her clothes.

The first time they'd been together, he had never expressed any interest in S&M. The S&M had only started when they'd reunited in the fall. Sadie had been turned on, at first at least, and then slightly disturbed, unsure of the game they were playing and why they were playing it. Dov wasn't abusive. He always sought consent. But he liked handcuffs and other more complicated props and ordering her around. He liked making her strip and tying her up and gagging her on occasion; he liked to slap her and spank her and pull her hair. He liked shaving off her pubic hair, which he did with the care and consideration of an artist. He had peed on her once, but when she told him to stop, he had, and he'd never done it again. When he hurt her—and he never hurt her much—he was always tender and sorry after.

Dov also liked to be hit, which was not something she was at all into doing. On the night of his thirtieth birthday, he had asked her to slap him across the face. "Harder," he said.

She obeyed.

"Harder."

She obeyed.

Once she'd hit him hard enough, his eyes would tear and then, russet-faced, he would phone his son, back in Israel. She could hear him speaking tenderly to the boy, in lilting Hebrew that reminded her of birdsong. Sadie's Hebrew was at a Bat Mitzvah prep, High Holy Days level, so the only word she could understand wasn't even Hebrew. It was his son's name: Telemachus, who Dov mainly called Telly. Telly was three.

On the night he asked her to start seeing him again, he'd poured her a glass of wine and told her that his wife had finally agreed to a divorce.

"That's good," Sadie had said carefully. "If you've been unhappy."

"I have been unhappy," Dov said. "It will be difficult and costly for me, but it will be worth it in the end."

They spoke at the same time.

"I don't think we should see each other," Sadie said. "I'd like to keep it professional."

"I'd like to see you again," Dov said.

"You weren't here last year," Sadie said. "I don't think I can go through another breakup with you."

"You won't have to," Dov said. "I promise."

But, back to the night Dov first played *Ichigo*.

After they'd had what Sadie considered to be quick, enjoyable, prop-free sex, Dov opened his nightstand drawer, and snapped a handcuff around her wrist and another to the bed frame. It happened so quickly; she didn't even have time to protest.

"I don't want you to leave this bed until I'm done with *Ichigo*," he said.

"But Dov," Sadie called. "You've still got, like, thirteen hours left."

Dov ignored her and closed the door to the bedroom.

Even handcuffed to the bed, Sadie could reach the landline on the nightstand. She called Sam.

"Is he done yet?" Sam asked eagerly.

"He's reached Gomibako," Sadie said.

A great deal depended on Dov's reaction. Dov had connections and influence in the industry—if he liked it, he could take it to his or a different publisher. He could bring attention to *Ichigo* in a way and with a speed that Sadie, Sam, and Marx, on their own, couldn't.

"Why don't you come back here?" Sam said. "We can go to the movies. Marx says *Mars Attacks!* is playing at Sony Fresh Pond tonight."

"You're good to go out?"

"I have to go out sometime, Sadie. We'll take a cab. We'll go slow."

"No skipping?"

"No skipping, no reciting of poetry. I promise."

Sadie looked at her shackled wrist. "I should stay here," she said. "In case he needs me," she added.

She didn't have a book to read, and while she had recently urinated, she was already starting to be thirsty. She pulled the sheets up over herself, as best she could, and she tried to go to sleep, but she wasn't tired, and it was awkward to sleep with her arm over her head.

There was no question that they had needed Ulysses, but it still bothered Sadie that she had had to use it. Dov was a producer on *Ichigo*, and he was so well known that she worried that people would think *her* work was *his* work. That they wouldn't know where her work began and his work ended.

On this point, Sadie wouldn't end up being entirely wrong. Consider Dov, in an interview on the *Gamedepot* blog for the release of *Dead Sea II*.

GAMEDEPOT: Another game that's been making a big splash this year is *Ichigo*, which employs your Ulysses engine to great effect. Tell us the story of how you became involved with *Ichigo*.

D.M.: Well, Sadie [Green, programmer and designer, *Ichigo*] was my student. She's brilliant—always has been. I'm, like, not in the engine-selling business. I don't have a great interest in selling my tools to other so-called designers. Personally, I think the sharing of engines has had a chilling effect on creativity across all games. It's lazy. The games start to look the same, have the same mechanics and the same presumptive physics, etc. But I saw what she and Sammy [Masur, programmer and designer, *Ichigo*] were trying to do, and it seemed really special to me, and like something I wanted to be involved with. I thought that Ulysses could help them. Listen, Ulysses shouldn't take away from anything Sadie and Sammy did. The amount of work those two kids did was astounding. I cite them as an example to my students of how much two kids and a couple of computers can get done on their own. Game companies have gotten too big and impersonal. You have ten guys doing texture layers, and ten guys doing modeling and ten guys doing backgrounds, and someone else is writing the story, and someone else is writing the dialogue, and literally, no one ever talks to each other. They're like zombies, with their heads in their cubicles. It's a [expletive] nightmare.

GAMEDEPOT: But you can see your influence. In the opening storm sequence, for example.

D.M.: Meh. Maybe it's there, maybe not. It's there if you know to look for it.

When Dov finally came back into the bedroom after his first play of *Ichigo*, there were tears in his eyes. "It's fucking beautiful, Sadie."

"It's good?" she said. She wanted to hear him say it.

"Good?" he said. "You crazy brilliant kid. You astonish me. You amaze me. To think, this little, tiny person can make something like this." Dov let tears run down his face and he made no attempt to wipe them away. Seeing Dov cry made Sadie cry, too. She felt different than she had when she'd heard Marx's reaction—Marx was a fan. With Dov, she felt nothing short of relief. She felt as if the tension she had been holding in her body for ten months, since last March, when Sam had asked her to make the game, was suddenly gone. She didn't know what would happen with the game—if it would be a quiet shareware release, if it would get a big publishing deal. She almost didn't care. She had made something that Dov Mizrah admired, and for now, that was enough.

She wanted to go to Dov, but she was still handcuffed to his bed. She got on her knees, still naked, and she held out her free hand to him and he squeezed it. "I love you," he said.

"I love you," she said.

"And I love *Ichigo*. I want to talk to Sammy and Marx first thing tomorrow. We're all gonna make so much money." He started spinning out his plans for *Ichigo*, speaking as quickly as an auctioneer. He was pacing the room, bouncing on one foot, gesturing passionately. She had never seen him so excited about anything.

"Dov," she said. "Would you mind . . . ?" She shook her chain.

III

———

UNFAIR GAMES

1

No one was entirely sure who had come up with the name Unfair Games, though all three of them, at various times, took credit. Marx thought he'd named it after a line he liked from *The Tempest:* "Yes, for a score of kingdoms, you should wrangle, and I would call it *fair play.*" Sadie didn't think this made any sense—"fair" was not "unfair"; "play" was not "games." She was sure Unfair Games derived from the fact that "It's unfair" had been the unofficial mantra of her childhood. Sadie repeated it so often that her mother had threatened to deduct a quarter from her allowance each time the phrase was uttered. Sam, for his part, was certain that he had named Unfair Games: when he had woken up in the hospital with that broken ankle, he could remember thinking that the best thing about games is that they could be fairer than life. A good game, like *Ichigo,* was hard, but fair. The "unfair game" was life itself. He swore he'd written the name on a sheet of paper by his bedside, but no one would ever locate this sheet of paper. And where credit was concerned, Sam's stories were often apocryphal, or at the very least, reverse engineered.

2

When he'd gone to speak to Unfair about his grand plan for selling *Ichigo*, Dov had one question: "So, Ichigo's a boy, right?"

"We didn't see them that way," Sam said.

"*Them?*" Dov said.

"What Sam thought, and I agree, is that gender doesn't matter at that age. So, we never identify Ichigo's gender," Sadie explained.

"That's clever," Dov said, "and it absolutely will not work. You want to sell this game in Walmart, right? You want to sell this game to people in the heartland. Marx, you're practical, what do you think?"

"I'm completely down with what Sadie and Sam are doing," Marx said carefully, loyally. "And it didn't affect my play at all. I'm a guy and I saw Ichigo as a boy."

"There!" Dov said. "That's exactly it. That's exactly my point. Ichigo should be a boy. Guys, I admire your creativity, but why put yourselves at a disadvantage for some bullshit Harvard thesis idea that no one will ever notice anyway?"

"Dov, why is Ichigo definitely a boy? Why can't Ichigo be a girl?" Sadie said.

"You know perfectly well that games with female main characters sell fewer copies," Dov said.

"But *Dead Sea* has a girl MC," Sadie protested. "And it's sold, what? A million copies?"

"Worldwide, yes, more than that even. But in the States, only about 750K."

"That's an enormous hit," Sadie said.

"It would have sold twice that if I hadn't made the Wraith a girl. But I didn't have *me* as an adviser."

Sadie was shredding a piece of notebook paper into a tidy pile. Dov put his hand over her hand to stop her.

"Listen guys, it's not my game. It's up to you. It's just my advice. If the 'them' thing is important to you, leave it. If you want Ichigo to be a girl, fine. The great thing for you is, it's a brilliant game and you have all the options. We can table this issue until the publishers weigh in, if you want."

Ichigo's top two offers were from Cellar Door Games, where Sadie had been an undistinguished intern, and Opus Interactive, the gaming division of the Austin, Texas–based PC company, Opus Computers.

Cellar Door didn't see Ichigo's gender as an issue. Cellar Door was a young company, run by recent MIT grads, and they thought the genderless Ichigo was "edgy and cool." They offered a relatively modest advance, a generous profit-sharing agreement, and an additional advance for their next game, which did not have to be a sequel to *Ichigo*. "We don't just want to be in the *Ichigo* business," Jonas Lippman, the twenty-nine-year-old CEO of Cellar Door, said. "We want to be in, uh, *your* business. Sorry, that came out weird. I didn't know if your company has a name yet."

Opus Computers offered a much larger advance—five times as large. They were launching a new gaming laptop, the Opus Wizardware, and their plan was to preload *Ichigo* on every Opus Wizardware PC sold during the Christmas 1997 season. They thought *Ichigo*, with its stylish, clean graphics and character design, and its emotional, family-friendly story, was the perfect game to sell gaming laptops to those who didn't think it was possible to play great games on anything but a console. They wanted a sequel to *Ichigo*, delivered in time for the Christmas 1998 season, for which they would pay twice as much money. And yes, to the all-male acquisitions team from Texas, Ichigo was definitely a boy—there had never been a question.

Sadie wanted to go with Cellar Door. She preferred the looser terms of their deal, and the truth was, she hadn't liked the Opus guys. Opus had flown the four of them down to Texas to meet the heads of the gaming division. Aaron Opus, the fifty-year-old, handlebar mustachioed, cowboy-hat-boots-bolo-tie-silver-bullhorn-buckle-Canadian-tuxedo-wearing head of the company, had surprised everyone by showing up at the meeting. Later, back at the hotel, Sadie commented to Dov that Aaron Opus looked like he did all his shopping at the barn-sized western wear stores that dotted the road from the Austin airport. But Dov found Aaron Opus delightful. "I love that Americana shit," he said.

"It's a costume," Sadie protested. "Opus is from Connecticut. He went to Yale."

"I love this guy! I'm stopping at one of those stores before we go back," Dov said. "Real men wear at least three different kinds of dead animals."

"Gross," Sadie said.

At the meeting, Aaron Opus apologized if he looked haggard, but he'd stayed up for two nights playing *Ichigo*. "Everyone knows you already, Mr. Mizrah," he said to Dov. Then he turned and addressed himself to Sam, "So, you're the programmer?"

"I'm *a* programmer," Sam said. "But Sadie's *the* programmer."

"We designed the game together," Sadie said.

Aaron Opus nodded. He studied Sam's face, and then he studied Sadie's face, and then he turned his attention back to Sam.

"The little fella, Ichigo. He looks a lot like you," Aaron Opus said. He nodded some more, as if deciding something. "Mm-hmm. You're the face of the game, I reckon."

When they got back to Cambridge, they exhaustively went over the two offers. Sadie said she liked Cellar Door because it didn't require them to make a sequel, and because she'd felt Cellar Door was more of a chemistry fit. Sam said he didn't even understand why they were considering Cellar Door when Opus had offered so much more money. Dov said both were good offers, but different paths, and it depended on what they wanted. He added that since the profit-sharing terms Cellar Door was offering were better, they might even make more money with Cellar Door in the long run. Marx said he, too, liked the creative freedom of the Cellar Door offer, but he felt the Opus deal had the potential to make *Ichigo* bigger. Opus had guaranteed that *Ichigo* would be featured prominently in the multimillion-dollar advertising campaign for the Opus Wizardware PC. If the game did what they thought it could do, Opus saw animation, Macy's Thanksgiving balloons, and tons of merch in *Ichigo*'s future. Cellar

Door didn't have the apparatus or the money to make that happen, not anytime soon.

By the end of the night, Marx, Dov, and Sam were on the side of Opus. Sadie was the only holdout for Cellar Door.

"It's life-changing money," Sam said. "Honestly."

"But I don't want to spend another year of my *changed* life making an *Ichigo* sequel," Sadie said.

"I get that," Marx said. "And I support Sadie, if that's what she wants. You guys are the creatives on this, so the two of you have to decide."

Sam asked Sadie to go out onto the balcony, so they could collogue. He was still in a cast and he couldn't get around very well; otherwise, he would have preferred to go on a walk with her. He felt like he thought better and was more persuasive when he was in motion.

Sadie spoke first. "The Cellar Door advance is fine, and they truly understand the game we're trying to make," she reasoned. "And we'll be able to spend next year making something new, something better. And how can you be so quick to sell out the thing we were trying to do with Ichigo's gender? I thought that was important to you."

"It is, but it's so much money," Sam said.

"Why do you suddenly care about money? You're twenty-two, how much money do you need? If you wanted to make money, you never should have made the game. You could have done Harvard recruiting, and ended up with a six-figure job at Bear Stearns, like everyone else in your class."

"You've never been poor," Sam said, "so you don't understand." Sam paused. He hated admitting vulnerabilities, even to Sadie. "I've got student loans. I owe a ton of money for the emergency room visit and the surgery on my ankle and foot, and if I don't start paying it back, the bills will go to my grandparents. At the moment, I've got negative dollars in my bank account. Marx is paying the rent, and I'm eating off the butt ends of credit cards. If we take the Cellar Door offer, I won't have anything to live on while we make the next game. I need this, Sadie, but honestly, I also think it's the better offer, the one that can really blow *Ichigo* up. And I know you must see that. I think the real reason you don't like them is because they thought I was the programmer."

Sadie sat down on the balcony. She loathed the Opus guys, and the thought of making an *Ichigo* sequel for them made her feel like she was being shackled and blindfolded and gagged and locked into a duffel bag and tossed into the bottom of the sea.

Sam was struggling to lower himself to sit down next to her. Sadie gave him her hand, but even with her assistance, he still landed a bit hard. He put his head in the crook of her shoulder; the freight was in proportion to the groove.

"I'll do whatever you want," he said.

"Okay, Sam," she said. "Opus it is."

Once Ichigo had become a real boy, his identity and Sam's identity became more and more inseparable. People beyond Aaron Opus started to say Sam *looked* like Ichigo—he did, somewhat. They ate up Sam's colorful and tragic biography: the childhood injury and playing video games as a way to be invincible, the Korean grandfather with the pizza parlor and the *Donkey Kong* machine. They tried to find ways in which Sam's biography and Ichigo's overlapped. Both had been separated from their parents at young ages. Sam was Asian, and Ichigo was Asian—in 1997, no one made the distinction between Japanese and half-Korean; that Sam was Asian was good enough. Because people—critics, gamers, the Opus marketing department—could more easily find Sam in the game, *Ichigo* became Sam's creation, not Sadie's, and as such, he became the game's auteur. (As for his relationship to Sadie, they were neither siblings nor married/divorced people nor dating nor had they ever dated, and thus, people found their relationship too mystifying and non-relatable to be worth exploring.)

As part of their promotion, Opus sent Sam to all the game conferences, which were much smaller affairs in those days. Sadie could have chosen to go along with him, but she felt as if her time was better spent at the new Unfair Games offices (fluorescent lighted and industrial carpeted, but no longer in Marx's living room at least). She was simultaneously supervising the *Ichigo* sequel and completing her BS at MIT. Besides, Sam liked the attention more than she did. She didn't begrudge him this: he liked interviews; he liked bloviating to a crowd; he liked having his photo taken. Someone had to do it, and Sadie felt uncomfortable speaking about the work—the work, she naively felt, should speak for itself. Sadie was twenty-two when *Ichigo* was launched, and she hadn't figured out who she was in public yet. (She barely knew who she was in private.) There were so few prominent female game designers, and there wasn't exactly a playbook for how a female game designer was supposed to present herself. But the fact is, no one at Opus was pushing Sadie to put herself forward either. The men at Opus *wanted* Sam to be the face of *Ichigo,* and so he was. The gaming industry, like many industries, loves its wonder boys.

Still, Sadie had to concede, if only to herself: it wasn't only that Sam *liked* promotion; he was better at it than she was. Before the game's launch, they had done a joint appearance at a sales conference in Boca Raton. It had been the biggest crowd they had ever spoken to, around five hundred people. Sam had been nervous, but Sadie hadn't been nervous at all. He had paced around the makeshift greenroom up until the moment they were called on stage.

"I think I'm going to throw up," Sam had said.

"You'll be fine." Sadie had squeezed his hand and poured him a glass of water. "It's a hotel ballroom and a couple of hundred nerds."

"I don't like so many eyes on me," Sam had said. He raked his fingers through his hair, which had become a Jewfro in the Florida humidity.

But as soon as they got on the dais, Sam's nerves disappeared, and he transformed into the world's most entertaining talk-show guest. When Sadie was asked a question—something like "How did you two meet?"—she gave a specific answer, usually no more than two sentences. "Well, we're both from Los Angeles," Sadie said. "And we both liked to game."

When Sam was asked a question, he turned it into a novella. The story could go on for fifteen minutes and take an extended detour into childhood without anyone ever seeming the slightest bit bored. "On the day I met Sadie, I hadn't spoken to anyone for six weeks, literally six weeks. But that's a whole other story. I'll tell you some other time when we're better friends. But the main thing you need to know is, Sadie couldn't get Mario on top of the flagpole. This was before the internet. You couldn't just cheat. You had to know someone who *knew* . . ." The crowd leaned forward when he spoke, laughed at his jokes, spontaneously broke into applause. They *loved* him. He was more handsome in front of a crowd; his limp, less apparent; his voice, warm and authoritative. It was as if all these years Sam had been waiting for an audience. Sadie marveled at his transformation. Where had her introverted partner gone? Who was this raconteur? Who was this clown?

And next to him, Sadie felt herself diminish.

3

Ichigo II: Go, Ichigo, Go came out in November 1998, almost a year after *Ichigo: A Child of the Sea.* In the second game, Ichigo's little sister, Hanami, is lost in yet another storm, and Ichigo, now age eleven, must find her. The second game sold modestly better than the first, but it was largely seen to be coasting on the original's reputation and strong sales. Most critics, including Sadie and Sam, thought the game was creatively a step backward. It wasn't that the second *Ichigo* was a bad game, but what it felt like was more of the same. *Ichigo II* didn't take the Ichigo character in a new direction; it didn't push things graphically, technically, or story-wise.

On the night Sadie told them that she didn't want to make a third *Ichigo,* Marx and Sam had just returned from a monthlong *Ichigo II* promotional tour. It was one of the longest separations the three of them had had since the summer when everything had begun. "I feel like the series has run its course," she said. "I feel like there isn't anything left for us to do creatively." They were having dinner back at the Kennedy Street apartment that Sam and Marx still shared.

"So, what do you want to make instead?" Marx asked.

"I have a couple of ideas," Sadie said. "But I feel like this is a different discussion."

"We can get out the old whiteboard anytime," Marx said.

"Hold on," Sam said. Up until this point, he had been listening quietly. "We can't leave Ichigo this way, Sadie. We didn't have time to make a great *Ichigo II* because of Opus's arbitrary timeline. Don't you want to make a third game that's great?"

"Maybe someday," Sadie said.

"I mean, he's our child," Sam said. "You can't abandon our child in a shitty sequel."

"Samson," Sadie said, in a warning voice. "I can."

Sam stood up, wincing.

"Are you all right?" Marx asked.

"Just tired," Sam said. "Sadie, you don't get to determine by yourself what we do next. If we aren't going to make *Ichigo III*, which I think we should, you have to give us some idea of what it is you'd like to do instead."

"Sam, your foot is bleeding through your sock," Marx said.

"Yeah, it's been doing that a little," Sam said, unconcerned.

"You need to have a doctor look at that."

"Marx, fuck off about my foot, okay? I'll take care of it." Sam hated when his maladies became a topic of discussion.

"Don't abuse Marx. He's trying to make sure you don't end up unconscious in the street again," Sadie said.

"I'm fine," Marx said. "Honestly."

"You should apologize," Sadie insisted.

"Sorry, Marx," Sam said without conviction. He immediately turned back to Sadie. "Seriously, don't you want to run these ideas by me, your partner?"

Sadie began stacking dishes. "If everyone's done, I'm going to clear."

"You don't have to do that," Marx said.

"I'm a guest," Sadie said. "It's polite."

Marx began clearing alongside her.

She went into the kitchen, and Sam trailed behind her, limping. "Don't you want to run these ideas by me, your partner?" he repeated.

"I would," Sadie said in a controlled voice. She set the dishes in the sink. "If you were ever here."

"You could have come," Sam said. "I *repeatedly* asked you to come."

"We couldn't all go on vacation for two years."

"Sadie, it was real work," Sam said.

"I did real work, too," she said. "I had to make the *shitty* sequel."

"Well, you certainly did that," Sam said.

"Hey Sam, kindly fuck yourself," Sadie said.

"Friends, Romans, countrymen," Marx said, "calm down."

Sadie walked out the door and straight back to the apartment she shared with Dov. Dov was in Israel, visiting his son and his wife, who two years later, he still hadn't managed to divorce.

When Sadie arrived at the apartment, the phone was ringing, but she didn't answer. Whoever it was didn't leave a message. She knew it was Sam or Dov, and she didn't want to speak to either of them.

It wasn't as if she didn't have other options. If Sam was committed to making *Ichigo III*, she could leave Unfair. Unfair had fulfilled its obligations to Opus, and she didn't have an employment contract with Unfair; none of them did. She didn't need Sam or Marx. She could strike out on her own, make a new game by herself. The phone rang again, and it went to the answering machine: "Sadie. Dov here. Pick up."

Sadie answered the phone. They spoke about domestic matters, and then, Sadie said, "If I wanted to make a game by myself, without Sam I mean, would that be a huge mistake?"

"What happened?" Dov asked.

"Nothing," Sadie said. "We had a fight."

"Sadie, that's completely normal. The best teams are constantly at each other's throats. It's a part of the process. If you aren't fighting, then someone doesn't care enough about the work. Say you're sorry. Move on."

Sadie didn't feel like explaining to Dov that she *wasn't sorry*, and that he hadn't answered the question she was asking. "Okay," she said. "Thanks, Dov."

By eleven-thirty, Sadie was in her pajamas, teeth brushed and flossed, ready to go to bed. She wondered if this was what other twenty-three-year-olds' Friday nights were like. When she was forty, would she lament that she hadn't had sex with more people and partied more? But then, she didn't enjoy many people, and she had never gone to a party that she wasn't eager to leave. She hated being drunk, though she did enjoy smoking a joint every now and then. She liked playing games, seeing a foreign movie, a good meal. She liked going to bed early and waking up early. She liked working. She liked that she was good at her work, and she felt proud of the fact that she was well paid for it. She felt pleasure in orderly things—a perfectly efficient section of code, a closet where every item was in its place. She liked solitude and the thoughts of her own interesting and creative mind. She liked to be comfortable. She liked hotel rooms, thick towels, cashmere sweaters, silk dresses, oxfords, brunch, fine stationery, overpriced conditioner, bouquets of gerbera, hats, postage stamps, art monographs, maranta plants, PBS documentaries, challah, soy candles, and yoga. She liked receiving a canvas tote bag when she gave to a charitable cause. She was an avid reader (of fiction and nonfiction), but she never read the newspaper, other than the arts sections, and she felt guilty about this. Dov often said she was bourgeois. He meant it as an insult, but she knew that she probably was. Her parents were bourgeois, and she adored them, so, of course, she had turned out bourgeois, too. She wished she could get a dog, but Dov's building didn't allow them.

But the reason she was bourgeois was so she could make work that wasn't bourgeois. If she were cautious in her life, she could avoid compromising in her work.

The buzzer sounded.

She ignored it.

She could hear Sam's reedy voice calling from the street. "SADIE MIRANDA GREEN, I CAN SEE YOUR LIGHT ON."

She ignored him.

"SADIE, IT'S COLD OUT HERE. IT'S SNOWING AGAIN. PLEASE LET YOUR OLDEST AND BEST FRIEND COME UP."

Sadie continued to ignore him. If Sam froze, it was his own fault.

Sadie peeked out the curtain, and she looked onto the street. Sam had his cane, which he had been using more and more often. She could not remember the last time she had seen him without it. She buzzed him in.

"What do you want?" she said.

"I want to know your ideas," Sam said. "I really want to know them. I love hearing your ideas. That's my favorite thing in the world.

"And I don't want to force you to make a sequel you don't want to make. You're my partner, and I haven't forgotten what you did for me when you agreed to the deal at Opus. But I love Ichigo. I love what we made, and lots of other people love Ichigo, too. I think we should, at some point, send him out on a high note. But I can understand why you'd be tired of him for the moment."

"*Ichigo III: Sayonara, Ichigo-San,*" Sadie said.

Sam laughed. "It's not that bad."

Sam was leaning on his good foot, in the increasingly lopsided way he had to stand, and Sadie felt a swelling of love and of worry for him—what was the difference in the end? It was never worth worrying about someone you didn't love. And it wasn't love if you didn't worry. "Did you at least take a cab here?"

"Yes, ma'am, I can afford them now."

"Marx let you go out in this?"

"Marx isn't my keeper."

"But he's the sensible one."

"Ah, don't blame Marx. He didn't know I left. He went to Zoe's," Sam reported.

"Is he still seeing her? That's a long one for him," Sadie said.

"I think they're in love." Sam sniffed, as if the idea of it, love, was ridiculous.

"You disapprove, I take it?"

"Marx is always in love. He's an emotional harlot. What does love even mean when you can find it with so many people and things?"

"Marx is great," Sadie said. "I think he's lucky."

"There is no luck," Sam said.

"Sure there is. It's that ginormous polyhedral die that you throw when you're playing Dungeons & Dragons."

"Very funny," Sam said. "Where's Dov anyway?"

"He's already gone for the break," she said.

Sam studied Sadie. He was an expert in her moods and colors. "Are you still in love?"

"Was I ever?" Sadie said.

"That's bleak."

"I adore him. I want to kill him. It's normal. It's complicated," Sadie said. "I don't want to talk about Dov." She yawned, and she shifted over on the sofa to make room for Sam. "Well, you're here now. You may as well stay. Marx'll kill me if I send you home in this weather."

Sam sat down next to Sadie. She turned on the TV, and they watched Letterman for a while. When stupid pet tricks came on, Sadie pressed mute, and Sam turned to her, waiting for her to speak. She studied Sam's moon face, which was so familiar to her. It was almost like looking at herself, but through a magical mirror that allowed her to see her whole life. When she looked at him, she saw Sam, but she also saw Ichigo and Alice and Freda and Marx and Dov and all the mistakes she had made, and all her secret shames and fears, and all the best things she had done, too. Sometimes, she didn't even *like* him, but the truth was, she didn't know if an idea was worth pursuing until it had made its way through Sam's brain, too. It was only when Sam said her own idea back to her—slightly modified, improved, synthesized, rearranged—that she could tell if it was good. She knew if she told him her new idea, it would instantly become his, too. They'd be walking down the aisle all over again, blithely stamping on another glass, come what may. She took a deep breath. "The game I want to make is called *Both Sides*."

4

Sadie came up with the idea for *Both Sides* on the night Sam went missing, and she'd been turning it over in her head ever since. It wasn't much then. A glimmer of a notion of a nothing of a whisper of a figment of an idea. When she'd been retracing the walk she'd taken with him on that promise-filled dawn, she had been struck by how the exact same route could look and feel so different. One minute, Sam was there, the game was completed, and the world was filled with potential. Twelve hours later, Sam was gone, the game was far from her thoughts, and the world was grim and murderous. *It is the same world,* she thought, *but I am different. Or is it a different world, but I am the same?* For a moment, she felt dangerously untethered from her body and from reality, and she had to sit down to feel the ground beneath her, before she could continue searching for Sam.

She had had feelings like this before. During her senior year of high school, a formerly close friend had died from an eating disorder. Long before Sadie knew about the eating disorder, Sadie and the friend had sometimes played what they referred to as eating games. The friend would declare it "lettuce day" or "granola bar day" or "canned soup day" or "matzoh day" and she and the friend would try to eat nothing but that item for twenty-four hours. At fourteen, Sadie had thought it was a joke, and the one-item eating game appealed to her organized and obsessive nature. She had not realized that this game meant something else, something ultimately deadly, to the friend. It was Alice who finally told her, "This is screwed up, Sadie. You can't go a whole day eating lettuce." The game ended not long after—Sadie's participation in it at least—and Sadie and the friend drifted apart.

At the friend's funeral, there was an open casket. When Sadie looked in the coffin, she almost felt as if she were looking at herself. She felt as if she had died, as if she were the one who was supposed to have died, and that somehow, she and the friend had switched places. She was so disturbed, she ran out of the service, apologizing to the friend's ruined parents on the way out.

On the night Sam went missing, it occurred to Sadie that nothing in life was as solid-state as it appeared. A childish game might be deadly. A friend might disappear. And as much as a person might try to shield herself from it, the possibility for the other outcome was always there. *We are all living, at most, half of a life,* she thought. There was the life that you lived, which consisted of the choices you made. And then, there was the other life, the one that was the things you hadn't chosen. And sometimes, this other life felt as palpable as the one you were living. Sometimes, it felt as if you might be walking down Brattle Street, and without warning, you could slip into this other life, like Alice falling down the rabbit hole that led to Wonderland. You would end up a different version of yourself, in some other town. But it wouldn't be strange like Wonderland, not at all. Because you would have expected all along that it could have turned out that way. You would feel relief, because you had always wondered what that other life would have looked like. And there you were.

But Sadie didn't say these things to Sam.

"Have you ever heard of *Colossal Cave Adventure*?" Sadie began.

"Sure, but I've never played it. It's old-school, right?"

"It's *ancient* school," she said. "Entirely text, no graphics."

"You're not saying you want to make a game like that, are you?"

"No," Sadie said. "Of course not. But there's this one part of the game that haunts me. You know how you have to go through all these caves?"

"Right, I assumed."

"So, it's a huge pain because you have to go back to the cabin at the beginning to access your inventory. In order to solve the problem of going from the caves to the cabin, the programmers invented this special command, Xyzzy."

"Zizzy?" Sam repeated.

"Yes. It's spelled X-Y-Z-Z-Y. When you use the Xyzzy command, you can magically switch between two places."

"Sounds like a cheat." Sam hated games that made a physical process too easy.

"No," Sadie said, "it's genius, actually. It's the best part of the game, because it acknowledges that the world you're playing is *not* the real world. And since you're not in the real world, you don't have to move as if you are in the real world. But that's what I want our game to be like. I want it to be like Xyzzy. Only instead of toggling between two places like in *Adventure,* the game should toggle between two worlds. Like, in one world, you're this ordinary person living an ordinary life, and in the other world, you're the hero. And the game lets you play both sides. I haven't worked everything out yet. It's early."

Sam took off his glasses and set them on the coffee table. "I get it," he said. "So, the two worlds should be different stylistically, and have different kinds of game mechanics."

"Yes," Sadie said. "Exactly. It's like Oz and Kansas, if Dorothy could switch between them the whole time."

"One side is like the new *Zelda* and the graphics are 3D, first person, high quality, the kind of thing that eats up a hard drive. And the other side is simple. Not eighties arcade simple, but a throwback to Sierra-style *Kings Quest IV,* or what have you. Third-person perspective. Simple enough so that you could possibly play it online."

"Right," Sadie said.

"What's the story?"

"Maybe it's about a girl. She has a bad home life. She's bullied at school. But in the other world, she's—"

"Hold on," Sam said, "I'll take notes."

The next afternoon, Sam took a cab back to Kennedy Street. He and Sadie had stayed up all night, and he felt tired and content. He'd been away promoting the *Ichigo* games so much that he hadn't had time to realize how much he had missed their collaboration. Sadie may have thought Sam had been on a vacation, but promoting their games *had* been real work. Some of it had been fun—the interviews with the more observant gaming journalists; the Ichigo mascot Opus had made for Game Developers Conference; the children who had begun to dress up like Ichigo and Gomibako; the fans who couldn't get enough of Sam Masur, the creator who looked just like his creation! Most of promotion had been a grind. It had been telling the same stories over and over again but acting as if he were telling them for the first time. It had been listening to stupid people make stupid observations about *Ichigo*, their baby, and having to act as if these observations were delightful, trenchant, and original. It had been dragging out his personal traumas for the amusement of the game-buying public. It had been seedy sales conferences. It had been signings in run-down game stores in strip malls. It had been smiling for photographs until he had a headache. It had been endless airplane travel and rental car lines. It had been his foot hurting more and more as the year went on, and Sam trying to ignore it. Sam was practiced at disregarding pain, but two weeks earlier, the foot had begun to bleed. Blood was harder to overlook. He'd been at a promotional event at the FAO Schwarz in New York City. A little kid had tugged at Sam's sleeve. "Mr. Ichigo, you're bleeding." Sam looked down. Indeed, his white tennis shoe had a large bloody spot right in the middle.

"I think it's paint," Sam had said, embarrassed.

Back in his hotel room, he'd bandaged himself up, making sure not to get any blood on the hotel carpet, and then he threw his sneakers in the trash.

The point was, someone needed to promote the games, and Sadie had made it clear that she didn't want to be that person.

What Sam loved best was being alone with Sadie and filling a blank slate with their grand ideas. He loved building a world with her. They had agreed to reconvene in the evening, and he was excited to start work.

He took a shower, but when he got out of the shower, he found that his foot would not stop bleeding. One of the seven metal rods that made up the structure of his foot had gotten out of alignment again and it was, inconveniently, poking through his flesh. The pain was sharp, but bearable. It was the nuisance that bothered him. As he sat on the bathroom floor, trying to make the bleeding stop, he found a second hole in his foot. When he poked his finger in the second hole, he could feel the end of one of the other rods. For a second, he allowed himself to feel scared. That was when Marx returned from Zoe's.

Marx found Sam on the bathroom floor, the damaged foot exposed. Marx hadn't seen Sam's foot for many years, as Sam took great pains to keep it concealed. But seeing it, Marx had no idea how Sam was even ambulatory. Sam's foot looked deathly—bruised and bloody and twisted and gory. Sam quickly threw a towel over it. "Jesus, Sam. You're going to the doctor right now," Marx said.

"I can't. I'm supposed to meet with Sadie in a couple of hours," Sam said calmly. "We're working on a new game. And it's not like I'm going to bleed to death tonight. Trust me, Marx. I've been dealing with this sort of thing for a while. Would you mind getting me some cotton and gauze?"

Marx went into their medicine cabinet, and he handed Sam the supplies.

"It'll heal in a couple of days. It always does," Sam said, with a confidence that he did not entirely feel. "Sadie and I are starting to get momentum with the new game."

After last night's argument, Marx was encouraged to hear that they were working on something and curious to hear what it was. "Fine," Marx said. "But I'm making you an appointment for tomorrow."

Sam's orthopedist was booked for the next week. By the morning of his appointment, the foot seemed neither better nor worse, though Sam was not walking on it almost at all, and he had, in the last several days, developed a fever. Marx went with Sam to the doctor, both to ensure that he went, and to offer his assistance on the way back.

At the doctor's office, Marx waited in the reception area and passed the time reading Joan Didion's *White Album*, which was not entirely pleasure reading. Zoe was thinking of moving to California. She had begun to find work scoring films, television, and advertising, and she thought she could find more work if she moved out to Los Angeles for a time. The idea appealed to Marx, not just for Zoe, but because he had always been drawn to living in California. He loved the West Coast. He had wanted to go to Stanford, but he hadn't gotten in. He appreciated Los Angeles, its skinny palm trees and its decaying Spanish-style homes and its occasional flocks of parrots and its smiling people who always wanted something from you. He liked hiking and running, and he wouldn't have minded living in a place where he could be outdoors most of the year. In terms of work, there were tons of game people on the West Coast, particularly in Los Angeles, and airy, stylish, modern office spaces that cost less than what they paid in Cambridge. After he'd returned from a business trip out there the prior year, Marx had floated the idea of setting up their office in California to Sadie and Sam. They were both from Los Angeles and neither had wanted to return. To return to the city of one's birth always felt like retreat.

About a half hour after he'd gone in, Sam emerged from the doctor's office. He was on crutches, his foot was wrapped in thick bandages, and he was carrying a prescription that needed to be filled for a course of antibiotics.

"What did she say?" Marx asked.

Sam shrugged. "Nothing I didn't already know."

"So, you're good?" Marx persisted. He could not get the visual of Sam's foot out of his mind.

"I'm the same as I've always been," Sam said. "I want to get back to work."

Marx and Sam went out to the parking lot to wait for a cab. Marx pretended to realize he had left *The White Album* in the waiting area. "I'll just be a second," he said.

Back in the office, he quickly claimed his book and then he went up to the desk to see if Sam's doctor had a moment to speak with him. He was Sam's brother, he said, and he had questions about Sam's condition. Because Marx was Marx—handsome, charming, polite—the nurse said she would try.

Marx went back to the doctor's office, and the doctor said she was quite glad to talk to him, because she wasn't always sure Sam was hearing her. She had cleaned, stitched up the wound, and realigned the foot as much as it was possible to do so. The largest wound on his foot had become infected, so Sam had to be given a course of antibiotics. But the news was not good. The doctor felt an amputation was inevitable.

"He says he can tolerate the pain, though I don't know how he is. But it isn't about the pain at this point. His foot is unsustainable. The rods are wearing out what's left of his bone and his skin is becoming prone to infection and resistant to healing. The only way to stop the damage is if he uses a wheelchair and puts literally no pressure on the foot, which I wouldn't recommend for an active twenty-four-year-old.

He will constantly be back here unless he takes serious action. The sooner, the better. He doesn't want to end up with sepsis, which could lead to a riskier emergency amputation. He's young and he's in good health—if it were my brother, I'd tell him it's time."

The cab was waiting for them when Marx got back out to the curb.

"That took a while," Sam remarked.

"Yes."

"Well," Sam said. "I can tell by your face and your dodgy timeline that something happened in there. What is it?"

"I ran into your doctor when I was in the lobby. She thought I was your brother. She seems"—Marx searched for the right word—"concerned."

Sam tightened his grip on his crutches. "She had no right to talk to you. My medical situation is my private business."

Marx knew that invoking friendship and personal history was never useful with Sam. "Sam, it arguably is my business. We're partners, and if you're going to need major surgery, Sadie and I need to be able to plan."

"People have been telling me that I have to do something about this foot for years. I get it. I get that it's probably close to time, but I need to make the new game with Sadie first."

"Sam! How long is that going to take? You haven't even started. I'm your producer and I don't know anything about it. A week ago, you two were still arguing about whether to make *Ichigo III*."

"We've resolved that now."

"This is madness. If you're scared, that would be entirely understandable. That would be—"

"I'm not scared. I simply can't make the game and be recovering from having an amputation at the same time," Sam said imperiously. "I don't have time for surgery and physical therapy and getting a prosthetic that fits. It's winter in Massachusetts, Marx. It's hard enough for me to get around as it is."

Marx and Sam didn't speak the rest of the way home.

"And I'd appreciate if you didn't mention any of this to Sadie," Sam said when the cab arrived at Kennedy Street.

Marx nodded. He got out first, so he could help Sam out of the cab.

. . .

Marx went to Zoe's apartment that night and he relayed what had happened with Sam. Zoe was sitting in the living room, cross-legged on an ikat-patterned cushion and playing the pan flute, which she was currently learning. Her Titian hair fell past her breasts and she wore only underwear. Zoe always kept the heat turned up in her apartment so that she could wear as little clothing as possible. She liked feeling the vibrations of her instruments, she said. She liked feeling the vibrations of the earth underneath her and the air around her. There was a secret music, she claimed, that she could only hear when there was nothing between her and the universe. (By "nothing," she meant "clothing.") Zoe joked—or maybe it wasn't a joke—that her first sexual experience had been with her cello. Before she'd become a composer, she'd been a child cello prodigy, and she'd loved nothing so much as going outside, stripping, and playing by herself. Her mother had once discovered her this way behind their house and had made Zoe see a therapist. (The therapist determined that Zoe had the healthiest body image of any teenage girl he'd ever met.) At this point in their relationship, Marx was so accustomed to Zoe's naked body that it didn't even feel sexual anymore. They still had frequent and playful sex, but Zoe's nudity was not an invitation to it.

"The solution is completely obvious," Zoe said. "You have to convince Sam and Sadie to go to California with us. The winter won't be a problem in California. Everyone drives out there, so Sam won't have to walk as much, and his recovery will be easier."

"I'm not sure I'm going to California yet," Marx said.

"Oh, you are," Zoe said. "I know it. Marx, look at you. You were meant for California. Unfair is between games, and Sam needs time off, so it's the perfect time to move your office to California, which you've told me for years is what you want to do. Sam will have plenty of time to have the surgery and recover, while you and Sadie set up the office and start hiring." Zoe clapped her hands together. "Done."

"Sadie might not want to go," Marx said. "Dov is here."

Zoe rolled her eyes. "Marx, Sadie is *dying* to have an excuse to leave Dov."

"She loves Dov," Marx said.

"She *hates* Dov. He will never get divorced. We all know this," Zoe said.

Marx laughed at Zoe's certainty—he had known Sadie for three years, half as long as he'd known Sam, and he still found her to be a mystery. "So how do I convince Sam?" Marx asked.

"Marx, my love, you are so innocent. *You* don't have to convince anyone. You tell Sadie that Sam needs to go to California—his foot is rotting; he needs to have the surgery and he won't do it in Massachusetts. You tell Sam that Sadie needs to go—she needs to find a way to break with Dov. Those two are thick as thieves; they'll do anything for each other."

Marx kissed Zoe on the lips. She tasted like cinnamon tea and mandarin oranges, and he wanted to have sex with her, but he could tell she was still in the middle of work. "You're being very Lady Macbeth tonight. Are you saying all these things because you want me to go to California with you?"

"Well, yes, partially. But it's also the absolute correct course of action," Zoe said.

It went almost exactly as Zoe said it would. He went to Sadie first and, ignoring Sam's prohibition against it, conveyed the information about Sam's disturbingly decrepit foot. Sadie said that she had not seen herself in California, but she readily agreed that it made sense for Sam and for the company. It was evident to her—as it would have been to anyone close to Sam—that something needed to be done about Sam's health, and all of that would be easier for him in California. "To tell you the truth," Sadie said, "I'm a little tired of winter myself."

When Marx went to Sam, he diverged from Zoe's advice. He began with the argument about the state-of-the-art office they could build in L.A., and the inspiring L.A. gaming scene, and he did not mention anything about Sadie. Sam had told Marx about *Both Sides*— Marx loved the idea, but then, no one truly cared about Marx's opinion of what they should do next. However, *Both Sides*, and its ambitious scale, fed perfectly into Marx's argument. They would require a larger office to accommodate the staff they would need to make it. Sam still wasn't convinced. "It'll take time to move and to hire decent people and to set up the office," Sam argued.

"Sadie and I can do that," Marx said. "And that would leave you time to have the surgery, no?"

Sam shook his head. "Sadie's willing to do this? She's willing to leave Dov?"

"She is," Marx said. "I think she wants to even, but she doesn't know how. It might help her if she had a reason to go."

"I'll do it," he said. "For Sadie."

Zoe was not the only one who had observed that all was not right between Sadie and Dov.

In addition to the divorce that never happened, Sadie sometimes showed up to the office with light bruising on her face and limbs, rope burns, small scratches; on one occasion, a sprained wrist. A series of minor injuries, nothing that serious or even noticeable, but enough so that Marx had once seen fit to ask her what the story was.

Marx and Sadie had gone to Austin by themselves to meet with the Opus team. The weather in Austin was murderously hot, so when they got back to their hotel, the two of them had changed into swimsuits and gone to the pool. Marx couldn't help but notice the number of bruises on Sadie's legs and arms, and later that night when they were sitting in the hotel bar, he, very gently, asked her about them. They were having hard, grown-up drinks—an old-fashioned for Marx and a whiskey sour for Sadie. It was kind of a joke, a play on being sad, middle-aged adults on a business trip. Marx lightly touched the welt on her wrist. "Are you okay?" he asked.

Sadie had laughed in that low breathy way she had when she was embarrassed. She covered the wrist with her other hand. Marx thought she wasn't going to tell him anything, but then she did.

"It's a game we like to play," she said.

"A game?" Marx said.

"Some bondage stuff," she said. "He never takes it too far. He always has my consent."

"Do you like it?" he asked.

Sadie considered the question. She took another swig of her drink. "Sometimes." She smiled her crooked smile, and there was an apologetic look in her eyes, as if she knew she had betrayed Dov by admitting that she only *sometimes* enjoyed sex with him. "But he's great. I mean, he's been really great for me," she said. "And for all of us, too."

5

It is relatively easy to pack up your life when you're twenty-three, and Sadie was significantly finished by the time Dov returned from the break.

"What the fuck is this?" he said.

"I'm . . . Well, I'm going to California," she said.

Unfair had acted quickly, she explained. Sam had already gotten a referral for a new team of doctors. He had left before Christmas so that he could get the surgery scheduled. Once he'd committed to this course of action, he said he wanted it done as soon as possible. New Year's Day, Marx and Zoe flew out to L.A. to find office space for the company, and an apartment for the two of them. They found both in Venice, where Marx determined the cool kids in tech were. Sam and Sadie didn't need apartments yet—Sam would stay with his grandparents until after he'd recovered from the surgery, and Sadie would stay with her parents and could house hunt from there.

Dov listened quietly until she was done. He was silent a moment before he said, "Like thieves in the bloody night. When were you planning to tell me?"

"It happened fast," she said. "It wasn't personal."

"We've spoken dozens of times since you must have *decided* all of this."

"Yes, but it's hard to talk to you when you're in Israel. You're always so distracted when you're with Telly."

Dov sat on the bed and watched Sadie empty the bureau. He

squinted, as if it were a problem with his eyes. He put his head in his hands.

"Do you want me to ask you to marry me? Is that what you want?"

"No," Sadie said. "You can't anyway."

"Do you want me to get a divorce right now? Because I will." He reached for the phone. "I will call Batia right now."

"No," Sadie said. "And I don't believe you. If you were going to do that you would have done it."

"Are we breaking up?" Dov asked.

"I don't know," Sadie said. "Yes, I think we are."

He pushed her down on the bed, and he pushed his tongue into her mouth, and she lay there limply. "You think you're a cool bitch now, don't you?" he said.

She looked Dov in the eye. "No. I just want to go to L.A., and help my friend, and make my game."

"Sam is not your friend, Sadie. Don't fool yourself."

"That's what my partners wanted to do, and that's what I'm doing."

"*Partners.* You wouldn't even have a company if it weren't for me," Dov said. "I gave you Ulysses. I set you up with publishers and industry people. I gave you fucking everything."

"Thank you," she said. "For fucking everything."

"Take off your clothes," he said.

"No."

"You think you're tough now, don't you?" She knew what was coming. He pushed her into the headboard, and he reached into his nightstand drawer and he snapped the handcuff around her wrist and to the bedpost, as he'd done so many times before. Sometimes, it had aroused her, and sometimes, it had annoyed her, and sometimes, it had frightened her. This time, Sadie felt nothing. She didn't fight him. She let it happen. He reached under her skirt, between her legs, and he yanked her underwear off, and then he threw it across the room. He wouldn't have sex without her consent, but he felt free to make her uncomfortable and embarrassed. He slammed the door to the bedroom, and she could hear him smacking something—the wall? the sofa?—in the other room. She picked up the phone with her free hand, and she called Sam. His grandmother answered the phone.

"Sadie Green! When do you arrive?" Bong Cha said.

"The day after tomorrow," Sadie said.

"It is so nice that you kids are still friends, and that you both are coming home. Your parents must be so excited," Bong Cha said. She was clearly delighted to have Sam home.

"They are," Sadie said.

"*Ichigo* is everywhere. Did you know there was a billboard on Sunset? Did Sam show you the pictures we took?"

"He did," Sadie said. "Thanks so much."

"Oh, it's no bother. Dong Hyun is so proud of you two. He tells everyone how Sam and his childhood friend made this big game all by themselves. He says that he always knew you two would do great things. He has a huge *Ichigo* poster at the pizza place, but of course, you'll see it soon."

"Definitely. Is Sam there?" Sadie tried to stretch out her shoulder, but it was hard with her arm over her head.

"Oh, I will give you Samson! One moment."

"How's California?" Sadie said once Sam was on the line.

"Dry. Hot. Traffic," Sam said. "I keep seeing coyotes everywhere. But the offices Marx rented are sweet."

"At least there's that," Sadie said.

"How'd Dov take the news?" Sam asked.

Sadie could hear Dov loudly playing *Grand Theft Auto* in the other room. "What I expected." She felt as if she were already in California.

"Do you want to talk about the game?" Sadie asked.

"I do," Sam said.

About a half hour later—Sadie was still on the phone with Sam, discussing *Both Sides*—Dov came into the bedroom, and he unlocked the handcuff. "Who are you talking to?" he whispered.

"Sam," she said.

"Tell him I say hello," Dov said, in a normal, professional voice. "And good luck."

She spent the next day packing up her life and intermittently arguing with Dov, going over the same ground. He told her she was nothing; she, in turn, said nothing. He apologized; she packed. He insulted her; she packed. He apologized again; she packed. The last thing she packed were the handcuffs. She slipped them into the zippered pocket of the large duffel she was planning to check. She didn't want Dov to use them on some other girl. She wasn't sure if this impulse came from a sense of sorority or sentimentality.

Dov drove Sadie to the airport even though she said she could call a car. In the best of moods, Dov was an unpleasant, belligerent driver—he gestured, cursed, honked excessively, cut people off, passed on the right, rarely signaled—and Sadie avoided car rides with him as much as she could. On this morning, Dov's driving was subdued, but he decided to pass the time lecturing Sadie about the folly of her exodus from Boston. He expressed his concerns through a series of histrionic rhetorical questions concerning L.A.'s shortcomings, all of which Sadie, a native Angeleno, already knew: Did she know about the earthquakes? The fires? The floods? The drought? The smog? The homeless? The coyotes? The general sense of looming apocalypse? Did she know that drugstores closed at ten? What would happen if she needed cough syrup or batteries or legal pads after ten? Did she know there weren't any all-night diners or bodegas or takeout? Where would she eat? Where would she get decent bagels or pizza? Did she know that the only things people in L.A. ate were avocados and sprouts? Was she ready to be into juicing? Was she aware that the tap water caused cancer? *Sadie! Whatever you do, do NOT drink the tap water!* Did she know how dry the air was, and was she prepared for the constant allergies? Did she know that cell phone coverage was terrible? Did she know that no one in L.A. read books or went to the theater or followed current events? That their brains were pulp because they all worked in entertainment and spent their spare time getting plastic surgery and going to the gym? Did she know that no one walked, not even one block? That they drove from their front doors to their mailboxes? Did she still know how to drive? And the traffic, Hashem, had she heard about the traffic? Was she prepared to spend the majority of her waking hours en route? Wouldn't she miss the seasons? Did she know that it never rained there, and when it did rain, there were mudslides? Wouldn't she miss the rain?

When they reached the airport parking loop, he said, "I feel like I've fucked everything up. I'm a fucking genius so I don't know why I fuck everything up all the time, but I do. I want to stop, but I don't know how." He took her suitcases out of the car, and he moved them to the curb. He pulled her tightly into him, crushing her head into his mesomorphic chest. "I'm a beast, but I fucking *love* you, girl," Dov said. "For better or for worse, you can take that on your travels."

. . .

For the flight to California, Marx had booked her a business-class ticket, and Sadie felt fancy. Even though her parents were wealthy, the family had always flown in coach. Her father, a business manager to movie stars, had seen too many of his clients go broke, wasting money on fripperies like luxury travel, divorces, restaurant investments, and second homes they never used.

Sadie settled into her seat. She accepted the heated washcloth, the orange juice in a glass flute, the small cup of warm nuts. She opened the window shade. It was not quite 7 a.m., and the sun was rising, a delicate, white blotch in a grayish sky. The plane took off, and she made sure to take a last look at Boston Harbor, which was covered in ice. She knew she wouldn't be back anytime soon.

It was only 10 a.m. when Sadie arrived in Los Angeles. Marx and Zoe picked her up at the airport. Zoe thrust a bouquet of multicolor gerbera into Sadie's arms. "Welcome home," Zoe said.

Zoe was wearing a long, white maxi dress, and Marx was wearing a white T-shirt and blue jeans. They looked, respectively, like Stevie Nicks and James Dean. Both wore sunglasses. "You guys are so Californian already," Sadie said. "I was born here, and I look way less Californian than either of you."

Marx and Zoe drove straight to the office—Zoe driving, Sadie in the front seat, Marx in the back. Sadie was tired from the flight, so Zoe did most of the talking. Zoe was the anti-Dov, eager to tell Sadie about her California discoveries: Had Sadie gone to the Griffith Observatory? Had she been to movie night at Hollywood Forever Cemetery? The Cinerama Dome? The Greek? The Hollywood Bowl? The Getty pavilions? LACMA? The Theatricum Botanicum? The Bob Baker Marionette Theater? The Watts Towers? The Museum of Jurassic Technology? Did Sadie have magic friends and had she been to the Magic Castle? Had she tried green juice? Had she ever gone to the donut place that looked like a donut? Hot dogs were gross, but had she been to Pink's? Had she taken one of those tours of celebrity homes on the double-decker buses? Had she been to the restaurant that was built around a tree? What was her favorite place to hear live music? The Whisky a Go Go? The Palladium? The Troubadour? What was her favorite part of town? Which canyon was her favorite for hiking? The sun was always out and it never rained, wasn't that so great?

"They say there's no culture here, but I'm finding plenty of things to do," Zoe said.

"She loves it." Marx was appreciative of his partner's exuberance.

It was a tourist's list, but Sadie liked Zoe anyway. She was intelligent, but her intelligence didn't get in the way of her enthusiasm.

"You're from Beverly Hills, right?" Zoe asked.

"The flats," Sadie said.

"The flat part of a place named for its hills?" Zoe said.

"You can't have hills without flats," Sadie replied.

"Yes," Zoe said. "That's the truth." Zoe turned to Sadie. "I've decided we're going to be great friends, by the way. Don't bother trying to resist me. I'll stalk you until you submit."

Sadie laughed.

The Venice office was on Abbot Kinney, which in 1999 didn't have a single high-end chain store to its credit (or deficit, depending on your point of view). The space was industrial and, aside from bathrooms and a half-dozen offices along its perimeter, undefined. Its significant architectural details were massive, steel-framed casement windows and concrete floors, which Marx had the customary plans to warm up with wooden furniture, rugs, and plants. Compared to the cramped space they had left, Abbot Kinney felt colossal, and its expansiveness caused Sadie to feel a fleeting anxiety bordering on kenophobia. When she spoke, her voice echoed. "We can afford this?"

"We can," Marx said. Venice was still relatively cheap—Santa Monica's shabby cousin—and Unfair Games was flush with cash. "The realtor said Charles and Ray Eames's office was down the street."

Sam emerged from one of the offices. "Hello, colleagues!" Sam turned to Sadie: "What do you think?"

"I think *Both Sides* better blow it out," Sadie said.

"If you go up to the roof," Marx said, "you can see a majestic, if terribly narrow, strip of ocean." His phone rang: It was the movers with their Cambridge office boxes. "I have to meet them. You two go on without me."

But when Sadie and Sam reached the landing, they found the only access to the roof was a steep spiral staircase. It was the kind of structure that gave Sam trouble, and Sadie was surprised Marx hadn't warned them. "We don't have to," Sadie said.

Sam sized up the staircase, and then he nodded. "No, I'll make it. I want to see this unimpressive vista for myself."

As they carefully ascended, Sam leaned on Sadie, but only a little. He talked as they went so she wouldn't notice his discomfort. "I was trying to remember the name of a game. It was around the time you started bringing the laptop to the hospital. There was a kid who's trying to save his girlfriend."

"But of course."

"And a scientist whose brain was taken over by, maybe, a—I want to say—a sentient meteor? And there was a character with a green tentacle."

"*Maniac Mansion,*" Sadie said.

"That's it. Of course, it's *Maniac Mansion*. God, we loved that game. I was thinking, we should make something set in a mansion sometime."

"And each room is a time-travel portal."

"Maybe all the people from all the different periods who ever lived there are there."

"And they're not happy about it," Sadie said.

By then, they had reached the top of the stairs.

"Thank you," he said.

"For what?"

"For the use of your arm."

On the roof, if she got on her toes and craned her neck, she could, indeed, see the Pacific. It wasn't a magnificent view, but it was there. And, in any case, she could feel that she was near the ocean—she could smell it and she could hear it and the air felt like it, too. She took a deep breath.

The space Marx had chosen was so immaculate. Sadie loved clean, bright things, and she felt hopeful. It was right that they should come to California. California was for beginnings. They would make *Both Sides,* and it would be even better than *Ichigo,* because they were so much smarter than when they'd made *Ichigo.* Sam would be healed, and she wouldn't be angry at him anymore—it wasn't his fault that people thought *Ichigo* was his. And Sadie would be brand-new.

. . . .

That night, Sadie borrowed her father's car and drove into K-town. She parked the car in the alleyway behind Dong and Bong's New York Style House of Pizza.

Framed posters for both *Ichigo* games were prominently displayed on the wall of the pizza parlor. The only other poster was for a Korean beer, JjokJjok. The poster was from the '80s and quite faded. It had a picture of a smiling Korean woman and the tagline "What's the most beautiful woman in Koreatown drinking?"

Sam was waiting for her at a booth toward the back.

When he saw Sadie, Dong Hyun came from behind the counter to hug her. "Sadie Green! Famous person!" he greeted her. "Same order? Half-mushroom, half-pepperoni?"

"I don't eat meat anymore," Sadie said. "So just mushrooms. And onions if you have them."

Using one of the many keys on the key ring attached to his belt, Dong Hyun unlocked the *Donkey Kong* machine. "You kids play as much as you want."

"Shall we?" Sam said.

As they approached the *Donkey Kong* cabinet, the Hall of Fame screen came up: Only one of S.A.M.'s scores remained—the top one. "Your record stands," Sadie said. "You think you can beat it?"

"No," Sam said. "I'm too out of practice."

While they waited for the pizza, they played several rounds of *Donkey Kong*. Neither Sam nor Sadie was good anymore.

"You know the best thing about *Donkey Kong*?" Sadie asked.

"That it's named for the villain? The innovative use of barrels as weapons?"

"The necktie," she said. "It's brilliant design. Without it, the question of his dick would always be *hanging out there*."

"Literally."

They both giggled at their adolescent joke, and they felt twelve again.

Dong Hyun served the pizza, and Sadie and Sam sat in a booth. Sam didn't eat—it was after seven and his surgery was scheduled first, the next morning. "You're seriously just going to watch?" Sadie said.

"I don't mind," Sam said. "I think you love pizza more than I do anyway."

"When I was a kid." Sadie made a face at him. "You sure you don't mind?"

"I mean, I mind a little, but there'll be other pizzas, Sadie."

"You never know," she said. "This could be the last pizza in the world."

Sadie hadn't eaten since the plane that morning, and she ended up eating almost the whole pie. "I didn't know it," she said, "but I was starving."

Around eight, Sadie drove Sam to the hospital. It was past visiting hours, so only immediate family were allowed to accompany patients into their rooms. But when the nurse asked Sam who Sadie was, Sam answered quickly, "My wife."

They went back to Sam's hospital room. Sam didn't feel like sleeping yet, so they sat side by side on the bed and looked out the window, which faced another almost identical building.

"A game that takes place in a hospital," Sadie said.

"Who's the main character?"

"A doctor, I guess," Sadie said. "She's trying to save everyone."

"No," Sam said. "It's a zombie attack, and this kid has cancer, and he's got to somehow get out of the hospital alive and save as many of the other kids as possible."

"That's better," Sadie said. She reached into her bag. "I found this in my desk at home and I was waiting for the right time to give it to you." She handed him several waterlogged sheets. Across the top it read: Community Service Record: Sadie M. Green. Bat Mitzvah Date: 10/15/88.

Sam was delighted when he figured out what it was. He flipped to the back to look at the total. "Six hundred nine hours."

"It was the most community service any Bat Mitzvah had ever done. I don't know if I ever told you, but they gave me a prize," Sadie said.

"You better have brought the prize with you!"

"What do you take me for?" She reached into her bag again and removed a small heart-shaped crystal paperweight that was inscribed: *Presented to Sadie Miranda Green, for Her Outstanding Record of Com-*

munity Service, June 1988, from Hadassah of Temple Beth El Beverly Hills. "They gave it to me when I hit five hundred hours. It drove Alice crazy, which is why I think she told you, though she denies that was the reason."

"This is a quality prize," Sam said.

"Those Hadassah ladies don't mess around. It's Swarovski or Waterford or something. Alice was so jealous!"

"Who wouldn't be?" Sam enclosed the paperweight in his fist. "This is mine now."

"Of course," Sadie said. "That's why I brought it."

"You're sentimental tonight," Sam said.

"Back in L.A. Back at the hospital with you. Starting all over again. No Dov. New game. New office. I guess I am."

"I thought you were worried I was going to die," Sam said.

"No. You'll never die. And if you ever died, I'd just start the game again," Sadie said.

"Sam's dead. Put another quarter in the machine."

"Go back to the save point. Keep playing, and we'll win eventually." She paused. "Are you scared?" she asked him.

"I'm *relieved,* more than anything, I think," he said. "I'm glad it'll be done. But it's strange because I'll also miss this useless foot. It's been with me my whole life, of course, and I can't completely deny that it's been lucky."

"How so?"

"Well, if I hadn't been in the hospital, I never would have met you," Sam said. "And we never would have become friends. And then enemies—"

"I was never your enemy. That's all on you."

"You were *my* enemy," Sam said. He held up the paperweight. "This precious proves it once and for all!"

"Don't make me sorry I let you have that." Sadie grabbed for it, but Sam held it away from her.

"I'll never give it back. But then we were friends again. And if I hadn't had a messed-up foot, we never would have made *Ichigo,* and we wouldn't be here, twelve years later, sitting in another hospital, less than a five-minute walk from the first one."

"You can't know that," Sadie said. "We could have met at some other time. Our childhood homes were five miles apart, and we went to colleges that were less than two miles apart. We could have met in Cambridge. Or we could have met before that, at one of those smart-kid things in L.A. that you were always shooting me those dirty looks at. Don't deny it—"

"You were my mortal enemy!"

"That seems strong. I remember it as a period of reserved cordiality. But returning to my original point, there were many other ways—indeed, infinite ways—we could have met."

"You're saying all my pain and suffering was for nothing?" he said.

"Complete waste," she said. "Sorry, Sam. The universe tortured you because it could, because it will. The enormous polyhedral die in the sky was rolled, and it came up 'Torture Sam Masur.' I would have shown up in the game of your life either way." Sadie yawned. She was starting to feel deathly tired. She'd been up for eighteen hours and she'd eaten so much pizza. She smiled sleepily at Sam. "I'm not your wife."

"My work wife," he said. "Don't deny it."

"Your work wife is Marx," Sadie said.

"And I was saying it so they'd let you come back," Sam said. "The key to getting what you want in a hospital is telling the right lies in an authoritative voice."

She yawned again. "I'm still so jet-lagged. I should drive home. I feel like I haven't driven in so long that I've become a bad driver." She shook his hand, which was their parting custom. "I'll be here when you wake up from surgery, okay? I love you, Sam."

"Terribly," he said.

After Sadie left, Sam wasn't tired, so he decided to take a last walk on his rotten foot. By this time, the foot could bear almost no pressure, and Sam was on crutches. But still, he wanted to remember what it felt like to be two-footed. He found himself walking over to the children's hospital, where he'd spent so much time, where they'd devoted so much effort to saving the thing that would, in several hours, be excised for good.

He went into the waiting room and a girl, not much older than Sadie had been when he met her, was playing a game on a laptop. In the perfect world, Sam thought, the game the girl is playing is *Ichigo*. He looked over at the screen: it was *Dead Sea*.

"Do you like that game?" Sam asked.

"It's kind of old, but I like killing zombies," the girl said. "My brother says I look like the Wraith."

As Sam walked back to his hospital room, he felt the surprisingly sharp point of Sadie's crystal paperweight in his pocket, poking his thigh. He reached into his pocket, and he took it out. He looked at the little paperweight and he laughed at himself. How angry he had been at Sadie! How much righteous passion he had devoted to holding this grudge! He had thought himself so mature when he'd decided to cut her out of his life, but his reaction had been embarrassingly childish and over-the-top. He'd once tried to explain the falling-out to Marx, and Marx had not even understood it. *No,* Sam had said, *you don't understand. It's the principle. She was pretending to be my friend, but she was just doing it for community service.* Marx had looked at Sam blankly, and then he said, *No one spends hundreds of hours doing anything out of charity, Sam.* Thinking of this and looking at the little paperweight, Sam's heart swelled with love for Sadie. Why was it so hard for him to say he loved her even when she said it to him? He knew he loved her. People who felt far less for each other said "love" all the time, and it didn't mean a thing. And maybe that was the point. He more than loved Sadie Green. There needed to be another word for it.

He wanted to call her right now and tell her, but he knew she was jet-lagged and would be sleeping in that mint green four-poster bed, under the rose-print sheets, her parents down the hall. The thought made him happy. His best friend had come back to their hometown for him. He wasn't a fool; he knew what Marx had been doing when he'd insisted they move their business here. Marx had let him think that they were moving for *Both Sides,* for Sadie, for himself, and for Zoe even. But the truth was, they had done it for Sam, because Sam had been afraid of facing the winter, because Sam had constantly been in pain, because Sam had been afraid of the surgery and it was obvious to everyone that the surgery could not be put off. They had been worried about him, and they had wanted to make his life easier. And so they invented reasons—some of them even compelling and real. And they had not done this for the game or the company, but because they loved him, and they were his friends. And he felt grateful.

He took off his clothes, carefully setting the crystal heart on the nightstand, and he changed into his pajamas. He took a last look at his foot—adieu, old friend—and then he got into bed, and he went to sleep. As was often the case when he was in the hospital, he dreamed of his mother.

For the first several months of being in Los Angeles, Anna did not work at all. She steadily auditioned for movies, soap operas, commercials, voice-overs, but hadn't received so much as a callback. When she asked her agent why she was striking out so much, he said not to worry. "You have to let them get to know you, Anna." Her agent insisted she had a *young* look, and he advised her to revise her résumé to say that she could play parts from thirteen to forty.

A few days after Sam's tenth birthday, she did get a callback for a Saturday-morning cartoon show about tiny singing blue trolls, but in the end, they decided that they wanted someone whose voice was less ethnic. Briefly, Anna wondered what was "ethnic" about her voice: she was a native Angeleno. It was never any use to dig down on rejection feedback, though. Maybe they didn't like her because she was no good, not talented, too short. Maybe they didn't like her because they were racist or sexist or harboring some other secret prejudice. In the end, they didn't like her *because* they didn't like her. She wasn't going to reason them out of their dislike. She wasn't going to teach anyone anything.

While she waited for her big West Coast break, she took classes: acting (voice, auditions, movement), dance, yoga, computer programming, memoir writing. She meditated. She went to therapy. She worked at her parents' restaurant when they needed the help. She watched her bank account diminish—she and Sam had far fewer expenses now that they were living with her parents, so it didn't go down as quickly as it might have. But there were expenses. Life was expensive anywhere you were. The classes cost money, though she considered them necessary. She'd bought a used car. She needed new headshots and clothes. She paid her parents room and board, even though they said she didn't need to. Eventually, she'd need money to find them their own place, in a good school district, better than the Echo Park one her parents were zoned for. And she needed to work, because if she didn't work soon, she'd lose her union health insurance, and Sam would lose coverage, too. She told her agent: Send me in for anything. I will literally do anything.

In September, she had three auditions. The first was for the national touring company of *South Pacific:* the minor role of Liat, with the possibility of understudying a larger role. Anna thought *South Pacific* was racist, and a national touring company would mean being away from Sam for the whole year. The second was for the role of an "ethnic" maid on *General Hospital* who would end up having an affair with the male lead of the show. The character's name on the sides was Ximena, but Anna's agent assured her that the producers were open to all colors: Ximena could be LaToya could be Meimei could be Anna (but probably not literally Anna, because that sounded too white). And behind door number three was a model/hostess gig on a newish game show called *Press That Button!* The program was meant to be a competitor to *The Price Is Right* and was hosted by Chip Willingham, who was famous, though Anna wasn't quite sure for what, maybe just being a host of things. The show was replacing one of their two spokesmodels. (Though they weren't really spokesmodels, in that they were rarely called upon to speak.) Anna was short to be a model—she was five-foot-five—but if she wore her highest heels, she was shapely enough and slim enough and high-cheekboned enough to present as a model. In addition to an Asian, they were looking for someone in her twenties with "a great sense of humor," which usually meant that some degree of humiliation would be involved. Anna didn't want the gig anyway. Game-show model was not *real acting*. Anna had gone to Northwestern and had even done a stint at the Royal Academy of Dramatic Art. Anna had been *on Broadway*. Anna was trained. Anna had craft.

At the audition for *Press That Button!* she was given a pair of red stilettos and a skintight black cocktail dress, and told to change. The producer, who was female, said, "We're the classy game show." The woman looked at Anna expectantly.

"Wow," Anna said. "That's . . ." She could not think of anything else to say.

The producer had Anna go through a series of exercises: opening and closing a curtain at the right pace, presenting an empty box, leading a contestant backstage, carrying out a big check, laughing and applauding politely.

"Bigger smile, Anna," the producer called. "With teeth and happy eyes!" Anna smiled bigger.

"That's great! Laughing is important, too. Chip needs to feel like you think he's funny, even when he's not being funny. Do you know what I mean?"

Anna laughed.

"Very good," the producer said. "Maybe a different kind of laugh? Something more genuine. Like *Oh Dad! You're so corny, but I still love you.* That kind of laugh."

Anna laughed, in a genuinely bemused way.

"Good, good! You're good. I completely believed that." The producer looked at Anna. "You're a little petite, but I like your look." The producer nodded. "Okay, so I'm going to have you meet with Chip now. The thing you need to know about Chip is that he's super old-school, right? He's not a bad guy, but he's not into, as he puts it, any women's lib stuff—he's fine with women, but he doesn't want to hear about it. Also, he went to Dartmouth and he likes people to know that. Your job is to laugh at his jokes, and be gorgeous like you are, and stay out of his way, as much as possible."

The producer led Anna into an office with a star on the door. The producer knocked. "Chip, I've got someone for you to meet. The girl that might replace Anna."

"I'm Anna," Anna said.

"Sorry. The girl before you was called Anne."

The first time Anna saw Chip Willingham, she thought that no one had ever looked more like a game-show host than this man. He was tanned and buttery, like a quality handbag; his hair had the color and rigidity of onyx; his teeth were enormous white rectangles. He gave the impression of being handsome without actually being handsome, and she could not begin to guess his age. He turned his head over his broad shoulders and looked Anna up and down.

"Go in," the producer instructed Anna before closing the door behind her.

"Short," Chip said.

"I am," Anna said.

"Tits." He paused. "Small." He paused again. "Apples. Some men like apples. Some men don't."

Anna laughed the *Corny Dad!* laugh. She couldn't wait for this to be over. With any luck, she'd get the national touring company of *South Pacific.* It would pay well enough, and while she'd miss Sam, at least he'd be with her parents.

"But women are the ones who watch our show. Your apple tits are perfecto for daytime."

"That's what my mother always told me," Anna said.

"You're funny." Chip did not laugh. "Come closer."

Anna didn't know why, but she did. He looked at her face. He ran his index finger down the bridge of her nose.

"Exotic. The last one was an Oriental, too."

"Orientals are rugs and furniture," Anna said. "Not people."

"Chinoiseries are furniture," Chip said. "Turn around."

Again, Anna didn't know why she did, but she did.

"Ass," he said. "Big apple." He smacked her on the rear and then he clutched her right butt cheek, his manicured fingernails penetrating her crack. "Firm."

Anna laughed, *Corny Dad!* And then she slapped Chip across the face.

She walked to the dressing room to find her clothes. She didn't cry.

The female producer stopped her as she was leaving. "How'd it go with Chip?"

Anna shook her head.

"For what it's worth, I think he really liked you," the producer said. "It wouldn't have gone that long if he didn't like you."

"What happened to Anne? The girl who had this job before."

"Anne. It's, well, it's a tragic story. Anne died quite suddenly."

"My God," Anna said. "Chip didn't murder her, did he?"

"It must have gone well in there," the producer quipped. "Anne was driving with one of her boyfriends on Mulholland, and they missed their turn, and . . . You know Los Angeles. She was a sweet kid. Only twenty-four. From Oakland."

"Her last name wasn't Lee, was it?" Anna didn't know if she could bear it if it was.

"No, it was Chin."

Anna started to cry. She was crying for the other Anna Lee, who threw herself from a building, and this Anne, who, no doubt, had also had Chip Willingham's fingers where they shouldn't have been, and herself: Had it come to this? She questioned her life choices—from auditioning for the school play her freshman year of high school, to deciding to come to Los Angeles because a woman, who had nothing to do with her aside from the coincidence of her name, had thrown herself from a building on a frigid night in February. The producer patted Anna on the shoulder. "It isn't as bad as all of that. She didn't suffer." She handed Anna a tissue.

Three days later, Anna's agent called. "Great news!" he said. "You booked *Press That Button!* They loved your 'feistiness.' That was the word they used."

"What happened to *South Pacific*?"

"Who cares?" the agent said. "You hate *South Pacific*."

"What about the soap?"

"They decided to rewrite the role as a poor-white-trash type. Forget about it. *Press That Button!* will pay better than either of those other gigs, and if the show runs forever, you can afford to send that son of yours to Harvard-Westlake or Crossroads. And if something better comes along, I'll get you out of *Press That Button!* I promise. It's easy money, Anna."

For its three-year run, *Press That Button!* was a completely nondistinctive version of a 1980s daytime game show, a completely nondistinctive form. Its variations included regular people paired with celebrities to answer trivia questions; an abusive, flame-haired mascot called the Button Monster; carnival-style games; the studio audience maniacally chanting *Press! That! Button!* as directed by the prompter. The handful of times Sam had gone to watch tapings, he had found the whole thing delightful—far more entertaining than the theater his mother had been doing in New York.

For her contributions, Anna was paid $1,500 a week, more than she had made when she'd been in *A Chorus Line,* and though the job had little to do with the work she had trained for, the only difficult part of it was avoiding Chip Willingham's advances. The more she avoided him, the more he sought her out. The more aggressive she was in rejecting his advances, the more determined he seemed to make them. He seemed to like the rejection, though he also liked telling her how replaceable she was. "There are a million Anna Lees in this town," he'd say. In order to get through it, she began to imagine herself in a parallel game show. Winning was, among other things, keeping her job.

Even if there were "a million Anna Lees," this Anna Lee was still one of a handful of Asians on American network television, and there turned out to be great value to this. She became a local celebrity in K-town, something she had not expected. She found herself with an endless array of paid-appearance opportunities: celebrity judge for Miss Koreatown, ribbon cutting for a Korean grocery store, ads for Korean beauty products, the openings of restaurants. She became the spokeswoman for a Korean beer called JjokJjok, and her face was on a fifty-foot-wide billboard on Wilshire, with the slogan "What's the most beautiful woman in Koreatown drinking?"

Anna, her parents, and Sam drove to Wilshire to take pictures with the billboard. Dong Hyun pulled out his bulky Minolta 35mm film camera. His eyes teared, and he patted Anna on the arm, and mumbled something about the American Dream. He had not known what the American Dream was or when he would know if he had attained it, but the American Dream might very well be his daughter on a billboard, selling JjokJjok beer to other Koreans. Who was to say it wasn't? "Dad," Anna said, "it's just a billboard. It's not a big deal." Anna was embarrassed by the attention, embarrassed by the work she was doing. Simultaneously, she was proud that she had recently signed a lease on a town house in Studio City, which would put Sam in a superior public-school district. She was proud that her dad was proud.

"The most beautiful woman in Koreatown," Dong Hyun said with reverence.

"It's an ad guy, trying to sell beer," Anna said. "I'm not the most beautiful woman in Koreatown."

"She isn't," Bong Cha said. "There are many beautiful women in Koreatown."

"Thanks, Mom," Anna said.

"I don't want you to get a swelled head," Bong Cha said. "All this attention."

"Let Sam settle it," Dong Hyun said. "Do you think your mom's the most beautiful woman in K-town?"

Sam looked at Anna. "I think you're the most beautiful woman in the world," Sam said. He was twelve, on the verge of being more man than boy. Every day, Sam became more of a mystery to Anna, even his smells, once so familiar, were a mystery, and there was a feeling of mourning to this. Yet, still Sam knew with certainty that his mother was the most beautiful woman in the world. It was on the billboard because it was true.

Anna and Sam drove back to Studio City, and she got a bit lost in the Hollywood hills. Maybe she had extended the drive on purpose. Maybe she had wanted to get lost. It was pleasant to drive with the top down, with your son on a warm California night in June. She had recently bought the car. A silly emerald-green sports car that had been her first real splurge.

"Did you know I went to the performing arts high school?" Anna said. "It's not that far from here."

Sam nodded. "Yeah."

"Maybe you'd want to go there?"

"I don't think so, Mom. I'm not really a performer."

"True. But the thing that's cool about it is that kids from all over L.A. go there, so you meet everyone. I don't know if you've noticed, but L.A., well, it can be a bit tribal. The eastsiders stay on the Eastside, and westsiders stay on the Westside. And the east, where we stayed with Grandma and Grandpa, isn't the east, it's the west. Because technically, anything west of the L.A. River is the west."

Sam and Anna shared a laugh at the expense of the people who cared whether they lived on the east or the west.

"So, when I was at performing arts school, I had a boyfriend," Anna said.

"Only one?" Sam teased.

"This particular one was the grandson of one of the old studio heads. Family money, you know? And he lived on the west, in Pacific Palisades, which is about as west as you can get, but he was always driving over to the house to see me. And he could get across town really fast. Like, lightning fast. Like, I'd call him, and then he'd be at my house in seven minutes. And you know how long it takes to get places around here. So, I ask him, 'Bro, how are you getting to my house so quick?' And he gives me this crazy look, and he says he can't tell me, 'It's a secret.'" Anna, a good performer, paused for dramatic effect, and to make sure Sam was still listening.

"So, did he ever tell you?" Sam said.

"No. He was kind of a jerk, and we were always fighting, so we ended up breaking up not long after that. But last week, I told this story to Allison, the other model on *PTB,* and Chip overheard us, and he said, 'He was obviously using the secret highways.'"

"Secret highways?"

"Yes, that's exactly what I said. According to Chip, when L.A. was first being developed, the heads of the studios built secret highways. Highways that only *they* knew about, so they could get places fast. Chip thought my old boyfriend, who you'll recall was the beloved grandson of a studio head, probably knew about the highways. Chip said there was one that supposedly ran from east to west, from Silver Lake to Beverly Hills, and another that ran north to south, from Studio City to Koreatown. Chip offered me ten thousand dollars if we could find them. Like I'd ever tell Chip if I found a magical secret highway."

"We should find it," Sam said. "That way, we can get to Grandma and Grandpa's house fast."

"We should!" Anna said.

"We can be methodical about it," Sam said. "We'll take a slightly different route back to Studio City each time we go. And I'll draw a map, and eventually, we'll find it. I know we will."

They were winding up toward Mulholland, when all at once, a blur of fur darted in front of their car. Anna hit the brakes and swerved a little. The animal froze. In the headlights, Anna could see it was a medium-sized dog, or perhaps a coyote, with blondish fur. An all-American.

The animal scurried away.

"Oh my God," Anna said. "Do you think we hit it?"

"I don't," Sam said. "It looked fine when it ran off. Just scared."

"Was it a dog or a coyote?"

"I don't know," Sam said. "How can you tell the difference?"

Anna laughed. "I don't honestly know myself. We'll look it up in Grandpa's encyclopedia next time we're over there."

"Does it matter which one it was?" Sam said.

"I guess not." She paused. "Maybe I'd feel a bit worse if I had killed someone's pet. A coyote belongs to no one. A coyote is wild. But it's probably wrong to feel that way. A coyote has as much right to its life as anyone else."

She turned off the car to steady herself. Anna and Sam were left in darkness. Anna was unfamiliar with the new car, so she could not easily locate the emergency lights. Her hands were shaking. "God, it's dark," Anna said.

Sam would remember the lights first. Two of them, like a pair of eyes, growing quickly wider, larger, seeking them out in the night. Sam would remember having an irrational thought: *We're fine, because the car can't see us. We're protected by the darkness.*

Then, the high-pitched squeal of tires, the metal crumpling, the glass shattering like a scream.

It will turn out that the driver had been speeding, but the accident won't have been his fault. The streets were narrow—barely room enough for two cars to pass. He took the turn a bit wide and crashed his heavy sedan directly into the hood of Anna's lightweight sports car, most of the impact on the driver's side and on Sam's left foot. How could that driver have been expected to know that a car was there? Why would a car be stopped just below Mulholland, without any lights on? How could he know a boy and his mother would be in that car?

From the passenger seat, Sam could see his mother's face, illuminated by the other car's headlights. Her skin had particles of glass on it, and she looked as if she were sparkling. He tried to reach for his mother to clear the glass from her face, but he found that his left leg was pinned against the dashboard. He felt no pain—that would come later—but he couldn't get free enough to reach her face, and the constriction panicked him. He could smell her blood, mingling with her tuberose perfume, and he could see that her chest and abdomen were crushed by the caved-in dashboard. But it was the glass. It was the glass on his mother's pretty face that disturbed him the most in that moment, and he tried again to reach for her to brush it off. He felt a strange shifting in the bones of his foot as he pulled for her. And with that last unsuccessful reach, he began to feel his body again. He began to shake violently, and he felt like he couldn't breathe. "Mom," he said to the still-warm body next to him, "it hurts." He craned his neck so that he could rest his head in the groove of her shoulder, and then he closed his eyes.

The man in the other car walked toward Sam in a daze. He called to them desperately. "I'm so sorry. I didn't see you there. I didn't see you. Is everyone okay? Is everyone okay? Is anyone alive? Anyone?"

Sam opened his eyes: "I'm here." These were the last words he would say until the day he encountered Sadie Green in the game room.

In games, the thing that matters most is the order of things. The game has an algorithm, but the player also must create a play algorithm in order to win. There is an order to any victory. There is an optimal way to play any game. Sam, in the silent months after Anna's death, would obsessively replay this scene in his head. If she doesn't take the job on *Press That Button!* and if Anna can't afford to buy the new car. If Anna buys the new car but drives directly home after dinner. If the first Anna Lee doesn't jump from that building and if Anna never comes to Los Angeles. If Anna doesn't stop driving after she hits the coyote. If Anna finds the emergency lights. If Anna never sleeps with George. If Sam is never born. There are, he determines, infinite ways his mother doesn't die that night and only one way she does.

6

The morning of Sam's surgery, Sadie drove out to Venice to organize her office. Marx had brought in cheap tables and bookshelves, enough furniture so that they could get started working before the space was properly finished. The last box Sadie unpacked contained her collection of PC games, which she always kept on hand for reference. She arranged the games, which were in a combination of jewel cases and book-like cardboard containers, on the shelf: *Commander Keen, Myst, Doom, Diablo, Final Fantasy, Metal Gear Solid, Leisure Suit Larry, The Colonel's Bequest, Ultima, Warcraft, Monkey Island, The Oregon Trail,* and three dozen others. At the bottom of the box was *Dead Sea.* She still loved *Dead Sea* even if her feelings about its creator were more complicated. She took the CD out of the package. Dov had signed it: *To Sadie on her 20th, the sexiest, most brilliant girl in Adv. Games—Love, D.M.*

Sadie had forgotten Dov had done that, and she wondered when the last time she'd looked at the disk was. Years, probably. The last time she could remember even seeing the disk was the day Marx and Sam had been playing *Dead Sea.* The day Sam had said, *Our game should look like this.*

Sadie clearly remembered Sam saying that he hadn't known Dov was her boyfriend or her teacher. But if he had used this disk to play *Dead Sea*—and she knew that he had—he would have read this inscription. He wouldn't have been able to miss it, and Sam never missed anything anyway. And if Sam had known that Dov was her boyfriend, had he turned to *Dead Sea,* not randomly, but specifically?

Had he shown her the game because he'd *wanted* Sadie to go to Dov, because he knew she *would* go to Dov? And didn't it follow that he would have guessed that the bad breakup she had had was with Dov, and that Sam hadn't paused, even for one moment, to consider what going back to him would mean for her? How different would the last three years have been if Dov hadn't had so much professional and personal power over her?

If it was true, it was absolutely a betrayal. Sam had wanted what he wanted, and he hadn't cared what it would mean for Sadie. He had wanted Ulysses, in the same way he had wanted the deal with Opus, in the same way he didn't truly care if Ichigo was a boy, in the same way he let everyone in the world believe *Ichigo* was *his* game, in the same way he had renewed their friendship for the sole purpose of making a game in the first place. She let herself think Sam was her friend, but Sam was no one's friend. It wasn't as if he was dishonest about it—when she told him she loved him, he never once said he loved her, too. She had made excuses for him—his absentee father, the death of his mother, his injury, his poverty, and the obvious insecurities these things had caused. But what if her mistake had been in imbuing Sam with emotions and sentiments that he was incapable of feeling?

Sadie sat down at the table in her office. She put the *Dead Sea* CD in her laptop. She skipped the haunting, opening cutscene—the plane crash inferno, where the Wraith becomes the lone survivor, scored to "Clair de lune." She felt like killing something, so she went straight to the first level—the entrance to the underwater world, which looks like a Vegas lobby. The zombie in the plaid shirt and leather pants limped to the center of the lobby, and Sadie as the Wraith picked up the log. She walloped the zombie repeatedly in the head. Dov had done amazing things with blood spatter. For example, the Wraith could even see herself reflected in the blood of the zombie she had just killed. A small detail like that is a mind-blowing amount of extra work. *Dead Sea is a great game,* she thought.

Sadie was still playing *Dead Sea* when Marx poked his head in the office. "He's out of surgery," Marx said. "His grandfather said it went well."

"Good news," Sadie said. Her mind was black. The Wraith dropped the log and traded it for the hammer.

"I'm driving over now," Marx said. "Is that *Dead Sea*?" The Wraith smashed a pregnant-looking zombie with the hammer. The hammer was so much more effective than the log.

"Yes." The Wraith tested out the hammer by smashing a window.

Suddenly, the zombie's baby crawled out of its dead zombie mother's abdomen. The Wraith paused—for the briefest of moments—before she walloped the baby in the head. Blood and brain flotsam exploded across the screen.

"The first time I played *Dead Sea*," Marx said, "this is where I died. I didn't kill the baby fast enough, and it threw itself at my face."

"People usually die there, or they die in the scene with the dog. Dov hates sentimentality."

"He's so dark," Marx said dryly. "It's hard to believe that *Ichigo* and this were built from the same engine."

"You see it in the water. You see it in the light," Sadie said. "You see it everywhere, if you know where to look."

The Wraith, with her unnatural, bouncing gait, crouched behind a statue. She panted, waiting for the next zombie.

"Have you ever played the game all the way through?" Sadie asked Marx.

"No."

"The twist of *Dead Sea* is that the Wraith did not survive that plane crash. She's a zombie, too. She just doesn't know it yet. So in essence, she's spent the whole game killing her own kind."

"Screw you, kids!" Marx joked. "Killing zombies might seem fun, but you'll feel bad about it later."

"It's so Dov," Sadie said. "Where there is pleasure, there is pain."

"You're coming to the hospital, right?" Marx said. "We should probably get going if we want to beat traffic."

"I think I'll stay here for a while," Sadie said, without turning her head from the screen. The Wraith traded her hammer for a screwdriver. The screwdriver was less satisfying for killing, but if you didn't take it, you wouldn't be able to open the panel that led to the elevator. And if you didn't take the elevator, you'd be stuck in the first part of the game forever. "I still have a few things I need to unpack."

IV

BOTH SIDES

Sam rented a one-bedroom bungalow, near his grandparents, on the precise, if disputed, eastern border between Silver Lake and Echo Park. Originally, he had planned to move out to Venice, to be near the Unfair office, but his recovery had taken longer than he'd expected, and in the end, it had seemed simpler to stay on the Eastside near his grandparents and the hospital, with its many doctors and physical therapists that he was forced to interact with multiple times a week.

One of Sam's new neighbors—a Popeye-armed woman with a pride flag on her porch and a rotating assortment of rescue pit bulls, always female—had referred to the neighborhood as HaFoSaFo, or Happy Foot Sad Foot, after an advertisement for a podiatrist that spun on the corner of Benton and Sunset, just below their houses. Each side of the sign depicted an anthropomorphized brown foot. "Sad Foot" had a Band-Aid on its big toe, bloodshot eyes, a mouth gaping in pain, crutches, hands and feet. "Happy Foot" was miraculously healed through the power of podiatry: two thumbs up, a manic smile, and the feet of the foot in pristine white high-tops. The sign was suspended high above the parking lot of a Comfort Inn, whose ground floor contained a Thai vegetarian restaurant and the podiatrist in question. The sign pirouetted slowly, making approximately one revolution every twelve seconds. Legend—though perhaps this was too grand a word for a spinning sign over a budget hotel—had it that whichever side of the sign you saw first would determine how the rest of your day went.

For over a year, Sam never encountered anything but Sad Foot. He tried to see the other side: he varied the speed of his approach to the sign; he came upon it, both walking and driving, and from all four cardinal directions. No matter how he varied his routine, it was Sad Foot every time. It did not take a former Harvard math major to know that this result was statistically unlikely, and he could not help but feel as if the universe was mocking him.

1B

Sadie rented an apartment in the Clownerina building in Venice, a six-and-a-half-minute walk from Unfair. The building had a thirty-foot-tall mechanical sculpture of a male clown dressed in a ballerina's tutu and toe shoes. Once upon a time, the ballerina had kicked, but either seawater had rusted his gears or tenants had complained that his motor was too loud. During the years Sadie lived in the building, Clownerina just stood there, his right red toe shoe demurely extended, waiting for the day when he would dance again

Clownerina may have been kitsch, but Sadie adored him. He represented the spirit of California to her—and for the first time in her life, she fully embraced her native city. She donated her winter coats to Goodwill, and she started wearing floppy hats and maxi dresses. She went to flea markets with Zoe, and they shopped for vintage vinyl and long necklaces and artisanal pottery. She burned incense and gave up caffeine. She grew her hair long, down to her waist, and parted it in the middle. She started doing Pilates, and she threw Dov's handcuffs into the sea. She dated—a scruffily handsome guy in an indie rock band, a scruffily handsome actor who was mainly known for indie films, a scruffily handsome tech guy who had sold his dot-com to a bigger dot-com. She threw elaborate dinner parties and prided herself on knowing the new bands before anyone else did. She bought a used VW bug the color of the California sky. She had brunch with her family every Sunday. She woke early, slept very little, and routinely worked eighteen-hour days. If California was a costume that could be worn, Sadie wore it as easily as Clownerina wore his tutu and derby hat.

Sadie didn't know why Sam had chosen to live on the Eastside.

What native Angelino would willingly subject themselves to a fifty-minute commute? In those days, they rarely spoke of anything but the game they were making, so she did not ask him for an explanation. She had stopped devoting any time to imagining her partner's motivations.

While Sam had been recovering through the winter, spring, and part of the summer, Sadie, and her core group of programmers, built Oneiric, the engine that would power *Both Sides'* mechanics and graphics.

Oneiric would become known for its innovative volumetric lighting techniques, which allowed for particularly haunting fogs, subtle clouds, and God rays. The graphical innovations were necessary because Myre Landing, the fantasy world of *Both Sides*, is covered in fog, until the very end of the game. As one reviewer would put it, "The weather in Myre Landing is truly a character." Sadie had been amused by that review: clever reviewers across all media liked to refer to things that were *not characters* as *characters*. But, in her initial design document, she had ambitiously written the same thing: "The weather in Myre Landing must feel like a character."

Sadie was proud of Oneiric. She was proud that she had been able to accomplish that which she hadn't been able to accomplish five years earlier. She called Dov for the first time in months.

"I did it," she said.

"It feels fucking good, doesn't it?" Dov said.

"It does," she admitted.

"I told you it would," Dov said. "You don't need Ulysses anymore. It's ancient now anyway."

"Hey, I was playing *Dead Sea* a couple of months ago, and I wondered, how'd you get those reflections in the blood?"

"Oh, that? It was ridiculous."

"In 1993, it was insane," Sadie said.

"I probably wouldn't do that today." He described his technique, a jury-rigged variation on adaptive tile refresh. "I burnt out a lot of graphics cards and processors, getting that going."

"Still looks good, though," Sadie said.

"I was thinking of coming out to L.A. in a couple of weeks. Some director wants to jerk me off about a movie version of *Dead Sea*. Will you be around?"

"I'm really busy," she said. "Also, well . . . I've got a boyfriend now."

"Who is this guy?"

"He's in a band," Sadie said, apologetically.

"Would I have heard of this band?"

"They're called Failure to Communicate."

"Failure to Communicate," Dov repeated. "He sounds fucking awful."

"He's great," Sadie said.

"I didn't mean I'd need to stay with you. But I would like to see the work," Dov said. "You're my most accomplished student. I brag about you constantly."

"Stop by the office," Sadie said. "I'm always here."

Sam had not been around for almost any of the work on the engines, and when she showed him Oneiric, he seemed bored and unimpressed. "Cool," he said. "These are going to work really well." Sadie had killed herself building Oneiric, and she was irritated by his muted reaction.

Sam had originally said he would be back to work in March, but he had not returned full-time until May, and even then, he was, Sadie felt, half there. Sam would arrive at 7 a.m., to beat traffic, and usually he was gone by 4 p.m., to beat the other side of traffic. Sadie kept crunch hours—she worked from 9 a.m. to 1 a.m. or often even later. Some days, Sam would not come in at all. He was always late, always in the car, always on his way.

Sadie discussed Sam's attendance with Marx, and Marx speculated that Sam was still struggling with his recovery, though he didn't know for sure—Sam never spoke of it to either of them.

"The difficulty is," Sadie said, "I can't wait for him to make decisions. It goes too slowly with him out of the office as much as he is."

Marx was the one who suggested that the work should be divided so that Sam could lead the team that built the simpler Mapletown "real world" side of the game and Sadie could run the Myre Landing "fantasy" side—that way, Sadie wouldn't be slowed down by waiting to confer with Sam. The Myre Landing sequences were more complicated in every way—and Sadie felt resentful that once again, she would have the greater portion of work and the same amount of credit. But it was what made sense for the game and for Sam, so she agreed to it.

2B

In May, relatively late in the development process for such a significant change, Sam had the idea that the main character should be a sick kid instead of a girl who was being bullied, which had been part of Sadie's original conception.

"I'm not making another game with a boy main character," Sadie said.

"No, I'm not saying that. But maybe, she could have cancer," Sam suggested. "And she should be disabled and in pain. That way, it's even more powerful when she is omnipotent in the other world."

Sadie considered this. "You mean like *my* Alice?"

"Yes," Sam said. "Like Alice."

"It's an interesting point," Sadie said, "but isn't bullying more relatable? Won't actual sickness and pain turn off gamers?"

"Bullying is psychological pain," Sam countered. "Physical malady gives our character more obstacles in the real world, and more contrast with her avatar in the fantasy world. What is the point of having two worlds, if not to draw these contrasts?"

They named the main character Alice Ma, and her idyllic, suburban American city, Mapletown. Once they knew Alice Ma had cancer, the fantasy world was brought into relief. Myre Landing became a medieval-looking, northern European village in which a plague had descended. No one can breathe; the skies are coated in a grayish green fog and seem to be growing darker by the day; the sea is murky with a viscous yellow phlegm, chunks of which keep washing up on the beach; everything is dying—the old first and then the young; animals, nature. It is up to Alice Ma's alter ego, Rose the Mighty, to figure out what (or who) is causing the plague and how to save Myre Landing. If Rose the Mighty can save her village, then maybe Alice Ma can save herself from lung cancer. The two stories are linked but proceed along separate tracks. You can only advance in one by advancing in the other. The gameplay was incredibly intricate, and ultimately, Sadie informed Sam that the most efficient way for them to build the game was to work on each side separately.

Once this division of labor had been established, Sam was happy to lose himself in the ostensibly less ambitious Mapletown project. Mapletown General Hospital was based on every hospital he'd ever stayed in, and Alice's illness and treatment, which comprised many of the Mapletown side quests and levels, was given the kind of corpuscular detail that could only have come from someone who had been chronically ill and understood the indignities of hospital life. In the fourth level, for example, Alice, after a major operation, becomes separated from her body, and she has to chase through the hospital to catch it, like Peter Pan and his shadow. This dissociation was something Sam had experienced many times—the feeling that your body, when it was sick, was no longer your own.

Within Mapletown, Sam created two distinct worlds: there was the hospital, but there was also everything outside of it, Mapletown itself. Sam directed his team to make Mapletown time and seasonally responsive—it was dark if you played at night, and light if you played in the morning. There would be leaves in the fall, and snow in the winter, and cherry blossoms in the spring. The world had always looked painfully beautiful to him when he was sick. It was only when he was alone and he couldn't participate in the business of living that he tended to notice how lovely being alive was. It was his friends through a glass window in a hospital door; it was Sadie's sweet twelve-year-old face, handing him a maze she'd completed; it was the nostalgia he felt when he watched the healthy and the able-bodied leave a world that they had only been visiting, but of which he was a permanent resident.

Because Sadie was wrapped up in Myre Landing, Marx was the first playtester of Mapletown's opening levels.

The first level of Mapletown takes place outside the hospital. Alice is a hurdler in a high school track meet. A text box states that she is the top-ranked hurdler in the state and that she is expected to win. The crowd is cheering; Alice's boyfriend and her dads are in the stands.

Marx ran the race, hitting the jump button every time Alice encountered a hurdle. He lost once, and then he lost again, and then he lost a third time. He turned to Sam. "Am I doing something wrong?"

No matter how well the gamer runs the race, Alice will lose every time. The tumor that is growing in her lungs is slowing her down, but she doesn't know that yet. Each time Alice loses, the gamer is given the option to restart the game. But the gamer will never "win" the first level. Winning is accepting that there are some races a person cannot win.

Throughout his life, Sam had hated being told to "fight," as if sickness were a character failing. Illness could not be defeated, no matter how hard you fought, and pain, once it had you in its grasp, was transformational. Mapletown was, for Sam, the story of his pain, in the present and in the past. It would be the most personal game he ever made, though of course, it was only half the game, and his partner, Sadie, understood it to be about her own sister.

"Sam," Marx said, once he'd figured it out, "I love what you're doing here. It's exceptionally smart. Has Sadie seen this?"

"Not yet," Sam said. "She knows the basic design, but she's been so busy with Myre Landing, I didn't want to bother her."

Marx studied his friend. Sam was thinner than Marx had ever known him to be, and his eyes were lightly bloodshot. He'd grown a mustache and a beard, and it looked as if his hair hadn't been cut in months. He seemed tired, subdued. When had Sam ever avoided "bothering" Sadie? "Is everything all right with you?" Marx asked.

"Sure," Sam said. He smiled at Marx, and Marx noticed that Sam had chipped his right canine tooth.

Sam hadn't wanted to make a *thing* of his twenty-fifth birthday. Since his surgery, he had avoided making any plans that didn't involve work or a doctor's office. At Marx's insistence, Sam had consented to go to dinner with Sadie, Marx, and their significant others. Sam had just reached the doorway of his house and was turning the lock when he felt a blinding, merciless pain. He fell to his knees and ripped off the prosthetic, throwing it so hard against the wall that it damaged the plaster.

He tried to call the restaurant, but his fingers were unable to manipulate his cell phone.

He lay down on the floor and he closed his eyes. He tried not to move, because moving was painful. But he could not fall asleep.

Around nine-thirty, a knock at his door. "Sam," Marx called, "it's me."

Sam's front door was unlocked, so when Sam didn't respond, Marx went inside. Marx did not express surprise at what he saw: the foot thrown across the room, Sam on the floor. "Please leave," Sam managed to say. Marx helped him out of his sweat-covered clothes and into his bed, which was a mattress on the floor.

"Can I do anything for you?" Marx said. "I'd like to help."

Sam shook his head.

"It's harder for me to help you now that we don't live together, so you have to tell me what you need."

Sam shook his head again.

"All right, my friend." Marx sat on the floor by Sam's bed. He turned on the television, and when he didn't find anything to watch, he looked through Sam's DVDs. Marx selected a recording of the 1981 Simon and Garfunkel concert in Central Park.

They'd been watching about a half hour when Sam said, "I don't know where this DVD came from."

"It's mine," Marx said, laughing. "My mom's actually."

By the time it was over, Sam's pain had abated somewhat, and he could speak more easily; he turned to Marx. "It's called phantom limb pain. I think my foot is still there, and when I put on the prosthetic, sometimes, I think it's being crushed. I can feel my bones crumbling, and my flesh turning to liquid. They say it's all in my head."

Marx thought about this. "But what pain isn't?"

Sam sat up in bed. "Please don't tell Sadie."

"Why?"

"I don't want to distract her from finishing the game. And honestly, the pain isn't real so it's not that bad."

At first, Sam had healed quickly from the surgery. The wound, though larger and rawer than wounds he had had before, seemed no more unmanageable, and he did not feel residual limb pain. He was allowed to check out of the hospital several days early to recover at his grandparents', and he anticipated a quick return to work. From his childhood bedroom, he began to look at online real estate listings for apartments in Venice and Santa Monica, apartments on the Westside, near Unfair. He called Sadie, and they continued to refine the complicated *Both Sides* level design. He told her he'd be back no later than March first.

The second night he was at his grandparents', the pains began. He woke up in the middle of the night screaming, drenched in sweat and urine, frantically kicking the foot that was no longer there. Sam was scared and ashamed, because he felt as if he had no control over his body, no understanding of what was causing the pain and thus, no means to ameliorate it. He kept reaching for the foot with his hand. The pain was so intense that he could not speak or explain when his terrified grandparents came into his room to ask him what was wrong. He tried to get out of bed so that he could throw up in the toilet, but he forgot that he didn't have the foot, and he fell hard onto the floor, chipping one of his canines, bloodying his lip. He got up on his knees so that he could vomit. He felt helpless and like a child again. At the same time, he felt savage, less than human. His grandmother cradled him in her arms until Sam was able to fall into a fitful sleep.

The next day, he went to the doctor, and she diagnosed Sam with phantom limb pain. "You had a particularly violent episode of it," the doctor said. "But it isn't uncommon with amputees."

For a second, Sam hadn't known to whom the doctor was referring. No one had ever called him an amputee before. In Sam's mind, amputees were war heroes or cancer survivors.

"Someone probably warned you about it before the surgery," the doctor continued.

Sam nodded. If they had, he'd barely paid attention. He had assumed that once he'd committed to the amputation, the issue of his foot would be resolved.

The doctor gave him a photocopied handout that had exercises to combat the pain. For example, he was told to look at his stump in the mirror in order to reprogram his brain to accept that he was now footless. Sam hated doing this exercise. Even before the amputation, he had avoided looking at his foot. He had always felt that if he didn't look at it, it couldn't possibly be that bad. The doctor also gave him a prescription for an antidepressant, which he did not end up filling.

For several weeks, the pain did not return, and Sam was hopeful that it never would.

The first time the prosthetic was put on, the pain came back with an even greater fury. He knew it was more than the pressure of the stump against the prosthetic, though the physical therapist kept encouraging him and insisting that that was what it was. It felt as if his old foot were being crushed by the prosthetic. He felt dizzy and for a few seconds, he lost the ability to see or hear. He could taste bile in his mouth.

"I'm feeling some discomfort," he said weakly. Sam's superpower had always been his ability to conceal and ignore pain.

"You're okay, Sam," the physical therapist tried to encourage him. "You're doing fine. I've got you. Just take one step."

Sam took one step, smiled weakly, and then he fell to his knees and vomited.

Sam was sent to a therapist, a hypnotist, an acupuncturist, and a masseuse, and while all these things worked to an extent, nothing could stop the pain when it decided to emerge. Sam was told to look for patterns and triggers. The only triggers were when Sam went to sleep or when Sam tried to walk—and it was challenging to live a life that involved neither sleeping nor walking. Adjustments were made to the prosthetic. Socks were added, socks were taken away. But mainly, whenever he wore the prosthetic, he was in an agony so consuming he could not think. Thinking, for Sam, was necessary, and the pain made him feel stupid, an entirely new phenomenon for him.

Sam's doctor said to him, "The good news is that the pain is in your head."

But I am in my head, Sam thought.

Sam knew the foot was gone. He could see it was gone. He knew what he was experiencing was a basic error in programming, and he wished he could open up his brain and delete the bad code. Unfortunately, the human brain is every bit as closed a system as a Mac.

He couldn't hold food down in those first months, and he ate very little. He lost twenty pounds, which scared his grandmother. Eventually, the pain decreased, or his ability to tolerate it grew. He returned to work. Disturbingly, for the first time in his life, games proved neither distraction nor comfort. The pain seemed to occupy spaces in his mind that had heretofore been untouched or reserved exclusively for imaginary endeavors.

3B

"Is it strange that your friend didn't show up for his own birthday dinner?" Sadie's boyfriend, Abe, asked. They were standing outside the Silver Lake restaurant Marx had selected because of its proximity to Sam's place. The restaurant had a tree growing in the center of it, and it was famous for being the best place on the Eastside to break up with someone.

"No," Sadie said. "I used to waste a lot of time worrying about him, but he's the kind of person who tends to go missing."

"Everyone's got friends like that," Abe said. "You want to go back to my place? Now that I've got you on my side of town, it would be a shame if you didn't see it."

Abe Rocket was the lead singer and second guitar player of Failure to Communicate, one of a thousand or so bands that resided in the three-square-mile area of Silver Lake circa 1999. By the night of

Sam's birthday, Sadie had been seeing him for about a month, but she had never gone to his house. The drive was too long, and it didn't seem worth it to Sadie to drive across town for Abe when the relationship was not that serious. She had not been with him long enough to know any of his stories or to know if Abe Rocket was a stage name or the name he'd been born with. She had met him at a concert that Zoe had taken her to. She liked Abe because he was a gentle and courteous lover ("Sadie, may I put my hand on your breast?") and because he didn't play games—video or personal—and because he didn't mind driving to Venice.

Abe's house was tidy and smelled like sandalwood, and he had around a thousand vinyl records, neatly organized into white lacquer Ikea shelves. Abe's collection included LPs, but Abe's passion was 45s. He loved B-sides, and the history of A-sides and B-sides, which Sadie knew nothing about. Originally, Abe explained, the record companies had put the "hit" on the A-side and the lesser track on the B-side. At some point, the record companies started calling 45s double A-sides so that there'd be less conflict in bands. According to Abe, John Lennon and Paul McCartney had been at each other's throats over which of their songs would be called the A-side. McCartney's "Hello Goodbye" (A) versus Lennon's "I Am the Walrus" (B), for example.

"But there is no double A-side. The A-side is still the A-side," Abe said. "Doesn't matter what some evil record company tries to pretend."

Abe and Sadie smoked some pot, and he put on one of his favorite 45s, the Beach Boys' "God Only Knows," which was the B-side to "Wouldn't It Be Nice." Abe particularly liked incidents where the B-side had become more significant than the A-side.

"Can you believe that?" Abe said. "Who would ever think 'Wouldn't It Be Nice' was better than 'God Only Knows'?"

"I get it, though. 'Wouldn't It Be Nice' is definitely more upbeat," Sadie said. "You sort of want to kill yourself when you hear 'God Only Knows.'"

"That's my favorite kind of music," Abe said. "I call it afternoon music. You don't want to listen to it too early in the day, or the day'll be lost to you." Abe put his arms around Sadie. "You're an afternoon woman, sexy Sadie. You don't want to meet someone like you too early in your life, or you won't ever like anyone else."

"I bet you've said that before," Sadie said.

Several months later, Abe would go away on tour, and that marked the end of that particular relationship. She did not regret having dated Abe, or that it had ended. She felt, in a way, that she finally understood Marx (though he was now effectively settled down with Zoe). Long relationships might be richer, but relatively brief, relatively uncomplicated encounters with interesting people could be lovely as well. Every person you knew, every person you loved even, did not have to consume you for the time to have been worthwhile.

She expressed some of this to Marx at the office, and he laughed at her. "I'm afraid I've given you the wrong impression, Sadie," he said. "I rather like to be consumed."

Sadie took a long look at Marx. They had worked together for five years, but she sometimes felt as if she had all the wrong ideas about him. "And you're consumed by Zoe?" Sadie liked Zoe. They'd never been friendly in Cambridge, but in L.A., they had become instant best friends in the way people can in their twenties.

"I devour, and I am devoured," Marx said.

"After Dov, I think I'm through with devouring," Sadie said.

"I understand why you'd say that, but I also don't think you should give up on the devouring yet." Marx growled at her and pretended to bite her, and then he kissed her on the cheek.

Lola Maldonado left her phone number for Sam at the pizza place. "Mr. Lee, I don't know if you remember me," she said to Dong Hyun, "but Sam and I went to high school together. I heard he's back in town. Tell him to call me, if he wants."

Dong Hyun passed the message on to Sam. "You should call this girl," Dong Hyun said. "Nice-looking. Nice manners."

"Work is crazy right now," Sam said.

"It will make your grandmother happy," Dong Hyun said. "She worries you don't do anything but work."

"I don't," Sam said.

"It will make me happy, too," Dong Hyun said. "Don't you want to make an old man happy?"

"Fine, old man. I'll try to call."

Sam called Lola about a month later. They were about to begin the debugging phase on Mapletown, so there was a brief lull in the schedule.

"Yo Masur!" Lola greeted him. "Took you long enough. What are we doing tonight?"

They agreed to go to the Arclight to see *The Matrix*. Lola had already seen it three times, but Sam hadn't seen it yet.

Lola and Sam had been in all the same classes in high school— they had dated briefly their senior year (one had to go to prom with someone) and drifted apart when they'd gone to college (Lola, to study computer engineering at UCLA). She was smart, funny, tough, pushy, a little mean. But smart was the main thing Sam liked about Lola. She wasn't *special* smart, like Sadie, but she was smart.

Although it hadn't meant that much to him, Sam had lost his virginity to her. They'd been studying differential equations on an oppressively hot day in September. The power went off and his grandparents' house became Palm Springs, and Sam and Lola ended up taking off their clothes. "We gonna do this, Masur?" she had said. And he thought, *Why not?* His foot hadn't been bothering him that much. He did not love Lola, but he really liked her, and he was comfortable around her.

"It's not your first time, is it?" he asked. In those days, Lola wore a cross around her neck, and he knew her family was Catholic. He didn't want the occasion to be too significant for her if it wasn't going to be significant for him.

"No," she said. "Don't worry about that."

They had serviceable, unmemorable sex, using a condom his cousin had given him as a joke, and when it was over, Sam's foot burned.

"Was that *your* first time?" Lola had asked.

"No," Sam lied. He didn't want to grant her the power of his virginity.

Including Lola, Sam had had four different sexual partners in his life, and he had never enjoyed sex with any of them. He had slept with one boy and three girls. While no one had ever mistreated him, sex had given him considerably less pleasure than masturbation. He did not like to be naked in front of other people. He did not like the messiness of sex—its fluids, its sounds, its smells. He worried that his body could not be relied upon. He could not imagine wanting to have sex with, for instance, Sadie or Marx, people he adored. The boy who had been his lover attributed it to Sam having low self-esteem because of his foot, but Sam felt that was reductive. He wasn't sure he would have liked sex, even if everything on his body had been in perfect working order. Though there was some truth to what the boy had said. Sam did not believe his body could feel anything but pain, and so he did not desire pleasure in the same way that other people seemed to. Sam was happiest when his body was feeling nothing. He was happiest when he did not have to think about his body—when he could forget that he had a body at all.

Lola was unchanged from high school, except for her hair, which was now a viridescent bob. She had big, brown eyes and was tiny, busty, and strong-looking. She was wearing a tight, red-and-white poppy-print skater dress and lug-soled Mary Janes, and she smelled like the same orange blossom–scented drugstore shampoo she'd been using as long as he had known her. The only makeup she wore was bright red lipstick that felt almost like a warning to Sam—weren't red things in nature dangerous?

"What did you think?" Lola asked him when the movie was over.

"It's like *Ghost in the Shell*," Sam said. "The anime, you know? It's kind of a rip-off."

"I've never seen it," Lola said.

"Well, if you like *The Matrix*, you should see it," Sam said.

They decided to drive to a rental store in Hollywood to pick up *Ghost in the Shell*, and then they went back to Sam's place to watch it. He hadn't had anyone over except his grandparents and Marx that once.

"Masur, what is up with your pad?"

"What's wrong with it?"

"Nothing, except it looks like a serial killer lives here," Lola said. "Or someone in witness protection, who might have to leave at any moment. You don't have anything on your walls. You're sleeping on a mattress on the floor. You're a grown-ass successful man with a *futon*. Half your stuff is still in boxes."

"Yeah," Sam said. "I've been busy."

"You should buy, like, a poster, or a plant, or something. Act like you live here, why not?"

Sam put in the DVD. Lola took off her shoes and curled herself into Sam, and he let her. No matter how hot it was in the day, L.A. was always cold at night.

It was pleasant to be near Lola. It was pleasant to feel her warmth against his warmth. He had been profoundly lonely since he'd come to Los Angeles, though he hadn't wanted to admit it to himself.

After the surgery, he hadn't wanted to be with other people. He had wanted to be alone with his pain. But then as the months passed and he began to feel somewhat better, he wondered where Sadie had gone. At first, he had assumed Sadie was respecting his need for privacy, but as time went on, he felt something off between them. She had not visited him in the hospital or come to see his new place. He wondered if she was repulsed by his amputation, though that didn't seem like Sadie.

She never spoke of anything but work with him, and at work, they were, literally, in two separate worlds. They had a staff of twenty working on *Both Sides*, and days could pass without them needing to speak. Their company had grown, so it was inevitable, he supposed—but sometimes, he longed for the intimacy of the apartment on Kennedy Street.

He missed Sadie more than he had missed her in the years he hadn't spoken to her, because there she was, every day. It looked like Sadie and it spoke like Sadie, but somehow it was no longer Sadie. Something was wrong, but he decided he would wait to find out what it was until they had finished the game.

Lola and Sam reached the end of *Ghost in the Shell*. "Yes," she conceded, "it's like *The Matrix*, but I still love *The Matrix*." Lola drew her knees up under her and she turned to face Sam. "I hope this won't come off as too fangirl, but I loved *Ichigo*. Those are great games. I tell everyone I know that I went to prom with Sam Masur."

"That's flattering," Sam said.

"I'm not flattering you. It's the truth."

"It's not just my game," Sam said. "I made it with my partner."

"Oh yeah, sure. The chick from L.A., right?"

"Yes."

"I remember her from high school. She won the Leipzig Family Scholars Prize for our region, right? I was up against her, but she won. I doubt she even needed the five thousand dollars. She was smart, but always had a stick up her ass, honestly."

"What'd she do?"

"Nothing. She seemed kind of cold, I guess. It was a long time ago. Forget I said it."

"Sadie can be cold," Sam conceded. "She's an introvert."

"I remember that she had great hair, though," Lola said. "That shiny Beverly Hills blowout that all the Jewish Westside girls get."

Sam wasn't sure if this comment was anti-Semitic or not. "I think her hair just looks that way," Sam said.

"No one's hair just looks that way," Lola said. She leaned in to kiss him, and he kissed her, and then she put her hand between his legs, wrapping her fingers around the cylindrical chamber of blood sponges that was his (and every) penis. He felt the corpora cavernosa, commanded by nerve messages from his subconscious brain, fill up with blood, and the tunica albuginea membrane, the penis's straitjacket, trap the blood inside. He pulled away.

"What is it, Masur?" Lola said. "We've done this before. You don't have a girlfriend, right?"

"This kind of thing is complicated for me." Sam sat up. "You remember about my foot?"

Lola rolled her eyes. "We did have sex, Sam."

"A couple of months ago, I finally had to have it removed and the recovery has been pretty gruesome, and I'm not the type of person that's ever been much good with intimacy in the first place, I guess."

"Sure," Lola said. "I get that. Does it hurt right now? One to ten."

"Maybe a six, or a seven, if I move?"

"That's no good," Lola said, nodding. "It's cool. We can have sex next time." She took his hand. "You want to smoke some weed? I've got a joint in my purse."

"I'm not into drugs. I like being able to have a clear head."

"How clear a head can you have when you're always in pain? Masur, trust me on this, no one has ever needed pot more than you."

Lola lit the joint, which they passed back and forth while watching *Ghost in the Shell* for the second time. It was Sam's first joint, and he could feel his mind gently slipping away, but at the same time, he wanted to act as if the drug was having no effect.

"You're so high," Lola said.

"I'm not," Sam insisted.

Toward the end of the movie, Lola said to him, "Do you want to show it to me?"

"My penis?" Sam laughed uncontrollably.

"No, your stump." Lola shrugged. Sam could not help but notice that she seemed a lot less high than he was. "It might help you. Plus, I saw what it looked like before, so I can offer you a point of comparison."

For whatever reason (maybe his inexperience with marijuana), this seemed like a solid argument to Sam. He took off his shoes, and then he took off his pants, and then he took off the prosthetic, and the two socks he had over the stump.

Lola looked at the stump appraisingly, and then she shrugged again. "It's not that bad. It was probably worse before. Now it's finished-looking, at least." She put her warm hand over the stump, and it felt different than when he touched it or when a doctor touched it. She ran her index finger along the red-and-pink scar that looked like a firmly closed mouth, and a slightly pleasurable, slightly painful electricity coursed up and down his spine. She bent down and kissed it once, leaving the red stamp of her lips. He was going to tell her to stop, but he really was too high, and then it was over anyway. She squeezed the stump with her hand and she sat back up. "You're going to be okay, Masur. I swear."

Sam felt like crying, but instead he started to laugh.

4B

Both Sides was completed a week before Sadie's twenty-fifth birthday. Marx threw a party at the office to celebrate both occasions. The game had taken twenty-two months and like *Ichigo,* would come out in time for the holidays.

At the beginning of the night, Zoe had given Sadie a dose of Ecstasy. "This is a great night," Zoe said. "I want to celebrate with my best friends." Sadie usually didn't do anything but pot, but she was in such a good mood and momentarily free from responsibility, so she took it.

The X made Sadie less inhibited to where she could enjoy the accomplishment of finishing *Both Sides*. She felt that she'd never made a better game. With *Both Sides,* as opposed to *Ichigo,* she felt that she had been able to push the boundaries, technically and narratively. And what was the point of making games if you weren't going to do that? She felt she'd reached a point where her ambitions and abilities were finally aligned. She was exhausted, as she always was after having made a game, but she had never felt more at peace with her own efforts. She felt in love with everyone in attendance at the party. She felt in love with Marx, who had been such a calming and wise presence at every step, and Zoe, who had written a moving and dramatic score for the game. She felt in love with her whole team of designers and coders. She felt in love with California. She forgave Dov and she felt less resentful of Sam.

Sam's work on the game had exceeded her expectations. When

she'd conceived of the game, she had thought the Mapletown story would be a clean frame on which the star attraction, Myre Landing, was mounted. Sam had surprised her. There was real depth to his side, and she had found herself in tears when she played Sam's side together with her side for the first time. As she played, she realized that the thing that gave the fantasy world of Myre Landing emotional resonance was Mapletown. The last few months of the game had passed in such a blur that Sadie hadn't had a chance to tell Sam how much she had liked his work. She was planning to take him aside tonight.

Though she was still resentful of him, they had fought less on *Both Sides* than they had on either of the *Ichigo*s. When disagreements arose, he conceded quickly, and Sadie had concluded that Sam was disengaged. He could not bother to come to the office some days; he could not bother to fight. When Sadie saw the work he had done on Mapletown, she realized that he had more than conceded. Somehow, Sam was able to bend to her criticism in a way that he had never been able to before. There was a particular scene that they had briefly fought over. It was the penultimate scene on Mapletown, in which Alice Ma, who is as sick as she has ever been, discovers that Myre Landing is a game that she has been playing the whole time. Sam, at first, had argued that it would be better if Myre Landing wasn't a game, but a book or a story that Alice Ma had been writing. He felt that it was too meta, too clever, if Myre Landing was a game, and that it would cause an unnecessary ludic dissonance in the gamer. But Sadie had held her ground, and Sam had conceded. He had rewritten the penultimate scene so that when we finally see Alice playing Myre Landing on her laptop (for the first time, Myre Landing is rendered as a screen within a screen), Alice loses the game. She dies in battle, as Rose the Mighty. The restart prompt of Myre Landing comes up: *Ready for a new tomorrow, Paladin?* Alice returns to the save point, and the second time she plays, she dies again. The restart prompt of Myre Landing comes up for the second time: *Ready for a new tomorrow, Paladin?* Alice returns to the save point, and she tries one more time. This time, she wins, and the final scene of the game is launched. It was Sam's idea that Alice should die twice in the game within a game before she could win the game properly. It was the inversion of the opening scene of Mapletown, in which moving forward meant giving up, and Sadie thought it was brilliant.

In a couple of weeks, she would be heading out on the road to promote *Both Sides*. Sam had a new girlfriend—some girl from high school—and a dog—and he had said he didn't want to travel for a while. Sadie would be taking the lead for the interviews and the cons this time. She wanted to make things right with Sam before she headed out.

Sadie was still looking for Sam when Zoe asked Sadie and Marx to come up to the roof to look at the late September stars, which she promised were "spectacular, truth-telling stars."

On the roof, the view was as distant as ever, but the stars were clear. Zoe pointed up at the sky. "That one's called Capricornus," Zoe said. "And that's Indus. And that's Cygnus the swan."

"How can you tell?" Sadie asked. "To me, constellations never look like what they're supposed to be."

"Honestly, I don't know which is which. I just know what's supposed to be up there in September," Zoe admitted.

"Look up there!" Marx said, pointing his right arm and putting his other arm around Zoe's shoulders. "It's Smurfus! You can tell by the bluish tinge."

"And that's Gandalfus," Sadie said, joining in. "The three stars represent the wizard's hat."

"And there's Frodus and Bilbus Bagginsus," Marx said.

"And Smeagolous looks like a ring," Sadie said.

"The magical ring of Smeagolous."

"You guys are being mean," Zoe said, but she was smiling.

"No, this is a great game. That's Cobainus. The eleven stars of Cobainus form a fuzzy grandma sweater," Marx said.

"And that's Donkey Kongus," Sadie said.

"How lucky we are to see the ethereal necktie of the sky!" Marx said. "But I think technically, it's known as Donkus Kongus."

"*Donkus Kongus.* I always mess that up," Sadie said.

"I didn't want to correct you," Marx said.

"No, it's good you should correct me when I'm wrong," Sadie said.

Without warning, Zoe kissed Sadie on the mouth. "Is this okay?" she asked. Zoe ran her fingers through Sadie's hair.

Sadie looked at Marx. "Is it okay with you?"

Marx nodded, and Zoe said, "We don't believe in ownership." Zoe kissed Sadie again. "Your lips are so soft. Marx you have to feel Sadie's lips."

Marx shook his head. "I'll watch," he said, with a sly grin.

"My favorite two people on the planet," Zoe said. "I'm so in love with both of you right now."

Zoe pulled Marx to her, and she held each of her friends' heads in her hands, and then she pushed the two of them together like dolls, and then she made the dolls kiss. The kiss lasted seven seconds, though it seemed longer to Sadie. Marx tasted like mint and the fruity Hefeweizen beer he'd been drinking and himself. She had expected kissing Marx to be strange, but it felt entirely natural, as if they kissed all the time. Sadie pulled back first, and Marx was laughing in his gentle way and covering his mouth with his elegant, long fingers.

"Was that weird?" Marx said.

"It was," Sadie said. "But we're on drugs so it doesn't count." (Marx hadn't been.) "It felt like kissing my brother." (Sadie didn't have a brother, just Alice, and it did not feel like kissing a sibling.)

"We won't even remember it in the morning," Marx said. (They did.) Marx sighed, as if resigning himself to something. "I love you, Sadie," Marx said.

"I love you," Sadie said. She turned to Zoe. "We love you, Zoe."

"You guys, I'm so in love with both of you right now," Zoe said. She put her arms around them. "I wanted to know what that would look like and now I do." She nodded to herself. Her eyes looked enormous and moist, and then, Zoe started to cry.

"No, Zoe!" Sadie said. She took Zoe in her arms. "You're not supposed to cry on X," Sadie said.

"Happy tears," Zoe said.

Although professional reviews did not entirely determine a game's fortunes in 2000, the reviews for *Both Sides* ranged from mixed to bad:

"For those of you who have been eagerly awaiting the next release from Mazer/Green, let's get this out of the way: *Both Sides* is *not* a game for fans of the delightful *Ichigo* series."

"Some of the graphics in Myre Landing are among the most beautiful visuals I have ever encountered in a game, but unfortunately, Myre Landing shares space with the maudlin Mapletown."

"While I enjoyed aspects of my play, the game is twice as long as it needs to be."

"*Both Sides* suffers from a major identity crisis."

"*Ichigo* fans should skip it."

"... the game seems schizophrenic, as if it has been designed by two different people, and the play is unsatisfying."

"The weather in Myre Landing is the best character in it."

"The game's ending is twice as clever as it needs to be."

"We can all agree that we need more games with female MCs, but I didn't like either Alice Ma or Rose the Mighty."

"*Ichigo* is so different from *Both Sides* that it is hard to believe that the same set of designers made it. Maybe *Ichigo* is more Mazer's game, and *Both Sides* more Green's? Mazer, usually the more public of the team, was curiously absent during the promotion, while Sadie Green was definitely front and center. Maybe Mazer knew he had a flop on his hands?"

"*Both Sides* thinks it's blowing your mind, but mainly what it induces is a minor headache."

"I guess I was expected to feel emotion at the end of *Both Sides*, but the only thing I felt was the strong desire to throw my controller across the room."

"There is so much technically right with *Both Sides*. Amazing graphics in the Myre Landing section, a haunting score by Zoe Cadogan, great sound design, a reasonably clever concept. So why did I hate it so much? Because it's pretentious, it's boring, and it's not that fun. Better luck next time, Unfair."

During its first week of release, *Both Sides* sold approximately one-fifth of the units *Ichigo* had sold in its first week. Marx was still optimistic. "It's a great, special game," Marx said, going into Sadie's office. "Maybe it'll take longer to find its audience?"

"People hate it," Sadie said.

"They don't hate it. They just don't understand it. They expected *Ichigo*, and marketing and publicity didn't do a good enough job telling them that it wasn't going to be *Ichigo*," Marx said. "And I haven't given up yet. We're going to buy more ads. We're going to send out more copies to gamers and reviewers. The retailers are still excited about it and you guys. It isn't over yet."

"They hate it." Sadie put her head on her desk. "I've got a headache."

Marx bent down, and he lifted Sadie's chin up. "Sadie, this isn't over. Believe me."

She did not. "It might be a migraine. I think I'll go home for the day."

"Okay. Take the afternoon. I'd come with you, but I'm having lunch with the boys," Marx said. The boys were Antonio "Ant" Ruiz and Simon Freeman. While Sadie and Sam had made *Both Sides,* Marx had begun expanding Unfair's producing efforts. The first team he'd brought on was Simon Freeman and Antonio Ruiz, who were both juniors at CalArts. The boys—as Marx called them—were making a Japanese-style RPG, inspired by their favorite game, *Persona.* The game took place in a high school, and each character could summon alternate versions of themselves through a complicated system of wormholes. *Love Doppelgängers,* its tentative title, was part romance and part science fiction. "Do you want to come? Sam said he was going to try to join."

"No." Sadie took the *Dead Sea* disk from the shelf. *Dead Sea* was her comfort game. She decided she'd go back to her apartment and kill zombies for a while.

Sadie left the office and walked home to Clownerina, who now seemed to be mocking her with his foot that wouldn't kick. She drew the curtains, and she got into bed, without taking off her clothes or her shoes. She felt ashamed and foolish. She felt covered in failure and she felt sure that people could smell and see it on her. The failure was like a fine coating of ash, after a fire. But it wasn't only on her skin; it was in her nose, in her mouth, in her lungs, in her molecules becoming part of her. She would never be rid of it.

Dov called her and she let it go to voicemail: "Critics are vile," he said. "The game's brilliant. The atmospheric effects on Oneiric are *fucking* great. Hope you're doing okay. Call me." Sadie listened to the message, and then she hit delete.

Sam called her, and she let that go to voicemail, too: "Sadie, pick up. We need to discuss this. This isn't just happening to you."

Delete.

Sadie fell asleep. About fifteen minutes later, someone was knocking on her apartment door. She could hear Sam's muffled voice.

"Sadie, let me in. We have to talk," Sam said.

Sadie didn't answer.

"Sadie, come on. This is stupid. Talk to me. They mostly hated *my side,* not *your side.*"

Sadie still didn't answer.

"Sadie, please. This is ridiculous. How long is this going to go on?"

Sadie got out of bed. She swung her front door open, and Sam walked in.

5B

"Say what you came to say," Sadie said.

Sam sat down on Sadie's couch. "I like your apartment building. I like that strange clown."

"Can't you leave me alone? I told Marx I'd be back to work tomorrow."

"We tried to do something big," Sam said. "We swung for the fences, and people didn't like it. But I don't care. *I* like what we did."

"That's easy for you to say," Sadie said. "Everyone thinks it's *my* game, and you supported me in my folly. They think *your* game, *Ichigo*, is the good game, and *my* game is the failure."

"That isn't true."

"And maybe you thought *Both Sides* was going to flop, like that reviewer wrote. You let me go out and promote it. If you'd thought it was any good, you would have been front and center, wouldn't you?"

Sam looked at Sadie. "Wait. What?"

She glared at him. "If you'd thought the game was good, you would have taken all the credit." She paused. "Like you always do."

Sam had been proud of her work and of his own. He'd stayed home because his foot was unreliable and pain management would have been difficult on the road. Sam opened his mouth to explain himself, but then he changed his mind. He went into her kitchen and poured himself a glass of water from her fridge.

"Help yourself," she called, sarcastic and unrelenting. "What's mine is yours. Except when it's something no one else likes."

"Come on, Sadie. You *wanted* to promote *Both Sides*."

"I didn't *want* to. I was willing to, because you wouldn't. And it wasn't easy. I'm not Sam Mazer. Strangers don't naturally love me."

"So I'm clear: It's work when you do it. But it's a vacation when I do it."

"Yes, I think it's easier for you."

"Easier for me, or you could even call it something I'm *good* at. Something I'm good at that, maybe, you're not good at," Sam said.

"You're saying the game flopped because I was bad at promoting it?" Sadie asked.

"No, of course not. I was trying to get you to admit that promoting *Ichigo* had been work. Stop looking for an argument. And for the record, I put everything I had into Mapletown. I've never put more of myself into a game."

"Sam, you couldn't have put everything into it. You were never here!"

"I worked my ass off," Sam said. "And I've had a hard year, not that you ever asked. And what is *wrong* with you?"

"What do you mean?"

"Come on, Sadie. There are only two of us in this relationship. I want to know what is wrong with you. You've had some problem with me ever since we moved back to California."

Sadie didn't say anything. She shook her head.

"You're a complete bitch all the time for no reason?"

"Screw you, Sam."

"Say it," Sam said. "It's worse for me not knowing what it is."

"I don't care what's worse for you," Sadie said.

"That is so typical of you," Sam said. "Sit there and suffer and don't tell anyone what's wrong."

"You're the one who does that," Sadie said.

Sam banged his hand on Sadie's coffee table. "What is it? Sadie, this is unfair. I have no idea what I've done. Clearly you think I've done something."

"You have no idea?"

"No idea," Sam said.

She took the *Dead Sea* CD out of her bag, and she flung it at him. "What is this?" Sam asked.

"You tell me."

He looked at the CD. "It's Dov's game. So?"

Sadie looked him in the eye. "You knew Dov had been my boyfriend, and that's why you wanted me to go to him. You pretended like you didn't."

"So what if I knew? Ulysses was perfect for *Ichigo*. Sadie, this is crazy."

"You already said that."

"But it is *crazy*."

"Stop calling me crazy. I thought you were my friend, but—"

"Sadie, I am your friend. You're my best friend. Or I was until you decided two years ago that I wasn't."

"I thought you were my friend, but you're a liar and a manipulator."

"That isn't true."

"Isn't it? You let everyone think you made *Ichigo* by yourself."

"That isn't true. I can't control how they wrote the stories. I tell everyone you're my partner. I tell everyone you're brilliant."

"You made us take the Opus deal because it was better for *you*."

"You know why we took the Opus deal. We talked about the reasons."

"*I* got stuck making the sequel. I got stuck doing the work while you went on a coronation tour."

"That isn't what happened."

"But the worst thing you ever did to me was making me go to Dov for Ulysses."

"I didn't make you."

"I know I could have built that engine, if I'd had more time. If you hadn't pushed me to go to Dov, I wouldn't have ended up in a relationship with him for three years. Do you know how much power he had over me and how hard it was to leave him?"

"It's not my fault you got back with him. You can't blame me for his actions or for yours. You can't blame me for everything, but it seems like you do."

"Admit it, Sam," Sadie said. "You wanted Ulysses, and you didn't care about me."

"I care about you more than anyone," Sam said. "But do I regret that I wanted you to get Ulysses? Do I regret that we got rich, and we get to make basically whatever we want now, even ill-conceived, pretentious art games like *Both Sides*? No, if Ulysses led to that, I would tell you to go to Dov and get Ulysses every time."

"You think *Both Sides* is ill-conceived and pretentious?"

"I think it was pretty obvious that it was *never* going to be *Ichigo*, but it was what you wanted to do, so I supported you."

"You're saying it's my fault?"

"No, I'm agreeing maybe it was more your idea than mine."

"*Ichigo* was my idea, too. They're *ALL* my ideas."

"It's nice that you see it that way, and if it helps you to make a villain out of me, go for it. But if I hadn't pushed you to make *Ichigo*, where would you even be? You'd be one of a hundred programmers at EA working on *Madden Football*, if you were lucky. There aren't that many girls in our field, you know. You'd probably be working for Dov. He'd probably have you handcuffed to your desk."

Sadie's eyes grew wide. She had never told him about the handcuffs. "How do you know about that?"

"Christ, Sadie, it was obvious. You had welts around your wrists for, like, two years. Marx and I used to—"

"You're such an incredible asshole. Sometimes, I hate you."

Sam realized he might have gone too far. "Sadie, I shouldn't have said that last thing. Please. Do you remember that day in your old apartment at MIT? You said we would forgive each other, no matter what we did or what we said."

"I didn't know what I was agreeing to," Sadie said. "I was young and stupid."

"You've never been stupid."

Sadie turned away from Sam. "Did you ever ask yourself why I was depressed?"

"I . . . I thought you'd broken up with your boyfriend. That's what your roommate said, I think. I didn't even know it was Dov."

"Yet," she said. "You didn't know *yet*. But yes, it was Dov. But that's not the reason I was depressed." She pulled her head to her knees, her head buried under the habit of her hair. "Everyone thinks *Ichigo* is about you, but it's really about me."

"What do you mean?"

"*Ichigo* is about a boy who has been lost at sea, but it's also about a mother who has lost her child. I never had a child, but I might have . . ." She turned away from him. She hadn't told anyone about the abortion, not Dov, not Alice, not Freda, and even now, she struggled to say the word to Sam.

Sometimes, it seemed as if it had never happened. On a snowy day in January, she had taken the train to a clinic in Back Bay. They had told her to bring a friend, but she went alone. The whole thing had taken an hour; the procedure itself, ten minutes. The nurse had warned her about possible pain, but she had felt nothing. (She wouldn't even end up bleeding as much as she did for a regular period.) She rode the

T back home, and that night, she went out for drinks with her room-mate. She had a White Russian, a rum and Coke, and a seven and seven, treacly college-girl drinks, and when she returned to her apart-ment, she passed out in her bed. At first, the roommate had thought she was hungover, but after Sadie had been in bed a week, the room-mate finally demanded, "What's wrong with you?"

"I broke up with Dov," Sadie had lied.

"Good riddance."

Sadie had been in bed for eleven days when Sam showed up in her room, demanding to talk about *Solution*.

"I felt so ashamed," Sadie said. "And maybe that's why I let him do the things he did."

"Sadie." Sam's voice was filled with tenderness and love for her. "Sadie, why didn't you ever say?"

"Because we never say anything *real* to each other. We play games, and we talk about games, and we talk about making games, and we don't know each other at all."

He was about to tell her that that was bullshit, that no two people had ever shared more of their lives together. That if *she* didn't know him, no one knew him, and he might as well not exist. But at that moment, Sam started to feel the phantom pain. He hadn't had an epi-sode in several months, and he didn't want to have one right now, in Sadie's apartment. He didn't want to be weak and vulnerable when she hated him this much. He had become practiced at sensing the signs of it: the tension in his jaw and his forehead, the hyperawareness of every scent (the ocean, Sadie's hand cream, rotting fruit in a garbage can outside), the bile in his throat, the electric pulses up his spine, the throb, the ache, the pulse of the missing limb. He opened his back-pack, and he took out a joint. He lit it and then he inhaled deeply.

Sadie observed him, suddenly bemused, as if she were watching an animal do something unexpected: an elephant paint a picture, a pig use a calculator.

"You don't mind if I smoke in here?" Sam said.

"Do what you want," Sadie said. She stood up to open the gauzy cotton curtains and the window behind them. The sun was setting over Clownerina. "Since when do you smoke pot?"

Sam inhaled and then he shrugged.

She returned to the couch, positioning herself as far away from him as she could. The tendrils of smoke reached across the sofa to her, like sepulchral fingers beckoning, and a pleasant haze began to fill the room, turning everything that had been sharp, soft-focused. The pot's miasma was strong and spicy, and despite herself, Sadie could feel herself mellowing.

"What is this?" she asked.

"Some kind of sinsemilla," he said. "I don't remember the name." He did remember the name. It was one of those puerile names that growers gave pot—Bugs Bunny, Magic Kitten, Rollergirl—as if the only reason anyone smoked pot was for childish hijinks. He didn't want to say the name out loud in that moment.

She shifted closer to him and she reached for the joint, palm up. Sam looked at her outstretched hand, which he knew as well as any hand except his own—the precise pattern of the lines that made up the grid of her palm, the slim fingers with the purplish veins at the knuckles, the particular creamy olive hue of her skin, her delicate wrist, pinkish, with a penumbral callus that must have come from Dov, the white gold bracelet she wore that he knew had been a gift from Freda on her twelfth birthday. How could she honestly think he wouldn't know about the handcuffs? He had spent hours sitting next to her, playing games and then making them, staring at her hands as her fingers flew across a keyboard or jabbed at a controller. *Tell me I don't know you,* Sam thought. *Tell me I don't know you when I could draw both sides of this hand, your hand, from memory.*

"Sam?" she said.

He passed her the joint.

V

—————

PIVOTS

1

Everyone knew *Love Doppelgängers* was a terrible title, but no one knew what to call it instead. They had lived with the title for so long that it had almost become good by sheer virtue of repetition and familiarity. It was not, in fact, good. As Sam said to Marx, "*Love Doppelgängers* is an excellent title if we want twelve people to play this game." Unfair couldn't afford that. After the modest performance of *Both Sides, Love Doppelgängers* needed to work commercially.

The one person who didn't know *Love Doppelgängers* was terrible: Simon Freeman, the person who had come up with it. Simon had studied German in school and had had an adolescent obsession with all things Kafka. "I don't think it's that bad," Simon said, feeling offended at Sam's utter certainty that it was terrible. "Why won't it work?"

"No one knows what a doppelgänger is," Sam said.

"Lots of people know what a doppelgänger is!" Simon defended his title.

"Maybe not enough people know what a doppelgänger is," Marx amended Sam.

Sadie thought she'd quite possibly lose her mind if one more person said doppelgänger.

"If kids know one German word, it's 'doppelgänger,'" Simon said.

"What kids are these?" Sam said. "Are they all in AP English?"

"Well, then, they can *learn*," Simon said. "We can put a definition on the cover, a footnote—"

"A footnote? Are you kidding? You know what says, *Get ready for a great time gaming*? A cover with a footnote," Sam said.

"You're an asshole," Simon said.

"Whoa, Simon. Calm down," Ant said.

"He went to Harvard. He should stop pretending like he's down with the people." Simon turned back to Sam. "You're being perverse. There are tons of cryptic titles in games: *Metal Gear Solid. Suikoden. Crash Bandicoot. Grim Fandango. Final Fantasy.* They work because they sound cool."

"But *Love Doppelgängers* does not sound cool," Sam said.

"The whole game is literally a love story with doppelgängers, so we should have a title that reflects that," Simon said. "And people do know what a doppelgänger is."

"Honestly, I don't think most people do," Sam said.

"Well, maybe we don't want those people to play our game, then," Ant said, coming to his partner's defense with exactly the wrong argument.

"No, we want *everyone* to buy this game," Sam said. "Simon. Ant. Listen, we love this game. It's your game, and we completely believe in you as artists. But we want the game to sell a million copies. Do you want to cut off the game's legs over a completely unsubstantiated conjecture that kids in Montana know the word 'doppelgänger'?"

Sadie thought Sam sounded exactly like Dov the day he'd told them Ichigo needed to be a boy. She felt a bit sorry for Simon and Ant.

The boys turned to her. "Sadie," Ant said, "what do you think?"

Sadie knew they trusted her more than Sam, and she wanted to side with them. "I think," she said, "that Americans hate umlauts. Sorry, guys."

Simon and Ant exchanged looks. "She's right," Ant said.

"Fine," Simon said. "What are we going to call it, then?"

Sam called a company meeting to brainstorm new titles. He rolled out the trusty whiteboard that had traveled with them from Cambridge to Los Angeles. At this point, the whiteboard was no longer white, and its permanent palimpsest was an archive of Unfair's last five years. Marx said to Sam, "We can afford a new whiteboard, you know."

But Sam resisted throwing the whiteboard out. He felt it possessed a talismanic power. "Not one that says 'Property of the Harvard Science Center' on the side."

"Well, right," Marx said. "Even better, then, because it won't be a monument to your moral turpitude."

"Okay," Sam said to the assembled employees of Unfair. "No one leaves until we've got a new title. No idea too stupid." He brandished his dry-erase marker like a sword, and he wrote their suggestions on the board.

Love Doubles
Love Strangers
Love Stranger High School
High School Love Doubles
The Doppelgänger
The Doppelgänger Who Loved Me
Doubles High
Couples High
Wormhole Love Story
Wormhole High
I Am in Love with a Doppelgänger
The Doppelgänger's Love Story
Love Tunnels
Dirty Love Tunnels
Dark and Dirty Love Tunnels
Dark and Dirty High School Love Tunnels
Sexy High
Dirty Sexy High
Dirty Crazy Sexy High

And about two hundred more titles that were variations on, or de-evolutions of, the same.

"These are awful," Sam said, after they had been at it for around two hours. "They're great for a porno or an unpublished German novel about pedophilia, but horrible for a four-quadrant video game."

During sex with Zoe that night, Marx was still ruminating about titles for *Love Doppelgängers,* and that made him think about his own high school years at the International School of Tokyo. Marx had been the captain of the chess team, and the team had gone across town to compete with another high school chess team. (Marx's school was number two in Tokyo; the other team, number one.) When they arrived at the other high school, they found that the building was almost identical to their high school, but with everything in reverse. The high schools must have been built at the same time and from the same architectural plans. The team had joked that maybe they would find alternate versions of themselves and their teachers in the buildings. The captain of the other chess team had introduced himself to Marx quite formally: "Team Captain Watanabe, I am your counterpart." He could still hear the Katakana in the way the boy had pronounced the English loanword "counterpart."

For the rest of their lovemaking, Marx could barely concentrate. He didn't want to forget the word "counterpart," but he also didn't want to interrupt sex with Zoe to write it down. But Zoe could sense Marx's distance. "Where are you?" she asked.

Counterpart High came out the second week of February 2001 and was an instant best seller for Unfair. By its third week of release, *Counterpart High*, or *CPH*, as it was known by fans, had significantly outsold *Both Sides*, and Marx immediately set the boys to making a sequel. Unlike Sadie, Simon and Ant liked sequels and didn't see them as a sellout. They claimed that they had imagined *CPH* as a quartet anyway—a game for each year of high school.

By its tenth week of release, *CPH* was the best-selling PC game in America. PlayStation and Xbox ports were already in the works, and there was talk of porting it to Nintendo.

By the end of the year, *CPH* would outsell the original *Ichigo*.

The staff who had worked on *Both Sides* were moved over to *CPH2*. Until they could lease additional office space, Sadie ceded her office to Simon and Ant, and moved down the hall, to share with Marx. When Marx needed privacy, Sadie would use Sam's office, or she would walk home to Clownerina. Sadie didn't mind losing her office. She and Sam hadn't settled on an idea for their next game, and she wasn't working much anyway. They occasionally tossed concepts back and forth, but nothing seemed to inspire either of them to action. Sam occasionally floated the idea of making *Ichigo III*, but Sadie thought that felt like retreat. For the first time in five years, they didn't actively work on a game.

Sadie was not, by nature, ungenerous, and she didn't begrudge *Counterpart High* its success. She felt excited for Marx, her partner,

216

and his ability to spot talent. She felt excited that her company was going to be significantly in the black for 2001, despite the disappointing sales of *Both Sides*. She felt, perhaps, old. She was still only twenty-five, but until that point, she had always been the youngest in any room she'd been in, and she had derived power from that. Even though Simon and Ant were only a handful of years younger than her, they seemed like they were from a different generation than Sadie and Sam. They didn't have the same issues she had. They *liked* sequels! They didn't care about building their own engines, or who got credit for what, or where a good idea came from. They had been playing games since they were in diapers. Their presence, in combination with the failure of *Both Sides*, made her feel ancient and out of touch.

Though Sadie didn't see it that way, *Counterpart High* was her accomplishment, too. The game had been built, in part, using Sadie's engine, and *Counterpart High: Sophomore Year*, would be built on an improved version of Oneiric. The tech Sadie had created was worth more than the game she had created it for. When Marx came to her with the idea to use Oneiric for *Counterpart High*, Sadie agreed. She liked the game's pitch, and she liked Simon and Ant. How could she not like them? They reminded her of Sam and herself. Although a difference between the boys and her team was that Simon and Ant were lovers, too. She'd watch them working and would feel a touch of . . . It was hard for her to articulate what. A nostalgia for something that had never been? An envy at their intimacy? She wondered what it would have been like if Sam had been her lover. It wasn't as if she had never thought of it. But Sam had always been so guarded—he was a boy, and also a windowless and doorless tower. She had never found his entrances. She had never kissed him except on the cheek or the forehead. She had, in fourteen years, only intentionally touched him a handful of times, and he had always seemed uncomfortable when she did. And in the end, she had decided she preferred being his creative partner to being his lover. There were so many people who could be your lover, but, if she was honest with herself, there were relatively few people who could move you creatively. Still, when she watched Simon and Ant, she felt that their personal relationship was riskier than her and Sam's, though maybe it was more rewarding, too.

Sometimes, she would see them at the end of the day when they were heading back to their apartment in West Hollywood, and she would notice Ant carry Simon's bag or offer him some other small kindness, and she would think, *It must be nice to have that, to have someone to share your life and your work with.* She had been so lonely in the months since *Both Sides* had come out. But it was different for Simon and Ant, she decided: Simon and Ant were both men. If Sadie and Sam had been lovers, Sadie was certain she would have been seen as Sam's helpmate, and not as an artist in her own right. Many people saw her that way already.

Because they had built the game using her engine, Sadie was intimately involved in the making of *Counterpart High,* and she knew the boys viewed her as a mentor. She had liked advising them, though it was a new experience for her to be generous in that way. It was strange to invest yourself in work that was not your own. She felt a new appreciation for Dov—for how willing he had always been to share his knowledge and his time, for what a good teacher he had been, if nothing else. When *Both Sides* had failed, the world had gone so quiet. One of the few people who had called her was Dov, and she owed him a callback. Marx was on the phone, so she went into Sam's office.

"Brilliant one! I saw the California area code, and I was hoping it was you."

Dov told her a bit about what he was working on: a new game, and he was consulting for an AI company in Silicon Valley. He asked her about her work, and she mentioned producing for Simon and Ant and how popular *CPH* was. "It's to Marx's credit," Sadie said. "And to a lesser extent, Sam's. They both wanted to use California as an opportunity to produce for other people. Maybe they knew before I did that *Both Sides* would tank? We've got seven games currently in production or postproduction."

"And many of them are using your engine, yes?"

"Some of them," Sadie said. "At least it's good for something." Sadie paused. "Were you ever jealous when *Ichigo* started to take off?"

"No," Dov said.

"Not even a little?"

"I saw you as an extension of myself," Dov said. "I have an enormous ego. Your accomplishments were my accomplishments. You'll probably think this makes me a monster."

"You were a garbage boyfriend—"

"Thank you. It's not a lie."

"But you were a great teacher. That's what I was thinking today. No one took my work seriously until you did."

"I just wanted to have sex with you."

"Don't say that!"

"It isn't true anyway. You're exceptional, kid. You know that."

Sadie paused. She looked at Sam's shelves, which were a veritable museum of Ichigo history and merch: Ichigo hats, books, comic books, coloring books, T-shirts, figurines, paper dolls, stuffed animals, dishes, rice cookers, cookie jars, costumes, handheld games, board games, bobbleheads, bedsheets, beach towels, tote bags, bath balls, teapots, bookends, etc. There was not a product in the world that couldn't be stamped with Ichigo's likeness. "I want your advice about something," Sadie said.

"Of course."

"How do you get over a failure?"

"I think you mean a *public* failure. Because we all fail in private. I failed with you, for example, but no one posted an online review about it, unless you did. I fail with my wife and with my son. I fail in my work every day, but I keep turning over the problems until I'm not failing anymore. But public failures are different, it's true."

"So, what do I do?" she asked.

"You go back to work. You take advantage of the quiet time that a failure allows you. You remind yourself that no one is paying any attention to you and it's a perfect time for you to sit down in front of your computer and make another game. You try again. You fail better."

"I don't know if I have a better game in me than *Both Sides*," Sadie said. "I don't know if I can be that vulnerable again."

"You do and you can. I believe in you. And you aren't failing, Sadie. Your game failed, yes. But you just told me: your company is succeeding. This is a company built on your technology, your good judgment, your labors. Embrace that."

Sadie picked up a squishy Ichigo stress ball and she squeezed until Ichigo was buried in her palm.

"Seeing anyone?" Dov asked lightly. "The guy in the band with the pretentious name?"

"Dov, that was a million years ago," Sadie said. "I haven't spoken to Abe Rocket in years."

"Abe *Rocket*, gross. So, what else is new? You can't be all games and no play."

What had she been doing? Working on games that weren't her own. Improving Oneiric. Endless office meetings about things she didn't care about. On the weekends (mostly), smoking copious amounts of weed. Playing *Grand Theft Auto*, *Half-Life*, *Mario Kart*, *Final Fantasy*. Reading *Harry Potter* or whatever book Oprah had told her mom to buy. Sneaking out of the office in the middle of the afternoon to go to the movies with her grandmother—Freda favored romantic comedies with the misadventures of "hapless goyish blond girls." Weighing which breed of dog she should get, but not doing anything about it. Googling former rivals and games that had come out the same season as hers. Reading online reviews of her games (insisting that she wasn't). Generally, obsessively, licking her wounds. What a funny turn of phrase, she thought. Licking your wounds would only make them worse, no? The mouth was filled with so much bacteria. But Sadie knew it was easy to get addicted to the taste of your own carnage. "My older sister is getting married," Sadie said. She let the Ichigo stress ball return to its normal size.

Dr. Alice Green, in her final year as a cardiology resident, was getting married to another doctor, not coincidentally a pediatric oncologist, and she had appointed Sadie the maid of honor. Consequently, Sadie and Alice were spending more time together than they had since they were kids. Sadie was bored with the mundanity of wedding planning, but glad for the distraction and the time with Alice.

The prior week, the sisters had been at the stationer in Beverly Hills, looking at *Oxford English Dictionary*–sized binders of white invitations.

"There are so many variations on white," Alice commented.

"But this white one is great," Sadie said.

"It's so different than the myriad other white ones. How will I ever choose?"

But Alice and Sadie did manage to choose a white invitation and then, to reward themselves, they went to lunch at Freda's favorite Italian restaurant.

"Oh! I wanted to tell you!" Alice said. "I played your game!"

"I'm impressed. How did you ever find the time?"

"It's my sister's game. Of course I found the time." Alice paused.

"I didn't know if I would like it when I heard what it was about. But it was so good, Sadie. I'm honored that you gave the character my name. I loved the Mapletown parts especially. I didn't know until I played the game how much you understood about what I was going through back then. I thought you were just resentful that you couldn't go to Space Camp and that Mom and Dad essentially ignored you for two years."

"For the record, I *was* resentful. I will always regret Space Camp. But Alice? Mapletown was all Sam. I had pretty much nothing to do with it."

"That can't be true."

"Honestly, it was Sam. He made Mapletown; I made Myre Landing."

"Well, whose idea was it to call the main character Alice?"

"Honestly, I don't remember, but I think it was Sam's."

"I liked the whole game," Alice said. "Truly."

"Thank you."

"I'm so proud of you." Alice grabbed Sadie's hand across the table. "But when Alice Ma dreams of her funeral, there's a tombstone in the graveyard that reads 'She died of dysentery.' You must have put that there for me. That's our joke."

"Nope. Sam again. He's kind of coopted that joke to tell you the truth."

"Well, give Sam my compliments," Alice said, as she paid the check. Alice always insisted on paying even though Sadie made more money. "Maybe I should invite him to the wedding?"

Alice was not the only person who preferred Mapletown to Myre Landing. Marx, who followed online discussion of all Unfair's games, had found groups of gamers who avoided playing the Myre Landing side and *only* played the Mapletown side as much as possible. They called themselves Mapletownies. Although critics had generally preferred Myre Landing, the gamers had embraced Sam's work. Marx did not discuss any of this with Sadie—Sadie, of course, already knew.

2

When he had booked the tickets to Tokyo, Marx had planned to go with Zoe, but two weeks before they were set to travel, Zoe received a fellowship to study opera in Italy. She claimed that she had not been the fellowship's first choice, which was why she had been left with almost no time to pack up her California life. It had also derailed their trip to Tokyo.

Marx had left quite early to take her to the airport, considering that their house was only a twenty-minute drive. They were halfway there when traffic came to a complete stop.

"Do you think I should try to get off the freeway?" Marx asked.

"Maybe it'll clear," Zoe said. "We have plenty of time."

"We do," he agreed. "We have plenty of time."

For the next five minutes, they volleyed this phrase back and forth to each other.

"We have plenty of time."

"We have plenty of time."

After ten minutes of saying it, they became aware of how often they were repeating the phrase, and it became a joke.

"We have so much time."

"So much time. I won't even know what to do with this never-ending span of time."

"You'll have so much time, you'll be one of those people getting a massage in the middle of the airport."

"I'll be looking at the airport art."

"You'll probably have time to visit another terminal."

"Another? I'll ride that party bus and I'll visit *every* terminal." Abruptly, Zoe began to cry.

"What is it?" Marx said.

"Tension," she said, waving her hand. "I'm stressed about leaving, I guess."

Marx squeezed her hand.

"I'm getting off the freeway," he said. "We can get back on closer to LAX." Marx changed lanes.

"I think we should stay where we are," Zoe said. "It could be worse on the surface roads, and we're almost there. It can't take much longer. And don't they say that changing lanes never makes a difference anyway? It takes the same amount of time whether you change lanes or not."

"I'm not changing lanes," he said. "I'm rerouting us. If I'm wrong, we'll still have plenty of time." Marx changed lanes again. "You'll be getting a pedicure in Terminal One before you know it."

"I'll be eating a sugar pretzel and waiting in the Starbucks line."

"You'll be buying an inflatable pillow and a snow globe."

"I think we should break up," she said.

Once she had said this, he recognized that the strange feeling in the air between them for the last several months was denouement. After *Both Sides* had come out, there had been a series of mundane skirmishes. She had accused him of spending too much time at the office, something that she had never cared about before. She accused him of loving Sam more than he did her. (She did not mention Sadie.) She had yelled at him for being bourgeois—for caring too much about Danish furniture and wine ratings. (He had spent some time shopping for a dining room table, but the wine struck him as unfair—he preferred beer.) Suddenly, she seemed to loathe California, complaining about allergies and vapid people and bad theater. And then the arguments had ceased as abruptly as they had begun. A month later, she informed him about the opera fellowship in Italy. It was too good an opportunity to pass up.

"You don't love me," she said.

"Zoe, of course I love you."

"But you don't love me *enough*," she said.

"What's enough?" Marx asked.

"Enough is . . . Maybe this is selfish, but I don't want to love more than I am loved. And I don't want to be with someone who loves something or someone more than me."

"Why are you speaking in riddles? Say what you mean. If you know something I don't know, I'd love to be told what it is. And I like our life, Zoe. Why do you want to burn everything to the ground?"

"Like," she said. She wiped her eyes on her sleeve, and she pushed her chin out, as if resolving something. "It's my fault. Let's not make this some awful thing," she said. "We've had good times, right? My trip to Italy is a natural break, and if at the other end of it, it becomes a permanent one, then . . ."

The drive ended up taking four times as long as it usually did, but Zoe did make her flight. It was the first time Marx had ever *truly* been broken up with. He knew he should be devastated, but what he felt was relief. The relationship, without him noticing, had been the longest one he had ever had. He had seen no reason to end it. He had never tired of coming home to their place and finding her naked, playing some new instrument. Why end something that worked over the vague notion that he could love someone more deeply than he loved Zoe, who was by every measure fantastic? It was a strange moment in Marx's personal development. He was no longer the boy who wanted to taste everything at the buffet, and he considered it a sign of his own maturity that he had not thought to end things with Zoe. But his disdain for his former itinerancy had made it so he could not recognize the reasons a person should stay.

Had it only been a visit to his family, Marx might have canceled the trip to Japan, but he had also scheduled business meetings. Marx first asked Sam if he wanted to go to Japan with him. Sam said he didn't want to travel, which had become Sam's standard answer since they'd moved to California. And when Sam declined, he asked Sadie. Sadie, too, was going to decline, but then she thought, *Why not go?* She and Sam weren't getting anywhere on the new game, and Sadie had never been to Japan before. Marx thought it would be helpful for some of their creative team to be present at the meetings, which were about the possibility of Unfair collaborating with Morikami Publishing to adapt the popular *Osaka Ghost School* anime series into a game. Morikami was interested in working with an American partner, and they liked Unfair because of the work they had done on *Ichigo*, which seemed to be agreeably Western and Eastern to them.

When they arrived in Tokyo, both Marx and Sadie were jet-lagged. They slept two or three hours, and then, independently, they both woke up and passed the quiet predawn hours working, which to them often meant gaming.

For the holidays, Simon and Ant had given Sadie a Game Boy. She hadn't had time to use it until the trip to Tokyo, and the first game she played on it was *Harvest Moon*. *Harvest Moon* is a farming, role-playing game: You are a farmer whose job is to raise crops, find a wife, make friends with people in the community. It was one of the first, if not the first, farming games. Sadie found its simplicity reminiscent of what she and Alice had liked about *Oregon Trail*. The game was gentle, peaceful. It was the opposite of a game like *Dead Sea*—it was a protected world in which nothing bad would ever happen to you.

Down the hall, on the same floor of the hotel, Marx was playing *EverQuest* on his PC laptop. *EverQuest* was a massively multiplayer online role-playing game, known by the bulky acronym MMORPG. *EverQuest* is a riff on *Dungeons & Dragons*, and like *D&D*, its emphasis is on building characters. Marx had spent more hours than he cared to admit customizing his avatar, a half-elf bard named Hella Behemoth. It reminded Marx of his days playing D&D with Sam, though nostalgia was not Marx's primary reason for playing it. Marx was interested in *EverQuest* because it was the first MMORPG to utilize a 3D graphics engine, and he was hoping the next iteration of *Counterpart High* would have an online component, too.

Around 5 a.m. (still too early to go to breakfast), Sadie knocked on Marx's hotel room door. He had sent a group email about *CPH2* around 4:45, so she knew he was awake. "Have you played *Harvest Moon*? It's not the kind of thing we make, but I'm finding it pretty addictive."

Marx and Sadie traded devices. "I'm trusting you with Hella Behemoth," Marx said. Sadie sat beside Marx on his bed. They gamed companionably for maybe an hour or two, until breakfast opened. It was six in the morning, and the city was still sleeping, the only sound the occasional grumble of one of their stomachs.

At breakfast, they heaped their plates with food, and then they went to a quiet corner of the dining room to eat.

They spoke of whether *Osaka Ghost School* was something Sadie and Sam would want to work on, if Morikami made them an offer. "Maybe?" Sadie said. "But wouldn't it be better for Simon and Ant? High school is their thing."

"Well," Marx said gently. "Simon and Ant are busy."

Sadie laughed ruefully. "Sam doesn't know we're the B-team now."

"Never," Marx said.

They spoke of Zoe.

"Are you devastated?" Sadie asked.

"Not as much as you'd think," Marx said.

"I'm devastated," Sadie said. "She was my best L.A. friend."

They spoke of *Both Sides*.

"Are *you* devastated?" Marx said.

"I want to say, 'Not as much as you'd think.' I want to be blasé like you." Sadie paused. "I am devastated, but more what I feel is ashamed. I got you and Sam and everyone to follow me down the road of making this. And I completely believed. I completely believed it would work. I feel like the guy who built the *Titanic*."

"You are not naval architect Thomas Andrews Jr."

"I *am* naval architect Thomas Andrews Jr."

Sadie and Marx laughed.

"*Both Sides* is not the *Titanic*," Marx said. "No one died playing *Both Sides*."

"Just my soul. A little," she said. "Maybe the worst part is, I don't trust myself anymore. I'm not sure my instincts are good."

Marx reached across the table and he took her hand in his. "Sadie, I promise you: your instincts are good."

On the second night of their trip, they went to a Noh theater, with Marx's father. Noh had been Watanabe-san's idea—it was the kind of thing Japanese brought their esteemed gaijin visitors to do. The performance had come with a printed English libretto, but Sadie misplaced hers before the play had even begun, and she found herself quite lost. She understood neither the conventions of Noh nor the language.

Marx would occasionally whisper poetic, cryptic commentary into her ear: "The fisherman's ghost was killed for fishing in the wrong river." Or "The drum is silent, and the gardener is killing himself."

Once she resigned herself to not understanding anything, she enjoyed Marx's commentary and the plays themselves. The theater was warm and smelled of lacquered wood and incense, and it felt like a dream to her. As Sadie was still quite jet-lagged and additionally tired from a long day of meetings, it was an effort to stay awake. She felt her eyes begin to close, and then, not wanting to be a rude white person, she would sternly wake herself.

After the show, they had dinner with Marx's father at a nearby tempura place. Sadie had not seen Watanabe-san since that long-ago dinner to celebrate Marx's performance in *Twelfth Night*.

Watanabe-san and Sadie exchanged gifts. She brought him a pair of carved wooden Ichigo chopsticks that their Japanese distributor had had made to celebrate the release of the second *Ichigo* in Japan.

In return, he gave her a silk scarf with a reproduction of *Cherry Blossoms at Night,* by Katsushika Ōi, on it. The painting depicts a woman composing a poem on a slate in the foreground. The titular cherry blossoms are in the background, all but a few of them in deep shadow. Despite the title, the cherry blossoms are not the subject; it is a painting about the creative process—its solitude and the ways in which an artist, particularly a female one, is expected to disappear. The woman's slate appears to be blank. "I know Hokusai is an inspiration for you," Watanabe-san said. "This is by Hokusai's daughter. Only a handful of her paintings survive, but I think she is even better than the father."

"Thank you," Sadie said.

Watanabe-san bowed deeply to Sadie when they parted. "Thank you, Sadie. Without you and Sam, Marx might have become an actor."

"Marx was a fantastic actor," Sadie defended him.

"He's better at what he's doing now," Watanabe-san insisted.

Sadie and Marx took a cab back to the hotel. "Do you mind what your father said?" she asked him.

"No," Marx said. "I loved being a student actor. I was fully devoted to it, and now I'm not. I think if I'd become a professional, I would likely have fallen out of love with it anyway. It isn't a sadness, but a joy, that we don't do the same things for the length of our lives."

"Are you saying I get to quit making games?"

"No," Marx said. "You're stuck. You're doing this forever."

On the third morning of their trip, early, before any of their meetings, Marx took Sadie to the Nezu Shrine. The Nezu Shrine has a tunnel of red torii gates for visitors to pass through. Sadie asked what it meant when you passed under the gates, and Marx said in Shinto tradition, a gate represented passing from the mundane to the sacred. But Marx was not Shinto, so he did not entirely know. "I used to come here when I was a teenager and I had a problem I needed to solve."

"What problems did you ever have?" Sadie said.

"Oh, the usual angst. I didn't feel like anyone understood me. I wasn't Japanese enough, but I wasn't anything else either."

"Poor Marx."

"Don't pass under the gates too quickly," Marx warned. "It works best for me when I go very slowly."

Sadie walked under the gates, one by one by one. At first, she felt nothing, but as she kept moving ahead, she began to feel an opening and a new spaciousness in her chest. She realized what a gate was: it was an indication that you had left one space and were entering another.

She walked through another gate.

It occurred to Sadie: She had thought after *Ichigo* that she would never fail again. She had thought she arrived. But life was always arriving. There was always another gate to pass through. (Until, of course, there wasn't.)

She walked through another gate.

What was a gate anyway?

A doorway, she thought. A portal. The possibility of a different world. The possibility that you might walk through the door and reinvent yourself as something better than you had been before.

By the time she reached the end of the torii gate pathway, she felt resolved. *Both Sides* had failed, but it didn't have to be the end. The game was one in a long line of spaces between gates.

Marx was waiting for her, and he was smiling. He was standing in the center of the path, his arms held slightly open. How nice it was to have Marx waiting for her. He was a perfect traveling companion.

"Thank you," she said. She bowed her head to him.

On the fifth night of their trip, they had dinner with Marx's mother at her apartment. Marx's parents were not divorced, but they lived separately. Marx's mother was a textile designer and teacher. She wore stylish, shapeless, boldly patterned garments and had her hair cut in a severe bob. The dress she was wearing on that evening was a cotton polka-dot print that precisely matched the curtains that were behind her.

Mrs. Watanabe had gotten the wrong idea about who Sadie was. She thought Sadie was Marx's longtime girlfriend, and that Marx and Sadie were on the verge of marriage. "No, Mom, this is Sadie, not Zoe. Sadie is my business partner."

Marx's mother took a long look at Sadie, and then she said, "Are you certain?"

Marx said, "I'm too dumb for Sadie, Mom."

"It's true," Sadie said. "Marx is pretty, but shallow."

Under the table, she squeezed his hand.

But Mrs. Watanabe was relentless. "Do you have a boyfriend, Sadie?"

"I don't," Sadie admitted. "At the moment."

"You should ask Sadie out, Marx. The window of opportunity might close."

"In America," Marx said, "it's frowned upon to date your colleagues, Mom."

"I'm American. I know that," Mrs. Watanabe said. "But Sadie is the boss, right? It's fine if she says it's fine. You two would make a pretty couple."

"Mrs. Watanabe," Sadie pivoted. "Marx says you teach textile design. I'd be interested in hearing about that."

Mrs. Watanabe loved hand painting, quilting, and the discipline of woven textiles, but she worried these techniques were a dying art. "Computers make everything too easy," she said with a sigh. "People design very quickly on a monitor, and they print on some enormous industrial printer in a warehouse in a distant country, and the designer hasn't touched a piece of fabric at any point in the process or gotten her hands dirty with ink. Computers are great for experimentation, but they're bad for deep thinking."

"Mom, you know Sadie and I work in computers, right?"

"A great textile, like the William Morris Strawberry Thief, is a piece of art, but it takes a lot of time to make a piece of art. It isn't simply design either. You have to understand the fabrics and what they can bear. You have to understand the dyeing process and how to achieve certain colors and what will make the color last through the ages. If you make a mistake, you might have to begin again."

"I don't think I know Strawberry Thief," Sadie said.

"One moment," Mrs. Watanabe said. Mrs. Watanabe went into her bedroom, and she returned with a little footstool that was uphol-stered in a reproduction of Strawberry Thief. The pattern depicted birds and strawberries in a garden, and although Sadie hadn't known the name, she recognized the print when she saw it.

"This was William Morris's garden. These were his strawberries. These were birds he knew. No designer had ever used red or yellow in an indigo discharge dyeing technique before. He must have had to start over many times to get the colors right. This fabric is not just a fabric. It's the story of failure and of perseverance, of the discipline of a craftsman, of the life of an artist."

Sadie caressed the thick cotton.

Back at the hotel, early the next morning, Marx knocked on her door. "I have an idea," he said.

She surprised herself by hoping that the idea would be sex. It turned out to be business.

"I had a dream about Strawberry Thief. It was kind of a night-mare," Marx began. In the dream, Marx is back at his mother's apart-ment. His mother tells him to retrieve the stool, but when he gets it, the Strawberry Thief design is rendered in the graphic style of Mapletown. And when he walks out to the living room, his mother is wearing a Strawberry Thief dress rendered in the graphic style of Mapletown, too. And then Marx notices that the whole apartment has been digitized to look like Mapletown. His mother is an adorable

Mapletown sprite. A bubble comes up over her head: *Ask me about my Textiles.* He dismisses the bubble, but another comes up: *Did you know William Morris took one hundred tries to get the dyeing process right for his most famous print textile, Strawberry Thief?*

"Is that true?" Sadie asked. "I don't remember your mother saying that."

"I have no idea," Marx said. "That's what was in the bubble."

Marx continued describing the dream. "I walk into the kitchen to get some air, and I look out the window. Outside the kitchen window is a man-sized thrush, stealing a strawberry. The scene is quite beautiful, and I'm happy watching the bird. The bird and I make eye contact for a moment, and a text bubble comes up over the bird's head: *Go ask Sadie what it would take to turn Mapletown into an online role-playing game.* And here I am. I obey the giant bird of dreams."

Sadie considered Marx's question. She could tell where Marx was going without him having to say. Cut out the cancer that was Myre Landing. Give Mapletown away for free, and monetize its maintenance (servers, new quests and levels) through additional purchases—upgrades for the characters, the furnishings, the residences and expansions. If people liked it, the game could be a cash cow. It could be like *EverQuest,* but without the fantasy story line. It could be like *Harvest Moon,* but less provincial and not centered on farming—just a pleasant small town in America. Let people build their own characters in the gorgeous, evocative backdrop Sam had created. Sadie could see the merit in this strategy. She knew that people preferred Sam's world to hers. Seeing Marx in the doorway, it was clear that he knew it, too. "Nothing. Except a ton of work," Sadie said.

They spent the next several hours brainstorming ideas for a rebooted Mapletown. Around four in the morning, they called Sam back in California. Marx explained to him what they had been discussing.

A long pause, before Sam responded, "I like this idea a lot, but Sadie, you're cool with this?"

"I am," she said. "Myre Landing will still exist to those who bought the original game, but I think this is an opportunity to bring Mapletown to a larger audience. If it doesn't work, all we've lost is a lot of time and money."

Sam laughed. "Let's do this," he said.

They spoke with Sam a little longer, and then they hung up. Once again, it was too early to go down to breakfast. "I'm starving," Sadie said.

He took her to an all-night conbini that was a short walk from their hotel. He bought egg salad, chicken croquette, and strawberry-and-cream sandwiches; inari; two liters of Royal Milk Tea. "These are my favorites," he said. They took the sandwiches up to Marx's hotel room and they spread their convenience-store feast on a towel on the bed.

The sun was rising over Tokyo.

"This is the best egg salad sandwich I've ever had," Sadie said.

"You're easy to please," Marx said. He wiped a smudge of egg salad from the side of her mouth.

On the seventh night of their trip to Tokyo, Marx went to an izakaya with two of his closest high school friends: Midori, who was half-Japanese, and Swan, who was full Japanese but had been born in England. As was their tradition, they consumed profuse amounts of greasy appetizers, yakitori, and warmed sake. The izakaya was a dive; it was the same place they'd frequented in high school, only the guy running it now was the son instead of the father.

Marx asked Sadie if she wanted to come along. Normally, she would have absented herself from such a meeting of old friends, but since they'd come up with the idea to reboot Mapletown, she felt more relaxed and celebratory.

When they arrived at the izakaya, it became clear to Sadie that the friends, like Marx's mother, had the impression that Sadie was Marx's longtime girlfriend, Zoe.

"No," Sadie said. "Sorry. We just work together."

"Darn it," Midori said. "We thought we were finally going to meet the girl who made Marx settle down."

"What was Marx like in high school?" Sadie asked.

"Well, since you're supposedly not his girlfriend, we can tell you," Swan said. "Everyone dated Marx."

"And Marx dated everyone," Midori said, laughing. Sadie recognized the vaudevillian rhythm of an oft-repeated joke.

"If he'd been a girl," Midori said, "everyone would have called him a slut, but he was just a stud."

"He was like that in college, too," Sadie said. "Not news to me. Did either of you ever date him?"

"He took me to a school dance once," Midori said. "He was an excellent date, but it was a friends' thing."

"That's Marx's redeeming feature," Swan said. "He is a great friend, and that's why no one can ever hate him."

"Did you ever date him?" Midori asked Sadie.

"God, no. He was friends with my friend," Sadie said.

"She didn't like me much," Marx said. "She may still not like me."

"How can anyone not like Marx?" Swan said.

"What did he do?" Midori asked.

"It's a long story," Sadie said. "He said we could use his apartment for the summer and then he ended up staying in it."

"Is that why you didn't like me? I think I made up for it in the end," Marx said.

"Well, I didn't know that you'd be producing *Ichigo* until we were at dinner with your dad. Sam never told me."

"Sam," Marx said, shaking his head. Marx held up his tumbler of sake. "To Sam! Kanpai!"

"To Sam! Kanpai!" Sadie, Midori, and Swan repeated.

"Who's Sam?" Midori said, laughing.

They drank several rounds of sake, not enough liquor for Sadie to be drunk, but enough for her to feel pleasantly warm inside.

Midori went outside to have a smoke, and Sadie went with her. "I was so in love with him, you know," Midori said.

Sadie nodded, because she didn't know what to say.

"Never ever ever sleep with Marx. Whatever you do, don't do it," Midori warned. "At some point, he'll look at you with those eyes and that hair, and you'll think he's harmless. He's hot. I should sleep with him."

"I've known him for six years," Sadie said. "I doubt that's going to happen."

Ah, but Sadie Green was a gamer! In a game, if a sign warns you not to open a certain door, you will definitely open that door. If it

233

doesn't work out, you can always go back to the save point and start again.

Sadie and Marx took a cab back to the hotel. They rode the elevator up to their rooms, which were on the twentieth floor. While walking her to her room, Marx said something about twenty being a significant number and that when a person turned twenty (not eighteen, or twenty-one) in Japan, they were considered an adult. "It's called hatachi."

"I was twenty when I met you," Sadie said.

"Indeed."

They were standing outside her door, and he turned to go to his room. "Marx?" she called. "I'm not looking to get into a relationship right now."

"No, me neither," Marx said.

"But I do think it would be a good idea if we slept together," she said. "We're in a different country, and the sex you have when you're away doesn't have to count, in my opinion."

"I'm unfamiliar with that custom." He walked back to her door.

Sadie had often reflected that sex and video games had a great deal in common. There were certain objectives that needed to be met. There were certain rules that shouldn't be broken. There was a correct combination of movements—button mashes, joystick pivots, keystrokes, commands—that made the whole thing work or not work. There was a pleasure to knowing you had played the game correctly and a release that came when you reached the next level. To be good at sex was to be good at the game of sex.

Sadie did not remember much about the first time she had sex with Marx, but she remembered afterward how profoundly comfortable she felt, how easy. His body molded naturally against hers; his scent, barely there, just soap and clean skin; the feeling that there was the right amount of companionable space between them. *I am here with you,* his body seemed to say, *but I acknowledge that we are separate beings.* But in the end, she did not know if these feelings were attributable to Marx himself, or all the sake and yakitori she had consumed, or the crisp white hotel duvet, or the fact that she was 5,500 miles from home.

She closed her eyes for a second, and she imagined herself back under the red gates of Nezu.

A gate and a gate and a gate.

And at the end of all the gates, Marx. Marx, in a white linen shirt and rolled-up khakis and a silly straw fedora that Zoe had bought him at the Rose Bowl Flea Market. He takes off the hat, and he tips it to her.

She turned onto her side to smile at Marx in bed. "I love this city," she said.

"Maybe we could live here someday?" he said.

They flew home the next day, and they said their goodbyes, as working Angelenos do, by the baggage carousel. There is always a point where one despairs of one's luggage ever arriving, but not long after the siren, Marx's bag came. He asked Sadie if she wanted him to wait for her, though this was mainly a formality. Marx's meeting was at a gaming company in the Valley, and Sadie was headed back to Venice, in the opposite direction. After customs and the shuttle to long-term parking, Marx would barely make his meeting in the Valley as it was. Sadie told him to go on ahead. He kissed her on the cheek. *Friends,* he said. *Always,* she said. A half hour later, Sadie's suitcase was the second-to-last one on the conveyor belt. Everyone else was gone except an old Japanese couple, whose powder blue vinyl suitcase marked the actual end.

Sadie dragged her big suitcase through customs. When they asked her if she had anything to declare, she repeated the things she had listed on her customs form: a silk scarf for Freda, a necklace for Alice, packaged sweets for her parents. She always felt as if the customs agents were trying to catch her in a lie.

"What kind of work are you in?" the customs agent asked her.

"I make video games," she said.

"I love video games," the customs agent said. "Would I have played anything you made?"

"Ichigo," Sadie said.

"Nope, haven't heard of it. I mainly like racing games. Like *Need for Speed.* And *Grand Theft Auto.* Even *Mario Kart.* How do you get into making video games anyway?"

Sadie hated answering this question, especially after a person had told her that he hadn't heard of *Ichigo.* "Well, I learned to program computers in middle school. I got an eight hundred on my math SAT, won a Westinghouse and a Leipzig. And then I went to MIT, which by the way is highly competitive, even for a lowly female like myself, and studied computer science. At MIT, I learned four or five more programming languages and studied psychology, with an emphasis on ludic techniques and persuasive designs, and English, including narrative structures, the classics, and the history of interactive storytelling. Got myself a great mentor. Regrettably made him my boyfriend. Suffice it to say, I was young. And then I dropped out of school for a time to make a game because my best frenemy wanted me to. That game became the game you never heard of, but yeah, it sold around two and a half million copies, just in the U.S., soooo . . ." Instead, she said, "I liked to play games a lot, so I thought I'd see if I could make them."

"Well, good luck to you," the customs agent said.

"Thanks," she said. "Good luck to you, too."

Sadie dragged her suitcase out to the cab line, and was about to get in it, when she saw Marx.

"What are you still doing here?" she asked.

"Well, it's a funny story," he said. "I got all the way out to my car in long-term, and I was about to drive away, when I decided to turn around and drive back. I'm in short-term now."

"So, why are you here again?"

He reached for the handle of her large suitcase, and he started rolling it toward the parking lot. "I thought maybe you'd need a ride home."

3

"Sadie! Marx! Get in here! We're ten minutes away!" Sam called.

Marx came into the newly appointed Mapleworld server room, carrying a tray of champagne flutes.

"Where's Sadie?" Sam asked.

"She's around somewhere," Marx said. "I'll try her cell phone." He hadn't been sure if champagne would set the right tone, but in the end, he thought, screw it. Everyone had worked their asses off to get Mapleworld online. They were entitled to celebrate, no matter what the mood of the world in general was.

Unfair called the reboot of *Both Sides: The Mapleworld Experience,* or *Mapleworld* for short. Although they had been able to employ many of the graphics, environments, sounds, and character designs of Mapletown, the work to transform it into an MMORPG had been more extensive than Sadie had thought. Sadie's metaphor was that it was like buying a house you liked in a bidding war, and then moving that house to a different country by boat, and then once you got the house to the other country, deciding that you liked the materials the house was made from but not, in fact, the house itself, and then building an entirely new house after painstakingly disassembling the old house piece by piece.

The team had worked through the spring and summer to prepare it for online play—everything from creating currency systems to figure out how the game would be monetized in the real world, to setting up its dedicated servers, to renting more office space to accommodate the additional staff. The additional staff (ten people to start, more if the game took off) would be engaged in programming new side quests, levels, and challenges; moderating the game world; and keeping it all going 24/7. Internet ads ran that looked like Alice's hand-lettered wedding invitations: "Attention: poets, dreamers, worldbuilders! On Midnight, October 11th, 2001, Unfair Games cordially invites you to The Mapleworld Experience." A newly hired outreach manager had contacted each Mapletownie individually to make sure they were the first members of the *Mapleworld* community, and a letterpress paper version of the invitation had been created to send to the Mapletownies' houses. All that was left to do was flip the switch.

Exactly one month before the launch, terrorists had flown planes into skyscrapers and other buildings, and in the wake of that, Unfair had debated whether it was the right time to launch *Mapleworld*. Whether it felt in bad taste, and whether people would even want to play a game like *Mapleworld* at this moment in history. The world seemed so chaotic, people so tribal, and their game was so soft. In the end, they decided that there was never a good time to do anything. *Mapleworld* would launch as planned.

Sadie came into the server room with a case of champagne. After she set the bottles on the table, she joined Marx and Sam and the rest of the *Mapleworld* team, who were huddled around the pristine servers.

The IT guy whispered in Sam's ear, "Mazer, we need to power up the network before midnight, if we want it to be running *by* midnight, and not *five after* midnight."

"Good point. Five minutes, everybody!" Sam announced.

"Dammit," Sadie said, "I forgot the corkscrew." She ran back up the stairs.

"Sadie!" Marx called after her, a beat later, "Champagne doesn't need a corkscrew!"

But Sadie hadn't heard him. Marx went up the stairs to retrieve Sadie as Simon and Ant were descending. Sam shook their hands. "Guys, really nice of you to come."

"We wouldn't miss it," Simon said.

"*Mapleworld* looks amazing," Ant said. "Sadie was showing us some of it yesterday. We're both going to join, and reach out to the *CPH* community to join, too."

"We definitely need to go now," the IT guy said to Sam. "We can't wait, if it's important to you to be on time."

Sam knew so many horror stories about games being dead on arrival because they weren't online when they said they were going to be. *Mapleworld* was his world, and it would be punctual.

"You wanna do the honors?" the IT guy asked.

Sam reached over and flipped the switch. "I feel like God," he joked. "Let there be light!"

The group of tired programmers cheered. Sam thanked everyone for their efforts, and Ant opened the champagne bottles. This was when Sam noticed that Sadie and Marx hadn't returned.

Sam thought that things had been good between him and Sadie during the months they'd worked on *Mapleworld*. Not exactly like old times, but not actively hostile either. Still, he felt irritated at Marx and Sadie for having missed the turning on of the server, even if the whole thing had been ceremonial.

As the *Mapleworld* support staff quietly retreated to their desks to attend to the business of moderating the newborn game, Sam headed toward the stairway. He could see Sadie and Marx at the top of the stairs. Sadie appeared to be removing a runaway eyelash from his cheek; Marx was looking at her and laughing. Sadie's gesture was not especially intimate. Sam had not caught them making love, or kissing, or with their clothes in disarray. And yet, there was a tenderness to Sadie's gesture that almost made Sam have to sit down, right where he was, at the base of the stairs. He could feel the distant throb of his foot, which he had not felt for over a year.

Sadie and Marx were in love.

She had said that Sam didn't *know* her, but he knew her well enough to know what her face looked like when she was in love. Her eyes were softer and her expression was less arch and self-conscious; her hand, entitled, as if she owned Marx's cheek; her posture, slightly canted toward him, relaxed and pliable; her cheeks flushed. She was pretty all the time, but she was beautiful in love. He knew her well enough to know: it must have been going on for some time.

"Samson," Marx called down the stairs to him, "did we miss it?" He was all good spirits. They both were.

"Champagne doesn't need a corkscrew," Sadie said, laughing.

Sam could confront them now or wait to be informed later. But why did he need to be told? To have confirmed what he could plainly see? If it hadn't been serious, they would have already told him. "I'm thinking about asking Sadie out," Marx would have said. "What do you think?" Or Sadie might have said, "Funny thing. I'm seeing Marx. Don't know what will happen." The omission let him know it was fatally serious.

Sadie and Marx's whole future was revealed to him. Sadie would probably marry Marx, and the wedding would be in Northern California, Carmel-by-the-Sea or Monterey. And at the wedding, Sadie's grandmother would shoot sympathetic looks at Sam, because she had always been nice to him, and she would know he was brokenhearted. Freda would grab his hand with her soft, old hand, and pat it gently, and say, "Life is long" or some other unhelpful, old-lady wisdom. Sadie and Marx would buy a house together, somewhere in Laurel Canyon or maybe Palisades. And they'd get a dog—a big, rangy, mixed-breed thing, or if not that, a Borzoi called Zelda or Rosella. They'd throw big dinner parties. The house would be the kind of place where everyone wanted to congregate because Sadie and Marx had great taste. They were both great. And at some point, there would be children, and Sam would become sad bachelor uncle Sam, expected to give presents for birthdays and holidays. And every day, he'd have to see Marx and Sadie at work. He would watch them arrive together, and leave together, and he could imagine the drive, and the jokes, and the references that you only had with the person you shared your life with. And eventually, Sadie would be a stranger. And this would be a disaster for Sam. A tragedy. He would know that if he hadn't been the person he was, terrified and cowardly and petty and insecure and sexually panicked and broken, Sadie might have been his. It wouldn't have even been a question. He would have leaned across a desk and kissed her, and she would have led him to a soft surface somewhere, and they would have made love. Maybe the sex wouldn't have been exceptional, but it wouldn't have mattered. Because the other things they had were finer than sex. Because he loved Sadie. It was one of only a handful of things that he knew to be a constant about himself. The greatest pleasures of his life had been when he was by her side, playing or inventing. And how could she not feel that as well? There would never be another Sadie, and now this one was lost to him. It wasn't her fault.

He had had years to figure out the solution, but he'd wasted his time making games with her instead. He had had years to contemplate the puzzle of himself. And now the old puzzle would be replaced with a new puzzle: *How do I go on when the person I love most in the world is in love with someone else? Someone tell me the solution,* he thought, *so I don't have to play this losing game all the way through.*

"You didn't miss anything," Sam said. He smiled, but he could not bring himself to look at either of them.

He walked up the stairs and past them.

"Where are you going?" Marx asked.

"I'll be back down in a minute," Sam said.

At first, he thought he'd go to his office to clear his head, but then he decided that wasn't sufficient separation from Sadie. He decided to take a drive. Once he got in his car, he found himself heading east, back home to his grandparents and his dog, Tuesday, a stray he'd taken in the prior summer.

The drive from Unfair to Echo Park took about forty minutes, if traffic was good, which it rarely was. The first time he attempted it in the opposite direction, he had a panic attack where he could not feel the brake under his prosthetic. He had to get off the freeway and pull over to the side of the road. He pumped the brake overly hard, slamming his stump into the prosthetic and badly bruising his leg. He drove the rest of the way to Unfair on surface roads, and he was a half hour late to his first day back, and after that first day, he did not return for another month.

He went to see another therapist to help with his driving anxiety. Sam hated therapy, but he needed to get places, and so, therapy it was. The easiest way to conquer a driving phobia, the therapist said, was to drive. Sam began to drive around Los Angeles at night, after work, and when he drove, he thought of his mother.

He remembered what she had said about there being secret highways that went from east to west and north to south, and he started to look for them. He had nothing else to do, and if he found one, he could spend less time commuting. He blasted classic rock that reminded him of Anna—the Rolling Stones, the Beatles, Bowie, Dylan—and he wound his way through Los Angeles and its hills, looking for dead ends that might somehow turn into secret roads.

On one of his drives, a coyote darted out in front of his car. This was Sam's second first summer in L.A., and the coyotes were every-where. He would see them in the front yard, sunning themselves, lan-guorously eating fallen fruit from the cherimoya and loquat trees. He would see them loping down the streets of Silver Lake and Echo Park, sometimes in couples or in families, sorting through the trash outside the vegan place on Sunset, hiking stoically in Griffith Park, nursing their young. The coyotes felt capable, canny, and strangely anthropo-morphized, as if they had been endowed with human features by a team of animators. Their hair seemed artfully disheveled, the haircut of a hot, young actor playing a drug addict in an independent film. The coyotes felt more human than most of the humans Sam encountered, more human than Sam himself felt back then. Their constant presence made the city feel wild and dangerous, as if he weren't living in a city at all.

Sam slammed on his brakes, and the coyote paused, but did not move. Sam opened the window. "Get!" he called. When the coyote still did not move, Sam got out of the car. The coyote was not a coyote. Or, maybe it was a coyote. Sam still didn't know what the difference was. In any case, it was young, not much older than a puppy. It had the shaggy look of a coyote, but the muscular build of a pit bull. Its back leg was bleeding, and Sam worried he might have grazed it with the car. The coyote/dog looked scared. "If I pick you up," Sam said gently, "will you bite me?"

The coyote/dog looked at him blankly, terrified. It was shivering. Sam took off his plaid shirt, and he scooped the little dog into his arms, and he put it into the back seat of his car. They drove to an emergency veterinary clinic.

The dog had broken its leg. She needed stitches and would have to be in a cast for a couple of weeks, but she was strong, and she would recover.

When Sam asked the vet whether the dog might be a coyote, she rolled her eyes. She was just a dog, a mutt yes, but likely some combi-nation of German shepherd, Shiba Inu, and greyhound. You could tell by the elbows, she said. Coyote elbows were higher than dog elbows. She brought up a graphic on her computer: a coyote, next to a wolf, next to a domesticated dog. *See,* she said, *isn't it obvious?* It did not seem obvious to Sam. Nothing seemed obvious to Sam. *Yes, it's obvi-ous,* Sam said.

Sam paid the vet, and then he took the hurt little dog home with him.

He posted flyers with her photograph around the area in the eastern Hollywood hills where he had hit her, but he was glad when no one responded. He decided he liked having a dog. She distracted him from the discomfort he was in. Having never lived alone before, Sam was lonely, but contradictorily, his pain made him not want to be with people. He named the dog Ruby Tuesday, after the song that had been playing in his car when he'd hit her. He ended up calling her Tuesday.

After Tuesday had recovered from the broken leg, she could not sleep. Sam also had insomnia, so he couldn't tell if she was just keeping him company. She paced his one-bedroom bungalow, looking haunted, occasionally baying. He took her to the vet again. The vet gave them a prescription for dog Prozac and suggested that they take even longer walks. That was what they did. They moved past the familiar landscape of their block and traveled uphill, into the winding, sidewalk-less hills of eastern Silver Lake. Sometimes, they would pass a coyote. The coyotes always seemed collegial with Tuesday, though Sam didn't know if that was his imagination.

Tuesday was often mistaken for a coyote. When they were out on walks, people would regularly stop their cars to ask him why he was walking a coyote. He would inform them that she wasn't a coyote, merely a dog. Sometimes, they would laugh at them; sometimes, they would argue. Sometimes, they would insist on knowing what she was, as if they might trick Sam into admitting that he had lied and Tuesday was a coyote. Sometimes, they would seem angry, as if Tuesday and Sam were deliberately trying to make fools of them. For her part, Tuesday seemed unaware that she was the cause of so much controversy. "People," Sam would say to Tuesday, shaking his head. In her silence, Sam sensed agreement.

They walked uphill and then downhill, until they were spit out at Silver Lake Boulevard, with its small strip of upscale stores and cafés. They would then head north around the reservoir, stopping when they reached the dog park.

On one occasion, Tuesday was socializing with an Akita and a standard poodle. The three of them took turns chasing each other, an interaction both complicated and dazzling.

The Akita was sniffing Tuesday's ass when a woman's voice called out, "There's a coyote attacking other dogs in the dog park! Everyone! Get your dogs! NOW!"

There were twenty-five or thirty dogs in the dog park that day. Sam didn't immediately see the coyote, but that didn't mean it wasn't there. Sam called Tuesday and leashed her. It had been her turn to reciprocally sniff the Akita's ass, so she was reluctant to come. When they reached the entrance to the dog park, the woman who had warned of the coyote incursion looked from Tuesday to Sam. She laughed loudly and self-consciously then said, "Oh my God, is that *actually* your dog?"

Her laughter was irritating to him, as was her use of the word "actually." "Yes," he said.

"I honestly thought it was a coyote." On the woman's leash was a small, grayish, yapping thing, possibly a bichon. "I thought it was *attacking* those dogs."

Sam told her *it* was a she, and *she* had been playing.

"Well, from where I was, it looked different. It looked like a vicious attack." She petted Tuesday on the head. "Good girl," she said, as if she were offering Tuesday a benediction. "What even is the difference between a coyote and a dog?"

Sam stammered something about elbows.

"Well, these days, you can't be too careful." She said that her dog had been attacked by a coyote the week before. She described yelps, coyote saliva, a desperately hurled yoga block. Sam made noises of assent. "I need to go," he said.

"Oh sure. Sorry about the confusion."

It was annoying that she attributed her mistake to a collective confusion, but Sam wasn't going to pick a fight in the dog park. The woman looked at him, waiting for Sam to say that he was sorry, too, but he couldn't bring himself to do it. She continued, "But if you don't know what something is, it's better to be safe. It's better to have information, right? She could be, like, half-coyote, right?"

His heart pounded murderously. He hadn't slept much that week on account of Tuesday's insomnia and the pain he was in, and he felt a disproportionate rage come over him, the facade of civilization beginning to crumble. "Maybe you should look more goddamn closely at a thing before deciding what it is and running off your mouth."

"Hey, screw you, man! I was trying to prevent people and dogs and children from getting hurt! You shouldn't bring a dog that looks like a coyote to the park, asshole!"

"You're the asshole. You're an ignorant asshole," he said. He gave the woman the finger. Tuesday and Sam headed back home. Sam felt defeated and an inane comeback kept echoing through his head: Would you have her wear an I AM NOT A COYOTE sign around her neck? Would that make things easier for you? But that would have required her to read the sign, and the woman had not seemed like a reader. Los Angeles, he decided, was a profoundly stupid city, and he felt a palpable, if irrational, longing for all things Massachusetts.

He walked back to his house, and he realized two things: Throughout the encounter, he hadn't felt any pain. And the woman who'd yelled at him must not have noticed or known he was disabled, and that had not happened to him in years. He decided he was ready to go back to work.

When Sam told this story to Sadie, she laughed, though she barely seemed to be listening. He had framed the story in a humorous way, smoothed off some of the edges of his hostility toward the woman in the park. But as he told it, he could feel himself back in that dog park. He could feel the dry California heat and the murderous pounding of his heart. Without warning, an anecdote he had meant to be amusing did not feel amusing. Anyone who had truly looked at Tuesday could not have possibly seen a coyote. But the woman had not truly looked, and the injustice of this hit him. Why was it acceptable for apparently well-meaning people to see the world in such a general way?

Sam was put off by Sadie's laughter. He asked her what was funny. She was confused for a moment—hadn't he wanted her to laugh?—and then she said, annoyed, "You get that this is a story about you, right? That's why you lost your mind at a dog park. You're Tuesday. You're the incredibly special dog that no one can classify." It was not long after their huge argument, and things were quite strained between them.

Sam told her that she was being reductive, and that her interpretation was insulting to both him and the dog. "It's a story about Tuesday," he insisted. "Maybe it's a story about L.A., too. Maybe it's a story about the kind of people that go to the dog park in Silver Lake. But it's mainly a story about Tuesday."

"The text," she said, "perhaps."

When he knew he would be out late, Sam left Tuesday with his grand-parents. It was after 1 a.m. when he got to their house, but Sam knew Dong Hyun would just be getting home from the pizza place anyway. He let himself into their house, and Tuesday greeted him, soft and warm, and then Dong Hyun trailed behind her, still smelling of garlic, peppery red sauce, olive oil, and dough.

"I thought you'd be out all night," Dong Hyun said.

"It's over," Sam said. "Nothing for me to do now. They'll call me if they need me."

"Are you okay?" Dong Hyun asked.

"I've been better."

"Do you want to talk about it?" Dong Hyun's kind, old face look-ing at him was almost more than he could bear.

"No." Sam picked up Tuesday and put her on his lap. He realized he was crying when the dog started licking the salt off his face.

"What is it?" Dong Hyun asked.

"I love Sadie Green," Sam said helplessly. He felt childish saying this, but there it was.

"I know," Dong Hyun said. "She loves you, too."

"No, she loves someone else."

"Maybe it won't last."

"It's Marx. And I think it's pretty serious, and I don't know what to do. Sadie and I had a fight about a year ago, but I always thought it would come around eventually."

Dong Hyun put his strong, dough-throwing arms around Sam. "You'll find someone else to love."

"Please don't say there are a lot of fish in the sea."

"I wasn't planning on it, but now that you mention it, there are. What about Lola?"

"She's nice, but she's no Sadie. I don't feel like anyone in the world knows me except Sadie."

"Maybe you need to let more people know you."

"Maybe."

"Sam, when your grandmother and I first opened the restaurant, did you know it was a Korean place?"

Sam shook his head.

"But there were too many Korean places in K-town, so we had to come up with something else. And that's why we decided to make pizza. There weren't any other pizza places in that part of K-town. It was scary, at first, because we didn't know anything about pizza, but then we set ourselves to learning about pizza. We didn't have any choice. We had two babies and bills to pay.

"Your cousin Albert told me that, in business, they call this a pivot. But life is filled with them, too. The most successful people are also the most able to change their mindsets. You may not ever have a romantic relationship with Sadie, but you two will be friends for the rest of your lives, and that is something of equal or greater value, if you choose to see it that way."

"I am familiar with the concept of the pivot," Sam said, "though I don't think it technically applies here." He laughed gently; Dong Hyun was often regaling Sam with Albert's business school curriculum.

But the unapt metaphor made him feel a little better, nonetheless. Sam could see that Marx had left him a message on his phone—he was needed, the *Mapleworld* team had questions. Sam kissed Dong Hyun on the cheek, and he and Tuesday got in the car to drive back to Abbot Kinney.

They were about a tenth of a mile from the freeway entrance on Rampart when Sam spotted a curious turnoff, near Filipinotown. It was the peculiar 2:30 a.m. light that enabled him to spot it—a broad, flat, dirt road, partially concealed by a flowerless jacaranda tree. As he drove closer, he noted that the road did not have a named street sign, but a dark green hexagon whose lone markings were a group of three dots in a triangle shape:

$$\therefore$$

In a mathematical proof, this mark indicated "therefore," but Sam didn't know what it meant on a road sign. He'd never seen a sign like it before. He stopped the car, so he could look down the road. There was no definitive vanishing point. The road seemingly led to nowhere. Alternatively, the road could lead to somewhere. He could end up dead, or he could end up in Beverly Hills. (Though it was rarely so binary, was it? Most of the time, when Sam pursued an unnamed road, it was a U-turn, and then back to where he'd started from.) "Should we try it?" Sam asked Tuesday. The little dog snored in the back seat and offered no opinion. Sam flipped on his turn signal.

VI

MARRIAGES

1

Sam's avatar, Mayor Mazer, was the first person who greeted a new visitor to Mapletown. He was styled like a grunge-era rock star—ripped blue jeans, a red plaid shirt, Doc Martens—and meant to evoke plainspoken, folksy icons like Jiminy Cricket, Andy Griffith, Woody Guthrie. Sam didn't use a cane anymore, but he gave Mayor Mazer a cane—a gnarled wooden staff—and Mayor Mazer had also been programmed to have Sam's slight limp. The Samatar had Sam's glasses (thick, black frames) and mustache (chevron shaped). No one remembered whether Mayor Mazer or Sam had grown the mustache first.

"Welcome, friend, I'm Mayor Mazer," the Samatar introduced himself. "You must be new here. We've got our problems like everywhere else, but Mapletown's a fine little burg, once you get to know it. I've lived here my whole life, I should know. Moving is hard. Here's five thousand Maplebucks to get you started. My advice to you would be to walk around. The foliage in the Magical Valley is beautiful this time of year. And our shopping district is small for now, but you'll find most anything you need there. I'm fond of our artisanal cheeses. Greet a couple of your new neighbors while you're moseying about. It's truffle season, so keep your eyes out. The super-rare rainbow truffle fetches a high price if you can manage to get your hands on one. Everyone's real friendly here. If you run into any problems, come back and see me. You can always find me at Mapletown City Hall."

By 2009, Mayor Mazer ranked number seven (in between the Serta Counting Sheep and the Coca-Cola polar bears) on an *AdWeek* list of most recognizable branded characters of the new millennium. The description of Mayor Mazer read: "We debated about whether to add Mayor Mazer to this list. A cross between game character and branded character, the little hipster mayor of the little hipster town (Portland? Silver Lake? Park Slope? Where the hell *is* Mapletown anyway?) ultimately makes the list because he's been on about a million Etsy products, and isn't he the mayor everyone wishes they had? Guns are verboten; socialism rules; gameplay rewards conservation (try chopping down too many maple trees without replanting); same-sex marriage was legal in M-town way before it was in the U.S. Mapletown is probably the first MMORPG your mom played, and that's thanks in large part to the branding of Mayor Mazer. He's friendly, he's hip, he knows the best places to buy pottery in Mapletown and how to get that fiddle leaf fig tree to grow in your living room. Sure, he's mining your data like everyone else, but he's one of the good guys, right? Love him or hate him, there are very few characters or brands that have become more associated with a utopian vision of Americans online than Mayor Mazer."

But this would come later.

Two months after its launch, more than a quarter of a million people had set up accounts at *Mapleworld*, and the servers routinely overloaded. When the site crashed, a screen with the Samatar would come up: *Looks like the weather's bad in Mapletown. Grab your umbrellas, and we'll be back real soon.* It wasn't long before fan-generated "When Mayor Mazer tells you the weather's bad in Mapletown . . ." graphics spread across the internet as a meme for expressing tedium and frustration.

Sam, Sadie, and Marx had debated whether it was the right time for a game as "soft" as *Mapleworld*. As it turned out, in the late fall of 2001, *Mapleworld* was exactly what people craved. A virtual world that was better governed, kinder, and more understandable than their own.

On or about the tenth anniversary of *Mapleworld*'s launch, Sam gave a TED Talk titled "The Possibility of Utopia in Virtual Worlds." "Despite everything that transpired at Unfair Games on December 4th, 2005, and despite evidence to the contrary, it is not an inevitability that we should be our worst selves behind the mask of an avatar. What I believe to my very core," he concluded, "is that virtual worlds can be better than the actual world. They can be more moral, more just, more progressive, more empathetic, and more accommodating of difference. And if they can be, shouldn't they be?"

2

Not long after New Year's 2002, Dov called Sadie with two pieces of news: (1) he was, at long last, getting divorced, and (2) he was getting married in Tiburon to a former student, a young woman a few classes behind Sadie at MIT.

"I don't know if you'll want to come, but I'm inviting you, Sammy, and Marx to the wedding," Dov said. "I didn't want you to get the invitation without us having spoken. It would mean a lot to me if you were there."

On the approximately nine-hour road trip to Tiburon, Sam, Sadie, and Marx took turns driving. The mood was celebratory, relaxed: *Mapleworld* was a success, and Sadie and Marx were in love, though they were still keeping this a secret from Sam.

"Were you mad when he told you he was getting divorced?" Sam asked.

"Mad?" Sadie said. "I was terrified he was going to ask me to get back with him."

"He's such an asshole," Marx said. From the back seat, he reached over the front seat to squeeze Sadie's hand.

"Hey," Sam said. "You guys are seeing each other, right?" This was said casually, as if Sam was barely interested in the answer: *Hey, should we stop for food?* Or *Hey, you mind if I turn on the radio?* He was the one driving the car at the time, and they were about halfway to Tiburon, on the high elevation of the Pacific Coast Highway, five miles south of San Simeon.

Marx and Sadie had been discreet at the office, and they had had no reason to believe that Sam knew. For several months, Sadie had wanted to tell Sam, but it had been Marx who had resisted. "He'll take it harder than you think," Marx had said.

"I don't think he'll take it that badly. Sam and I have never dated or been lovers or any of that. And these days, I would describe us as colleagues, more than friends. You're better friends with him than I am," Sadie said. "Trust me, the lying is worse."

"We're not lying. We just haven't told him yet," Marx said.

"So, let's tell him."

"Maybe we should pull a Dov. Let's send him an invitation to the wedding," Marx said.

"Dov did actually tell me first," Sadie said, smiling. "And you and I aren't getting married."

"Why not?"

"Maybe I don't believe in marriage," Sadie said.

"There's no *believe*, Sadie. It's not like God, Santa Claus, or whether Lee Harvey Oswald acted alone. It's a civic ceremony, with a piece of paper. It's a party, with your friends—"

"Our friends who you refuse to tell."

"Only Sam."

"And everyone who knows Sam. And that's almost everyone we know. You'd rather marry me than have to tell Sam? Am I understanding you correctly?"

"I don't see the issues as entirely related," Marx said.

The conversation was a roundelay of inaction that they dutifully repeated every couple of months. Sadie found the whole thing out of character for Marx—as a person, he was remarkably transparent. He was honest. He loved the things he loved, and he made no secret of what those things were. And in the end, she attributed Marx's inertia to a touching, if naive, devotion to Sam. She, too, used to feel such devotion, before she'd seen Sam for who he really was.

By the time of Dov's wedding, they had been together almost an entire year. Marx still had the bungalow he'd shared with Zoe, but he had effectively moved into Clownerina. Sadie and Marx were even thinking of buying a house together.

"It's fine, if you're seeing each other," Sam said. "I'm not going to lose my mind if that's what you both are worried about. I'm not going to drive this car off the highway into the Pacific." He swerved the car a little, as a joke. "But I would like to know. I mean, it's obvious. I know you both, so it's obvious. And it's honestly rather insulting that you haven't told me."

"We are seeing each other," Sadie said.

"I love her," Marx added. "I love you," he said to Sadie.

"I love you, too," Sadie said.

Sam nodded. "Good. That's what I thought. Mazel. Do you guys want to go see the Hearst Castle? We're about to pass it and I've never been."

Sam was quiet on the tour of La Cuesta Encantada, the most quixotic, stately pleasure dome in California, land of the quixotic, stately pleasure domes. Sadie had trained herself not to cater to Sam's moods, not to feel too much for him, but nonetheless, she could sense his agitation.

When the tour was over, Sadie told Marx that she wanted to speak to Sam alone, so they went out to a half-moon-shaped patio that faced the Pacific. It was two o'clock and the sun, reflecting against the water, was blinding. Even with sunglasses on, it was difficult for Sadie to see Sam.

"I thought this place was so beautiful when I was nine, but now it seems ridiculous," Sadie said, mainly to fill the silence.

"Why? Hearst had the money, so he built himself exactly the world he wanted. There were zebras and swimming pools and bougainvillea and picnics, and no one ever died. How is it different than what we do?"

"Are you okay?" she asked.

"Why wouldn't I be?" Sam said.

"I don't know," she said.

"I might have loved you once," Sam said. "And I'll always care for you in my way, but we wouldn't *work* together. I've known that for years."

"Yes," she agreed.

"If you and I were going to be a couple, one of us would have done something about it by now, don't you think?"

"Yes."

"It's strange when your two closest colleagues keep a secret like that, though," Sam said. "It's arrogant of you both to assume I would care so much."

"I think," Sadie said, "Marx was scared that you would take it badly. And we didn't know if it was serious at first, so we didn't want to upset you if it wasn't serious."

"But now you know it's *serious*?"

"The way you say 'serious,' it sounds like a disease."

"'Serious' was your word."

"Your tone, then."

"But now you know it's serious?" Sam repeated.

"Yes, now we know."

Sadie studied Sam. The sun had changed angles in the time they'd been standing there, and she could see him again. He was twenty-seven and he had a mustache, but whenever she allowed herself to think of him as the kid from the hospital, her heart could not help but soften for him. It was easy to dislike the man; it was harder to dislike the little boy who existed just below the surface of the man. Though his voice was cool and disinterested as they spoke, his brow was lightly furrowed. His mouth was set in a determined way, as if he had been asked to take a bitter medicine but was determined not to complain. His expression reminded her of a time when he'd recently had surgery, and he hadn't realized that she had come into his hospital room yet. He was clearly in a lot of pain—his eyes were unblinking, and his jaw was slack, and he was panting softly, and he looked feral. For a second, she didn't recognize her friend. The face she knew, the face she thought of as Sam, was nowhere. And then he saw her, and he smiled, and he was Sam again, as if he had put on a mask. "You're here!" he had said.

"I must say," Sam said, "I'm not surprised that he would be into you. He's always had a thing for you. He asked me about it that first summer we were making *Ichigo*. I told him that you would never be into someone like him. So maybe, if anything, I'm surprised that I was wrong."

"Why wouldn't I be into him?" She knew she shouldn't ask this question.

"Because he's boring." Sam shrugged, as if Marx's banality was an indisputable fact. "That's why he's always dating someone new. He gets bored with people, but it's not about them, it's because *he's* boring."

"You're an incredible asshole," Sadie said. "Marx loves you. Can't you ever just be nice?"

"It's not cruel to state a fact."

"It isn't a fact. And sometimes, it is cruel to state a fact."

"When we took Heroes for Zeroes at Harvard, you know what his favorite part of *The Iliad* was?"

"It's not something we've ever discussed," Sadie said, trying to contain her rising irritation.

"The end, which is incredibly boring. 'Thus *blah blah blah* they buried Hector *blah blah blah* the tamer of horses *blah blah blah*.' Hector is boring. He's not Achilles. Marx is boring like Hector, so he ate that shit up."

Marx came onto the patio. "What's everyone talking about?"

"The end of *The Iliad*."

"That's the best part," Marx said.

"Why is it the best part?" Sadie asked.

"Because it's perfect," Marx said. "'Tamer of horses' is an honest profession. The lines mean that one doesn't have to be a god or a king for your life to have meaning."

"Hector is us," Sadie said.

"Hector is us," Marx repeated.

"Hector is *Marx*," Sam said. "Boring," he coughed. "We should put 'Tamer of Horses' on Marx's business cards."

They decided to stay the night near San Simeon and drive the rest of the way in the morning. They checked into the first hotel they came across, which was old and un-air-conditioned. The night was uncommonly balmy for the central California coast, and the rooms were airless and stale, even with the windows open.

In the morning, when Sam came down to the car, he had shaved his black curly hair down to a buzz cut. "What happened?" Marx asked. He petted Sam's shorn head.

"I got hot," Sam said.

"It looks good," Marx said. "Right?"

Sadie knew there was probably some message in this for her, but she couldn't be bothered to decipher it. It made her feel egomaniacal and ungenerous to think this way, but wasn't there always some game Sam was playing? Wasn't there always some maze for her to solve? He was an exhausting person. "Sure," she said. "We should get on the road."

"It wasn't an aesthetic choice," Sam said. He seemed almost embarrassed. "I honestly was hot."

"Yes," Sadie said. "Our room was hot as well, though we both woke up with the hair we started with."

Sadie felt that everything Sam did was an aesthetic choice. Not long after they'd moved to California, he had had his name legally changed from Samson Masur to Sam Mazer. The explanation he gave her: the name Masur had never meant much to him, and Mazer sounded more like the name of a Master Builder of Worlds. In the last year, he had begun asking them to refer to him just by Mazer, like he was Madonna or Prince. "You can still call me Sam in private," Sam had said to Sadie, "but in public, I'd prefer to go by Mazer. That's my name now."

Mazer had extensively promoted the *Mapleworld* launch. He loved being a showman; he loved declaiming to an audience of rapt fans about the state of games. And, as he was no longer in chronic pain, he was much better at doing these things than when he'd promoted *Ichigo*. But, as the promotional schedule had stretched on, Sam had started shifting his appearance away from Mayor Mazer's. He took to wearing denim coveralls with a name pocket patch embroidered MAZER and a white undershirt underneath. He often wore an army green Breton hat. For years he'd tried to conceal his disability; now he was never photographed without a cane. The cane was used for pointing at things, clearing crowds, grand gestures as needed. He had recently gotten braces and had started wearing contact lenses. For the first time in his life, he was working out with weights, and he became thick with muscle, like a wrestler. He got a tattoo on his right upper arm: umma (in hangul; Korean for *mom*), accompanied by the round yellow head and pink bow of Ms. Pac-Man. The Mazer character that Sam fashioned would become almost as iconic to gamers as Mayor Mazer, his avatar, was. But Mazer, circa 2002, looked nothing like Sam, circa 1997.

And now his hair was gone, too. Sadie was driving, Marx was sleeping in the passenger seat, and Sam was in the back seat. For a second, she looked in the rearview mirror at Sam. The first time she had met him, she had imagined the circles it would take to draw his glasses, his face, his hair. She had to admit it; she would miss the circles of his hair. He caught her eye for a moment, and then he looked away. A second later, he put on his Breton cap.

Once Sadie and Marx's personal relationship was out in the open, Sadie and Sam's working relationship further deteriorated. Perhaps this was to be expected. The conflicts were the same as they'd always been, but they became less civil with each other.

Sadie had little interest in working on or promoting *Mapleworld*. She had absolutely no interest in being the "face" of Unfair, and she was happy to cede those duties to Sam. What she wanted to do was get back to work on a new game, something that would put *Both Sides*, *Mapleworld*, and *Ichigo* solidly in their rearview mirror.

For his part, Sam enjoyed the process of building out *Mapleworld*, and he wanted to work on another *Ichigo*. "We've got so many eyes on us right now, Sadie. Imagine what we could do with the resources we have. It's the perfect time to do a new *Ichigo*."

"I don't want to be making *Ichigo* until I'm forty, Sam. I'm not like you. I don't get off on doing the same things over and over again."

"Why do you always want to cast off our successes? Why does something have to be *new* for it to interest you? It's almost pathological."

"Why are you so afraid to do anything else but the things we've already done?"

And so it went.

The game Sadie wanted to make was *Master of the Revels. Master of the Revels* was a simulation set in the theater world of Elizabethan London, centering on solving the murder of Christopher Marlowe. Sadie had been inspired by a comment Marx had made about how there weren't ever any good games about theater.

From the moment Sadie described it, Sam detested *Master of the Revels*. He felt it was pretentious and not likely to be embraced by a mass audience.

Still, Sadie kept insisting that *Master of the Revels* should be their next game.

"You can't be serious, Sadie. People hate Shakespeare. People hate history. And the world you're proposing is so dark. What are you even trying to prove?"

"I don't want to make bubble gum like *Mapleworld* forever."

"*Mapleworld* is not bubble gum. But it's like you took the experiences we had on *Both Sides*, and you want to repeat the worst parts of it," Sam said. "It's perverse."

"That's a shitty thing to say," Sadie said. "And is the point of everything we do to reach as broad an audience as possible? Is that the only reason to do anything? I'd like to know."

"It is, if we're going to spend millions of dollars on it. Not to mention, the limited time of our very finite lives."

"Not every game has to be *Mapleworld*, Sam. Not every game has to appeal to everyone."

"I'm so bored of having this discussion with you."

"I'm bored of having it with you."

"You're pretentious, Sadie."

"You're a pandering asshole."

At this point, their conversation was audible to all who worked on the second floor.

"If you're going to work on this," Sam said, "you can work on it alone."

"Fine. I will, then. I was *praying* you would say that."

"You *can't* work on it alone! I still need to sign off on it as a producer," Sam said. When they had founded Unfair, Sam, Sadie, and Marx had agreed that every game they made needed to be approved by at least two of them. "You can't unilaterally decide to work on it."

"Marx'll back me."

"I bet he will."

"He'll back me because it could be a great game, Sam."

"He'll back you because he takes your side in everything. Because he's *screwing* you."

"Get out of my office."

"No," Sam said.

Sadie physically pushed Sam out the door.

"GET OUT!"

"No, let's go see the Tamer of Horses," Sam said, "and settle this once and for all."

Sadie pushed past Sam, and they both went into Marx's office.

"I assume she's told you her idea," Sam said. *"Masturbator of the Revels."*

"Screw you," Sadie said.

"Yes," Marx said.

"Well, I think it stinks," Sam said. "It's like a multimillion-dollar version of *EmilyBlaster*."

"If this was anyone else's idea but mine," Sadie said, "you would talk about it with more respect."

"I'm refusing to work on it with her. I don't think we should do this game at all," Sam said, to Marx. "Every penny we spend on it, we'll lose. But you've got the tiebreaker, so . . . Not that you're exactly objective."

"I think it's a good idea," Marx said.

"Surprise, surprise," Sam said.

Sam walked out of Marx's office. He went into his own office and slammed the door.

"It's settled," Sadie said. Her face was flushed. "If you agree to it, I'm making *Master of the Revels* as my next game, and I'm doing it without Sam." Sadie nodded to herself. "I'm so done with him."

She, too, left Marx's office and returned to her own office.

For a second, Marx debated about which of them to follow. He took a right and went toward Sam's. He knocked on the door.

"Do you want to talk about it?" Marx asked.

"You're pussy blind," Sam said. "This is exactly why I told you that you shouldn't date Sadie back in 1996. It throws the balance of power, or whatever, off."

"I'm not going to dignify that," Marx said. "You're being childish and insulting, Sam. Unfair is my company, too. I wouldn't say we should do this if I didn't think it was worth doing. *Master of the Revels* has intrigued me since the first time Sadie told me about it. The Elizabethan theater world. The murder of Christopher Marlowe. I think these are interesting details and an interesting world could result. Even if two high school kids at a game jam showed up with a demo of the game Sadie described, I'd be tempted. And honestly, I've always wanted to make a game about theater."

Sam shook his head and he sighed. "Marx, don't you think I know Sadie a little? *Master of the Revels* is all of her worst instincts. I told her it was like *EmilyBlaster*, but honestly, it's *Solution*."

"We both loved *Solution*," Marx said.

"*Solution* is awesome for a college kid. *Solution* is awesome if the idea is to piss off your classmates, and if it costs no money."

Marx pondered Sam's point. "I don't think it is like *Solution*."

"Sadie wants to make something *dark* and *intellectual* so that people will take her seriously. She's trying to impress people like Dov. She's trying to win back the people that wrote bad reviews of *Both Sides*. The best colors of Sadie are not her darkness."

"I don't know, Sam. I think all her colors are worth exploring. Professionally speaking. And this game could be great. If you could have seen the way Sadie looked when she first described it. She was so excited."

Sam looked at Marx, and for a second, he despised him: *You, who could have anyone, why did you have to pick Sadie Green?*

Sam could imagine them in bed, in Clownerina. Sadie wakes up, and she turns over to look at Marx, and she says, *I've had an idea.* And she describes the idea for *Master of the Revels* to Marx—her hands flying through the air the way they do when she is excited, her words rapid-firing. She gets out of bed, and she has to pace around the room, because when Sadie has a great idea, she can't stay still. Sam couldn't remember a time when he hadn't been the first to know about one of Sadie's ideas.

"You know what? It's fine, Marx," Sam said. "I don't care what she does."

That night, in bed at Sadie's apartment, Marx asked Sadie if she was certain she wanted to make *Master of the Revels,* sans Sam.

"Are you saying you don't think I'm capable?" Sadie was ready for a fight.

"No, of course not," Marx said.

"Because I was making games without him, long before we started making games together."

"I know that," Marx said. "I think the games"—he chose his words carefully—"have a different energy when the two of you work together."

"We're barely speaking," Sadie said. "And when we do speak, it's not that creative, as you and everyone else at Unfair can plainly hear, and things haven't been good for us for some time. I don't see how we can work together. He hates the idea for *Master of the Revels,* and I love the idea, and I think we'll honestly kill each other if we work on this. I don't think we're breaking up forever. But I do think the two of us need some time apart so that we can like each other again.

"And, maybe it's more me than him. But I *want* to do something on my own. Something that is fully mine. Something that no one can attribute, for better or for worse, to Sam."

"I understand that, and I support you. *Master of the Revels,* a game by Sadie Green. Let it be known! But I'm curious about something. I've been here the whole time, and I've never understood what happened between you and Sam. You two were so tight that Zoe once told me that if I needed to get you to do something, all I had to do was tell you it was for Sam, and vice versa."

"It's not one thing," Sadie said. "For a long time, I thought it was one thing ... But it's everything."

"But is there one thing?" Marx persisted.

"This will sound crazy. Sam thought it sounded crazy when I told him. You remember when we went to Dov for Ulysses? Sam claimed he didn't know that Dov had been my teacher and my lover, and I found out that he had known both of those things."

"How?"

"Dov had signed the CD-ROM you both were playing."

Sadie went to her desk, and she took out the CD-ROM, and she showed it to Marx. Marx read the inscription. "God, Dov was the worst," he said.

"I know."

"Explain it to me. What difference does it make that Sam knew that?"

"Well, it means that he cared more about making *Ichigo* than he did about my well-being. For many years, I was the reverse—I loved our games, but I cared about Sam more. And for me, this betrayal came to be emblematic of all the other times I felt that Sam had chosen the games and himself over everything."

"But that's Sam," Marx said. "You two aren't that different. You're both obsessed with the work."

"I am different. I moved to California *for him.* I know there were other reasons, but you and I both essentially moved to California for him."

"I don't mean to dig up fossils, but Sam believed he was, in part, moving to California for you. He was worried about you. About your relationship with Dov . . ."

"We never spoke of that," Sadie said. "I don't see how that can even be true."

"But he and I did," Marx said. "Often."

Sadie shook her head.

"And Sadie? Not that it necessarily matters, but I'm not certain Sam would have ever seen that *Dead Sea* CD-ROM. I remember that afternoon very clearly. You were sleeping in the bedroom, and Sam was going through all the games we had to look for graphical references for *Ichigo*, and he'd worked his way through his pile, so I went over to your bookshelf to get your games. I'm certain I would have been the one to get up and put *Dead Sea* in the drive, because I was always worried about Sam's foot, and it would have been easier for me to get up and sit back down. And I know that I didn't look at the CD, and Sam wouldn't have had time to either."

Marx would have liked this to be true, but Sadie knew he was mistaken.

"I know it's not only that . . ." Marx continued.

"It isn't. It's *Ichigo II*, and Sam always taking credit, and maybe, as I said before, it isn't even Sam. I just want something of my own, and I don't want to negotiate with him. I'm only twenty-six, Marx. I don't have to work with him on every little thing I do for the rest of my life."

The phone rang, and Marx answered it. It was their realtor. Sadie's lease was almost up in Clownerina, and they had put in an offer on a house in Venice, a grayish-purplish, weather-beaten two-story, with clapboard siding, east of Abbot Kinney. The house had been built in the 1920s, like most everything in L.A., and it had a dangerous, banister-less staircase, French doors everywhere, wide plank floors, and a living room with an A-frame that looked like a church. (In fact, the house had been briefly occupied by one of the many cults that pass through Southern California on the road to Enlightenment and Nirvana.) The house was in an appealing, but livable, state of decay. A thirty-foot-tall bougainvillea was in the process of strangling a palm tree out front; the fence that surrounded the property was at a 45-degree angle in places; the roof would need repairs sooner rather than later. The listing had called it a "Boho Dream"—Boho, meaning "overpriced for the work you're about to do." Marx spoke with the realtor, and then he covered the mouthpiece and turned to Sadie.

"She wants to know if we're willing to come up with our offer," Marx said.

In the time since she and Marx had been looking, they'd lost out on several houses. California real estate moved briskly. Sadie had accustomed herself to disappointment, and she didn't get attached to any of the houses anymore. "It's a great house," Sadie said. "But I guess there'll be other houses. It's up to you."

"I like this house," Marx said. "I think this might be our house."

"Let's do it, then," Sadie said. "We'll come up a little, and we'll see what happens."

A few days later, their offer had been accepted.

Two months later, post tenting and lock changing and the endless signing of papers, they moved in.

"Should I carry you over the threshold?" Marx asked.

"We're not married, so I think I'm good to walk on my own two feet," Sadie said.

She unlocked the door, and they walked through to the small backyard. It was fall, and two of their three fruit trees were in season: a Fuyu persimmon tree and a guava tree.

"Sadie, do you see this? This is a persimmon tree! This is my favorite fruit." Marx picked a fat orange persimmon from the tree, and he sat down on the now termite-free wooden deck, and he ate it, juice running down his chin. "Can you believe our luck?" Marx said. "We bought a house with a tree that has my actual favorite fruit."

Sam used to say that Marx was the most fortunate person he had ever met—he was lucky with lovers, in business, in looks, in life. But the longer Sadie knew Marx, the more she thought Sam hadn't truly understood the nature of Marx's good fortune. Marx was fortunate because he saw everything as if it were a fortuitous bounty. It was impossible to know—were persimmons his favorite fruit, or had they just now become his favorite fruit because there they were, growing in his own backyard? He had certainly never mentioned persimmons before. *My God,* she thought, *he is so easy to love.* "Shouldn't you wash that?" Sadie asked.

"It's our tree. Nothing's touched it except my grimy hand," Marx said.

"What about the birds?"

"I don't fear the birds, Sadie. But you should have one of these." Marx stood, and he picked another fruit for himself and one for her. He walked over to the hose at the side of the house, and he rinsed the persimmon. He held out the fruit to her. "Eat up, my love. Fuyus only yield every other year."

Sadie took a bite of the fruit. It was mildly sweet, its flesh somewhere between a peach and a cantaloupe. Maybe it was her favorite fruit, too?

3

Once upon a time, in the great simulation beyond *Mapleworld*, the mayor of San Francisco instructed his City Hall to grant marriage licenses to same-sex couples. It was a few days before Valentine's Day, and Simon and Ant were deep into postproduction on *Counterpart High: Junior Year*. While both agreed that this was an interesting political development, they had never discussed marriage as it pertained to them personally. Had they been inclined to marry, there could not have been a less convenient time for them to take off from work. *CPH3* had been playtested too long, and they'd added so many new elements that the game was extraordinarily buggy. To ensure the game would be delivered on schedule, they were regularly putting in eighteen-hour days.

"Do you think we should go, though?" Simon asked. It was four in the morning, and Ant was driving them back to their apartment to shower, change clothes, and perhaps, even sleep for an hour or two.

"Go where?" Ant said, yawning.

"To San Francisco," Simon said.

"For what purpose?"

"To get hitched," Simon said.

"I didn't know you *wanted* to get married."

"Well, it wasn't an option before," Simon said. "You can't know you want something until it's an option."

"I think we have to finish the game before we can even think of doing anything else," Ant said.

"You're right. Of course you're right."

By 8 a.m., they were on the congested road back to Unfair.

"I'm feeling Torschlusspanik," Simon said. He was the one driving, while Ant tried to catch some extra sleep.

"Nope," Ant said, without opening his eyes. "You can't throw German at me when I've only slept two hours."

"Who knows how long before they stop giving out marriage licenses?" Simon said. "While we're busy making a wormhole prom fantasy, we could have completely squandered our chance to get married in the real world."

"I'm sleeping, Simon."

"Fine. Go to sleep."

Two minutes later, Ant opened one eye. "I honestly didn't know you were so conventional. Next you'll be wanting a white picket fence."

"If you mean a house in Santa Monica or Culver, that sounds about right. I'm so bloody tired of driving to and from West Hollywood."

And, at 3 a.m., Ant drove them home again.

"I think I want to go to San Francisco," Simon admitted, sounding pissed off about the whole situation. "Will you come with me, Anthony Ruiz?"

They had met six years ago, as freshmen, in a character animation class. Initially, Ant had not been attracted to him, thought he looked like a muscular genie, not his type. Worse than his looks, Simon was obnoxious. He corrected their professor, hated American animation, had a habit of dropping long German words and making references to obscure films, had a laugh like a leaf blower.

About two weeks into class, Simon had presented his first twenty-second, animated project. "The Ant" began with a repulsive kid holding a magnifying glass over an ant. The camera zooms in on the ant, a leather jacket–wearing, eye-rolling, proto-hipster. The ant delivers a mordant monologue detailing his final thoughts about existence, and then he combusts spectacularly. No one in their class had anything nice to say about it, and although Ant thought it was the best student work he'd seen, he hated speaking up during critique. At the end of class, he went up to Simon. "That was brilliant," Ant said.

"Thanks, man," Simon replied. "I based that character on you, you know."

Ant rolled his eyes and zipped up his leather jacket. "I don't know how to take that."

"Not the combustion," Simon said. "The rest of it. The sexy ant." He grinned, causing the eruption of a heretofore unseen dimple, and Ant thought, *God help me, he's cute when he smiles.*

They asked Marx to go to San Francisco with them in case they needed a witness and, also, so he couldn't possibly be angry that they were taking off in the middle of finishing the game. Once Marx was going, Sadie decided to go, too—someone needed to take pictures. And then, since everyone else was going and the event was of civic and historical interest, the mayor of Mapletown decided he, too, wished to attend.

They flew to San Francisco on Tuesday morning. By the time they arrived at City Hall, the line stretched around the perimeter of the building and only grew longer as the day progressed. Despite the cold, damp weather, there was a low-key music festival vibe— not like Coachella, more like Newport Jazz—mixed with the giddy bureaucratic tension of a day in traffic court. Simon feared that marriage licensing could be suspended without warning, and that cops, lawyers, homophobic protesters might show up to spoil everything. "Torschlusspanik," Simon said.

"Okay," Sam said. "I'll bite."

"Don't encourage him," Ant said.

"What's Torschlusspanik?" Sam said.

"It means 'gate-shut panic,'" Simon said. "It's the fear that time is running out and that you're going to miss an opportunity. Literally, the gate is closing, and you'll never get in."

"That's me," Sam said. "I have that constantly."

When the rain picked up, Sam and Sadie were dispatched to go buy umbrellas, which the group from eternally sunny Los Angeles had not thought to bring. The vendor in front of City Hall was sold out of umbrellas, and so they had to walk farther down Grove Street. The second vendor they encountered was selling dodgy, used/stolen umbrellas. *It's our friends' wedding. We can do better than this,* they told each other. A half mile or so farther, they arrived at a sporting goods store that sold colossal umbrellas designed for golf spectators. By then, Sam and Sadie were both drenched, and they agreed that they probably should have settled for the dodgy umbrellas a half mile back. *Why are our standards always so high?* they joked. Lacking other options, they bought three of the monster umbrellas. They opened two of them and began the trek back to City Hall.

Thirty seconds later, they came to the realization that it was impossible to share the sidewalk when deploying two umbrellas with five-foot-wide canopies. Sadie told Sam to close his umbrella and come under hers, and then, she offered him her arm. Sam interpreted the arm as an indicator of improved relations between them, and he decided to mention that he'd seen some of the *Master of the Revels* work. "I like the desaturated color scheme. Not quite black-and-white, but very stylish. It's smart."

"Thanks," Sadie said. "That's nice of you to say, considering how much I know you disapprove of it."

"I don't disapprove of it," Sam said. "And anyway, it didn't matter what I thought, did it? You were going to make that game no matter what I said. And now you're making it. Which is good."

"So, you don't think *Master of the Revels* is the worst idea ever, and it's going to single-handedly destroy our company?"

Sam shook his head, no.

Four hours later, Simon and Ant were the 211th couple to be married that day. After the ceremony, everyone was starving so they went to a nearby dim sum place, where they stuffed themselves with dumplings. Marx ordered an expensive bottle of cheap champagne, and Simon, who liked bloviating as much as Sam did, decided to give a toast. "Thank you to our friends and colleagues for taking the day off to bear witness to our nuptials. And for producing three *CPH*s with us. I think we can agree, once and for all, that it should have been called *Doppelgänger High*."

"Agree to disagree!" Marx called out.

"Contrary to popular belief," Simon continued, "my favorite German word is not actually doppelgänger. It's 'Zweisamkeit.'"

"The alternative title was *Zweisamkeit High*," Ant said. "I talked him out of it."

"Thank you," Sam whispered.

"'Zweisamkeit' is the feeling of being alone even when you're with other people." Simon turned to look in his husband's eyes. "Before I met you, I felt this constantly. I felt it with my family, my friends, and every boyfriend I ever had. I felt it so often that I thought this was the nature of living. To be alive was to accept that you were fundamentally alone." Simon's eyes were moist. "I know I'm impossible, and I know you don't care about German words or marriage. All I can say is, I love you and thank you for marrying me anyway."

Ant raised his glass. "Zweisamkeit," he said.

By the time *Counterpart High* dropped in August, Simon and Ant were no longer married. The California Supreme Court declared that the City of San Francisco had overstepped, and the marriages that had been performed based on those licenses were now void. Strangely, Ant took it harder than Simon. Simon had felt the Torschlusspanik for a reason, and he wasn't surprised to find that his legal marriage was now over, considering the country and the times they lived in. He did a few lines of old coke, which he had been saving for a special occasion, and he went back to work. "I'm sorry if this whole thing has been a Verschlimmbesserung boondoggle," Simon said to Ant, who had decided to take the day off.

Ant pulled the blanket over his head. At first, he had wanted to call their congressman, go to Sacramento to protest, write angry letters and op-eds, but in the end, he had to resign himself to the reality that he wasn't a protester, an organizer, or even a political person.

After he'd missed a week of work, Sadie drove to Ant's house to see him. "I didn't think it would feel different to be married," Ant told her, "but somehow, it did. And now I feel as if I've been tricked."

Back at the office, Sadie called Marx and Sam into her office. "There should be marriages in *Mapleworld*."

"I thought you didn't believe in marriage," Marx said. "Why force an antiquated institution on innocent digital people?"

"There will be some people for whom *Mapleworld* will be the only place they *can* get married," Sadie said. "And what is the point of having your own world if it can't right a few injustices of the real one?"

Three years after *Mapleworld* had launched, Marriages was quietly introduced as one of a handful of new features in *Mapleworld*. Marriages, much like marriage in the real world, allowed residents to combine property and Maplebucks. In *Mapleworld*, marriage was defined as between two consenting adults, no explicit mention of sex or gender. And indeed, it would have been foolish to define sex or gender as a requirement for marriage in *Mapleworld* when so many of its residents adhered to neither binary nor human characteristics. There were many hipsters, like Mayor Mazer, but there were also elves, orcs, monsters, aliens, fey, vampires, and a variety of other supernatural-presenting, nonbinary folk.

On a rainy October morning in Mapletown, Anthony Ruiz and Simon Freeman were married for the second time in a Special Mapleworld Event. Sam and Sadie did not have to go for umbrellas. The programmers had added them the night before.

Because he wanted the wedding to have verisimilitude, Sam had gotten ordained as a minister in the real world, and after he had completed Simon and Ant's ceremony, Mayor Mazer invited anyone else who wanted to be married to step forward. Before closing shop, he had married 211 couples.

In the weeks that followed, fifty thousand people canceled their *Mapleworld* accounts. An additional two hundred thousand joined.

The hate mail began immediately. Death threats—emailed and paper—for Sam mainly. A convincing bomb threat that forced everyone to evacuate Unfair for an afternoon. Boycotts from various anti-equality organizations that felt *Mapleworld* was being needlessly political. Boycotts from equality groups that felt Sam had made a jest out of a serious issue and had then used that issue as promotion. A handful of op-eds in the usual places, both in support of Mayor Mazer and against him. (*Newsweek:* "Should Games Be Political? Mayor Mazer Thinks So.") Sam on TV talk shows, quoting Marshall McLuhan, "The games of a people reveal a great deal about them."

Marx decided to hire security, and for a few weeks, Olga, a Russian former weightlifting champion, dutifully followed Sam around.

Sam made a point of writing back to everyone who wrote to him, responding to even the vilest hate mail. Once, Sadie found him at his desk, replying to a letter that began with the salutation, "Dear Chink Jew Faggot Lover."

"I like that the person writes 'Dear,'" Sadie said. She tossed the letter across the room. Sadie felt guilty. Marriages had been her idea, but Sam, because he was the face of *Mapleworld*, took the abuse.

If anything, Sam was encouraged by the hate mail, and because of his experience with Marriages, he would use *Mapleworld* to make even more political statements. He did not consider them to be political statements but sensible governance and, not insignificantly, an excellent source of promotion. He banned user-created gun stores and the sale of weapons. He supported conservationism and the building of an Islamic cultural center by a group of Muslim Mapletownies. He arranged mass avatar protests about the war in Iraq and offshore oil drilling. He held town halls where he'd talk to residents about the issues facing Mapletown and the country. Every time he took a controversial stand, there'd be the same flurry of hate mail and cancellations of accounts, and then life would go on in *Mapleworld,* and the world beyond it as well.

4

After Sam played *Master of the Revels* for the first time, he called Sadie and asked her if he could come over to discuss it. It was Labor Day weekend, and when he called, she was at her grandmother's house in Hancock Park. As she was more than halfway across town, she offered to drive over to his house instead.

Sadie drove down Sunset, and past the Happy Foot Sad Foot sign (Happy Foot, but about to become Sad Foot), and then she turned onto Sam's street. He still lived in the little bungalow he'd rented when he'd first moved to L.A.

"So?" she said. "Let's have it."

"So, I absolutely detest," he paused, "that you made this without me." Sam smiled at her self-consciously. "It's great, Sadie. It's art. It's the best thing you ever made."

"I didn't think that's what you were going to say." Sadie could feel herself blushing with pleasure. She didn't know she still cared what Sam thought.

"Why?"

"Because I thought things had to come from you for you to even be able to see them," Sadie said.

At Unfair, everyone—Sadie included—was worried about how they were going to market *Master of the Revels,* a spectacular but aggressively erudite game. In *Master of the Revels,* the gamer plays from the point of view of multiple characters, all linked in some way to the murder of Christopher Marlowe: Marlowe's lover; a rival playwright; a twenty-first-century Shakespearean scholar researching the murder of Christopher Marlowe; Christopher Marlowe himself; and finally, the Master of the Revels, the man in charge of revels (and censorship) for the queen of England. *Master of the Revels* was part interactive mystery drama, part action-adventure game. Sadie had painstakingly re-created Elizabethan England, and in addition to murder and mystery, the game had a great deal of sex.

Ultimately, they decided that the only way to market it was to be honest about what they thought they had. The press release read: "From the studio that brought you *Counterpart High,* and visionary game designer Sadie Green, the creator of *Ichigo* and *Mapleworld,* comes another groundbreaking adventure. *Master of the Revels* is unlike anything you have played before. Part mystery, part love story, part tragedy, it is a game for those who believe that games can be art."

Unfortunately, by invoking Unfair, *Ichigo,* and *Mapleworld,* the press release had led game journalists to believe that *Master of the Revels* was Sam's game as well. And when they began to book publicity for *Master of the Revels,* it became obvious that there would be more opportunities to promote the game if Sam was involved. Because of the Mayor Mazer character and the Marriages hoopla, Sam was significantly more famous than Sadie. On some level, *Master of the Revels* was his game, too. His company had produced it; his name was on it; Sadie was his partner. The marketing people broached the idea of Sadie and Sam going on the road together with Marx first. Marx said he wasn't sure if either of them would want to do it. But Sam surprised Marx by saying he'd be glad to, if it would help *Master of the Revels.*

When Marx spoke to Sadie, she was more resistant. "This is going to sound awful and petty, but I don't want people to think it's his," Sadie said.

"They won't," Marx said. "I promise you, they won't. Sam'll make a point of telling people that he's just a producer, and that the game was your brainchild."

In November, Sam and Sadie flew around the country, promoting *Master of the Revels* at the various cons and retailers. Sam was true to his word. He did not take credit, though journalists were still more interested in talking to him than to her. "This question is for Mazer," a journalist would say. "Should games be political?" It was more than irritating that a solid 25 percent of the interviewers assumed that Sam and Sadie were a couple. The journalists would seem slightly taken aback when they were told that they weren't. Why would a man, *in games,* work with a woman he wasn't married to or at least sleeping with? But Sadie took it in stride. The work was the thing, she kept reminding herself. The work was the thing that lasted, but the work only lasted if people knew it existed.

They had been on the road for four days when Sadie came down with a stomach flu. She threw up in the morning, just after lunch, and again after dinner, though she claimed she felt fine the rest of the time, and it didn't interfere with her ability to promote the game. She suspected the culprit was oysters she'd eaten at a buffet in Vegas. "Perhaps not the best idea to have oysters, from a buffet, in a landlocked city," she admitted to Sam.

Two days later, they were driving from the Dallas–Fort Worth airport to Grapevine, Texas, when Sadie asked Sam to pull over: she needed to throw up again.

Sadie vomited under a recently planted crepe myrtle tree, and then she told Sam that she wanted to drive, because she thought it would ease her motion sickness. "You drive too slow," she said.

"Sadie," Sam said, "do you think there's any chance you might be pregnant? By my count, this is the seventh time you've thrown up in the last three days. It can't still be the oysters, can it?"

"No, it was the oysters before, but it's definitely motion sickness now," she insisted. "And it definitely can't be morning sickness because I've had it the whole day."

On the way to the hotel, she spotted a drugstore. "I'm going to pop in to get Gatorade and Dramamine," she said. She also bought a pregnancy test.

The hotel in Grapevine turned out to be an annoyingly charming B&B, with seven rooms, all named for historical figures from Texas. Their travel agent had accidentally booked them into the Parker and Barrow suite instead of two separate rooms. "Do you want me to see if there's another hotel?" Sam whispered.

"It'll be fine. It's a suite in Texas," Sadie said. "Isn't everything in Texas supposed to be giant?"

The Parker and Barrow was disappointingly un-Texas-sized: a tiny bedroom, and a tiny sitting room with a convertible couch, and a tiny bathroom that seemed to be in the center of everything. "Our first dorm room at Harvard was like this," Sam commented.

About a half hour after they'd arrived, she went into the bathroom, and she came out with the box, and the stick in a glass. "I'm sorry," she said. "This is gross. That bathroom has, literally, no counter space. It's just a pedestal sink. This hotel is so cute. I want to murder everyone. And I'm also sorry that I've been the most disgusting traveling companion ever." Sam laughed, and Sadie sat down on the couch next to him, and they watched what was playing—that old Disney movie *Swiss Family Robinson* about the castaway family who live in the tree house—and they waited for the test to work its magic.

Sam saw it change first. "What do two blue lines mean?" He picked up the box to decode it, and Sadie, having already grasped its meaning, went into the bathroom to throw up again—this time it was more mental than physical, but emesis can take on a certain momentum. She brushed her teeth, came back out to the couch, and retook her place next to Sam. Her phone, which was sitting on the coffee table, was ringing. Sam could see it was Marx: she let it go to voicemail. "I want to live in a tree," she said. "Can we do that for a little while?" She put her head on Sam's shoulder, and he did not move or say anything, though she still smelled lightly of acid and bile. "We've got two hours before we have to be at GameStop HQ," she said. "Wake me, if I fall asleep."

A month later, December, they went to New York to do even more press, which included a photo shoot for *Game Story*. The magazine was doing a cover feature on Sam and Sadie, for which the headline would be "Masters of the Revels: Behind the Scenes with Mazer and Green." For the shoot, they had both agreed to wear over-the-top Elizabethan-era costumes. Sadie was made up to look like Queen Elizabeth I; Sam, like William Shakespeare. The situation was absurd, and Sadie and Sam could not stop laughing. The photographer, an Italian man in his sixties, didn't know anything about gaming, or who either of them were.

"You two are married, right?" the photographer said.

"She doesn't believe in marriage," Sam said.

"It's true. I don't," Sadie said.

"It'll be different when you have children," the photographer said.

"People like to say that," Sadie said.

When they had finished taking the photos, Sadie removed her costume and rushed off to the bathroom.

Sam was taking off his doublet when a text came in on the publicist's phone. "Unfair's in Venice, isn't it?" she said. "My friend says there's an active shooter at a tech company in Venice. You should tell your people to stay inside."

"That's awful. Which one?" Sam asked. Though he was concerned for whichever of his Silicon Beach neighbors had met with misadventure, he did not think this information had much to do with him. Unfair was a *game* company, not a *tech* company.

"That's all I know," the publicist said.

"I'll call Marx," Sam said. "Maybe he'll know what's up?"

Sam took out his phone: there were several missed calls from Marx in the last fifteen minutes. He tried calling Marx back, but his phone went to voicemail. He called the landline at the office, but despite it being morning on the West Coast, no one picked up.

He went into the ladies' room to ask Sadie to call Marx. He could hear her throwing up. He knocked on the door of the stall. "Sadie?"

"Samson, why are you in the ladies' room?"

Sadie came out of the stall. She was growing so accustomed to throwing up that she could get over it quickly. She was about to tease him for following her into the bathroom, but then she saw Sam's face.

5

In 2005, people from the U.S. sent, on average, four hundred sixty text messages a year.

Texts were treated and written more like telegrams than like conversations. The brevity lent these early texts an almost poetry.

Sadie and Marx had texted only a couple dozen times during their relationship. They had no need for texting. They were usually together, at work or at home.

After Sadie's first call to Marx went to voicemail, she tried sending a text:

Are you OK?

A minute later, he replied:

I love you. all ok.

Just kids. Talking. TOH.

Sadie's hands were shaking. She showed Sam her phone. "What's TOH mean?" Sadie asked. "I don't know any of the acronyms."

"Tamer of Horses," Sam said.

VII

THE NPC

You are flying.

Below, a checkerboard of country life. A pair of Jersey cows graze in a lavender field, tails swatting at imaginary flies. A woman in a chambray dress rides a bicycle over a stone bridge. She hums the second movement of Beethoven's Emperor Concerto, and as she passes, a man in a Breton cap begins whistling the tune. From a hive you cannot see, the susurrus of bees. In the valley below the bridge, an ink-haired boy feeds a sugar cube to a horse with a wild look in her eyes. A grove of apple trees waits patiently for fall. Unobserved, a graying man watches two teenagers swim in a pond. You can smell the man's longing, stronger than lavender, and you think, *Humans want so much. I am glad to be a bird.* In a field of strawberry plants, waxy berries companionably mingle among white flowers.

You have never been one to resist a strawberry, so you descend.

As a winged creature, you are occasionally called upon to explain flight to the flightless. Your standard answer is that it's a combination of Newtonian physics, concerted flapping, weather, anatomy. But honestly, it's best not to think of the mechanics of flight while you're doing it. Your philosophy: Surrender to the air, enjoy the view.

You have arrived at your destination. Your small beak surrounds the berry, and you are about to snatch it when you hear the click of a trigger.

"STOP, THIEF!"

You feel the bullet penetrate your hollow bird bones.

An explosion of brown and beige feathers, like dandelion seeds dispersing. Blood on the berries—red on red—but to you, a tetrachromat, the two reds are distinctive.

You land in the dirt: an almost imperceptible thud, an unimpressive dust cloud that only you can see.

Another shot.

Another shot.

Your wing is flapping. You choose to interpret this as an attempt at flight, and not an involuntary death spasm.

Some hours later, you become aware of someone holding your hand, which means you have a hand, which means you are not a bird, which means you must be on some pretty terrific drugs, like LSD, which you have never done even though Zoe always wanted you guys to do LSD together, said she knew the perfect guide. For a second, you experience competing melancholies: sadness that you cannot fly, sadness that you didn't do LSD with Zoe, sadness that

You are dying.

No, that came out wrong. What you meant to express was the existential grief that comes with the knowledge that all things die. You are not dying, except insofar as you have always been dying.

To repeat: You are not dying.

You are thirty-one years old. You are the only child of Ryu and AeRan Lee Watanabe—respectively, a businessman and a design professor. You were born in New Jersey. You have two passports. You work at Unfair Games on Abbot Kinney Boulevard, in Venice, California. The nameplate on your desk reads:

MARX WATANABE
TAMER OF HORSES

You have had many lives. Before you were a tamer of horses, you were a fencer, a high school chess champion, an actor. You are American, Japanese, Korean, and by being all of those things, you are not truly any of those things. You consider yourself a citizen of the world.

You are currently a citizen of a hospital. A machine is breathing for you. Regularly spaced chirps indicate that you are still alive.

You are not awake, but you are not asleep either.

You can see and hear everything.

You cannot remember everything. You don't have amnesia, per se, but you don't immediately recollect how it is you have ended up in a hospital and why it is you cannot wake up.

You pride yourself on your memory. At the office, someone is always saying, "Ask Marx. He'll know." Often, you do know. You remember the usual. People's names and faces, birthdays, song lyrics, phone numbers. You remember the slightly more unusual: entire plays, poems, character actors, the meanings of obscure words, long passages of novels. You remember the names of people's parents, children, pets. You remember with granularity the geography of cities, hotel room floor plans, video game levels, the scars of ex-lovers, times you've said the wrong thing, and the clothes people wore. You remember what Sadie was wearing the first time you met her: a black tank dress, with a white cap-sleeved T-shirt underneath it, a red flannel tied around her waist, burgundy oxfords with lug soles, sheer socks with a rose print on them, those tiny oval-shaped, yellow-tinted sunglasses that everyone was wearing that spring, her hair parted in the middle, in two Brunhilda braids. "You must be Marx," she said, holding out her hand to you. "I'm Sadie."

"I know you already," you replied. "I've played two of your games."

She surveyed you over the top of her yellow sunglasses. "You think you can know a person from playing their games?"

"I do. No better way, in my humble opinion."

"So, what do you know about me?" she asked.

"You're smart."

"I'm Sam's friend, so that is to be assumed. I could guess the same about you. What specifically do you know about me from playing my game?"

"That you're a little bit wicked. And your mind is an interesting and unusual place."

Sadie may have rolled her eyes, but it was hard to see them beneath those sunglasses. "Do you make games, too?"

"No, but I play them."

"How will I ever know you, then?"

Memory, you realized long ago, is a game that a healthy-brained person can play all the time, and the game of memory is won or lost on one criterion: Do you leave the formation of memories to happenstance, or do you decide to remember?

So, where were you when this began?

You are in a meeting with Charlotte and Adam Worth.

They are blue-eyed innocents, brand-new to Los Angeles, strapping and healthy, like pioneers or folk singers. They remind you of Sam and Sadie, if Sam and Sadie were tall, married ex-Mormons from Utah.

The Worths are pitching their game, tentatively titled *Our Infinite Days*. (You used to joke that if you ever wrote a memoir, the title would be *All Titles Are Tentative*.) *Our Infinite Days* is an adventure shooter about the end of the world. A woman and her young daughter travel through a desert apocalypse, fending off people and a gauntlet of what the Worths were calling "desert vampires"—a cross between a vampire and a zombie. The woman has amnesia and the young daughter, who is only six years old, must act as her memory. The daughter believes her brothers and fathers are on the West Coast, but can you trust the memory of a six-year-old?

"Amnesia is a gaming chestnut," Charlotte apologizes, "but we know we can make it work."

"Actually, we were inspired by the original *Ichigo*," Adam says. "The challenge of having to rely on a child's memory and perceptions to win a game. It's brilliant."

"We can't wait to meet Green/Mazer," Charlotte says. "We're huge fans."

"She even loves *Both Sides*," Adam says.

"Don't say *even*. It's my favorite game of all time," Charlotte says. "Myre Landing is genius. I cosplayed Rose the Mighty."

"No one knew who she was," Adam says

"I'm somewhat obsessed with Sadie Green."

"Not Mazer?" you ask, amused.

"They're both great, but Sadie Green's Myre Landing and *Both Sides*, Sadie Green's *Solution*, and those are the kinds of thing I want to make," Charlotte says. "I cannot wait to play *Master of the Revels*."

"Solution," you say. "That's deep. You really are a fan."

Maybe this is a fan service vaudeville, but you still appreciate it. It's amazing how many people you meet—people who want things from you, after all—who can't be bothered to research any of Unfair's games.

You thank the Worths for coming in and you tell them that you will discuss *Our Infinite Days* with Sadie and Sam when they're back from New York. You promise they'll hear from you no later than the end of next week. You look at Charlotte and Adam, and you see how much they need you to make this game with them. You see how many times they must have been told no, the wanting in their eyes. You wonder what they're doing for day jobs and how long their relationship will survive if it isn't bolstered by some success. (They say success kills relationships, but the lack of it will do it just as quickly.) One of the absolute best parts of your own job is being able to tell an artist, *Yes. I see you. I get what you're doing. Let's do this thing.* Even though it's a breach of professional protocol, you contemplate telling them your company is going to make *Our Infinite Days* right now. You like these people; you want to play this game; it's a no-brainer.

You are about to walk them to the elevator bank when you hear what sounds like thunder, or a car driving over a metal plate, or a wrecking ball hitting the side of a building a block away.

It is loud, but not necessarily grave.

It is a bang, but Los Angeles is filled with sounds and furies signifying nothing. It's famous for them.

You do not think it's a gunshot.

You hear a muffled shout, but you cannot say whether it is coming from the lobby a floor below, or outside.

You smile at the Worths, and you laugh and, to put everyone at ease, you say, "The never-ending excitement of working in video games."

The Worths laugh at your weak joke, and momentarily, everything is normal. "Should we leave our concept art so that your partners can look at it?" Charlotte asks.

You're about to reply when your office phone rings. It is Unfair's receptionist, Gordon. "Hi, Marx. There's someone down here to see Mazer."

You sense tension in Gordon's voice. "Is something wrong?"

"I—I can't talk," Gordon says. "They say they need to talk to Mazer."

"Okay, hold on." You smile in the Worths' direction. You lower your voice and whisper into the phone, "I'll ask questions. You say yes or no. Should I call the police?"

"Yes," Gordon says.

"Do they have a gun?"

"Yes."

"Is there more than one?"

"Yes."

"Is anyone hurt?"

"No."

Through the earpiece, you can hear someone yell, "Get the fuck off the phone! Tell that faggot-lover to get down here."

"Tell them Mazer isn't here, but that the CEO of Unfair is coming down to see them, and that's just as good."

"Okay," Gordon says, sounding dazed. He repeats what you've said.

"It'll be okay, Gordon." You hang up the phone.

You turn around, and the Worths are staring at you, awaiting instruction. "What can we do?" Adam Worth asks. Like their characters in *Our Infinite Days*, the Worths are prepared for imminent apocalypse.

You explain the situation and you ask him to call the police. Adam Worth picks up the phone.

As you're leaving, Ant comes toward you. "What's going on?"

You repeat what you know, and Ant offers to accompany you. "Sadie'll kill me if I let you go down there alone."

"There are things for you to do up here," you say. You tell Ant to contact maintenance to get them to turn off the building's power, so the elevator won't work. You tell him to block off the stairwells. You tell him to keep everyone calm and make sure no one comes downstairs. You tell him to take the staff up to the roof and block the door.

"But Marx, for God's sake, are you sure you have to go down there?"

"They just want to talk to someone. They probably have some grievance with the company. I've talked people off the ledge before."

Ant says, "I don't know. Maybe you should wait for the police. Sadie and Sam'll *both* kill me if anything happens to you."

"I'll be fine, Ant. And it isn't right to leave Gordon down there alone. Whatever these peoples' grievances are, they're with Unfair, not our receptionist."

Ant embraces you, and you walk toward the stairs. "Be careful, my friend," he says.

Charlotte Worth calls after you. "Marx, should you take a weapon?" This is the question of a serious gamer. A gamer should never enter a potential combat situation without checking one's inventory and confirming the availability of a weapon.

"What weapon?" you say. You have no weapons. You have lived an easy life that has required no defenses of any kind. Your privilege probably makes you reckless. "I'm going to have a conversation. I'm sure this will just turn out to be a person who needs someone to listen to them."

Before you descend, you take a quick, final look at your office. You feel as if you've forgotten to do something. In a game, the out-of-place object is often the solution. You notice the Worths' portfolio, which Charlotte has left on your desk, and you scribble on a Post-it: s., TELL ME YOUR THOUGHTS. —M.

You hand the portfolio to your assistant, and you run down the stairs, and that is all you want to remember for now, because Sadie is in your hospital room.

"Are you his wife?" the doctor asks.

"Yes," Sadie lies.

This strikes you as funny because Sadie has a thing about marriage—i.e., she doesn't believe in it. You don't know where this comes from exactly—her parents have been happily married for thirty-seven years; her grandparents for longer than that. If anyone should have a problem with marriage, it should be you. Your parents have been unhappily married for nearly as long as Sadie's have been happily married. You can't remember the last time you saw your parents together. After your freshman year in college, you came back home to find that they had moved into separate apartments in Tokyo.

"Where's Dad?" you'd asked your mother.

Your mother seemed unconcerned. "He said he wanted to be able to walk to work."

Over a decade later, they still aren't divorced, and you can't explain this either.

You proposed to Sadie last year. You asked her father for permission, which he granted. You bought a ring. You got down on one knee.

"I don't see myself being someone's wife," she said.

"You wouldn't be a wife. I'd be your husband," you said.

She was not convinced by this argument. Her resistance was surprising, so you asked for reasons. She said that you already owned a house together, so you didn't need to be married. She said that she didn't want to be married to her business partner. She said that marriage was an antiquated institution that oppressed women. She said she liked her name.

"I like your name, too," you said. "I love your name."

But now, here Sadie is, telling a doctor that she is your wife. If you could speak, you would say to her, "All I had to do was fall into a coma for you to marry me. If only I'd known it was so easy."

You have not, technically, fallen into a coma.

The coma has been medically induced.

From overhearing doctors, you have surmised that you have been shot three times: in the thigh, in the chest, in the shoulder.

The most problematic of those injuries is the bullet that went through your chest: it raced through your lung, your kidney, and your pancreas. The bullet is now chilling somewhere in your intestine, waiting until your body is well enough for it to be removed. They say it could be worse—you, like most humans, have redundancies built in. Your pancreas is, heartbreakingly, single. The trauma of the injuries has caused your body to go into shock, which is why you find yourself in the coma. You are young and healthy, or you were, and depending on the day, they say your chances for surviving this are *good, better than average, not bad*. You take some comfort in this.

Sadie leaves, and a nurse comes into the room to deal with the dueling portmanteaus of waste and nourishment that hang by your bed. He carefully wipes down your body with a sponge, and despite everything, you find a small pleasure in being cared for.

· · ·

You are in the lobby of Unfair Games.

A white boy, dressed in black, with a red bandanna tied around the lower half of his face is holding a small gun to Gordon the receptionist's head. Another white boy, also dressed in black—this one, with a larger gun and a black bandanna, is pointing the barrel of his big gun at you. "WHO THE FUCK ARE YOU?" the boy with the red bandanna wants to know.

You have no idea why these boys haven't gotten into the elevator to come up to the main floor yet. Don't they want to wreak havoc on the most people possible? You have no idea how Gordon—sweet, baby-faced, ball-of-clay Gordon—has managed to contain them to the lobby. You remember Gordon at Halloween. He had modded his Pikachu costume so that he could make actual electric sparks.

You don't know much about guns, other than the guns you've used in video games, like *Doom*. And even when you play *Doom*, guns are not your weapon of choice. You prefer a chainsaw or a rocket launcher, weapons with more Grand Guignol–style thrills to them. You determine the smaller gun is a pistol, and the larger weapon is an assault rifle.

"Hi, I'm Marx Watanabe. This is my company." You hold out your hand in case anyone wants to shake it. The boys look mystified by this gesture. You bow your head slightly. "What can I do for you? Gordon says you want to talk to Mazer, but Mazer's not here."

Red Bandanna screams at you, "I don't believe you! You're a goddamn liar!"

"I promise you, he's not here," you say. "He's in New York, promoting our new game. But why don't you tell me what I can do for you?"

"Show me the office," Red Bandanna says. "I want to see for myself that little faggot isn't here."

"Okay," you say, desperately stalling to give Ant time to evacuate everyone to the roof. "I can do that, but can you do me a favor—"

"Boy, I cannot fucking do you a favor."

"Explain to me what you want with Mazer. Maybe I can help."

The one with the black bandanna has a slight stutter. "We don't want to hurt anyone else," he says. "We just need to talk to Mazer. If we wanted to go shoot up your office, we'd have gone up there already. We want Mazer to come down here."

"Let's call him," you suggest. You dial Sam's number, but Sam doesn't pick up. He must be in the photo shoot with Sadie. You leave a message, keeping your voice neutral: "It's Marx. Give me a ring when you have a chance."

You look at these two kids. You can't tell how old they are because of their bandannas. They're probably your age or younger, and you aren't afraid of them, though you are afraid of their guns.

"He'll call back," you say casually. "How about while we wait for Mazer to call, you let Gordon here go?"

"Bitch," Red Bandanna says. "Why would we do that?"

"He's not important," you say. "He's an NPC." They're gamers, obviously, so you know they will know this term.

"*You're* an NPC," Red Bandanna says.

"You're not the first person to call me that," you say.

You are in a hotel, just outside of San Simeon.

Sadie has fallen asleep, so you go down to the bar. Sam is there. Your friend, who never drinks, is drinking.

You ask him if he wants company, and he shrugs and says, "Do what you want." You sit down on the stool next to him.

"I don't know how it happened," you say lamely. "I don't think either of us meant for it to happen."

"I don't have even one iota of desire to hear the story," he says. He is drunk, but he doesn't sound drunk yet, only edgy and nasty. "What you have with Sadie is nothing like what I have with Sadie, so it doesn't even matter. You can *fuck* anyone," he says. "You can't make games with anyone, though."

"I make games with both of you," you point out. "I named *Ichigo,* for God's sake. I have been with both of you every step of the way. You can't say I haven't been here."

"You've been here, sure. But you're fundamentally unimportant. If you weren't here, it would be someone else. You're a tamer of horses. You're an NPC, Marx."

An NPC is a character that is not playable by a gamer. It is an AI extra that gives a programmed world verisimilitude. The NPC can be a best friend, a talking computer, a child, a parent, a lover, a robot, a gruff platoon leader, or the villain. Sam, however, means this as an insult—in addition to calling you unimportant, he's saying you're boring and predictable. But the fact is, there is no game without the NPCs.

"There's no game without the NPCs," you tell him. "There's just some bullshit hero, wandering around with no one to talk to and nothing to do."

Sam orders another shot of Grey Goose, and you tell him he's had enough. "You're not my father," Sam says.

The bartender looks at you, and you order a beer.

"I wish I'd never met you," Sam says. "I wish we'd never been roommates. I wish I'd never introduced you to Sadie." Sam is starting to slur his words.

"Sadie doesn't belong to you."

"She does," Sam says. "She's mine. And you knew that, and you pursued her anyway."

"No. People don't belong to each other."

"Why not?" Sam says. "Why not?"

"Sam."

"Are you going to *marry* her?" Sam asks. He says "marry" like he means "murder."

"Not at the moment."

"What's so great about marriage? What's so great about sex? What's so great about making babies or playing house? Why can't you belong to the person with whom you share your work?"

"Because there is life, and there is work," you say. "And they aren't the same."

"They're the same for me."

"Maybe they're not the same for Sadie."

"Maybe they're not," Sam says quietly. "I'm so screwed up, Marx. If I hadn't been such a screwed-up coward, maybe I'd be the one going up to Sadie's hotel room. I know it's my fault. I know I had time." Sam puts his head down on the mahogany bar and he begins to weep. "No one loves me," he says.

"I love you, brother. You're my best friend." You pay the bar tab, and you help Sam up to his room. He goes into the bathroom, and he closes his door, and then you hear him throwing up.

You sit on Sam's hotel bed. You turn on the television and a rerun of a medical show is playing. A man has brain cancer, and he is going to die, unless he has an experimental brain surgery. But in the end, the experimental brain surgery kills him anyway. It is strange, you think, how much people hate going to doctors, but how much they *love* watching shows about doctors.

Sam is taking longer than you'd expect so you call his name, "Sam?"

When he doesn't answer, you go into the bathroom, and he's standing in front of the mirror with a pair of grooming kit scissors. He's hacked off approximately half of his hair.

"I got vomit on it," he says, "And it wouldn't wash off, so I cut it. Now I want to shave the whole thing, but I'm too drunk."

Without commentary, you take the scissors from him, and you cut off the rest of his hair, and then you take out his electric shaver, and you shave his hair down as close as you can.

"Who's the NPC now?" you say to him. "I'm the one with the controller. I'm the one with the task."

"You find your crazy roommate in the bathroom. He's cut off half of his hair in a fit of nonsensical despair. What do you do?" Sam says, imitating the form of interactive fiction. He runs his fingers through his hair. "Don't tell Sadie about any of this."

"Brother, I think she'll notice." You take his head in your hands and you kiss him on the crown.

You are in the lobby of Unfair Games.

"You guys play a lot of games?" You're both stalling and you genuinely want to know.

"Some," Red Bandanna says.

"Which ones?" you ask. "Don't worry. It's a professional question. I'm interested to know what people are playing."

They report that they play *Half-Life 2, Halo 2, Unreal Tournament,* and *Call of Duty*. Gordon, who is sitting under the desk, comments, "You guys sure like shooters."

"No one asked for your opinion, fat-ass," Red Bandanna says.

Years ago, you were on a panel about violence and games, and the most knowledgeable among you was a guy in a corduroy jacket with elbow patches, who'd literally written a book on the subject. He said that most, if not all, gamers were able to make the distinction between playing a violent game and committing a violent act, and that kids might even become psychologically healthier from indulging violent fantasies through play. You are no expert, but what you know is this: No human has ever been murdered with a video game weapon.

You look at your phone. Five minutes have passed since you called Sam.

You go to the mini fridge underneath Gordon's desk. "You want a Fiji water? We have some PowerBars back here, too."

Red Bandanna shakes his head, but Black Bandanna accepts the drink. He lifts up his bandanna to drink, and you can see his face. Boyish, a gathering of tender, red marks, irregularly stubbled.

"So, what's your beef with Mazer?" you say. "From what I can tell, you guys aren't playing any of our games."

"It's *Mapleworld*," Black Bandanna says.

"Don't fucking tell him," Red Bandanna says.

"Why? He'll find out soon enough," Black Bandanna says. "His wife got married to a woman in *Mapleworld,* and now she left him for the woman she married, and . . ."

"Fuck you," Red Bandanna says to his partner. "That's none of his fucking business."

"So, you blame Sam."

"Who's Sam?" Red Bandanna says.

"Mayor Mazer."

"I blame Mazer. And I will have my vengeance," he says, speaking like a character in a video game that has been poorly translated.

You turn to Black Bandanna. "And you? Why are you here?"

"Because I don't think it's right," Black Bandanna says. "Little kids play *Mapleworld*. I'm not prejudiced, but why should all this gay stuff be forced on kids?" He looks at you to see if you're agreeing with him. You keep your face impartial. "Also, I'm his best friend since kindergarten, so I had to come."

You nod. These guys are saying this like it's perfectly reasonable to show up at an office with two guns and demand to shoot a game designer. They're acting like they're on a fishing trip, a groomsmen's weekend to Vegas. You imagine them choosing the bandannas they're wearing before they left the house, debating whether bandannas set the right tone for shooting up an office. "So, what's the plan?" you say.

"I want to kill Mazer," Red Bandanna says.

"But Mazer's not here. So, maybe the best thing for you to do is go home?"

"Fuck you," Red Bandanna says. He pushes the barrel of the gun into your cheek. "This is taking too long. I want to see the office now." He moves the gun to your spine, and you lead them up the stairs. It sounds promisingly quiet on the second floor, but you're still holding your breath when you go to open the fire door.

The entire floor is empty, and you try not to look relieved.

"Did you lie to me?" Red Bandanna says. "Where is everyone?"

You make up a story about a company retreat. "Look, Sam's office is right over here."

"If you're important, then why aren't *you* on the company retreat?" Red Bandanna asks.

"Because someone has to mind the farm. I'm an NPC, right?"

The Bandanna Boys begin to knock things off Sam's shelves. *Ichigo* memorabilia everywhere. "I hate that game," Red Bandanna says. "Fucking little boy in a dress."

The phone rings. Red Bandanna tells you to answer it: it's the police. They're outside, and they have a hostage negotiator with them. They want to speak to Red Bandanna. But before you hand over the phone, you cover the mouthpiece. "You should decide what you want out of this," you tell Red Bandanna. He has light brown eyes, and you can see fear in them. "No one's gotten hurt yet, and that's in your favor. So, ask for what you want, and move on with your life. You're not going to be able to shoot Mazer today."

Red Bandanna reaches for the phone, and then he hangs it up. He starts to weep, and he takes off his bandanna to wipe off his eyes, and for the first time, you can see his face and he looks like a boy. He looks like Sam the night he shaved his head. He looks vulnerable and, despite everything, you want to help him.

"It's okay," you say. You try to put your arms around Red Bandanna. This is a mistake. He pushes you against the wall with both of his hands.

"Get off of me, you goddamn queer."

"Jesus, Josh," Black Bandanna says.

"Don't say my *fucking* name," Red Bandanna says.

At that moment—what could he possibly be thinking?—Ant comes down the stairs into the office. He has his hands up. "Marx," he calls, "It's Ant. Are you all right?"

Red Bandanna points his gun at Ant.

"Is that fucking Mazer?" Red Bandanna says. "Did you lie to me?" He turns to you. "Has he been here this whole time?"

"That's not Mazer," you say. "That's another one of our employees. His name is Anthony Ruiz."

"It looks like Mazer to me," Red Bandanna insists. Maybe he truly believes that Ant is Sam. That day, Ant is unluckily wearing a red plaid shirt like the Samatar in *Mapleworld*. Sam and Ant don't look that much alike, other than being slightly built, dark-haired, and olive complexioned. They aren't the same races. You realize that, to the boy with the gun, it probably doesn't matter what particular "other" he is looking at.

Or maybe he doesn't mistake Sam for Ant. Maybe he just doesn't like the look of Ant. With his Mohawk and his tight jeans, Ant instantly becomes a symbol of the liberal agenda of game companies.

Maybe he just wants to shoot someone.

You hear Red Bandanna's finger move the trigger, and you jump between Ant and the gun. "Josh, don't shoot," you say.

You're too late. Red Bandanna fires the five bullets in his round. One hits Ant—you don't know where.

Three hit you.

```
I felt
SHOOT
a Funeral,
SHOOT
in my
SHOOT
Brain
SHOOT
```

The last one, Red Bandanna uses to shoot himself in the head.

"Oh my God, Josh," Black Bandanna says, "what'd you do? What'd you do that for? We said we were just gonna scare them a little bit." Black Bandanna falls to his knees, clasps his hands, and begins to recite the Lord's Prayer.

A few seconds before you pass out . . .

Your phone rings. It's Sadie.

Sadie, by the way, is pregnant. You thought you wanted the baby, but it's her body and you followed her lead. You discussed the impedimenta: what it would mean for work, for life. You are a game producer, and so you drew up a spreadsheet, the same way you would for a game you were thinking of producing. You listed pros and cons, divisions of labor, potential hazards, costs, benefits, dates, and deliverables.

You showed her what you had worked out on your laptop. "Our theoretical baby can't be called Spreadsheet1.xls," she commented. She retitled the spreadsheet "Green Watanabe Summer 2006 Game."

She requested a printout, and a day or two later, she said she wanted to have the baby. "It's never a good time, but it's also a good time," she said. "*Master of the Revels* is done. I can work on the expansion pack through the spring, and the baby will drop in the summer. With any luck, it'll fare better than your Tamagotchi."

You and Sadie began referring to the baby as Tamagotchi Watanabe Green.

You are in a hospital.

Down the hallway, carolers are singing, but you can't quite hear the song. As they travel closer to your room, you determine it's that Joni Mitchell song that makes everyone want to kill themselves, and if anything, the song is even more depressing when sung by carolers in a hospital. You can't remember the title, and this disturbs you. You always remember the title.

Someone has decorated the hospital room with a single string of star-shaped Christmas lights. You can't imagine who that could be. Everyone close to you is Jewish, or Buddhist, or atheist, or agnostic.

If it's Christmas, that means you've been in a coma for three weeks.

If it's Christmas, that means you didn't call the Worths.

If it's Christmas, that means *Master of the Revels* is in stores and available for download.

If it's Christmas, that means Sadie is almost in the second trimester.

Your mother and father are here. They are so rarely together that you know your condition must be grave.

You remember that the song is called "River."

Your mother is in the bedside chair. She is wearing a dress printed with strawberries and birds. Using a long needle, she is stringing brightly colored origami cranes into garlands. You know what she's doing: It's a Japanese custom called senbazuru. If you make one thousand paper cranes, you can restore someone to good health.

Though you cannot see him, you become aware of the fact that your father is sitting on the floor. He is folding cranes so that your mother can string them.

This is marriage.

After a while, your father leaves. Your mother continues to string the cranes, but without your father, her supply quickly diminishes. Cranes can be strung faster than they can be constructed.

When Sam arrives, he introduces himself. "You must be Marx's mother."

"Anna," she says.

"That's my mother's name," Sam says. "Marx never mentioned that our mothers had the same first name. I thought you had a different name."

Your mother explains, "AeRan is my Korean name. When I'm in the U.S., everyone calls me Anna."

"Anna Watanabe."

"Watanabe is my husband's name. I'm Anna Lee."

"Anna Lee was my mother's name, too," Sam says.

"Do I look like your mother?"

"Not at all," Sam says. "It's strange that Marx and I never discussed this."

"Maybe he didn't think it was notable," your mother suggests. "Lee is quite a common name, as is Anna." Your mother is not in the least sentimental about anything but fabric. "Maybe he didn't know?"

Sam walks over to the bed, and he studies your face. "No, Marx always knew everything about everything." When you figured out Sam's dead mother's name, you decided that it was fate, and from that day forward, Sam would be your brother. A name is destiny, if you think it is.

Sam turns back to your mother. "You're almost out of cranes," he says. "If you teach me how to make one, I can help." Your mother demonstrates, and then Sam sits down on the hospital room floor, and he begins folding cranes, as well.

· · ·

You are still alive.

Sadie is brushing your hair, and she is telling you that *Master of the Revels* is the best-selling game in America. "I don't think they even like the game," Sadie says. "People feel sorry for us, I guess."

You want to tell her to stop with the false humility, if that's what it is. No one drops sixty dollars on a game out of pity. Without warning, your mind flies away.

You are still alive.

"Ant's out of the hospital," Sam says. "He's going to be fine."

Good, you think.

"Gordon was here. He brought you lavender."

You can't see the flowers, but you think you can possibly smell them. There is an ungenerous part of you that wishes you had left Gordon in the reception area and gone up to the roof with everyone else.

Video games don't make people violent, but maybe they falsely give you the idea that you can be a hero. Without warning, your mind flies away again.

Still alive.

You wake in the middle of the night. Someone is in the room with you. You see her Titian hair. You hear the scratch of pencil against paper.

It's Zoe. You wonder what she's working on.

"It's a score for a movie," she answers, as if she's heard your question. "It's some dumb horror movie, but it's so hard to get it right. I had this intellectual idea, but I don't know if it will work. I want to limit the instrumentation to only percussion and brass, but I'm worried it sounds a bit high school marching band. I might have to throw everything I've done out and start again. And they're paying me about thirty cents. And deferrals, of course, which I'll never ever see. The movie's called *Bloody Balloons.*" Zoe rolls her eyes. "*Bloody Balloons* is never going to see deferrals." She smiles at you. "Marx, you had better be all right. I absolutely can't bear the thought of a world without you." She squeezes your hand and then she kisses your cheek. "No, I won't bear it. I refuse to bear it. Love you madly, my sweet friend."

Love you madly.

The way to turn an ex-lover into a friend is to never stop loving them, to know that when one phase of a relationship ends it can transform into something else. It is to acknowledge that love is both a constant and a variable at the same time.

You are going to die.

Some hours, days, or weeks later, you are listening to a doctor tell your mother and father, in an outrageously serene voice, that you, Marx Watanabe, citizen of the world, are going to die.

You are a gaming person, which is to say you are the kind of person who believes that "game over" is a construction. The game is only over if you stop playing. There is always one more life. Even the most brutal death isn't final. You could have taken poison, fallen into a vat of acid, been decapitated, been shot a hundred times, and still, if you clicked restart, you could begin it all over again. Next time, you would get it right. Next time, you might even win.

But it cannot be denied.

You *feel* the body. The blood is sludgy, moving through the circulatory system at the speed of the I-10 at rush hour. The heart is not beating on its own. The brain is

Slowing.

Down.

Increasingly, the brain is

Flying.

Off.

Soon, you will not be you. You, like all of us, are a deictic case.

You are a Tamer of Horses.

For your thirty-first birthday, Sam makes you a nameplate that reads:

MARX WATANABE
TAMER OF HORSES

You laugh when you see it. "Technically," you say, "some sources translate it as 'Breaker of Horses.'"

"But that's not what you are," Sam says.

The first time he had called you that, it was meant to be an insult, but over the years, the name had transformed into something loving, a joke between friends.

And so you accept it. This is what you are.

When you were a boy, you never thought you would be a producer of video games. You must admit there were times when you wondered if it was a mortifying passivity that had led you to this employment. Had you become a video game producer because Sam and Sadie had wanted to make video games, and you had nothing else you were doing at the time? Had you become a video game producer because you loved people who wanted to make games? How much of your life had been happenstance? How much of your life had been a roll of the big polyhedral die in the sky? But then, weren't all lives that way? Who could say, in the end, that they had chosen any of it? And even if you hadn't exactly chosen video game producer, you were good at it.

You are thinking of *Our Infinite Days*. How you wish you might play it. You can anticipate problems with the game, and you want to help the Worths solve them. For instance, they will have to choose vampires or zombies. They will have to choose a single mythology, or they will have to make a new one. Or . . .

But it is not your problem anymore.

Sam is holding one of your hands, and Sadie is holding the other. And your parents are there, but they are standing behind your friends. And this makes sense, because Sadie and Sam have been your family, as much as your family has been your family. Behind them, a thousand paper cranes festoon the room.

"It's okay, Marx," Sadie says. "You can let go."

As the brain is detaching from the body, you think, *How I will miss the horses.*

. . .

You are in a peach orchard.

Here is a perfect day. Your high school classmate, Swan, is in town, and he knows a guy who has adopted a peach tree on Masumoto Family Farm, near Fresno. Swan's guy says that you and your friends can take all the fruit they want from the tree, but the only day you're allowed to go is Saturday morning.

"People adopt peach trees?" you ask.

"These aren't ordinary peaches," Swan tells you. "The fruit is too delicate to be shipped to grocery stores. The farm has been owned by the family since 1948, since just after internment. My friend had to write an essay and fill out an application to be allowed to adopt the tree."

You tell Zoe, and she wants to go. And she invites Sadie, who invites Alice. And you invite Sam, who invites Lola, the girl he is seeing. And then you invite Simon and Ant, because they should take a day off from making *Love Doppelgängers* every now and again. The group leaves Los Angeles at 6 a.m. and by 9:30, you're in Fresno, but it seems like a whole other world.

The peaches are impossibly large and almost fluffy. They aren't engineered to survive the indignities of shipping, of grocery store shelves. Zoe samples one, and she says it's like eating a flower. And then she hands it to you, and you take a bite, and you say it's like drinking a peach. And then you hand the peach to Sam, who bites down and says, it's like a song about a peach more than it's like a peach.

And your friends begin to make increasingly absurd similes and metaphors about peaches.

"It's like finding Jesus."

"It's like finding out the things you believed in as a child are actually real."

"It's like eating the mushrooms in *Super Mario*."

"It's like recovering from dysentery."

"It's like Christmas morning."

"It's like all eight nights of Hanukkah."

"It's like having an orgasm."

"It's like having *multiple* orgasms."

"It's like watching a great movie."

"Reading a great book."

"Playing a great game."

"It's like finishing debugging on your own game."

"It's the taste of youth itself."

"It's feeling well after a long sickness."

"It's running a marathon."

"I'll probably never have to do a single other thing in my life, because I tasted this peach."

The last one to taste is Sadie. Somehow, the peach—what's left of it—makes its way back to you, and you hold it up to the tree, where Sadie has been industriously harvesting.

Sadie wears a big straw hat, and she has climbed up the ladder and set a wicker basket on the top step. She looks so fine and wholesome, like a girl in a WPA poster. She is smiling at you, exposing the narrow gap between her teeth. "Do I dare?" she asks.

"You dare."

You are in the strawberry field.

You are dead.

A prompt comes up on the screen: *Start game from the beginning?*

Yes, you think. *Why not?* If you play again, you might win.

Suddenly, there you are, brand-new, feathers restored, bones unbroken, sanguine with fresh blood.

You are flying more slowly than last time, because you don't want to miss any of it. The cows. The lavender. The woman humming Beethoven. The distant bees. The sad-faced man and the couple in the pond. The beat of your heart before you go onstage. The feel of a lace sleeve against your skin. Your mother singing Beatles songs to you, trying to sound like she's from Liverpool. The first playthrough of *Ichigo.* The rooftop on Abbot Kinney. The taste of Sadie mixed with Hefeweizen beer. Sam's round head in your hands. A thousand paper cranes. Yellow-tinted sunglasses. A perfect peach.

This world, you think.

You are flying over the strawberry field, but you know it's a trap.

This time, you keep flying.

VIII

———

OUR INFINITE DAYS

1

The first time Sam saw Marx die was in October of 1993. Marx had been cast as Banquo in a black box production of *Macbeth*. "So, here's the setup," Marx explained. "Fleance and I are on our way to a dinner party at Macbeth's. We dismount our horses, though I highly doubt there will be horses, this being college theater. I light a torch—how else will the murderers see me? The three murderers approach! They attack. I die spectacularly, cursing all responsible: *O treachery!* Etcetera, etcetera." Marx lowered his voice, "I can already tell the director's an idiot. I'm going to have to work out the blocking entirely on my own, or the whole thing will end up looking shoddy. Sam, you'll play the murderers, okay? I'll come in from the bathroom, and then you'll surprise me." Marx handed Sam his paperback *Macbeth*, open to act 3, scene 3.

Sam had only lived with Marx for twenty-three days, and he didn't feel he knew Marx well enough to pretend to murder him, or even run lines with him. He did not wish to be entangled in someone else's drama, someone else's life. The less he knew about his roommate and the less his roommate knew about him, the better.

The main thing Sam did not wish Marx to know about him was that he had a disability, though Sam did not think of it as a disability—other people had disabilities; Sam had "the thing with my foot." Sam experienced his body as an antiquated joystick that could reliably move only in cardinal directions. The way to avoid appearing disabled was to avoid situations in which one looked disabled: uneven terrain, unfamiliar staircases, and most analog forms of frolic. Sam demurred, "I'm not much of an actor."

"It's not acting," Marx said. "It's pretend murdering."

"And I've got so much reading to do. And a problem set due on Wednesday."

Marx rolled his eyes. He picked up a couch cushion. "This pillow will be Fleance."

"Who's Fleance?"

"My young son. He escapes." Marx flung the pillow toward the door. "*Fly, good Fleance, fly, fly, fly!*"

"Never a good idea to let the son of the man you've murdered escape," Sam said. "Is he Fleance because he flees?"

"Am I Banquo because I die on the way to a banquet? These are solid questions, Sam."

"What am I murdering you with?"

"A knife? A sword? I don't think it says. He—or they, whatever Shakespeare is—writes vaguely, unhelpfully, 'They attack.'"

"Well, I think the weapon makes a difference."

"I'll leave the selection of a weapon to you."

"Why don't you counterattack? Aren't you a warrior, or some such?"

"Because I'm not expecting to be attacked. That's where you come in. Surprise me." Marx smiled at Sam conspiratorially. "*Help me.* It's my big scene, so, you know, I want it to look cool."

"Your last scene, too, right? You die."

"No, I come back as a ghost, but I don't have any lines. I just show up at the banquet," Marx said. "I'm not even sure if they'll have me in the scene, or if it'll be an empty chair. It depends on how much we're in Macbeth's point of view."

"Is Banquo a good role?" Sam asked. "I'm not particularly familiar with *Macbeth*."

"It's the best friend. It's not Macbeth. It's not 'A tale told by an idiot, full of sound and fury signifying nothing.' But it has its moments. I have a name! I get to die! I have a ghost! And I'm only a freshman, so there's plenty of time for me to be the lead. The shame of it is, I've always wanted to play Macbeth, and I doubt anyone'll stage it again before I graduate."

For the next hour, Marx died a variety of ways. He fell back on the couch; he dropped to his knees; he staggered around the common room, clutching various parts of his body—his throat, his forearm, his wrist, his magnificent hair. He whispered his lines, and once, he yelled them so loudly, a prefect came by to make sure Marx wasn't actually being murdered. Sam found that he barely thought about his foot. He enjoyed saying the murderers' lines; hiding behind the door, then attacking Marx with a pillow from behind; pretending to put his hands around Marx's neck. If Marx noticed that Sam's attacks were always weighted toward the right, he did not say.

"You're not that bad. Have you done any acting before?" Marx asked.

"No," Sam said. He thought he would leave it at that, but then, scant of breath, flattered, and indiscreet, he found himself continuing, "My mom was a professional actress, so I used to run lines with her sometimes."

"What does she do now?"

"She ... Well, she's dead."

"I'm sorry."

"A long time ago," Sam said. It was one thing to concede having had a mother, but to tell the story of her death to a fantastic-looking person you barely knew ... "By the way," Sam said, "live animals are a bad idea for theater in general."

"True."

"Not just college theater. You mentioned before—"

"I'm right there with you, Sam," Marx said. "Maybe you should audition next semester?"

Sam shook his head.

"Why not?"

"I've got a thing ... Maybe you've ..." Sam began. "In here. This is fine, but I don't like being onstage. Shall we run it again?"

Sam had never been sure when he had become friends with Marx, but he supposed that night could reasonably be considered the beginning.

He had needed a starting data point in order to calculate the total number of days of their friendship. Once he settled on the night they rehearsed Marx's death, he determined the number to be 4,873 days, give or take. Sam normally took comfort in numbers, but he was disturbed by how paltry this particular number was, considering the presence Marx had maintained in his life. He performed the calculation twice to confirm. Yes, it was 4,873. This was the kind of baby math Sam did when he couldn't sleep.

Four thousand eight hundred seventy-three, Sam thought, *the dollars in a seventeen-year-old's bank account when he's flush, twice the number of passengers on the* Titanic, *the population of a town where everyone knows each other, the inflation-adjusted cost of a laptop in 1990, the weight of a teenage elephant, six months or so more than the number of days I knew my mother.*

Once, when he was fifteen—just old enough to acknowledge the inner lives of others beyond himself; not yet old enough to have a driver's license—Sam had asked his grandmother how she'd gotten through the time after his mother's death. She'd had a business to run, a sick grandson to care for, presumably her own grief to work through, though she was deeply unsentimental and never mentioned it. They were in her car on the way back from a math competition in San Diego, and Sam was giddy with the feeling of being better than everyone else at something that he didn't care about at all.

Despite having almost died in a car accident, Sam relished these car trips. He had his best conversations with his grandmother in the car, at night, and though Bong Cha and Dong Hyun alternated chauffeur duties, he preferred when his grandmother drove. She was fast, and the trips took two-thirds of the time if Bong Cha was behind the wheel.

"How did we get through?" Bong Cha had been baffled by Sam's question. "We got up in the morning," she said finally. "We went to work. We went to the hospital. We came home. We went to sleep. We did it again."

"But it must have been hard," Sam persisted.

"The beginning was the hardest, but then days passed, and months, and years, and you got better, and it was not quite so hard," Bong Cha said.

Sam thought she was finished entertaining the subject when she added, "Sometimes, I spoke to Anna anyway, and this helped a little."

"Do you mean like a ghost?" His grandmother was the least likely person in the world to see ghosts.

"Sam, don't be ridiculous. There are no ghosts."

"Okay, so you spoke to her. She was definitely not a ghost. Did she ever reply?"

Bong Cha narrowed her eyes at Sam, deciding if her grandson was trying to trick her into appearing foolish. "Yes, in my mind, she did. I knew your mother so well I could play her part. The same with my own mother and my grandmother and my childhood best friend, Euna, who drowned in the lake by her cousin's house. There are no ghosts, but up here"—she gestured toward her head—"it's a haunted house." She squeezed Sam's hand and inelegantly changed the subject. "It's time you learned how to drive."

Concealed by darkness, Sam felt comfortable admitting to Bong Cha that he was more than a little scared to begin driving himself.

2

Seventy-two days after the shooting, two days after Marx's funeral, Simon called Sam. "I know things have been awful," he began. This is the way everyone started a conversation with Sam that year. "But what are we going to do about the office? Ant's feeling somewhat better, and we had just started playtesting and debugging *CPH4* when everything happened. And if we don't get back in, we'll never make our release date in August—are we even still releasing the game in August? And people are wondering if they still have jobs, and I don't honestly know what to tell them . . . I don't want to overstep here, but we need to know what to do."

It had, of course, usually fallen to Marx to conduct the practical business of running their company. Sam and Sadie were creatives! They were grand schemes and big pictures! Marx kept the bills paid, the lights on, the plants watered. Marx was the one who talked to people. This wasn't to say that this was all Sam thought Marx did. The arrangement went largely unmentioned: Marx was Marx, so that Sam and Sadie could be Sam and Sadie. But Marx, of course, was no longer here.

Sam tried to imagine what Marx would say to Simon. "I'm glad you called, and you're completely right. Let me talk to Sadie," Sam said. "I'll have an answer for you by the end of today."

Sam called Sadie. When she did not answer, he texted her, *What should we do about the office?* Five minutes passed before Sadie replied, *Do what you want.*

He considered texting her something sharp in return. Because what Sam wanted to do was to stay in bed, like Sadie was probably doing. What Sam wanted to do was get stupendously high—find a great drug that turned his brain off for a year but stopped short of killing him.

His pain, a mortifyingly psychosomatic weathervane, had returned, and none of his usual strategies for tamping it down were working. The pain seemed to come on as he was arriving at the deepest part of sleep, when his foolish human brain was the most vulnerable to dreams. During this time, Sam's dreams usually featured a mundane task he had neglected: he'd be back in the Kennedy Street apartment, and he would realize that he had forgotten to debug a particular section of *Ichigo*. Or he'd be driving on the 405, and just as he wanted to brake, he'd become aware that he was missing his foot. Sam would wake up, covered in sweat, ghost foot throbbing, feeling panicked and guilty. He would be in such discomfort that he could not return to sleep. Sam had not slept for more than a two-hour stretch since December.

Still, unlike Sadie, Sam was answering his phone. Sam was replying to emails. Sam was talking to people.

He was about to press send on a strongly worded text to Sadie when he found himself asking for the second time that day, *What would Marx say?* Marx, Sam decided, would take a second to empathize with Sadie's situation. Sadie was pregnant. She had not only lost her business partner, she had lost her life partner. Unlike Sam, Sadie had had no significant experience with loss or grief. It was harder for Sadie. Marx, Sam concluded, would simply get whatever needed doing done.

In the three months since Marx had been shot, Sam had not returned to the office on Abbot Kinney, and when he finally did, he decided to go alone. He did not want to subject an assistant, or his grandfather, or Lola, or Simon, or even Tuesday, to whatever horror might be inside. The only person he would have wanted with him was Sadie. Though he told her he was going, he felt it would be cruel to explicitly ask her to come with him. She did not volunteer.

In front of the threshold of their office door, an impromptu shrine had been created: stuffed-animal effigies of Mayor Mazer and Ichigo, dead carnations and roses in plastic sleeves, satin ribbons of support tied wherever they could be tied, weather-beaten cards that seemed like they must have been outside for decades and not weeks, game boxes, votive candles. It was the kind of pointless accumulation one saw whenever a gun crime happened. All of it was meant to say, *We stand with you, we love you, we condemn what happened here.* In the face of this display, Sam felt nothing, except a passing desire to kick stuffed Mayor Mazer in the face. As he stepped over the shrine, he made a note: *(1) remove shrine,* and then he slipped his key into the door. Sam almost expected that his key wouldn't work, but it did not resist. He made notes: *(2) locks, (3) new security.*

The air inside was a tick colder than usual and had a staleness, though it did not, to Sam's nose, smell like murder or indeed, like anything. Standing in the lobby, Sam felt as if he had stepped into a little-used room at a museum. He could imagine finding a small, tasteful plaque that read: GAME COMPANY, VENICE, CALIFORNIA, CIRCA 2005. The tree in the lobby was dying: *(4) plants.*

Sam made his way through the space wearily, warily, like a character in a stealth game. In one of the wooden columns, a bullet hole: *(5) fill hole.*

The worst of the damage was a series of grisly bloodstains on the floor where Marx had been shot. Marx's blood had seeped through the polished concrete. The floor had been overdue for a refinishing, and the blood had been allowed to settle for too long. Sam tried cleaning it with a series of increasingly potent cleansers: water, Windex, iodine, Comet, bleach. The stain was too deep; the floor would need to be professionally refinished: *(6) floors.*

An untethered strip of police tape lent the room a festive feeling. Sam threw it in the trash.

Sam went into Marx's office. Though he had not run Unfair Games, he had some practical knowledge of business from his grandparents. In Marx's files, he found the contact information for their insurance company. The agent he spoke to said that their policy did not explicitly cover damage from mass shootings—*Did two constitute mass?* Sam wondered—and thus, it was unlikely insurance would cover repairs. *Do take pictures, Mr. Mazer. You're welcome to file a claim.*

Sam found the name of their cleaning service, and also, the flooring contractor who had done the floors when they first moved in, and then, in order to pay for these things, he located the name of their accountant. The accountant had apparently been their accountant since 1997, since Cambridge, though Sam had never had reason to speak to the man before. "Nice to meet you over the phone. It's a terrible thing that happened, but it's good you're getting back to work," the accountant said. "Unfair's a little cash poor right now."

"We are?" Sam said.

"You tied up a lot of cash purchasing the building on Abbot Kinney last October, and that was a major expense. In the long run, you'll be glad you did it, though."

For the first time in his life, Sam did not want to contemplate the long run.

Sam left Marx's office and went into his own office, where he was confronted by a *Guernica*-style massacre of Ichigo merchandise: disembodied heads with bowl haircuts, and chubby limbs, and round childish eyes, and waves, and boats, and torsos in football jerseys. Sam picked up a ceramic Ichigo head from the floor. The head had once been attached to a body, and together, they had formed a piggy bank that had been a promotional item for the game's Danish release. Sam considered the chipped ceramic head, and he shuddered: those men had wanted to kill him. They had wanted to kill him and had settled for destroying Ichigo merch and killing Marx instead.

A memory from Marx's hospital room: Without preamble, Sadie is screaming at Sam, *They wanted you. They wanted you. They wanted you.* She beats his chest with her fists, and he doesn't try to stop her. *Harder,* he thinks. *Please.* The next day, or the next week, or the next month, she apologizes, but the apology lacks the conviction of the attack.

Sam threw the Ichigo head in the trash can. He left his office and locked the door behind him. He was in no mood to deal with the dead Ichigo museum, and maybe, he no longer required an office filled with memorabilia. What did the memorabilia prove anyway? They had made games. Some people had promoted those games and tried to monetize them with gimcracks that no one needed.

He made a note: *(7) mazer office junk.* He returned to Marx's office. In his pocket, the buzz of his cell phone. It was Sadie, and her voice was tight and small. "Are you there now? Is it awful?"

"It's not so bad."

"Describe it," she said.

"I—there's not much to say."

"You have to be honest. I don't want to be surprised."

"It's still the office. They mainly messed up my office. I'll never be able to put that Ichigo piggy bank back together. There's some damage to the floor. There's a hole in a pillar."

Sadie didn't say anything for a beat. "'Damage' is obfuscation. What does 'damage' mean?"

"It's blood," Sam said. "It seeped into the concrete."

"How big is the stain?"

"I don't know. The largest section is a couple of feet in circumference."

"There's a spot several feet wide where Marx bled to death, you mean."

"Yes, I guess so." Sam felt existentially tired. A contrary part of him wanted to insist that Marx hadn't bled to death on that floor. He had died in a hospital, ten weeks later. But Sam was too tired for semantics. "I spoke to a flooring contractor. It can be refinished."

"Maybe I don't want it to be cleaned," Sadie said.

"You mean, you want me to leave it?"

"No, but it shouldn't be erased," Sadie said. "Marx shouldn't just be erased."

"Come on, Sadie. The stain isn't Marx. It's—"

She interrupted him, "The place where he died."

"It's—"

"The place where he was murdered."

"I think it will be hard for people to work around a huge blood-stain."

"Yes, it will be hard," Sadie said.

"How about a great vintage rug, then? Marx loved kilim rugs."

"That isn't even a little funny."

"I'm sorry. It isn't funny. I'm tired. Seriously, Sadie, do you not want people to return to work?"

"I don't know."

"Do you want to come and look at it?" he said hopefully. "We can decide what to do together. I can pick you up."

"No, I do not want to look at it, Sam. I do not want to fucking look at it! What is wrong with you?"

"Okay, okay."

"Just take care of it," she said.

"That's what I was trying to do, Sadie." A long pause. He could hear her breathing, so he knew she was still there.

"Considering this, considering the god-awful state of things, maybe it would be better to move offices?" she said. "Even if we clean the floor, will anyone ever want to work at those offices again?"

"I don't know if we can afford to move," Sam said. "We're behind on every project, and we've been paying people for three months but not getting much, or any, work done. Simon and Ant need to finish *CPH4* now. *Revels* expansion pack needs to be ready for December, too."

"Ant's coming back?" Sadie said.

"Yes. Simon thinks so."

"That's brave," Sadie said, but there was a meanness to her tone, and he could tell that she was about to commence a new argument. "Are you saying we can't move because you don't want the bother of moving? Or can we actually not move?"

"Sadie, I'm telling you the truth. I spoke to our accountant this morning. You can call him yourself."

"It's just you have a way of bending reality to suit your own agenda."

"What agenda do I have? Except to get our people back to work."

"I don't know, Sam. What agenda could you have?"

"I don't want our company to close. That's my agenda. Marx would want the same thing."

"Marx doesn't want anything anymore," she said. "You know what, Sam? Do what you will. You always do."

"Are you okay?"

"What do you think?" She hung up the phone.

(8) Sadie . . .

The only thing he could do for Sadie was to keep their business running until she was ready to return to it.

The day stretched impossibly long though it was only eleven, and it was two more hours until the floor guy would arrive. Sam lay down on the firm, orange sofa in Marx's office, and he closed his eyes but did not go to sleep.

The phone in Marx's office rang, and without considering who might be on the other end or whether he was even in a state to field Marx's calls, Sam answered.

"Great! Someone's here!" a female voice said. "The voicemail's entirely filled up. I tried sending an email, but the only address I had was Marx's, and . . ."

"This is Mazer. Who is this?" Sam asked impatiently.

"Mazer? Wow, it's honestly such an honor to meet you over the phone."

"Who is this?" Sam repeated.

"Oh! I'm sorry. My name is Charlotte Worth. My husband and I were meeting with Marx about our game when . . . when . . . Well, he was thinking of making it. Maybe he mentioned it? It's about this mother and her daughter after the apocalypse. The mother has amnesia, and the daughter is a kid like Ichigo, and there are vampires, but they're not really vampires, it's hard to explain, and—"

Sam interrupted her, "I wouldn't know anything about that."

"I know this is a bad time, but Marx had some of our original concept art for *Our Infinite Days*—that's what our game's called—and we left it at the office, and we need to get it back, if possible."

"I wouldn't know anything about that," Sam repeated.

"Well, if you see it . . ." Charlotte said. "Or if you could have someone look for it. It was in a black portfolio, with the monogram *AW* on it. *A* is for my husband, Adam."

"Honestly, what the hell is wrong with you?" Sam said. "Marx is dead. I have neither the time nor the desire to look for your husband's portfolio, or to hear your insipid game pitch."

"I'm sorry," Charlotte said. Her voice sounded weepy, and this pissed Sam off more than he already was. Sadie had been awful on the phone, but she hadn't cried. What right did this stranger have to cry? "I know it's a terrible time. I know. I just need our materials back. If you could—"

Sam hung up the phone.

In the Harvard-Radcliffe Dramatic Club fall 1993 production of *Macbeth,* the director ultimately decided that Marx wouldn't appear as Banquo's ghost. The director had the actor playing Macbeth stare at an empty chair at a long banquet table—an invisible Marx that only Macbeth could see—and then he directed Macbeth to throw dinner rolls, purloined nightly from the Adams House dining hall, at the empty chair. "Reduced to dinner rolls, Sam!" Marx complained. "The indignity of it!" By opening night, though, Marx had made peace with the decision. As he said to Sam, "If I've done the work in the scenes before I die, if I've made a real impression, they'll feel me in the scenes I'm not in anyway."

Sam's cell phone rang. The floor guy was early. Sam went downstairs to let him in.

Sam showed him the stain and the guy went cheerfully to work. "I remember when I did these floors, maybe five, six years ago, right?" the floor guy said. "Beautiful space. Great light. A pale girl with red hair let me in. What kind of company is this again? Something in tech, right?"

"Video games," Sam said.

"That must be fun."

Sam did not reply.

"What happened here?" the floor guy asked.

"Sorry," Sam said. He walked away and pretended to take a call. "Yes, this is Mazer. I'm here with the floor guy right now," he improvised lamely. "Yes, yes." He found himself facing the pillar with the bullet hole in it. A handyman was coming tomorrow, but looking at the hole, Sam thought maybe he should leave the scar. It wasn't gory, like the bloody floor would have been. The hole was perfectly symmetrical, round, clean. The wood was miraculously un-splintered, darker on the edges, like a knot that might have always been there. To an outsider, it didn't obviously signify the death of his partner.

It was just a hole.

3

The *Master of the Revels* expansion pack was scheduled for a December release, a year after the original game had come out, but by the end of April, no substantive work had been done. Mori, whom Sadie had put in charge of the project, was reluctant to complain about Sadie to Sam, but finally admitted that work was going slowly because Sadie was, for all practical purposes, unreachable.

"I'm sympathetic," Mori said. "She's going through a terrible time."

"Can you do the work without her?" Sam asked.

Mori considered the question before answering. "We could," Mori said. "But I would prefer not to."

Sam knew exactly how he felt. "I'll talk to her," Sam said.

In theory, Sadie was working from home. It was useless to phone her, so Sam texted her. He was starting to resent the elliptical nature of texting Sadie, the way she could ignore half of what he said and, often, the important half. *The Revels Ex team could use your input.*

I'll check in with them this afternoon, Sadie texted about an hour later.

Do you mean you'll come in? Sam replied.

No. I'll call.

They seem a little lost, Sam texted.

Sadie did not respond.

On the day the Unfair offices officially reopened, Sam had wanted the two of them to give a rousing we-shall-carry-on St. Crispin's Day type of speech to their returned employees. When Sadie agreed to the plan, Sam felt cautiously hopeful. *If they could get back to work. If she could get back to work.*

They had arranged to meet outside the offices an hour before the employees were to arrive. The locks had been changed and security had been updated, so he needed to let her in.

He felt relieved when she arrived a minute before the appointed hour. She was wearing a black jersey dress, and for the first time, he could see that she was pregnant. He surprised himself by having the impulse to do that awful, invasive thing that people did to pregnant women—to violate her personal space and touch her abdomen. But he wouldn't do that to Sadie. He waved to her. She waved back and she crossed the street, and Sam thought, *We will go inside. We will cross this threshold one more time. We will be fine.*

"Hello, stranger," he said, holding out his hand to her.

She looked as if she might take his hand, but then she grimaced. Her shoulders hunched slightly, her nostrils flared, and she turned to face the wall. He couldn't see her face. "I need a minute," she said.

Her breathing sounded fast and erratic. She rotated back to face Sam, though she did not look him in the eyes. Her forehead was covered in a fine sweat. "I can't," she said.

"Let's just go inside." Sam unlocked the door. "You'll see. You'll feel better once you're inside."

"You have to do this without me."

"Sadie, I . . ." For the usual reasons, he could not bring himself to say *need*. "People will want to see you." Sam paused. "I know it's asking a lot, but it's our company. It's ours and Marx's, and people are counting on us. You don't have to say anything, if you don't want to. Just come in and see people. Ant's up there already."

Sadie's face was pale and she was shivering. "I'm sorry, Sam," she said. "I simply can't. I—" Without warning, she threw up on the sidewalk. She clutched the side of the building to steady herself. He could hear her nails scratch against the brick.

"Hyperemesis gravidarum," she said. "The more pregnant I get, the worse it seems to get, though my ob-gyn keeps insisting it should end any day now." She had vomit on her dress, and on her face. Sam didn't know how to help her. "I can't go in there," she said.

She was six months pregnant. Sam wasn't going to force her

through the door. "It's okay," he said. "Some other day." Sam wanted to see her home, but he had employees to meet and a speech to give. "Are you good to drive?"

"I walked," she said.

He watched her cross the street, then he went back into Unfair Games, alone. He could not conceive of asking his assistant to clean up Sadie's vomit, but he did not want his skittish employees greeted by it either. Sam retrieved a mop and a bucket from the supply closet. He rolled up his sleeves.

As he cleaned the sidewalk, he imagined what he would say to the battered staff of Unfair Games. Should he explain Sadie's absence? Should he begin by saying that Sadie wanted to be here, too? Or was it better to let them draw their own conclusions? What would Marx say?

Sam, it's not so difficult as you think. People want to be comforted, and then, honestly, they want to carry on. Tell them that it's safe to go back to the office, and that their seemingly frivolous work is still worth doing in the face of a random, violent universe.

Sam poured water on the sidewalk, washing the vomit into the gutter.

Start with an anecdote. A funny story about me. Thank them for coming back and mean it. That's all you have to do. You make everything harder than it needs to be. You always have.

The next morning, Sadie texted Sam: *I'd like to start my maternity leave early. I'll check in with the Revels team by phone, and I'll supervise them from home.*

Okay, Sam texted. He knew this wouldn't work, but he agreed to it anyway.

That had been a month ago. Sam texted Sadie yet again: *I think we need to have an actual conversation. May I come over?*

Let's do it by phone.

Promise you'll answer if I call.

She didn't reply.

He called.

She did not answer.

He neither understood nor did he have the time to deeply contemplate what was happening inside of her. What he wanted was the work on *Master of the Revels,* or at least, for her to direct her team. It had been three months since Marx had died, and it was the only thing he had insisted that she do.

The expansion pack for *Master of the Revels* had been in the works since Sadie had conceived of the game. *Master of the Revels* had been almost as expensive as *Both Sides.* Additional content, utilizing the same game engines, had been a significant way the game would theoretically become profitable. The gameplay of the original *Master of the Revels* had centered on a production of *Hamlet.* The plan for the expansion pack revolved around *Macbeth.* For a variety of reasons, the expansion pack needed to hit no more than a year after the first game.

He drove to her house, and he walked up to the door, and he knocked. When she did not answer, he knocked louder, and then he called her name, "SADIE!"

Ever since Marx and Sadie had bought this house, Sam had harbored a grudge against it. His initial impression when Marx showed him the online listing was that it had a haunted, dilapidated look. But once he'd heard they were buying it (not long after they had confirmed that they were together), he had become somewhat obsessed with the house. He could not say how many times he had viewed the listing. He had studied the floor plan and the photos, as if he expected to be tested on them. He would go to his grave being able to draw the floor plan of 1312 Crescent Place. He had become certain that they had overpaid, based on the comps for the neighborhood, and though they were his closest friends, he looked forward to the inevitable depreciation of their investment. Several months after the sale, the listing and photos were removed from the website and Sam experienced panic, then palpable grief. When Sadie and Marx had him over for dinner the first time, he felt as if he were meeting a celebrity, but one whose fame seemed undeserved somehow. The house, in person, was charming. It was Marx and Sadie's house—of course it was charming.

All the curtains were drawn, but Sam could see a light on in the room he knew to be her bedroom. She was home.

"SADIE!" he called again.

Several minutes later, she came to the door, looking like herself, but very pregnant and very pale.

"What?" she said.

"May I come in?"

She swung the door open, barely wide enough for Sam to enter, and the house seemed airless, and distantly he could smell fresh paint.

"Are you painting?" Sam asked.

"Alice," Sadie said. "The room for the parasite."

She led him into the living room. The room wasn't dirty, but the houseplants had been neglected.

"So?" she said. "You're here."

"The *Revels Ex* team needs to know what to do for the expansion pack," Sam said.

"I said I'd call them," Sadie said.

"If we don't have it on the market this year, we'll have to upgrade the engine, because the tech will have lagged behind the—"

Sadie interrupted him. "I know how games work, Sam."

"It would be good if the work were finished before your due date."

"Yes."

"Do you want me to put someone else on it? You could tell me the broad strokes, and I could oversee it."

"It's my game, Sam. I'll finish the expansion pack."

"Yes, but everyone would understand. Under the circumstances."

"You'd love that, wouldn't you? Put your fingerprints all over my work. Find more ways to call it your game."

"Sadie, that is not what this is about. I want to help you."

"If you wanted to help me, you'd leave me alone."

"I'd positively love to leave you alone, but someone has to run our company."

Sadie pulled her hands into the arms of her sweater. "Why?" Sadie said. "Why do we have to do any of this?"

"For God's sake. Because it's our company." Sam stood up, and he almost thought he would collapse, the ghost foot beating like a heart. But instead of sitting down, or mentioning the discomfort he was in, he let the pain and lack of sleep power his rage. "I am so tired of your crap. Do you honestly think you suffer more than everyone else? Do you think you suffer more than I do? Do you think you're the first person to ever have a baby? Or lose someone? Do you think you're some goddamned pioneer when it comes to grief?"

Sadie shifted forward, and he could feel the momentum of their argument. He could feel the cruel thing she was about to say in response to the cruel thing he had said. But the cruel thing did not arrive. Disturbingly, she slumped forward, and started to weep.

He watched her, but he did not go over to her. "Snap out of it, Sadie. Come to the office. We work through our pain. That's what we do. We put the pain into the work, and the work becomes better. But you have to participate. You have to talk to me. You can't ignore me and our company and everything that came before. Everything isn't over because Marx is dead."

"I can't go back there, Sam."

"Then you're weaker than I thought," Sam said.

The sun was going down, and the air had turned abruptly cold in the way L.A. beach towns can. "In truth," she said in a low voice, "you've always made too much of me."

Sam walked toward the door. "Come in. *Don't* come in. I don't care how you do it. Just get the work done on *Revels*. It's your game. You wanted to make it so much that you were willing to end our relationship, if you can remember anything that happened before last December. You owe it to me, to Marx, to yourself. You owe it to the game, Sadie."

"Sam," she called as he reached the door. "Please don't come here again."

She did not ever admit he was right nor did she speak to Sam, except through the occasional strained text. She did not once go into the office, though she did have an extra computer moved into her house. She spoke to Mori regularly, and Mori reported to Sam that Sadie did a great deal of the work herself. Somehow, *Master of the Revels: The Scottish Expansion* was completed a week before she gave birth, and the expansion pack was released on schedule.

Sam heard the game was good, but he didn't know firsthand. It would be many months before he could bring himself to play it.

Naomi Watanabe Green was born in July. She, like the game her mother had been working on, arrived exactly on time.

Sam didn't know if Sadie wanted him to visit, and he had always been bad at going places where he was not certain he was wanted. Besides, he did not particularly want to meet this baby. He feared babies in general—their immaculateness was threatening to him. With this one in particular, he dreaded finding Marx's face in it.

You should go meet this baby, imaginary Marx admonished him. *Trust me on this.*

But Sam did not take his advice.

Still, he did what he could for Sadie. He went to work, even when he didn't want to, even when he was in pain. He called Alice, whom he disliked, to see how Sadie was. He drove past her house to make sure her lights were on, but he kept his distance because that was what she had asked. Maybe it wasn't enough, but it was what he could do.

On the day debugging was finished on *Counterpart High: Senior Year,* Simon announced to Sam, "The occasion demands a party, Mazer."

Sam admitted that it had not even occurred to him to have a party.

"You're kidding, right? God, I miss Marx. Hmm, why throw a party? I don't know, we finished the game. We survived the last year. They tried to kill us, they nearly broke us, but we're still bloody here! Why does anyone ever throw a party?"

Parties, like many other things, had fallen largely under Marx's purview, and Sam had never thrown one before. Marx's advice was to hire a party planner: *For God's sake, Sam, you don't have to do everything yourself.*

Since *Counterpart High* ended in a graduation ceremony, the party planner's idea was Grad Night. Guests could wear caps and gowns, or clothes from when they went to high school. A secret room for alcohol and spiked punch. A photo booth. A yearbook signing table. Sam thought it sounded jejune. "People love being jejune," the party planner assured him.

Sam had invited Sadie, though he knew she would not come. She was, according to Alice, overwhelmed. "She has a pretty good case of postpartum depression going, I'd say. And that's on top of the depression she already had," Alice said. He still had the impulse to go to her house every day, like he had done when they'd been in college. But Sadie was an adult, with a child. And Sam was an adult, with a business to run, mostly by himself.

· · ·

Four hundred thirteen days after Marx had died, Unfair Games threw a party to celebrate the launch of *Counterpart High: Senior Year*.

Simon, dressed in royal blue cap and gown, got a bit inebriated, and then, as often follows, a bit maudlin, and then he did a celebratory line of coke to wake himself up. He turned to reminiscing about what it had been like when Marx had discovered them. "We didn't have that much. We were still in college. The shittiest demo. A two-hundred-page, deeply clunky treatment, and a couple of pages of concept art."

"And the title," Ant added. He was wearing a baby blue tuxedo and a sash that said PROM KING.

"Yeah, which Sam immediately threw out," Simon said.

"Not immediately." Sam was also dressed in cap and gown, though his was crimson and gold. The party planner had racks of them at the door for anyone who hadn't come in costume. "So, why do you think Marx decided to make the game formerly known as *Love Doppelgängers?*"

"No idea," Simon said. "I wouldn't have given us money to make a game, that's for sure."

"But he was right to, wasn't he? If you look at how things turned out. It's our most successful series by a mile," Sam said. "What did he say to you? What did he see? I'd love to know."

Simon thought about the question. "He said he'd read through our materials, and he was intrigued. And then he said, I remember this clearly. He said, 'So tell me how you see it.'"

For the next several hours, Sam socialized with the people who had come to the party like it was his job, which, in point of fact, it was. Around midnight, he was exhausted from socializing, and he found himself looking for a place to recharge. To return to his or Marx's office would have required walking through the party again—past the gauntlet of journalists, gamers, employees, and well-wishers from other game companies—and so he went into Sadie's office, which was the farthest away from everything. Her office wasn't empty: Ant was sitting at her desk.

"What's the prom king doing in here?" Sam demanded.

"The king is tired," Ant said. "Also, I detest Simon when he's using coke." He explained sheepishly that he had often used Sadie's office when he needed a break from Simon, with whom he shared a large office on the second floor. For his part, Sam had not been in Sadie's office since before the shooting.

Ant was flipping through a portfolio of artwork that was sitting on Sadie's desk. "Something you two were working on?" he asked.

"No," Sam said, "I've never seen this work before."

"Well, it's not half-bad," Ant said.

Sam pulled up a chair next to Ant, and the two of them went through the pages. It was a series of drawings and storyboards of a postapocalyptic land somewhere in the American Southwest. The drawings were done in pencil and watercolor.

On the first page, a title: *Our Infinite Days.* Wildflowers grew over the crumbling stone letters.

The title was familiar to Sam, but he could not yet say why.

Ant read the text aloud: "Days 1 through 109: A Dry Season. Rain has not fallen for over a year, lakes have dried up, the sea level is fallen, and access to fresh water is not guaranteed. A plague, brought on by drought conditions, has swept through the United States, killing four in five people and much of planet earth's flora and fauna. Of those who survive, many are left as *desert vampires*—their brain chemistry altered by disease and dehydration. Some of the vampires are violent: the Parched. Some of the zombies are docile but lack memories: the Gentle. Without warning, the Gentle can turn into the Parched, and vice versa."

Sam laughed. "Of course, they can."

Ant turned the page to look at the next painting, which was a detailed watercolor of a female desert vampire in the process of feeding. The desert vampire is lunging at a man, and her tongue has morphed into a long proboscis, which she is plunging up the man's nose. A caption read: *Up to 60% of the human body is water. The heart and brain are 73%; the lungs, 83%; the skin, 74%; bone, 31%. It is not the human's blood the desert vampire seeks, but her water.*

"Conceptually, that's somewhat interesting," Ant said. He turned the page. A small girl and her mother walk across a surreally beauti-ful, Daliesque desert, their footprints leaving a trail in the caramel-colored sand. The mother has a gun; the daughter, a knife. The caption read: *Though she doesn't always have the words to express their situation, the six-year-old girl is the keeper of memories. That is why she is known as the Keeper. The player will toggle between playing Mama and the Keeper, but she will need to master both characters if she wants to get to the Coast, where the Keeper believes her brothers and father are waiting for her.*

"The artist is a fine draftsman," Sam said. "But these ideas are pretty clichéd."

"Still, I think there's something here," Ant insisted. "These images make me feel . . . I don't know the word. I guess they make me feel."

Ant turned the page: The Keeper and Mama are fending off a vampire attack. The caption read: *Day 289: The Burden of Memory. When we dream, we dream of the old world. Of rain, of bathtubs, of soap suds, of clean skin, of swimming pools, of running through sprinklers in the summer, of washing machines, of the distant sea which may just be a dream.*

Another painting. The Keeper makes a line on her calf with a Sharpie. The line joins rows of other lines. *If we did not mark the days, we would not know how much we had survived.*

"Maybe there is something here," Sam said. "I'm going to take it home with me." He closed the portfolio and lifted it from the desk. A green Post-it detached from the folder and fluttered to the ground. Marx's handwriting—small, evenly spaced letters, all caps: s., TELL ME YOUR THOUGHTS. —M.

At once, Sam remembered the woman who had called him the day he'd come back to the office. "I think I know who this belongs to," Sam said. "It's a team. A woman and her husband."

"If you end up meeting with them, let me know," Ant said. "Maybe I'll sit in. Reminds me of *Ichigo* in a weird way."

Sam slipped the portfolio under his arm. "Do you talk much to Sadie?" Sam asked.

"Sometimes," Ant said. "Not as much as I'd like. The baby's super cute, full head of hair, looks like her and Marx."

All babies are cute, Sam thought. "Do you think she'll ever come back to work?"

"I have no idea," Ant said.

"Someone who loved video games as much as Sadie can't have nothing to do with them forever," Sam said to himself as much as to Ant.

"I sometimes think about doing other things," Ant said. "I like video games, but are they worth getting shot over?"

"But you came back to the office," Sam said.

Ant shrugged. "What's better than work?" He paused. "What's worse than work?"

Sam nodded. He took a moment to look at Ant. In his mind, he always thought of Simon and Ant as kids, because they had been so young when Marx had taken on *Love Doppelgängers*. But Ant was no longer a kid, and his eyes reminded Sam of his own. They had the patina of a person who had felt pain and expected to feel it again. Sam put his hand on Ant's arm, imitating a gesture he had seen Marx use. "If I haven't said it before, I want you to know that I really appreciate you coming back here to finish the game. I know it must have been incredibly difficult."

"Truthfully, Sam, I was grateful for *Counterpart High*. I was grateful to not have to be in this world." Ant paused. "Sometimes, when I'm working on *CPH*, that world feels more real to me than, like, the *world* world, anyway. I love that world more, I think, because it is perfectible. Because I have perfected it. The actual world is the random garbage fire it always is. There's not a goddamn thing I can do about the actual world's code." He laughed at himself, then looked at Sam. "How are *you* doing?"

"Tired," Sam admitted. "All things considered, I'd say it's only been the second, possibly, the third worst year of my life."

"It's definitely been the worst year of mine," Ant said. "You must have had some outstandingly shitty years."

"Outstandingly," Sam agreed.

They were about to reabsorb themselves into the party when Ant added, "For what it's worth, she mentioned that she plays games at night. Stuff on her PC, maybe? Or even something on her phone? There was mention of a game in a restaurant. Something set in the Old West. Nothing too complicated. She called them 'dumb, garbage games,' and she said it relieved her anxiety. This is to say, I don't think she's entirely done with games."

Sam considered this information for a beat, and then he nodded. "Say, Ant, what do you think of the title *Our Infinite Days*?"

"It's okay, but it'll never sell in Montana," Ant said.

The DJ called out, "EVERYONE UP TO THE ROOF!" Two Decembers ago, this same instruction had meant something very different, and Sam had debated with the party planner about the taste of sending the party up to the roof again. Ultimately, he decided that it was best to reclaim the space. The roof had always been one of the best parts of the building on Abbot Kinney. Marx had loved the roof.

"Shall we?" Sam said.

Ant grabbed Sam's hand, and they let the momentum of the crowd push them up the stairs.

"IT'S TIME FOR THE CEREMONIAL CAP TOSS. ON THE COUNT OF THREE! 3 ... 2 ... 1 ..."

Sam tossed his cap, and Ant, his crown.

"CONGRATULATIONS TO COUNTERPART HIGH, CLASS OF 2007!"

"We made it," Sam said.

"We made it!" Ant screamed.

The DJ played "Everybody's Free (to Wear Sunscreen)," that oddball 1999 Baz Luhrmann spoken-word novelty track of the ungiven Kurt Vonnegut commencement address that turned out to not be by Kurt Vonnegut, but by a *Chicago Tribune* columnist named Mary Schmich. Unaware of these authority issues, Sam and Ant enjoyed the song, as they leaned over the side of the building, craning their necks so they could see that sliver of ocean the view from Abbot Kinney afforded.

"You know something funny?" Ant said. "I literally missed my senior year to make *Counterpart High*."

"Same with me," Sam said. "Except with *Ichigo*."

The party ended around 2:30 a.m., late for a party in L.A., the city that sleeps. Sam kicked out the stragglers and locked everything up, and then he got in his car to drive back home. He drove past Sadie's house, as he did almost every day after work. It was only a touch out of the way. He could see a light on the second floor, the guest bedroom, which he imagined had become the baby's room. He could imagine himself getting out of the car and going up to her door, but he never did. On this night, he decided to park outside her house and send her a text.

We missed you at the party. Can you imagine, me, Sam Masur the misanthrope, throwing a party? People seemed to enjoy themselves.

She did not reply. He sent another text.

Thinking about making a new game. Maybe something you'd be into?

Kind of a cross between Ichigo *and* Dead Sea. *May I drop the work off at your house? I think it's something Marx may have wanted to make, too.*

Sam, she replied, without pause. *I can't.*

∵

On the day Sam met with the Worths, it rained.

Sam's assistant let him know that the Worths were in the lobby. Sam said he would retrieve them himself.

"Thanks for coming back in," Sam said. "Apologies that it's taken us so long to get back to you. I think it's been about a year and a half since you met with Marx?"

"It feels like longer," Adam Worth said.

"And like no time at all," Charlotte embroidered.

Sam noted the easy way they finished each other's sentences, and he missed being part of a team.

Back in his office, he handed the portfolio back to Adam. "This belongs to you. Sorry we've had it so long. It's good work. I've gone through it several times now, and—"

Charlotte interjected quickly, "We've got other ideas, if this one's not for you."

"No, I like this, but I don't know if I understand it yet," Sam said. "Why don't you tell me how you see it?"

Five hundred three days after Marx had been shot, Charlotte and Adam Worth began work on *Our Infinite Days*.

To prepare for their arrival, Sam had packed up Sadie's office the night before and moved her personal items into his own office. An assistant was planning to drop off the boxes at her house that afternoon. And once that happened, Unfair Games would be a workplace officially devoid of both his partners.

Sam walked over to see how the Worths were settling in. Adam wasn't there, but Charlotte sat at the desk. A game was opened on her laptop. "I'm looking up a particular reference from *The Scottish Expansion*," she explained. "There's a way Sadie Green does blood that's so good. Maybe it's my imagination, but I feel like she has people bleeding slightly different colors and the blood has different viscosities even. It's a small thing, the idea that blood can have character, but I'm obsessed with it."

"I haven't played it yet," Sam admitted.

"Seriously?" Charlotte said. "Well, it's excellent. It's much gorier than the first one. The theater massacre level is one of the bloodiest, most thrilling things I've ever played."

"Yes, I read something about that." Sam moved to leave the office. "I'll let you get back to it."

"Wait," Charlotte said. "If you haven't played it, that means you haven't seen this. Hold on. It's an Easter egg. I think it's an Easter egg."

"She hates Easter eggs," Sam commented. Sadie thought they broke the reality of the game world.

"Do you mind spoilers?"

"No." Sam didn't believe it was possible to spoil a game. The point was not what happened, but the process of getting to what happened. He already knew the plot of *The Scottish Expansion:* Actors across London are getting picked off, one by one. You must successfully manage your theater company and solve the mystery of who's killing the cast.

"Okay, here it is," Charlotte said. She turned the screen toward him. "After the theater massacre scene, the actor playing Macbeth is murdered. You're the manager and you have to decide whether the play goes on, as scheduled, or if you cancel. So, the game warns you that attendance will be low, but the best decision is clearly to continue the performance as scheduled, right? The show must go on. At this point, you can choose from three different options: (1) the 'workman-like' actor playing Banquo, who has been understudying Macbeth, (2) Richard Burbage, 'who is demanding more and more money and may have the plague,' (3) an actor of 'unknown quality from a traveling theater company of unknown origin.'"

"It makes the most sense to choose option one," Sam said. "He'll know the play the best, and no one's going to go to the theater the night after the massacre anyway. But two or three sounds more fun."

"Well, I'm obsessive so I've played through all three options. The Easter egg is behind door number three." She clicked the third option. "In the course of regular gameplay, you can check in with the performance, or you can skip it, assuming it's a close variation of the same cutscene you've had before. But hey, the game designer, Sadie Green, put something here, so why not watch a little of the performance, right?"

Charlotte turned her laptop toward Sam.

Onstage, in the middle of white Elizabethan England, improbably stands a handsome Asian man as Macbeth. Macbeth has just heard the news that his wife had died, and he is giving the most famous soliloquy from the play, the "Tomorrow, and tomorrow, and tomorrow" speech.

When they had been deciding what to call their company all those years ago, Marx had argued for calling it Tomorrow Games, a name Sam and Sadie instantly rejected as "too soft." Marx explained that the name referenced his favorite speech in Shakespeare, and that it wasn't soft at all.

"Do you have any ideas that *aren't* from Shakespeare?" Sadie said.

To make his case, Marx jumped up on a kitchen chair and recited the "Tomorrow" speech for them, which he knew by heart:

> Tomorrow, and tomorrow, and tomorrow,
> Creeps in this petty pace from day to day,
> To the last syllable of recorded time;
> And all our yesterdays have lighted fools
> The way to dusty death. Out, out, brief candle!
> Life's but a walking shadow, a poor player,
> That struts and frets his hour upon the stage,
> And then is heard no more. It is a tale
> Told by an idiot, full of sound and fury,
> Signifying nothing.

"That's bleak," Sadie said.

"Why start a game company? Let's go kill ourselves," Sam joked.

"Also," Sadie said, "What does any of that have to do with games?"

"Isn't it obvious?" Marx said.

It was not obvious to Sam or to Sadie.

"What is a game?" Marx said. "It's tomorrow, and tomorrow, and tomorrow. It's the possibility of infinite rebirth, infinite redemption. The idea that if you keep playing, you could win. No loss is permanent, because nothing is permanent, ever."

"Nice try, handsome," Sadie said. "Next."

Sam watched through to the end of the cutscene. He thanked Charlotte for showing it to him, and then he returned to his office and closed the door behind him.

As soon as he was gone, Charlotte began to agonize: Had it been a mistake to bring the Easter egg to Mazer's attention? She'd been trying to share in an experience they had both had. Though nothing like what it must have meant to Mazer, Marx's death had been a trauma for her and Adam as well, and she had derived some comfort from Marx's appearance in *The Scottish Expansion*. But honestly, she'd also been showing off for the new boss. She wanted Mazer to see how knowledgeable she was about games, wanted him to know that he hadn't made a mistake in deciding to make *Our Infinite Days*.

What had she been thinking? Of course, it was inappropriate. She barely knew him. It was their first day. Adam often complained that she was too familiar with strangers.

When Adam returned, Charlotte had her head on their desk. "What happened?" Adam asked.

"I'm a fool," she said. She explained the situation.

"Maybe it was inappropriate," Adam said, "but in the end, he thanked you, right?"

"Yes, he barely said anything else. He might have been being polite."

Adam considered this. "No, I don't get the sense that Mazer's polite."

Sitting at his desk, Sam could not quite identify what seeing Marx in Sadie's game had made him feel. It was not just pain, or sadness, or happiness, or nostalgia, or longing, or love. What touched him the most was the sound of Sadie's voice, untouched and clarion, speaking to him through a game, across time and space. Others, like Charlotte Worth, might recognize Marx in the sequence, but Sadie was speaking to Sam. After a long silence, he could hear her voice again, and he determined that what he felt was hope.

An open crate contained Sadie's favorite games, the ones she had always kept on her shelf. The top game in the box was a '90s rerelease of *The Oregon Trail*. Sam decided to play it.

He lost himself in the minor stakes of the Old West world. How many wagon parts? How many sets of clothing? Do you raft across the river, or do you wait for the river conditions to improve? Do you shoot the bison for food, knowing that most of the meat will rot? How long does it take to recover from a rattlesnake bite? What happens when you get to Oregon?

It was easy to remember why this simple game had absorbed them so much when they were young. Many afternoons, they had lain side by side on his hospital bed, sharing one identity, making decisions together, passing a fifteen-pound laptop back and forth.

But it would be even better, Sam thought, *if the game hadn't been designed for one player.* "Hey Sadie," he said to the empty room, "what would you think of making *Oregon Trail* as an open-world MMORPG?"

I'd play that, imaginary Sadie replied. *But is it* Oregon Trail *you want or a steampunk version of* The Sims *or* Animal Crossing *or* Ever-Quest, *set in the Old West?*

Sam nodded.

Keep it simple, Sadie said. *That's always served you well. I'm the one who always makes games too complicated. Maybe you could even use the* Mapleworld *engines. There's no reason you shouldn't. They probably have one or two more games in them before they're completely obsolete.*

"I'm going to take notes," Sam said.

For the past two years, Sam had done almost no creative work. He had never made a game without Sadie. Although he had resigned himself to her reasons for working alone, he had never wanted to work without her.

He locked the door to his office. He took out a sketchpad. He sharpened a pencil.

"How does it begin?" Sam asked. His hand felt shaky. It had been so long since he had put pen to paper.

A train arrives, she said.

"I've missed this," he said.

A traveler disembarks from the train. The land is covered with a thin layer of frost, and the ground crunches beneath the traveler's boot. Look closely: Is that grass pushing through the ice? Could it be the white head of a crocus? Yes, it is almost spring. A text box appears on the screen: Welcome, Stranger.

IX

PIONEERS

HOMESTEADER SIGHTED IN UPPER FOGLANDS

The Stranger arrived in the early spring, when the thawing ground had the texture of crystalline silicon. Her inky hair had been customized into plaits, and she wore round, silver glasses that seemed as if they belonged to someone else. The Stranger wore black, and from a distance, her cleverly tailored velvet overcoat almost concealed the fact that she was with child.

When the Editor of the *Friendship Mirror* inquired, the Stranger revealed that her name was Emily B. Marks. Friendship was a town of pseudonyms, so no one made the mistake of assuming it was the name she'd been born with.

The Editor held out his hand for Emily to shake. "When will your spouse be joining you, Mrs. Marks?" the Editor asked, looking significantly at Emily's abdomen.

"It is Miss Marks, and I am alone and intend to stay that way," Emily said.

"I warn you: a comely young person like yourself never finds herself at a loss for company in these parts," the Editor said. "Life is quite difficult here, and even the most independent among us find it beneficial to pair up. Where will you be staying, if you don't mind my asking?"

She reported that she had selected a parcel of land in the northwesternmost part of Friendship. "I'm told it's on a high cliff, by the water," she said.

"Upper Foglands? Hope you like rocks! No one's kept a farm in Upper Foglands for as long as I can recall," the Editor said. "And the only folks nearby are—" The Editor searched his memory. "Alabaster Brown, the vintner, who has been married a dozen—"

"I have no interest in town gossip," Emily said. "*Skip.*"

"If you change your mind, be sure to take a gander at the town message board before you go. It has the latest Friendship happenings." The Editor indicated a hutch on which the community news and offerings of Friendship were posted. "I shall post a story about your arrival as soon as we are done speaking."

"Is it possible," Emily asked, "to opt out of such a posting?"

The question seemed too complicated for the newspaperman to consider, and so he ignored it. "Even Alabaster Brown's vineyard is closer than your plot in Foglands. If it were me, Miss, I'd find land nearer to town should the opportunity present itself. Verdant Valley would certainly be a fine place to raise a—"

"*Skip.*" Emily asked to be pointed in the direction of the stables so that she could procure a horse. The Editor obliged, and Emily was halfway down the street when he stopped her again. "Here," he said. Seemingly out of thin air, he produced half a baguette, spread with red sauce and sprinkled with greasy strings of cheese. "It's a gift. To help you get started."

"This is very generous," Emily said. "What is it?"

"I call it a panem et caseum morsu. It's based on a dish my grandparents made in the old count—"

"*Skip.*"

In the time it took Emily to add the offering to her inventory, the Editor had disappeared.

LOCAL WOMAN SHARES GIFT OF ROCKS

She had chosen the Upper Foglands plot for its solitude, but she had not been prepared for how remote and unaccommodating this land would be. The air was cold and damp, the soil was brackish, and the constant fog made it so there was almost no direct sunlight. Her waking hours were devoted to survival: buying seeds from the mercantile, sowing the tenaciously craggy earth, watering the crops, the endless trips on her azure mare, Pixel, to and from town.

Occasionally, she would run into one of her fellow residents in town, and even when they didn't know her, they would offer her modest gifts: a turnip or a block of cheese. Gifting was an important part of the culture of Friendship, and she felt shamed into reciprocation. She took to presenting her neighbors with rocks, the one product her farm produced in abundance.

She almost cried the first time she managed to grow a carrot. She washed and scrubbed the carrot, and then she set it on a white plate. She sat on the steps of her front porch, contemplating the carrot and watching the first fireflies of summer. She did not consume the carrot—it was too dear—but she was moved to write a poem.

In certain seasons,
We may be nourished by
The idea of the carrot
More than the carrot itself.

Alas, what is the point of writing a poem if there is no one with whom to share it? She decided to make a pilgrimage to her nearest neighbor's house. Alabaster Brown wasn't at home, so she left the poem, weighted beneath a rock, and she added the customary note of Friendship: *A Gift from Your Neighbor, Ms. Emily B. Marks, Myre Farm.*

Several days later, a lilac-eyed, lilac-haired person in overalls called on her. "Hmm, a rock," Alabaster Brown said. "I had heard rumors of a bespectacled woman spreading her gift of rocks. It's not many around here who are bold enough to give a gift as unpretentious as a rock. I shall happily add it to my collection. But I must warn you, Miss Marks, if you expect to bewitch me with your rocks, I have been married twelve times and I shall not be married again."

"I am not in search of such an arrangement," Emily said. "Yours is the farm nearest to mine, though, and so I hoped we might be friends."

"Good for you. This town is relentless in its desire to pair people up. I am tired of the combining of property, which is inevitably followed by the separation of property. And in these transactions, one will invariably end up with less than one started with." Alabaster thrust their hands in their pockets and spit on the ground. "Now, you'll pour me a glass of wine, and we can have a cigarette, too, and you can tell me the story of your life," Alabaster said.

"I'm pregnant," Emily said.

"Wait until we've decanted to begin the storytelling, if you don't mind."

"I meant, pregnant women don't generally smoke and drink."

"Where you came from, maybe. You'll soon discover that nothing affects anyone much here. Make sure you have enough hearts to get through your day, and that's all you'll need to survive."

"If nothing has an effect, then why bother smoking and drinking?" Emily asked.

"Aren't you a prickly one? My seventh wife was like that. A rogue and peasant slave to reality," Alabaster said. "I suppose we drink and we smoke for the same reasons it is done elsewhere. We must fill our infinite days with something."

Before they parted for the evening, Emily admitted to Alabaster that the rock had not been the gift: "It was the poem beneath the rock."

"A poem." Alabaster Brown laughed. "I wondered what that was. I assumed it was an advertisement for carrots. Several of my wives have reported that I can be emotionally obtuse, but I hope that won't get in the way of our friendship."

BOOKSTORE TO SELL CARDS AND GAMES

Alabaster Brown, for all their quirks, was one of the few people Emily felt she could have a conversation with, and they became frequent visitors to each other's homesteads.

"I feel I am not suited for this life," Emily confessed. "I have devoted months to growing a single carrot and I have no time to read. There must be more than farming."

"You don't have to have a farm," Alabaster counseled.

"Don't I, though?"

"Everyone here has a farm, and everyone here starts out a farmer.

We have more produce than we can bear in Friendship. Why not open a store in town instead?" Alabaster said. "Create a niche and trade for what you need. That's how I came to make wine. No one here cares what you have done before. You can be anything you want to be."

"As long as it is a farmer or a shopkeeper," Emily said.

Emily was five months pregnant when she decided to open the bookstore. Friendship didn't have one, and it would be a way for Emily to read more and farm less. She sold off her farm equipment at a 50 percent loss and she rented out her unused land to Alabaster. Emily allocated most of her remaining gold to the construction of a small building in town. She named the store Friendship Books.

The Editor interviewed Emily about the store's opening for the *Friendship Mirror*. "Our readers will want to know why you have decided to open a . . ." The Editor searched his memory. ". . . a bookstore, is it?"

"I am an occasional poet and an avid reader," Emily said.

"Yes, of course, *you* are," the Editor said, "but what does this have to do with the daily lives and struggles of Friendshippers?"

"I believe that virtual worlds can help people solve problems in the real one."

"What is 'virtual'?"

"Nearly appearing so. Like yourself."

"You speak in riddles," the Editor said.

By her sixth month of pregnancy, Emily knew the reason Friendship lacked a bookstore: it was not a town of readers. With the demands of farming and gifting, Friendshippers were left with little free time, and what free time they had, they did not wish to devote to reading *Walden* by candlelight.

By her seventh month, she was on the verge of closing the store— she did not possess the missionary zeal for converting nonreaders into readers—and perhaps even abandoning Friendship for good. It was Alabaster who suggested she expand her business by selling greeting cards. "In addition to the books, of course," Alabaster said.

"Will it make a difference?" Emily rejoined. "Do people like greeting cards?"

"Yes, I believe they do. There are numerous heads of cabbage and birthdays to acknowledge." Almost as an afterthought, Alabaster added, "You could also sell games. Reading is a chore, but I have heard told there is much money to be made in amusements."

Emily changed the name of the store to Friendship Books, Stationery, & Games, and she began to stock the store in kind. Board games and stationery proved slightly more popular than the books alone had been. Emily was perpetually at two or less hearts, but she was able to make a living.

One evening, Alabaster found Emily passed out on the front steps of her house. Alabaster roused her. "Is it the baby?"

She shook her head, but she could not speak.

"I fear that you are not eating enough. I can plainly see that you've let your hearts get too low." Alabaster gave her a can of PioneerAde from his inventory. "Drink."

"I have a pain that exists only in my head," she said, once some of her vitality had been restored. "I have had it my whole life. But when I feel that pain, I am incapacitated by it, and I am certain that I can't go on."

Alabaster studied Emily. "I think it is your glasses. They are far too small for your face. You should go see the optometrist."

"Does Friendship even have one?"

"Yes, her name is Dr. Daedalus, and her shop is a few doors down from your own. I'm surprised you didn't notice it before."

NEW OPTOMETRIST ACCEPTS INTERESTING TRADES

In the morning, Emily called on Dr. Edna Daedalus, whose office was, indeed, three doors down from Friendship Books, Etc. Dr. Daedalus was occupied with another patient, so Emily passed the time browsing. In addition to eyeglasses, the office carried a variety of glass objects in vivid colors: sculptural whimsies and more practical glassware as well. Emily picked up a miniature crystal horse to examine it more closely.

"Naaaayyyy." Emily started at the braying sound. She discovered the noise derived from the doctor. "She likes you," Dr. Daedalus said.

"Madame, this simulacrum bears an uncanny resemblance to my horse, Pixel," Emily said. "She is the precise shade of azure."

"It *is* your horse, though she never told me her name. She is always waiting outside your shop. Your horse and I, we're quite good friends," Dr. Daedalus said. "Pixel, you say? Is that P-I-X-L-E?"

"No. P-I-X-E-L. You are an artist, Dr. Daedalus," Emily averred. She carefully returned the horse to the menagerie.

"I amuse myself," she said. "My main occupation, of course, is the fabrication of lenses. I assume that's why you're here."

Emily looked at Dr. Daedalus. They were dressed identically, in the wardrobe typical of Friendship merchants: black skirt, white blouse with black tie. Dr. Daedalus was shorter than Emily, and her skin was pale and cast with undertones of verdigris. Her curly hair was the indigo black of comic book characters, and her round eyes, beneath her round glasses, were emerald and large. *To depict her,* Emily thought, *I would require a great many circles.* "Your eyes remind me of someone I used to know," Emily observed. "Where do you come from?"

"Isn't that the one question we're never supposed to ask each other around here?" Dr. Daedalus said.

"I forget myself! Of course, we were both born on the day we arrived in Friendship!"

Dr. Daedalus led Emily to the back office, where the doctor had Emily read the eye chart and then she shined a slim flashlight in Emily's eyes.

"May I ask the origin of your horse's name?" Dr. Daedalus inquired. "I have never heard the name Pixel before."

"It's a portmanteau of my own devising. A combination of pixie and axle," Emily said. "Pixel is fast to turn and light on her feet."

"Pixel," the doctor repeated. "How clever. I thought it had something to do with a tiny picture."

"I've invented the word," Emily said. "But you may invent the second meaning, if you wish."

"Thank you," the doctor said. "To restate. *Pixel.* Definition One: Noun. An animal that is fleet of foot. Definition Two: Also, noun. The smallest portion of an image on a screen."

"What is a 'screen'?" Emily asked.

"It is my own term for a length of land. It's very useful, so I'm hoping to force it into a broader parlance. For example, your house in the Upper Foglands is three screens from Alabaster Brown's house."

Emily and the doctor smiled at each other, as if they had a secret.

They did have a secret. The secret was the delight one feels when discovering a person who speaks one's native tongue.

"Are you and Alabaster friends?"

"I know of them," Dr. Daedalus said. "Your prescription is incorrect. I question if these glasses could have possibly been made for you. They seem as if they came from a menu of preset, aesthetic options, and glasses should never be obtained this way. Even considering that women experience vision changes during pregnancy, you will need a new pair." The doctor paused. "You are pregnant, aren't you?"

"No," Emily said. "What makes you say that?"

"My apologies, then! I shouldn't have assumed."

Emily laughed. "I am indeed eight months pregnant. Whatever that means in Friendship."

"Is time different here?"

"I think you know that it is."

"Give me a couple of days—"

"Whatever days are."

"Give me a couple of days to fabricate a new pair of glasses. We'll have you seeing all the pixels in no time."

"Is this proper usage of 'pixel'?" Emily admonished.

"I believe so. In this context, to see all the pixels means to have fine vision."

"That constitutes a third definition, then. How much do I owe you?"

Dr. Daedalus proposed a trade. "Your sign says that you also sell games. For some time, I've wanted to obtain a copy of the game Go. It's sometimes referred to as the Chinese version of chess. I played it with the nanny as a child, and I would like to play it again. Do you know this game?"

Emily had heard of Go, but she had never played it nor seen an edition offered for sale. "Let me see if I can get it for you. It will be a diverting side quest for me. It may take several weeks, if you don't mind waiting."

"Whatever weeks are," Dr. Daedalus said.

Through her usual channels, Emily could not find Dr. Daedalus's Go, though she did locate a book titled *Ancient Games for Fun and Amusement,* in which the basic setup for Go was described: a board with a 19 × 19 grid, and 361 stones (181 black, 180 white). Emily decided to manufacture the board herself. She cut down a Sequoia tree and fashioned the board from its wood. She added a secret drawer for storing pieces, and then she carved an intricate pattern of spectacles and Dr. Daedalus's name on the sides.

When she returned to the optometry, the doctor was not with a patient, but working on a small glass sculpture of still indeterminate form. Unexpectedly, Emily felt vulnerable as she presented Dr. Daedalus with her creation. "If it suits you to do so, I thought you could fashion the pieces out of glass."

Dr. Daedalus paused to consider the board. "It is a fine board. No one else will have anything like it, and I am intrigued by this proposal. But what if I made the dark pieces out of glass, and the light ones from stone? I am told you have an abundance of rocks on your land." Emily agreed to gather the rocks, and Dr. Daedalus offered Emily her hand to shake. "We are settled, then."

"It is an imperfect trade, Dr. Daedalus," Emily apologized. "I fear I've burdened you with an unequal portion of the work."

"There are no perfect trades," Dr. Daedalus countered. "And I shall enjoy the diversion."

"May I ask what you are making? It doesn't appear to be glasses."

"It will eventually be a prize for the most charitable person in Friendship," Dr. Daedalus said.

"How is the most charitable person in Friendship determined?" Emily asked.

"I believe it has something to do with the number of gifts you've given."

"This town." Emily shook her head. "I knew the gifting was fishy. I felt an ulterior motive to it all along."

"Miss Marks, that's quite a cynical way of looking at things. Do you think the promise of a glass object is motivation enough for a person to be charitable year-round?" Dr. Daedalus finished the sculpture. "Not to deprecate my talents, but I suspect this would be a rather minor motivation." She held out the heart to her. "It's still warm."

For reasons she could not explain to Daedalus, the crystal heart moved Emily deeply and she felt like she could cry, if it were possible for her to cry.

That night, she wrote a poem:

O crystal heart,
Unbeating lovely:
Such Beauty
Must have
Consequence.

In the morning, she left the poem under the bag of rocks, on the porch of Dr. Daedalus's store.

DOCTOR SEEKS GAMER

In her ninth month of pregnancy, Emily came across an advertisement on the Friendship board:

Doctor seeks Gamer, a person of sharp intellect, for competitive matches of the strategy game Go. Will teach you how to play, if necessary. Please arrive at my house in Verdant Valley, Tuesday nights, at 8 p.m., PST.

On Tuesday night, Emily rode Pixel to Verdant Valley. It was, in theory, getting more difficult to mount her horse. She once had read that pregnant women shouldn't ride horses, but she felt certain those rules didn't apply to her.

When she arrived, Dr. Daedalus was waiting in her doorway. "Welcome, Stranger," Dr. Daedalus called. The doctor did not seem surprised to see Emily, nor did she seem surprised that no one else had answered her advertisement.

The Doctor's house was Spanish style, with a red barrel-tile roof. Bougainvillea clung to the stucco, and there were two skinny palm trees in the front. "Your house and its flora are not typical of our region, Doctor," Emily observed.

The Doctor invited Emily into her library, which had wallpaper printed with oriental waves. She poured Emily a cup of tea, and then she explained Go to her. "The rules are simple," the doctor said. "Surround the other player's stones with your own stones. Within this simplicity is a near infinite complexity, and that is why it's a favorite with mathematicians and programmers." Dr. Daedalus gave the white stones to Emily, and she took the black stones for herself.

"What is a 'programmer'?" Emily asked.

"A programmer is a diviner of possible outcomes, and a seer of unseen worlds."

"*My.* Is this something they do where you come from?"

"Yes. I derive from a superstitious people." Dr. Daedalus hesitated. "But that is not how I came to Go. I used to dabble in mathematics, but I had no gift for it."

Emily lost the first three games, though she came closer to winning each time. "I should be heading back to Foglands now," Emily said. "I feel I've lost more than enough for one evening."

"I'll walk you," Dr. Daedalus offered.

"It's quite far. It's, perhaps, eleven screens away, and the path is labyrinthine. And actually, I rode."

"Do you not worry about riding your horse during your pregnancy?"

"I don't."

"Will you come next Tuesday, then?" the doctor asked.

"If weather permits, Dr. Daedalus," Emily said. "May I call you Edna, or Ed even? If we are to be friends, it is cumbersome to say Dr. Daedalus each time."

"I would prefer to be called Daedalus," the doctor said.

"It eliminates two syllables, so I shall count it a victory."

They played through the fall and into the winter. Emily steadily improved at Go, and in December, she beat Daedalus for the first time.

Emily's stomach was impossibly large at this point, and Daedalus insisted on walking her home.

"Why does a person choose to live in Upper Foglands?" Daedalus asked.

"It suits me," she said.

"That is a terse answer. Shall I admit I am curious about you?" Daedalus said. "One likes to understand the background of a woman who has destroyed you in Go."

"Daedalus, I have found that the most intimate relationships allow for a great deal of privacy within them."

Daedalus did not press her, and they walked in silence for a while. "My life was quite easy for a long time," Emily said. "It would be a lie to pretend that I have suffered more than anyone else. I had work I liked and was considered somewhat good at. But my partner died, and now I detest my work, and I have been blue. More than blue really. I have been in the depths of despair. My grandfather, Fred, who I adored, recently died. It begins to seem to me that life is little more than a series of losses, and as you must know by now, I hate losing. And I suppose I came to Friendship because I no longer wished to be in the place I lived and sometimes I no longer wished to even be in my body."

"What is meant by 'partner'? Like a husband or a wife?"

"Yes, of a sort."

"A helpmate?"

"Yes."

They passed a field in which a dozen or so American bison were grazing behind a fence. A sign in front of the field read: DO NOT SHOOT THE BISON.

"I don't remember encountering this field before," Emily said. She went up to the fence and she let the bison sniff her hand. "When I was a child, I saw so many dead bison on the Oregon Trail, and I remember feeling outraged. People kill them because they are slow moving and easy to hunt, but then the meat just rots."

"Yes."

"The greater world sometimes seems quite cruel to me, so I am glad we live in a world in which bison are protected." Emily turned to look at the doctor, but as they were almost to Foglands, the thick mists made it so they could barely see each other.

"Ms. Marks, I wish to make you a proposal."

"Go on."

"If it helps you, I would like to be a partner to you," Daedalus said. "I know I am an imperfect substitute for whoever you have lost. But we are both alone, and I think we could help each other. Sorrows can be shared, as easily as games of Go." She reached for Emily's hand, and she got down on one knee. "I would like to propose to you. Leave Foglands. Come to Verdant Valley."

"Do you mean marriage?"

"It doesn't have to have a name," Daedalus said. "It can have a name if you want it to have a name."

"What would it mean, then?"

"It means a very long game of Go, played without stops."

In the past, Emily had many reasons for not wishing to marry—among them her belief that marriage was conventional and a trap for women. She had rejected two engagements in her previous life, but at this juncture, she could see the facility of embarking on a different course. She discussed the matter with Alabaster.

"Verdant Valley is more fecund, but it's disgustingly crowded," Alabaster scoffed. "Would you honestly wish to live there? You will be constantly fending off gifts of turnips."

"Alabaster, I did not come here to discuss the merits of living in the Valley."

"What is your objection, then?"

"I barely know Daedalus. We have played several games of Go, that's it. She does not even allow me to call her by her first name."

"Oh, well, if that's your concern, I wouldn't worry about it. The most important thing is finding someone you wish to play with. And in any case, marriage is a more practical affair here. You join property, and if it doesn't work out, you separate property. I have done it—"

"Twelve times, I know."

"And I am no worse for the wear."

"This seems an about-face from what you told me several months ago. You went on and on about how wearying it was to join and separate property."

"There is a pleasure to the joining of property as well, otherwise why would we all keep doing it? 'Pleasure' might be too strong a word. If not a pleasure, let us say an interest. It develops the plot." Alabaster eyed Emily's still growing stomach. "How many months are you along now?"

"Perhaps eleven. I'm not sure. Soon, I shall be able to roll from Upper Foglands to town."

"I feel you have lived here longer than eleven months, and you were with child when you arrived. Is it possible your unborn child is *waiting* for you to be married?"

"No, I could never have a child so conventional," Emily said.

"Then, is it possible that it's a force greater than the will of your child? Greater than biology even?"

"What force are we speaking of?"

"The algorithm." Alabaster's eyes darted around the room, as if they were being spied on, and then they lowered their voice. "You know, the unseen force, al-Khwarizmi, that guides all of our lives."

"You are superstitious."

"Maybe so, but what if the algorithm doesn't allow children before marriage?"

"Oh, for God's sake. I can't believe Friendship would have such conventional morality baked into it. Who made the rules of this world anyway?"

And yet, that night, Emily had a lucid dream of her pixelated child, trapped in her pixelated womb. She cursed Alabaster for having put such provincial notions in her head.

For the next several weeks, neither wishing to accept nor reject Daedalus's proposal, Emily avoided her entirely. The commute felt longer than ever, and with the amount of weight Emily was carrying, she exhausted her hearts quickly.

When Daedalus finally came to the store, she did not mention the proposal. "I've made something for you, Em," Daedalus said. "I call it the Xyzzy portal. It's to help you travel through Friendship."

The doctor had installed a portal that connected Emily's store to her house, allowing her to bypass her commute. The portal was sage green and had three golden dots painted on the side:

∵

Emily studied the dots. "Is that an upside-down 'therefore' symbol?"

"When the dots are placed this way, they mean 'because.' I know my house is closer to town than yours. If you do ever decide to marry me," Daedalus said, "I did not wish convenience to be a factor in your decision."

That night, Emily showed Alabaster the portal. Alabaster stepped into it, and then they returned a moment later. "It works," they declared. "I'm going to need wine. Don't scrimp on the pours." Emily decanted and then they went out to the porch.

"Well, Emily, that odd little doctor is romantic," Alabaster said.

"Yes, I suppose so."

"And what is love, in the end?" Alabaster said. "Except the irrational desire to put evolutionary competitiveness aside in order to ease someone else's journey through life?"

WEDDING ANNOUNCEMENT

Ms. Emily B. Marks and Dr. Edna Daedalus were married by yours truly, in a ceremony attended by their small circle of intimates, including Pixel, the azure mare, and the vintner Alabaster Brown. Ms. Marks carried a bouquet of a dozen glass flowers, hand blown by Dr. Daedalus. Midway through the ceremony, snow began to fall, though Ms. Marks, who is two years pregnant, reported that she did not feel cold. In the months leading up to their nuptials, the couple had been playing games of Go, and Ms. Marks reported that the initial impetus for the marriage had been a desire to avoid interrupting their games with an eleven-screen winter commute.

As a wedding gift to Ms. Marks, Dr. Daedalus created a topiary hedge maze in the garden by her house. When asked why she had decided to make such a gift, the doctor replied cryptically, "To make a game is to imagine the person playing it."

BIRTH ANNOUNCEMENT

Emily B. Marks and Dr. Edna Daedalus are proud to report the arrival of their son, Ludo Quintus Marks Daedalus. Dr. Daedalus says the boy is healthy and has an area of 17 square pixels.

DOCTOR AND WIFE ARE HAPPY; BORED

Even after their marriage and the birth of their child, Emily and Daedalus decided to maintain separate residences. The doctor constructed an additional portal between their houses, so there was no real urgency to combine property. The baby, Ludo Quintus, grew used to living in both places.

LQ was an uncannily happy sprite. He never cried or fussed. He could be left unattended for long periods of time. He did not seek the company of other children, and he seemed content to be alone. In contrast with his long gestational period, his infancy was brief. He had the behavior and size of an eight-year-old by the time he was two. LQ was such an easy child that, to Emily, he sometimes seemed more like a doll than a human being. "He is easier to grow than a carrot," she remarked.

The house in the Upper Foglands was by the water, and as soon as LQ was old enough, Emily taught him to swim. LQ easily got the hang of swimming, and each time they went out, he wanted to swim farther. "You must always check your hearts, and make sure you use no more than half of them, before you return," Emily warned.

"Yes, Mama," LQ said.

LQ and Emily would swim exactly two screens out, and then they would return.

"How many screens is the ocean?" LQ asked.

"Nine or ten screens deep."

"How do you know?"

"I have swum to the end."

"And what is at the end?"

"A sort of fog, and then a nothingness that is like a wall. You shall grok it when you come to it."

LQ nodded. "Is it awfully frightening, Mama?"

"No, it's nothing to fear. It's just the end."

"I want to see it," LQ said.

"Why?"

"I don't know. Because I have never seen it."

"One day, when you are a stronger swimmer, and you have more hearts."

That night when LQ was sleeping, Emily reported this conversation to Daedalus. "What do you make of it?"

"I think it is natural to want to know the boundaries of your world," Daedalus said. "We should encourage him in his explorations. He is a strong child, and he cannot hurt himself very badly. Shall I get out the Go board?"

In most respects, it was an ordinary marriage, punctuated by competitive rounds of Go. Indeed, Emily felt the greatest intimacy with Daedalus when they were playing games together.

She confessed to Alabaster, "There must be more to life than working and swimming and playing Go."

"The boredom you speak of," Alabaster said. "It is what most of us call happiness."

"I suppose."

Alabaster sighed. "This is the game, Emily."

"What game?"

Alabaster rolled their lilac eyes. "You are happy, and you are bored. You need to find a new pastime."

"Did I ever tell you that I used to build engines?" Emily said.

"No, I don't think you did."

"Once, I built one that made the light of the sun. And I built another one that made the fog."

"Impressive. I did not know engines had these Promethean capabilities. Perhaps you should return to doing that, then?"

SPECIAL EVENT: SUPER BLIZZARD TERRORIZES FRIENDSHIP

At the end of March, Daedalus went to Eidetic Bluffs to perform eye examinations for the settlement's school. "It takes an entire day to get to the Bluffs," Emily grumbled. "If they want glasses so badly, why shouldn't they come to you?"

"It is thirty children, Em," Daedalus said. "What if it was LQ who could not see?"

"You are soft-hearted."

The blizzard began not long after Daedalus had left for the Bluffs. Emily didn't worry too much about the doctor because the worst that happened in Friendship was that one ran out of hearts. Even if Daedalus had gotten caught in the storm, eventually, the doctor would recharge and then she would return.

Three days after the blizzard, Daedalus still had not returned. The snow had begun to thaw, so Emily left Ludo Quintus with Alabaster, and she rode out to Eidetic Bluffs, where they informed her that Daedalus had never arrived.

On the fourth day, Daedalus's horse returned to the stable in the Valley without her mistress.

Emily spoke to the Editor, and despite her aversion to posting, she had him put a notice on the Friendship Hutch about Daedalus's disappearance. "Ms. Marks," the Editor said, "there are times when people leave our world without explanation. We must—"

"Skip."

On the fifth day, Emily searched again. This time, she took only roads she had never been on before. This led her to southwestern Undiscovered Friendship, where the land was cheap and sere. She rode past several ranches, an aviary, an exotic plant nursery, a piano store, a spa, a small amusement park, a museum devoted to old technology, a horse breaker, an arcade, a casino, an explosives warehouse, and other businesses that were too large, anachronistic, or aesthetically inappropriate to be contained downtown. No one that she encountered had seen Daedalus. At the arcade, a man in a seersucker suit suggested she try the caves, as people sometimes took refuge in them. "It's hard to find the entrance," he warned. "Some people say it moves."

She circled the perimeter of the mountain. The sun had gone down, but some light remained. She decided she would search until the light was gone before turning back. In the final moments of dusk, when she had almost given up, a reedy voice called out, "I'm here."

"I'm coming!" Emily turned Pixel around, and they backtracked slowly. She spotted an oddly shimmering place in the rocks. She dismounted her horse and she walked through the nebula, into a cavern. Inside was Daedalus, barely alive and her right hand a disturbing shade of black. Daedalus said her horse had been spooked and had thrown her, just as the blizzard had begun. She had gone into the cave for shelter. "I think there may be an injury to my hand," Daedalus said before she passed out.

Emily nursed Daedalus through recovery. Before long, it became clear to Emily that if Daedalus were to survive, her hand would need to be amputated. Daedalus said she would rather be dead than lacking her hand, to which Emily replied that she would be dead if she had both hands. The amputation could not be avoided.

The recovery was short physically, but long emotionally. Daedalus was quite despondent and refused to leave her house or even her bedroom. For a time, she would neither speak to nor even see Ludo Quintus.

"I honestly didn't know this could happen here," Emily said.

"You should leave me," Daedalus said. "I am now a useless person. I shall never be able to make lenses again."

"I don't think it's possible for me to leave you."

"Then I'll leave you. I'll swim to the end of the ocean, and I'll never come back."

"With whom would I play Go?" Emily began setting up the pieces on a table by Daedalus's bed.

"I don't wish to play," Daedalus said. And yet, when Emily placed the first white stone on the board, Daedalus could not help but place the next black one. Each afternoon, Emily would move the Go board a little farther from Daedalus's bed. In this way, Daedalus joined the world again, though she would not concede to leave the house or return to her optometry practice.

Several weeks later, Emily came to Daedalus with a proposal. "It is almost Christmas, and I was thinking how much I enjoyed making that Go board for you. I had a thought that we could make games for other people in Friendship. Even with the loss of your hand, I feel certain you could craft the pieces—the making of pieces requires a less precise craft than the making of lenses, I imagine. LQ is older now and he is fit to be your apprentice. I could make the boards, and we could sell our wares for the holidays. What do you think?"

"I think you are patronizing me," Daedalus said. "But I suppose I could try."

They made sets of Chinese checkers, checkers, chess, and Go. The games, with their carved boards and hand-blown, bespoke pieces, were art objects. They called their game company Daedalus & Marks Games. The games were a great success, and they sold every single board they created.

"I have missed making games," Emily said.

"Have you made them before?" Dr. Daedalus asked.

"Yes, with my brothers when I was a girl. They are not the sort of games you would understand."

"Tell me about one."

"One of the games was about a child who was lost at sea."

"It is hard to imagine that on a board," Dr. Daedalus conceded.

Emily pointed to the grid of Daedalus's Go board. "Imagine that this board is a world, and each of the places where the grids meet is a subdivision of that world. And imagine that each of these Go pieces represents a person."

"What are your hands in this metaphor?" Daedalus asked.

"My right hand is the lost child. And my left hand is God."

Daedalus reached across the table, but she could not touch Emily in the way she wanted to. "I love you," Daedalus said. "It is hard for me to say, because sometimes it doesn't seem like it is enough."

On Christmas morning, Daedalus and LQ presented Emily with a special board game that they had made. The board looked like a road, and the glass pieces were small covered wagons. There was also a polyhedral die and a deck of cards. On the side of the board, Daedalus had carved their son's name, Ludo Quintus. "It is also the title of the game," Daedalus said.

Emily asked how *Ludo Quintus* was played.

"It's easy, Mama," LQ said. "You can be a farmer, a merchant, or a banker. And you have to try to get from Massachusetts to California. But on the cards, there are many obstacles."

"Why is it called *Ludo Quintus*?" Emily asked.

"Because that is my name!" LQ said. "And because Mother says Ludo means 'game' in Latin."

Daedalus had been responsible for the naming of their child, and strange as it may seem, Emily had never put much thought into the meaning of Ludo Quintus. "What does Quintus mean?" Emily was reasonably certain she already knew.

"Fifth," Daedalus said, after a beat. "Fifth game."

PIONEERCHAT

You are now in a private chat with daedalus84.

EMILYBMARXX: Is it you?

DAEDALUS84: Yes, it's your beloved wife, Dr. Edna Daedalus.

EMILYBMARXX: Cut the crap. Samson, is it you? Be honest, for once in your life.

DAEDALUS84: . . . . Yes.

EMILYBMARXX: How did you find me?

DAEDALUS84: Find you? I built this place for you. Pioneers is a period extension of Mapleworld. I made it look like Oregon Trail because I knew you would like it.

EMILYBMARXX: You were trying to trap me?

DAEDALUS84: No, it wasn't like that. After Marx's death, I wanted to make things that reminded me of the old days, of you. I hoped you might join Pioneers, but I didn't know if you ever would. And when I figured out that you were Emily B. Marks, I had to be your friend. You seemed so lonely. Living by yourself at the far reaches of Friendship.

EMILYBMARXX: Be that as it may, these identities are supposed to be private. I didn't sign up with an identifying email address either, but you must already know that. Did you use my IP address?

DAEDALUS84: Yes.

EMILYBMARXX: I told you to leave me alone. Can't you respect any of my wishes?

DAEDALUS84: I was worried about you.

EMILYBMARXX: You tricked me.

DAEDALUS84: How did I trick you?

EMILYBMARXX: You invaded my privacy. You pretended you were a stranger.

DAEDALUS84: I didn't. I was myself. Except for the name and some of the details, I was exactly myself. And you were yourself. And I think you've known for a long time. Maybe you didn't want to admit it.

EMILYBMARXX: You know I'm going to have to leave Friendship now. You know that, right?

DAEDALUS84: Marx's death didn't just happen to you. He was my friend. He was my partner. It was our company. These things happened to both of us.

EMILYBMARXX:. . . . .

DAEDALUS84: I miss you, Sadie. I want to be in your life . . . A mistake I have made in the past. There is no purity to bearing pain alone.

emilybmarxx has left the chat.

Emily walked through the familiar landscape of Friendship. What was once beautiful and comforting now seemed like a brazen sham.

She mounted Pixel and rode down the hill to Alabaster's house.

Alabaster answered their door and invited Emily inside. She confessed to her friend that she thought she would have to leave Friendship soon. "Edna is not who she claims to be," Emily explained.

"Are any of us?" Alabaster asked.

"But it turns out she is someone I knew from before, and this spoils the game for me."

Alabaster nodded. "What I think you should consider," Alabaster said, "is the rarity of finding a playmate in either this world or the other world."

Emily looked at Alabaster, at their lilac eyes and their lilac hair. "Sam?"

"Who's Sam?" Alabaster said.

"Are you Sam as well?"

Alabaster lowered themself to their knees. "Sadie."

The figure of Emily disappeared from Alabaster's house.

A text box appeared on the screen:

Emily has left Friendship.

BOY REACHES END

Some days or months or years later, Emily logged back on to check on LQ. He had aged three years during her absence, and he was now a sturdy boy of eleven.

"Mama, where have you been?" LQ demanded. "Mother and I have been worried about you."

"Would you like to go for a swim?" Emily asked.

Emily and LQ swam out their usual two screens. LQ asked if he could keep swimming, and Emily thought about it for a moment. "Why not? You're much bigger now."

They swam until they reached the end of the ocean.

"It is so peaceful here at the end," LQ said.

"It is peaceful," Emily agreed.

"Mama," LQ said. "I'm worried. I don't think I have enough hearts to get back."

"Don't worry, my love. You aren't real, so you can't die."

LOCAL MERCHANT'S WILL READ

During the great blizzard of '08, while searching for Daedalus, Emily had come across a ranch in Undiscovered Friendship. The ranch's ice-coated sign read BREAKER OF HORSES and a smaller sign below that, GROOMING, SHODDING, HORSE TAMING, AND OTHER SERVICES OF AN EQUESTRIAN NATURE. NO HORSE TOO DIFFICULT. She had been occupied at the time with a more urgent mystery, and so she had not stopped.

Months later, even after she had ceased communication with Daedalus, the sign remained in her thoughts. The name suggested a place she had known when she was young, or perhaps, a dream she had once had. On or about her last day in Friendship, she decided it was time to see what lay beyond those gates. Even if it was a sign that signified nothing, the least she could do was get Pixel shod before she left Friendship for good.

When she zoomed out to the larger map, she found the location of Breaker of Horses was unmarked, and it took much unscientific backtracking and circling along anfractuous roads to find the place again. By the time she and Pixel finally passed under the gates, the sun was setting.

Emily rode through a grove of fruit trees and then down a long stone path, past stables and fields, and at the very back of the ranch, she arrived at a white A-frame house, almost like a church. She dismounted Pixel, and she rang the bell. A man in a white cowboy hat answered. He was in his sixties, noticeably older than almost everyone in Friendship; a bit bow-legged, befitting a person who had spent most of his life on horseback; not at all stooped. Under his hat, he had a shock of thick, dark gray hair. He looks, she thought, like his father, Ryu. The NPC tipped his hat to her. "Howdy, pilgrim. Having horse trouble?"

Emily explained that her horse needed shodding, and they discussed materials and horseshoe prices before coming to an arrangement. The NPC offered her his hand, and she kissed him on the cheek.

"You won't get a lower price that way," he said.

"I miss you," she said.

"Shucks, ma'am, you're making me blush."

"What's your favorite part of *The Iliad*?"

"What's *The Iliad*?" He paused, removed his hat, and a second later, as if possessed, the NPC had transformed into a different version of himself: "Then first of all came Andromaché, his wife, and cried—'O my husband, thou hast perished in thy youth, and I am left in widowhood, and our child, thy child and mine, is but an infant! . . . Sore is thy parents' grief, O Hector, but sorest mine. Thou didst stretch no hands of farewell to me from thy bed, nor speak any word of comfort for me to muse on while I weep night and day.'" When he was finished, he bowed and returned his hat to his head.

"It was good to see you," Emily said.

"Come back any time, little lady."

Emily found the exchange with the NPC unsatisfying, but then, most encounters with NPCs are.

And yet, were it not for the Breaker of Horses, Sadie may never have decided to set Emily's affairs in order.

One of Sam's innovations in *Pioneers* was the way a gamer could leave it. Sam hadn't liked the way a gamer, even someone who'd inhabited Mapleworld for years, could just vanish. A resident might one day decide to never log on again. It was healthier, Sam felt, to allow for the possibility that a person might want to leave a game. No matter how good an MMORPG was, gamers eventually did leave. They moved on to other games, other worlds, sometimes even the real one. When Sam built *Pioneers*, he expanded the category of Ceremonies to include Divorces, Wills, and Funerals.

The Editor read Emily's will: "My beloved son, Ludo Quintus, has swum out to seek the end of the sea, and I suspect he will be exploring for many years to come. I am but the avatar of a mortal woman, and since LQ's absence, I have been plagued by severe intestinal distress. I can only think this is my body saying that I no longer wish to live without LQ. I have, therefore, decided to leave Friendship. To my friend, Alabaster Brown, I bequeath my farm, my store, and both their contents. To my wife, Dr. Daedalus, I leave my horse, Pixel, and the glass simulacrum of same. I wish to add that I do not entirely regret the time I have spent in Friendship, nor do I regret the time I passed with Dr. Daedalus. I am resentful of her constant deceit—she knows very well what she has done—but I shall always remember those evenings playing Go with great affection. When I came here, I was as drained of hearts as I have ever been, and the tedium of Friendship and the kindness of its non-strangers gave me life. I am thankful to have come to a place as gentle as this, where the bison can be assured safe passage."

The Editor folded up the will. "She speaks in riddles," he commented.

A headstone for Emily was placed in Friendship Cemetery. The inscription read:

EMILY MARKS DAEDALUS

1875–1909

SHE HATH DIED OF DYSENTERY.

X

FREIGHTS AND GROOVES

1

"But, Sadie, be honest with yourself. On some level, you must have known it was him," Dov said.

At a certain age—in Sadie's case, thirty-four—there comes a time when life largely consists of having meals with old friends who are passing through town. Dov and Sadie were having brunch at Cliff's Edge, in Silver Lake. The restaurant looked like a tree house—an enormous, Ent-like, Ficus sprung from the middle of it, and the tables were on tiered wooden platforms that surrounded the tree. The waiters who worked at the restaurant were known for their epic calf strength and their feats of balance. Sadie had often thought that working as a waiter at Cliff's Edge must have been like being a video game character in a dull level of a platformer. As Dov was speaking, the tree caught his eye, and he grabbed one of its thick, smooth branches with his hand. "This is the most Californian place I've ever been. They must think it will never rain," Dov said.

"It never does," Sadie said.

"Do you think the restaurant was built around this tree?" Dov asked.

"I think it would have to have been."

"But the tree could have been brought in," Dov insisted.

"It's such a big tree. It's hard to imagine anyone moving a tree this large."

"Sadie, you're in California. It's a desert. Literally nothing should be here. If someone has a dream of a restaurant that looks like a tree house, Californians make it happen. I fucking love California."

"I thought you hated California."

"When did I ever say that?"

"When we were breaking up. I distinctly remember being regaled about all the apocalyptic ways I was going to die out here."

"Oh well, I'm full of shit. I didn't want you to leave. Let's ask the waiter about the tree when he comes," Dov said. "Marx was smart to move Unfair out here when he did. If I'd had an iota of sense, I would have followed you when you left, gotten on my knees, begged you to take me back."

"You're not the getting-on-your-knees type," Sadie said.

When the waiter came to take their orders, Dov inquired about the history of the tree. The waiter said he hadn't been working at the restaurant very long, but he'd ask the manager.

"Truly," Dov said. "You must have known it was him."

"I did and I didn't. I think it's like when you're watching a true crime show. People always think the cops are so hapless. How could they not see who the killer is when there are so many clues pointing in that direction? But you, the viewer, are looking at it from the point of view of knowing the solution. It isn't so obvious if you're walking into the situation, and it's dark and there's blood everywhere."

"But of all the games in the world, how did you end up playing an insipid casual game like *Pioneers*?"

"Well, unlike you, I play across the spectrum of games, and it had elements that attracted me."

"Such as?"

"I had heard it was an open-world, resource-gathering game with a social component. I heard it was loosely inspired by *Oregon Trail, The Sims,* and *Harvest Moon,* and so I wanted to play. Sam probably knew I'd be an easy mark."

"You've always had an immature fixation on *Oregon Trail.*"

"Yes, Dov. It is entirely possible for me to love a game that you don't get."

"So, Sam builds an MMORPG to lure one gamer? Brilliant. Crazy, but brilliant."

"No, he claimed he built the game because it reminded him of the games we played together when we were young."

"Farming and resource games are perennials."

"They are. I'm sure *Pioneers* made out fine financially." Sadie paused. "And, well, I'm not going to lie. After Marx's death and everything that followed, I really did crave something exactly like the thing Sam had made. But I guess Sam watched to see if I would join. And once I joined, he created a series of identities to keep me playing."

"What was the narrative?"

"Oh Lord. It was a ridiculous romance. I was Emily Marks, a pregnant woman with a dark past, and he was—wait for it—Dr. Edna Daedalus, the town's optometrist."

"Sounds incredibly hot."

"It was more tender and sad."

"Dr. Daedalus! Come on, Sadie. How could you not have known it was him?"

"Well, he was a she, for one."

"Why do you think he did that?"

"Maybe to throw me off his scent, I don't know? Maybe a Walt Whitman, we-all-contain-multitudes kind of thing. Do you always play the same gender when you game?" She knew, from experience, that when given an option, Dov always played the girl character.

"But eventually, I did know it was him. Maybe I always knew, but I didn't let myself know. He kept dropping, in retrospect, obvious clues. Edna loses a hand at one point."

"Life in the Old West is tough."

"Brutal," Sadie said. "She didn't know if she'd ever make lenses again."

Dov laughed. "I fucking love games. So, what now?"

"We still aren't speaking."

"You aren't speaking to him, you mean."

"I suppose that is what I mean."

"Sadie, for God's sake, why?"

"Because he tricked me." But, of course, there was more to it than that.

"Oh, to have the standards of Sadie Green."

"Said the man who handcuffed me to his bed."

"To my point, I did that, and you still have brunch with me whenever I'm in L.A.," Dov said. "And you weren't my student when I did that. I'm quite sure of that."

"What are my standards, and what does that have to do with Sam and me not speaking?"

"Sadie, you're how old?"

"Thirty-four."

"You're old enough to stop being so young. Only the young have such high standards. The middle-aged—"

"Like yourself," Sadie said.

"Like myself," Dov admitted. "I'm forty-three. I won't deny it." He beat his chest. "But I'm still sexy."

"You're okay."

He made a muscle with his arm. "Feel this muscle, Sadie. Is this muscle okay?"

She laughed. "I'd rather not." But then she did feel it.

"Impressive, right? I'm benching more than I did twenty years ago."

"Congratulations, Dov."

"I can wear the jeans I wore in high school."

"Which is useful for dating high school girls."

"I never dated a high school girl," Dov said. "Except when I was in high school. College girls, yes. Love 'em. Can't get enough of 'em."

"How you never got fired is beyond me."

"Because I'm a great teacher. Everyone adores me. *You* adored me. But to return to what I was saying, the middle-aged—"

"Those cursed souls worn down by the inevitable compromises of life, you mean?"

"Here is a thing to admit to yourself, if you're able: there will never be a person who can mean as much to you as Sam. You may as well let go of the garbage—"

"It's not just garbage, Dov."

"You may as well let go of your perfectly legitimate grievances, then. Find the mysterious Dr. Daedalus, shake his hand—"

"*Her* hand."

"Her hand and get back to the deadly serious business of making and playing games together."

The waiter came, and he set their food on the table. "The manager says the tree's been here for seventy years," he said before he left.

"Ah, so we have our answer," Dov said. "The restaurant was built for the tree. Thank you." Dov added hot sauce to his shakshuka.

"How do you even know that needs hot sauce? You haven't tasted it."

"I know myself. I like it hot. What are you working on now anyway?"

"Nothing much," Sadie said. "Taking my kid to nursery school. Trying to stay sane."

"I don't like the sound of that. You should be working."

"Yeah, I'll work eventually." She changed the subject. "What brings you to L.A.?"

"A couple of meetings, as usual." Dov said. "The director of some movie based on a Disney ride is interested in adapting *Dead Sea* for the cinema." Dov set down his fork in order to make a jerking off motion with his hand. "It'll never happen. Also, I'm getting divorced."

"I'm sorry to hear that," Sadie said.

"Inevitable," Dov said. "I'm fucking awful. I would never be in a relationship with me. The only good thing is that we didn't add children into the mess this time."

"What'll you do now?"

"Go back to Israel. See my son. Telly's sixteen now, if you can believe that. Work on a new game." Dov took a moment to eat his shakshuka, and he proceeded to get yolk and red sauce on his beard. "Oh yes, that's what I wanted to ask you. Since you're between games at the moment, would you have any interest in teaching my class at MIT for a semester? I'm happy to throw your hat in the ring, if it's something you'd at all want to do."

"Let me think about it," Sadie said.

"Up to you."

"When I first signed up for your class, I wondered what made you want to teach."

"Because teaching's fucking great."

"It is?"

"Sure. Who doesn't love puppies? And every once in a very long while, a Sadie Green comes along to blow your fucking mind." He tossed his head back and his chair teetered for a moment. "Boom."

Sadie felt herself blush. She still took an embarrassing pleasure in his compliments. "You curse too much."

At the end of brunch, Sadie drove Dov back to his hotel in the basin of the Hollywood hills. He kissed her on the cheek before he got

373

out of the car. "I know I'm middle-aged," Dov said. "And out of touch. And I have, apparently, no idea what women want. Twice divorced, etcetera. But I must tell you. To build a world for someone seems a romantic thing from where I stand." Dov shook his head. "Sam Masur, that fucked-up, romantic kid."

2

The Advanced Games seminar met once a week, Thursdays from one to four. Sadie did not vary the format from when she'd been a student in the seminar, sixteen years earlier. Each week, two of the eight seminarians would bring in a game, a mini game, or a part of a longer game—whatever could be feasibly programmed, given the time constraints. The students would play it, and then they'd critique it. They were responsible for making two games during the semester.

A difference from when Sadie had been in the class was that 50 percent of the students were women, or at least presented as such.

Sadie laid out her expectations for the class. "I don't care what programming languages you use, though I'm happy to give you advice about them. I don't care if you use a game engine—but I think it's good that you should understand what goes into building one. I don't care what kind of games you make. Good games and bad games are not unique to a particular genre. There are brilliant casual games made all the time, even though people think of casual games as a lesser form. I play every sort of game myself. There are great games to be made for phones, just as there are great games to be made for PCs and consoles. I don't expect your work to be super finished. I expect all of us to be honest and to treat each other with respect. It takes a lot of courage to put a game out there. As a designer, I've probably failed more than I've succeeded. And the one thing I didn't know when I was your age was how much I was going to fail. Sorry if that's a depressing note to end my introductory spiel on." Sadie laughed. "But yeah, you will definitely fail. It's okay. I absolve you in advance. This class is graded pass/fail, so you only have to succeed slightly more than you fail."

The class laughed at Sadie's joke. In the crucial moments that occur at the beginning of any class, she had succeeded in making them know she was on their side.

A dark-haired, dark-eyed girl named Destiny said, "You designed *Ichigo: Ume no Kodomo* in this class, right?"

"Japanese title, impressive. With my partner, Sam—"

"Mazer, right?" Destiny was on top of Sadie's résumé. "Was Mazer in this class, too? I know he went to Harvard, but kids sometime cross-register here, right?"

"Mazer wasn't in this class. As a game designer, he was completely self-taught. And I made *Ichigo* after I took this class. The games I made for seminar were a little simpler. It's a lot to program two games in a semester, by yourself."

Destiny nodded. "I love *Ichigo*. Seriously, it was my favorite game when I was a kid. Are you guys ever going to make an *Ichigo III*?"

"We used to talk about it, but I doubt it will ever happen," Sadie said. "Okay, so, to go back to Destiny's first question, I brought in a game I *did* make for this class. It's called *Solution*. Since I'm asking you to be vulnerable, I figured that the least I could do was show you the kinds of things I was making back when I was your age. The graphics are old, but give it a play, and tell me what you think. Bear in mind, I was nineteen, and this was about the best you could get done in 1994 in about four weeks, for no money. Also, I guess I should tell you that the game was inspired by my grandmother."

Sadie emailed her students a link to *Solution*.

The class opened their laptops and set themselves to playing Sadie's juvenilia. Sadie played a couple of levels, too. The game was technically obsolete, but she felt the concept was still strong.

As the kids began to discover the secret of *Solution*, they made appropriate sounds of outrage. At the hour mark, Sadie called time on play.

"Tell me your thoughts," Sadie said. "I want you to be candid. I can take it. Let's start with the aesthetics of the game."

They critiqued every aspect of the game. Sadie encouraged them to be ruthless, and she found she enjoyed defending herself and explaining the limitations of 1994. In general, the class appreciated the black-and-white graphics, though a boy in a beret asked Sadie if *all* games in 1994 were black-and-white. His name was Harry, and Sadie had memorized his name with the mnemonic trick Harr-ay with the ber-et. She would not be Dov. She would learn everyone's names in the first week.

"No, Harry," Sadie said, "we did indeed have color in 1994. It was an aesthetic choice. Something I've learned is that when you don't have many resources, you have to be even more rigorous with your style. Limitations are style if you make them so."

"That's what I thought," Harry said. "I didn't actually think all games in 1994 were black-and-white. I meant, was it common?" Sadie made a note on her class roster: *Black-and-White Harry*.

"I liked the game a lot," Destiny (*Ume no Destiny*) began. "I liked the idea of it, and I like that the game is political. But if I had a critique, it's that the game is too nihilistic. After you figure out what the factory is making, the game gets . . ." Destiny searched for the right word. ". . . well, repetitive, I guess. It should move on to a different part of the game instead."

"You know, Destiny, you're not the first person to say that. That's very astute, and I think if I'd had more time, I would have done exactly what you said. But sometimes, you have to make your game in the time that you have. If you're always aiming for perfection, you won't make anything at all.

"Mazer and I were best friends growing up, and we loved playing games together. We were obsessed with the idea of the perfect play. The idea that there was a way to play any game that had the minimal number of errors, the least moral compromises, the quickest pace, the highest number of points. The idea that you could play a game without ever dying or restarting. We'd be playing *Super Mario,* and if we missed even one gold coin, or got hit by one Koopa, we'd begin again. Yes, we were probably disturbingly obsessive and yes, we had a lot of time on our hands. Anyway, for a long time, I took this idea into the work I did as a designer, and it was absolutely paralyzing.

"You will inevitably bring games into this class that you aren't one-hundred-percent happy with, and that's okay. I want you to blow my mind. I want you to do great work, but I also just want you to work."

A student named Jojo, who was wearing a hole-filled Mapletown jersey, raised his hand. (*Jojo from Mapletown*—Sadie made a note.) "Nice shirt," Sadie said.

Jojo nodded, as if the wearing of the shirt had been a complete coincidence or something he'd been compelled to do by forces greater than himself. "I have a question: What did your classmates think of *Solution* back in the day?"

"Oh, I'm glad you asked that," Sadie said. "They hated it. One of them even tried to get me thrown out of school."

"For this?"

"Yeah, people don't like it when you call them Nazis. That's what my professor said, and it's probably good advice. I have never made another game where I called a player a Nazi."

The class laughed at Sadie's joke.

"On that note, it's four. I'll see you next week. Jojo, Rob, you're up first. Email your games to us no later than Sunday night, so we all have a chance to play them before next class."

Destiny hung around in the back until the others had left. "Is it okay? I wanted to ask you one more question, but not in front of everyone."

"Yes, of course," Sadie said. "Walk with me to my office. I've got to pick up my daughter from the sitter at five."

"You've got a kid?" Destiny said. "That's cool. I didn't think anyone in games had kids, because of the crunch hours."

"Some of that's changing a little," Sadie said. "And I've always owned the company, so . . ."

"So, like, all you have to do is own your own company?"

"Right. Then the men have to do what you want," Sadie said.

"Can I say? I'm so pumped that you're teaching this class? There still aren't that many women or people of color in the department. And I love *all* your games, not just *Ichigo*. I've played every single one. *Master of the Revels*? That game was my jam. I think you're completely brilliant."

They had reached Sadie's office, where the nameplate beside the door still said DOV MIZRAH. "So, this is me," Sadie said. "What was the question you didn't want to ask me in front of the class?"

"Oh, well, I didn't want to embarrass you," Destiny said. "When I was playing *Solution,* I definitely thought it was good."

"Yes?"

"But it's nowhere near as good as *Ichigo*. No offense. I seriously respect you so much, Professor Green."

"It's okay, I know it's true. And that's why I brought in the game. I wanted you to see what I was starting from."

"I guess the question I had was, how did you get from making something like *Solution* to making something like *Ichigo* not that much later? How do you get from *there* to *here?* That's what I don't know how to do."

"It's a long story." Sadie recognized the look in Destiny's eyes. She knew what it was to be ravenous with ambition but to have your reach exceed your grasp. "I'm not sure I have a simple answer," Sadie admitted. "May I think about it and get back to you?"

That night, Sadie tried to remember herself back in 1996. There were three things that had driven her, and none of them reflected a particular generosity of spirit on Sadie's part: (1) wanting to distinguish herself enough professionally so that everyone at MIT would know that Sadie Green had not been admitted to the college on a girl curve, (2) wanting Dov to know that he shouldn't have dumped her, and (3) wanting Sam to know that he was *lucky* to be working with her, that she was the *great* programmer in their team, that she was the one with the big ideas. But how to explain this to Destiny? How to explain to Destiny that the thing that made her work leap forward in 1996 was that she had been a dervish of selfishness, resentment, and insecurity? Sadie had willed herself to be great: art doesn't typically get made by happy people.

Sadie wanted to pose Destiny's question to Sam. He always had an answer for everything, and Sadie had come to see that one of Sam's gifts was his ability to cast the world—or at least her—in a more generous, flattering light. It was not the first time she had contemplated contacting him. Since she'd been back in Cambridge, every cobblestone reminded her of Sam and of Marx. But somehow, it felt impossible that a relationship as freighted as theirs could be resumed by simply picking up a phone. She knew he was alive. She often saw his name on group emails from Business Affairs at Unfair, but she had not directly communicated with him since *Pioneers.*

When she had downloaded *Pioneers,* she didn't notice anything about who had made it or have specific expectations for what the game would be. She had been postpartum, fuzzy brained, depressed, and alone, and she had turned to games for comfort, in the same way people turn to food. She favored casual games, the kind of thing that could be played while she was distracted with the business of keeping herself and a brand-new, insatiable creature alive. She had played a resource game about the Old West, a game about growing a tribe of villagers on an island, several games about waiting tables, a game about running a hotel, a game about magical flowers, a game about amusement parks, and then at last, Sadie had turned to *Pioneers*.

The degree of her investment in *Pioneers* had immediately been greater than her investment in those other games. The world, from the beginning, had seemed comfortable and familiar, but of course it had: *Pioneers* had been built using her own engine. If the players had seemed unusually clever, she attributed that to *Pioneers* attracting people like herself, people in their thirties with a nostalgia for the games of the 1980s.

On the day she found Daedalus blowing the glass heart, she had suspected Sam, but she had also allowed herself *not* to know. She wanted to play more than she wanted to know. Sadie told Sam he had tricked her, but the truth was, she had tricked herself. It was embarrassing how much that silly, exquisite world had meant to her.

A year and a half later, she could tell the story to Dov as an amusing brunch anecdote, and she realized she wasn't angry at Sam anymore. She began to feel a tenderness toward Sam and even an empathy for him. He had built that game for her, but he must have built it for himself as well. How alone he must have felt after Marx's death. How much of the business of running Unfair had she dropped in Sam's lap? Sadie had never gone back to that office, and she had never thanked Sam either.

A few weeks into the spring semester, she had been in the basement of the Harvard Book Store, where the used books were kept. She was shopping for used picture books for her daughter when she spotted a mis-shelved copy of a Magic Eye book. The book made her think of Sam in the train station, all those years ago. Even though it wasn't a picture book per se, Sadie decided to get the book for Naomi, who was four.

Sadie and Naomi read the Magic Eye book together at bedtime. "I can see it!" Naomi said.

"What do you see?"

"A bird. It's right there. It's all around me. It's amazing! Can we do another one? I think this might be my favorite book, Mom."

Two weeks later, Naomi had done the twenty-nine Magic Eye activities in the book multiple times, and she was ready for the next challenge.

Sadie decided to send the book to Sam. She was going to write a note, but then she changed her mind. He would know who it was from.

·.·

When Ant was passing through Boston, Sadie invited him to come speak to her class. *Counterpart High* was on its seventh installment, and most of her students were obsessed with it—for their generation, it was the Harry Potter of games. It was far more popular than *Ichigo,* and differently popular than *Mapleworld.* It was the kind of entertainment that evoked youth itself for the person who could remember playing it.

After class, she took Ant to dinner, and they gossiped about people they knew in the gaming industry: Who was embroiled in a sexual harassment scandal? Who was in rehab *again*? What company was on the verge of bankruptcy? What game's sequel completely sucked, and had clearly been outsourced to a disinterested team of programmers in a foreign land?

They had stealthily avoided subjects that were too personal or fraught. But over dessert, Sadie asked, "How's Sam doing?" It had been two or three weeks since she'd sent the Magic Eye book, and she hadn't heard back from him.

"The same, I guess. He's shutting down *Pioneers* at the end of the year."

"Poor *Pioneers.*"

"I'm not sure why Sam wanted to make that game. It was top secret at the company, at the time. Did you ever play it? It was this weird retro thing."

"Never played it," Sadie lied.

"Mayor Mazer stepped down from *Mapleworld,* too. Sam is holding a general election for his replacement."

"That's clever."

"I feel like whoever wins, the position will be largely honorary. Sam's working on some AR idea, I'm not sure what it is. His father died last week."

"George the agent?" As far as Sadie knew, Sam never saw him.

"No," Ant said. "The K-town pizza guy."

"No! Not Dong Hyun. That's his grandfather."

"Yes, I think the grandfather had cancer. I know he'd been sick

380

for a while. Sam's been gone from work a lot. Funny, I always thought that was his dad."

Sadie and Ant parted in front of the restaurant. Ant embraced her, and before they parted, he said, "I think of Marx every day."

"I do, too."

"No one believed in us as much as Marx did. We were college kids until he thought we had a game."

"So were we," Sadie said.

"I wish I could have saved him," Ant said. "I replay that day over and over again. If I hadn't gone down the stairs. If I hadn't let him go into the lobby. If—"

Sadie stopped him. "That's the gamer in you, trying to figure out how you might have beat the level. My brain is treacherous like that, too. But there was nothing you could have done, Ant. The game wasn't winnable."

After five years, she could finally hear Marx's name and not feel like weeping.

She had once read in a book about consciousness that over the years, the human brain makes an AI version of your loved ones. The brain collects data, and within your brain, you host a virtual version of that person. Upon the person's death, your brain still believes the virtual person exists, because, in a sense, the person still does. After a while, though, the memory fades, and each year, you are left with an increasingly diminished version of the AI you had made when the person was alive.

She could feel herself forgetting all the details of Marx—the sound of his voice, the feeling of his fingers and the way they gestured, his precise temperature, his scent on clothing, the way he looked walking away, or running up a flight of stairs. Eventually, Sadie imagined that Marx would be reduced to a single image: just a man standing under a distant torii gate, holding his hat in his hands, waiting for her.

Sadie got home from dinner around eleven-thirty. She paid the sitter and put her in a cab. Naomi was already in bed, but Sadie still went to look at her, sleeping. Sadie loved watching Naomi sleep.

Sadie was not a natural mother, though this was not a confession one was allowed to make. She craved solitude and personal space too much. But she loved this girl nonetheless. She was trying hard not to romanticize her daughter's personality. She didn't want to ascribe characteristics to her that were not truly hers. A good game designer knows that clinging to a few early ideas about a project can cut off the potential for the work. Sadie did not feel that Naomi was altogether a person yet, which was another thing that one could not admit. So many of the mothers she knew said that their children were exactly themselves from the moment they appeared in the world. But Sadie disagreed. What person was a person without language? Tastes? Preferences? Experiences? And on the other side of childhood, what grown-up wanted to believe that they had emerged from their parents fully formed? Sadie knew that she herself had not become a person until recently. It was unreasonable to expect a child to emerge whole cloth. Naomi was a pencil sketch of a person who, at some point, would be a fully 3D character.

Sadie had trained herself not to look for Marx in Naomi's face. Sometimes, unexpectedly, she saw Sam's there. Naomi was half-Asian and half–Eastern European Jewish, so Naomi was closer in background to Sam than she was to Sadie or to Marx.

Sadie closed Naomi's bedroom door, and she walked into her own bedroom.

She decided to call Sam. It was only 8:30 p.m. in California. His phone number hadn't changed. He didn't pick up—no one answered their phone anymore—and so she left a message. "It's me," she said. "Sadie," she added, in case he didn't know who "me" was. "I was having dinner with Ant here in Boston. I don't know if you've heard, but I live here now. Anyway, I was sorry to hear about Dong Hyun. I know how much he loved you. He was the nicest, gentlest man in the world."

She did not hear back from Sam.

A day or two later, she called the pizza place to find out if there were plans for a memorial for Dong Hyun. The young man who answered the phone told her that there was a service this weekend. He didn't bother to ask who Sadie was; Dong Hyun was friends with everyone in K-town.

3

The best you can wish for anyone, Sam decided, is a video game death. Which is to say, spectacular and brief.

When he put his final quarter in the machine, Dong Hyun had

been sick for nearly a year. Cancer—at first in the lung and then, fatally, elsewhere, everywhere—had reduced Sam's strong, marvelous grandfather to a helpless lump of misfiring cells. Sam had decided to step back from Unfair during that time to take care of Dong Hyun. How could he not? Dong Hyun had spent years taking care of him.

Sam watched as Dong Hyun suffered, as parts of him were cut away. And finally, when there wasn't anything left to take, Dong Hyun was gone.

Sam went back and forth. The fact that Dong Hyun had not died a video game death meant that Sam had been able to spend time with him before the end. The length of time it had taken Dong Hyun to die also meant he had said everything he wanted to say to Sam, his cousins, and his grandmother. Was this trade worth his suffering? Sam didn't know.

In the last weeks of his life, Dong Hyun barely spoke. He had grown quieter and quieter, and so Sam was surprised when Dong Hyun sat up in bed and grabbed Sam's hand. "Samson, you are a lucky boy," Dong Hyun said to Sam in a perfectly clear voice. "You have had tragedy, yes, but you have had many good friends as well."

Dong Hyun had been released from the hospital to die at home in the sunny Craftsman-style house that he had lived in for the last forty years of his life. It was disturbing to Sam that Dong Hyun's familiar pizza smell had been replaced by a variety of unpleasant medical ones.

"Have I?"

"Yes, Marx and Sadie. They loved you."

"Is two considered many?" Sam asked.

"It depends on how good the friendships are," Dong Hyun said. "And Lola? What happened to her?"

"She got married. She lives in Toronto." Sam paused. "I wish I had what you and Grandma have."

"You have different things," Dong Hyun said. "You were born into a different world than I was. Maybe you don't need what Grandma and I have." He patted Sam on the cheek. Dong Hyun began to cough one of his endless coughs.

"Marx is dead," Sam said.

"I know that," Dong Hyun said. "My mind is still good."

"Marx is dead, and Sadie has a kid now, and I don't know the kid."

"You could get to know the kid," Dong Hyun said.

"My point is, it's hard once people have kids. I don't understand kids really."

"You make games for a living," Dong Hyun pointed out. "You must know something about kids."

"Yes, but that's different. I think I don't like children because I hated being young."

"You're still young," Dong Hyun said.

"Well, she lives in Boston now," Sam said. "So . . ."

"You could visit her."

"I don't think she wants me to visit her."

"It doesn't take long to get to Boston anymore," Dong Hyun said.

"It takes about six hours by plane. Same amount of time as it's always taken."

"Faster than getting from Venice to Echo Park in traffic," Dong Hyun said.

"That's not true."

"I'm making a classic L.A. traffic joke."

"Oh, right."

"It was a good joke," Dong Hyun insisted.

"Nothing seems that funny to me lately."

"Are you kidding?" Dong Hyun laughed and that turned into another fit of coughing. "Everything is funny now." Dong Hyun closed his eyes. "When you talk to Sadie, tell her there's pizza for her. Friends of Sam's eat free."

"I'll tell her," Sam said. The pizza parlor had been renamed two years ago and had entirely new owners.

"Love you, Sammy," Dong Hyun said.

"I love you, too, Grandpa." For most of his life, Sam had found it difficult to say I love you. It was superior, he believed, to show love to those one loved. But now, it seemed like one of the easiest things in the world Sam could do. Why wouldn't you tell someone you loved them? Once you loved someone, you repeated it until they were tired of hearing it. You said it until it ceased to have meaning. Why not? Of course, you goddamn did.

The memorial was held at the Korean Cultural Center, and in addition to Dong Hyun's family and friends, many of his fellow shopkeepers and restaurateurs were in attendance. Sam and his grandmother spent hours being thanked and consoled.

As the afternoon went on, Sam softened his vision, allowing himself to be there and not there. It was a trick he'd had from the long convalescences of his youth. He could be in his body and not in his body. He looked at people, and he muttered thanks for coming ad nauseam, and without appearing to be, he gazed into the distance, as if the back wall of the KCC were a Magic Eye poster, in a train station.

At once, his eyes fixed on something. In a world of planar surfaces, someone became 3D. It was Sadie.

He had not seen her for almost five years, and the sight of her, in the flesh, seemed like an illusion.

She had called him two or three days ago, but he hadn't thought she would come.

She waved at him.

He waved at her.

She said something, but he was too far away to hear it.

He nodded as if he'd understood.

She left.

Two weeks later, Dong Hyun's will was read. As was to be expected, most everything passed to Bong Cha. There was one notable exception: "My *Donkey Kong* machine, which was in my pizza parlor for many years, I leave to Sadie Green. With much affection and gratitude for the years of friendship between my grandson and herself."

Sam had not called her number for many years. He did not get her immediately, but in the evening, she returned his call. He thanked her for coming to the funeral. "But that's not why I'm calling. Dong Hyun left you something in his will."

"Really? What is it?"

"It's the *Donkey Kong* machine."

"What?" Sadie's voice could not help but exude childish enthusiasm. "I love *Donkey Kong*! I was so jealous of you when you told me you could play as much as you want. Why would he do that do you think?"

"Well," Sam said. "You know, he was proud of us. Proud of our games. He always kept the posters in Dong and Bong's.

"And you were—well, just about my only friend for a significant portion of my childhood, as I'm sure you were aware ... so ... I think he probably thought I would have, like, given up without you, or something. Maybe I would have, I don't know. He was grateful to you."

Sadie considered this. "No, I can't accept this. You should have the machine."

"Why would I want it? You're the one who loves *Donkey Kong*. Just tell me what you want me to do with it. We can leave it in my grandmother's house, if you don't want it. I think it probably weighs a ton, literally."

"I'll get it shipped," Sadie said. "I definitely want it. It's a classic. Give me a couple of days to figure it out. I'm probably going to put it in my office at MIT."

"Dong Hyun would have loved his machine ending up at one of the best schools in the country."

"How are you?" Sadie said.

"I've been better. I've decided ... I prefer video game death, all things considered."

"Short, sweet, with the possibility of imminent resurrection," Sadie said.

"Video game characters never die."

"They die all the time, actually. It doesn't mean the same thing."

"What are you working on?" Sam asked.

"Raising a kid, teaching my class. That's about it."

"Are you harassing your students like Dov?"

"No," Sadie said. "I honestly can't imagine wanting to sleep with anyone in their twenties, forget about their teens. I always feel like I should add, Dov was a great teacher. I don't know what my impulse to defend him is."

"Do you like teaching?"

"I do," she said. "A kid wore a Mapletown jersey the first day."

"How'd that make you feel?"

"You mean, because *Mapleworld* was the phoenix that rose from the ashes of my failure?"

"Something like that," Sam said.

"The kid didn't know. It was a compliment. They think *Mapleworld* is my game."

386

"It *was* your game, wasn't it?"

"More yours," Sadie said. "I think that's been established. Considering my many concerns about credit, it turns out that no one remembers who's responsible for anything."

"Someone on the internet probably knows the truth," Sam said.

"Wow, that is amazingly naive," Sadie said. "The belief that someone on the internet knows the truth about anything."

"I've been blue, lately," Sam admitted. "And I wondered, how do you get over that sort of thing?"

"Work helps," Sadie said. "Games help. But sometimes, when I'm really low, I keep a particular image in my mind."

"What is it?"

"I imagine people playing. Sometimes, it's one of our games, but sometimes, it's *any* game. The thing I find profoundly hopeful when I'm feeling despair is to imagine people playing, to believe that no matter how bad the world gets, there will always be players."

As Sadie spoke, Sam was reminded of a winter afternoon, many years ago, and of commuters clogging up the train station, blocking his path. At the time, they'd seemed like impediments to him, but maybe he'd been thinking of them the wrong way. What makes a person want to shiver in a train station for nothing more than the promise of a secret image? But then, what makes a person drive down an unmarked road in the middle of the night? Maybe it was the willingness to play that hinted at a tender, eternally newborn part in all humans. Maybe it was the willingness to play that kept one from despair.

"I received the Magic Eye book, by the way," Sam said.

"So . . . ? Did you do it?"

"No."

"Come on, Sam. What the hell? You have to do it. Go get the book."

Sam walked over to his bookshelf, and he took the book off the shelf.

"I'm going to stay with you on the phone until you see it. My five-year-old can do it. I'll take you through it."

"It's not going to work."

"Hold the book up to your face," Sadie instructed. "Right against your nose."

"Okay, okay."

"Now let your eyes go soft focused, and slowly pull the book back," Sadie said.

"It didn't work," Sam said.

"Do it again," Sadie commanded.

"Sadie, these don't work for me."

"You have so many *ideas* about what works for you. Just do it again."

Sam tried again, and Sadie listened to Sam breathe.

"Sam?" Nearly a minute had passed.

"I can see it," Sam said. "It's a bird." His voice sounded shaky, but Sadie couldn't tell if he was crying.

"Good," Sadie said. "It *is* a bird."

"What now?"

"You look at the next one."

Sadie heard the rustle of a page being turned.

"We should make something together," Sam said.

"Oh God, Sam, why would we do that? We make each other miserable."

"That isn't true. Not always."

"It's not just you. It's me. And it's Marx. And too much has happened, I think. I'm not even sure I'm a designer anymore."

"Sadie, that's about the stupidest thing I've ever heard."

"Thanks."

"And there's no way it's true. Well, I had to ask. I always have to ask. Let me know if you change your mind."

Naomi came into Sadie's bedroom. "It's bedtime!" she announced. Sadie had invented a game where if Naomi called bedtime before Sadie did for seven nights in a row, Naomi received a prize. Yes, it was manipulative and basically bribery, but it was also effective at getting her five-year-old to bed. "Who are you talking to?" Naomi asked.

"My friend, Sam. Do you want to say hi to him?"

"No," Naomi said. "I don't know him."

"Okay, run along to your room, and I'll be there in a second." Sadie returned to Sam. "I've got to put my kid to bed. Good night, Dr. Daedalus."

"Good night, Ms. Marks."

∴

A *Donkey Kong* cabinet weighs approximately three hundred pounds. The crate, which will have to be specially built, an additional fifty. Freight shipping from a residence in 90026 to a university office in 02139 will run you about $400, or a little more if you want someone to carry the machine over a threshold.

Locally, you might find a classic *Donkey Kong* for cheaper. This will save you significantly in shipping, but the machine won't have the same memory. It will not know, for instance, that the best *Donkey Kong* player who ever played at Dong and Bong's New York Style House of Pizza on Wilshire Boulevard in K-town, Los Angeles, had the initials S.A.M.

When the cabinet arrived in Cambridge, the machine was still functioning, but the high scores were wiped. Memory on those early machines could be volatile, even when they were supposedly non-volatile. The backup battery, if it ever had one, probably died long ago.

When Dong Hyun's machine loaded the now empty high scores screen, Sadie could still faintly see S.A.M. The score had stood so long, it had burned into the monitor.

4

Not quite a year after Dong Hyun's death, ReveJeux, a New York–and Paris-based gaming company, approached Sam and Sadie about the possibility of making a third *Ichigo*. ReveJeux had several big hits, most famously *The Samurai's Code*, a stealth and parkour-style game about a non-gendered team of Samurai. Sadie and Sam both had admired this game, and so they decided to fly to New York to take the meeting.

The group from ReveJeux was young, as people in gaming tended to be, and, in Sadie's estimation, Sam and herself were the oldest people in the room by at least five years. How quickly you go from being the youngest to the oldest person in a room, she thought.

ReveJeux were self-described "huge fans" of *Ichigo,* and they wanted to preserve the style and emotion of the original game while using the technical firepower of today. Marie, an earnest French-woman who appeared to be seconds out of college, was the team's leader. She spoke of *Ichigo* with rising emotion in her voice. "I want you to know: *Ichigo* is the game of my heart. But ever since I played *Ichigo* as a young teenager, I have always felt that the story of Ichigo is incomplete," Marie said. "More than anything, I want to see Ichigo grow up."

In Marie's proposal for the third *Ichigo*, Ichigo is now a salaryman, the Japanese version of a suit who takes the train and works a nine-to-five job. Ichigo has a wife and a young daughter. When the daughter goes missing, Ichigo must shed his salaryman skin to go find her. He must once again don his number 15 jersey to set off on another adventure. The game's narrative would be split between Ichigo and Ichigo's daughter. Marie saw Ichigo as a Peter Pan character, and she wanted to make the story as emotional and immersive as *Uncharted* or *Journey*.

"I must know," she said. "Why have you never made a third *Ichigo*? The game is so brilliant. And you both are so brilliant."

Marie's colleague, a man in aquamarine glasses, answered for them. "I imagine they have been busy doing other things," the man said to Marie. On a second look, Sadie decided the man in the glasses might have been her and Sam's age after all.

If they agreed to let ReveJeux proceed with a sequel to *Ichigo*, Sadie and Sam would be involved as executive producers, and the game would be a coproduction of the two companies. Sadie and Sam would consult, but the work would largely be done by the team at ReveJeux.

At the end of the meeting, Marie gave them a zip drive with a sample level of the third *Ichigo* that her team had put together. "It isn't finished," Marie warned. "I need you to know, if you give me the honor of letting me make a new *Ichigo*, I will treat it like it is my child."

On the cab ride back to the hotel, Sam asked her, "So, what do you think? Do you want to let them have it?"

"I don't know," Sadie said. "They're a great company. I liked Marie, and I liked what she was saying, and Ichigo will be sixteen next year. I know people routinely license old IP. Still, it's strange to think of someone else making our game."

"It is strange," Sam agreed.

"But I'm circumspect about it. It could be great. If they make a third game, we could take the opportunity to update and re-release the old *Ichigo*s, bring them to a new audience."

Sam nodded.

"I'm starving. Let's get food and think about it," Sadie said.

They had not spent any time together for years, and at first, the conversation was as stilted as at any business dinner. There were long pauses, as Sam or Sadie tried to figure out the next thing they might discuss.

"I heard you're making interactive fiction, or something?" Sam said.

"Oh yeah," Sadie said. "I'm dabbling in that. I ran into one of my classmates from Dov's seminar, and she was trying to make visual novel games work for the U.S. market and asked me if I wanted to consult. So, I thought, why not? It's all made very quickly, and you don't have time to think, and that's good for me right now. And you?"

"I've been trying to do something in AR. It's hard to make AR work, but someone's eventually going to do it, and then people won't want to play anything else."

"I disagree," Sadie said. "People play games for the characters, not for the tech. Have you been playing anything great?"

"*Bioshock 2*," Sam said. "Great world building. Visuals, fine, that Unreal style. *Heavy Rain* does amazing things with point of view. *Braid* is brilliant. I was jealous the whole time I was playing. I kept wishing we'd made it. Have you played it yet?"

"I'm planning on it, but I don't have as much time to play since I had a kid," she said. "Naomi loves the Wii. Especially the sports games. So we play some of that."

"Do you have a picture?"

Sadie took out her phone. Sam nodded at the screen.

"She looks like Marx," Sam said. "And you."

"I took her to my seminar, and the kids in the class said she looked like Ichigo."

"They used to say that about me, too," Sam said.

"I remember. It used to piss me off."

"But now I'm old."

"You're not that old."

"Thirty-seven," Sam said. "Older than anyone at ReveJeux."

"I thought the same thing," Sadie said. "About myself, I mean."

They were walking back to the elevator when Sam said, "It's not late yet. We could play the sample level of *Ichigo III* together."

"Do you think we should?"

"I think we *have* to play it. We owe it to Ichigo."

Sadie and Sam went up to Sam's room. Sam set up the game on his laptop, and they played the level together, companionably passing the computer back and forth, as they had done when Sam was twelve and Sadie was eleven.

They finished the first level, which ended with a crowd scene that included digital avatars of the ReveJeux team and Sam and Sadie.

Sam closed the laptop. "The visuals are tight, considering how unfinished they are. The sound is tight." Sam shrugged. "These people aren't messing around. I think it's probably good. I can't complain. What do you think?"

"The same." Sadie paused. "I was a little bored, though. But I know that's unfair to say. They're not done yet, and maybe we're not the audience for it?"

"You're probably right." Sam turned to face Sadie. "You know what I keep thinking? I keep thinking how easy it was to make that first *Ichigo*. We were like machines then—this, this, this, this. It's so easy to make a hit when you're young and you don't know anything."

"I think that, too," Sadie said. "The knowledge and experience we have—it isn't necessarily that helpful, in a way."

"So depressing," Sam said, laughing. "What's all of this struggle been *for*?"

"There must be some other versions of us that don't make games."

"What do they do instead?"

"They're friends. They have a life!" Sadie said.

Sam nodded. "Oh, right. I've heard of those. They're those things where you sleep regular hours and you don't spend every waking moment tormented by some imaginary world."

Sadie walked over to the minibar and she poured herself a glass of water. Seeing her back, Sam thought there was no echt Sadie in this view in the way a gamer always knew Lara Croft from her braid.

"Maybe I should try that?" Sam said. "Having a life."

"I have a life now," Sadie said. "It's not so great. Do you want a glass of water?"

Sam nodded. "May I ask you something that I've often wondered about?"

"Oh God, this sounds serious."

"Why do you think we never got together?"

Sadie sat next to Sam on the bed. "Sammy," she said. "We *were* together. You must know that. When I'm honest with myself, the most important parts of me were yours."

"But *together* together? The way you were with Marx or Dov."

"How can you not know this? Lovers are . . . common." She studied Sam's face. "Because I loved working with you better than I liked the idea of making love to you. Because true collaborators in this life are rare."

Sam looked at his hands and at the callus years of gaming had left on his right index finger. "I thought it was because I was poor. And then, when I wasn't poor, I thought it was because you weren't attracted to me, because I was half-Asian and because of my disability."

"How awful do you think I am? Those were your things, not mine."

"Yes, they probably were."

"I'm still not tired," Sadie said. "Probably the excitement of being sans enfant. Do you want to go take a walk?"

"I do," Sam said.

Their hotel was in Columbus Circle, and they walked uptown, toward the Upper West Side. It was the end of March, and it was still cold, though one could feel the possibility of springtime.

"I used to live here with my mom," Sam said.

"That was before I knew you."

Sam nodded. "Yes, if you can believe there was a time when we didn't know each other. It doesn't seem possible to me. Did I ever tell you why my mom left New York?"

"I don't think so."

"A woman jumped from a building, and landed, splat, at our feet."

"Did she die?"

"She did. My mom tried to pretend that she didn't, but it was too late. I had nightmares about this woman for a decade."

"You never told me that story. I thought I knew all your stories."

"Not all of them," Sam said. "I hid so many things from you."

"Why?"

"Because I wanted to seem a certain way to you, I guess."

"It's so funny you should say this, because if you were one of my students, you'd be wearing your pain like a badge of honor. This generation doesn't hide anything from anyone. My class talks a lot about their *traumas*. And how their *traumas* inform their games. They, honest to God, think their traumas are the most interesting thing about them. I sound like I'm making fun, and I am a little, but I don't mean to be. They're so different from us, really. Their standards are higher; they call bullshit on so much of the sexism and racism that I, at least, just lived with. But that's also made them kind of, well, humorless. I hate people who talk about generational differences like it's an actual thing, and here I am, doing it. It doesn't make sense. How alike were you to anyone we grew up with, you know?"

"If their traumas are the most interesting things about them, how do they get over any of it?" Sam asked.

"I don't think they do. Or maybe they don't have to, I don't know." Sadie paused. "Since I've been teaching, I keep thinking about how lucky we were," she said. "We were lucky to be born when we were."

"How so?"

"Well, if we'd been born a little bit earlier, we wouldn't have been able to make our games so easily. Access to computers would have been harder. We would have been part of the generation who was putting floppy disks in Ziploc bags and driving the games to stores. And if we'd been born a little bit later, there would have been even greater access to the internet and certain tools, but honestly, the games got so much more complicated; the industry got so professional. We couldn't have done as much as we did on our own. We could never have made a game that we could sell to a company like Opus on the resources we had. We wouldn't have made *Ichigo* Japanese, because we would have worried about the fact that we weren't Japanese. And I think, because of the internet, we would have been overwhelmed by how many people were trying to do the exact same things we were. We had so much freedom—creatively, technically. No one was watching us, and we weren't even watching ourselves. What we had was our impossibly high standards, and your completely theoretical conviction that we could make a great game."

"Sadie, we would have made games no matter what era we'd been born in. Do you know how I know this?"

Sadie shook her head.

"Because Dr. Daedalus and Ms. Marks became game designers, too."

"They made checkerboards. It's not the same. And you knew who you were in *Pioneers*, so that doesn't count. You had your finger on the scale."

"You knew who you were as well."

"I did, and I didn't," Sadie said. "But I think there was some *trauma*—there's that word again—I was able to play out through that experience. I can't even explain it. Nothing was getting through to me, and I was so depressed, and I had a baby. And even Freda—God, I miss Freda—was fed up with me. She was like, 'Mine Sadie, bad things happen to everyone. Enough already.' But after *Pioneers*, I wasn't able to feel quite as terrible about things. The main thing it made me feel was not quite so alone. I don't think I've ever properly thanked you." Sadie looked at Sam's face. It was still as familiar as her own. "Thank you, my friend."

He put his arm over her shoulder. "I have a theory about why you confronted me after the 'fifth game' revelation. Do you want to hear it?"

"I suppose I'm about to."

"I think it was the stirrings of the designer in you, sensing the possibility for an elegant endgame. I wrote the beginning and the middle; you wrote the ending."

"This is a theory," Sadie said. "Do you need to turn around?"

"No, I'm good," Sam said. "Let's stay out a little longer."

They had made it up to Ninety-ninth Street and Amsterdam Avenue. Sam pointed up to a tenement building with exterior fire escapes. "This is where my mom and I used to live. Seventh floor. Back in 1984, it was a rough part of town, but now it doesn't look that bad to me."

"There aren't any rough parts of New York now."

Sadie looked up at the building. She imagined a child Sam, gazing out the window at her. He is perfect and unmarked, like her own daughter. But if Sam hadn't been as traumatized as Sadie now realized he had been, would he have pushed them so hard? Would Sadie have been the designer she became without Sam's ambitions for them? And would Sam have had those ambitions without the childhood trauma? She didn't know. The work had been hers, yes, but it had equally been his. It had been theirs, and it wouldn't have existed without the both of them. This was a tautology that had only taken her the better part of two decades to understand.

Since she'd started teaching and become a mother, she'd felt old, but that night, she realized she wasn't old at all. You couldn't be old and still be wrong about as many things as she'd been wrong about, and it was a kind of immaturity to call yourself old before you were.

She looked past the building to the sky. It was a deep, blue velvet night, and the moon hung heavy and supernaturally spherical in the sky. "I wonder who built this engine," Sadie said.

"It's good work," Sam said. "The God rays are nicely done, but the moon is almost too beautiful. The scale seems off."

"How is it so large and low? And it needs more texture. A bit of Perlin noise. It should look a little rougher, otherwise it doesn't seem real."

"But maybe that's the look they were going for?"

"Maybe so."

Sadie's flight back to Boston left an hour before Sam's flight to Los Angeles, but they had decided to share a cab to the airport. Since he had time to pass, he walked her to her gate. She seemed preoccupied to him, in the way that people are before a voyage, and though he had things he wanted to say to her, the manic energy of the airport did not lend itself to conversation. By the time they arrived at her gate, Sadie's boarding group was already being called.

"Well, this is me," she said.

"This is you," he said.

He watched as she joined the line, and it occurred to him that it might be years before he saw her again. "Sadie," he called, "I just want you to know. I think you should make more games. With or without me. You're too good at it to quit."

Sadie left the line, and she went back to where Sam stood.

"I haven't completely quit. I mean, for a long time I had. But I'm working some," she said. "There's no point in making something if you don't think it could be great."

"I agree. Still, I'd like to make a game with you again, if you ever find the time."

"Is that a good idea?"

"Probably not," Sam said, laughing. "But I want to do it anyway. I don't know how to stop myself from wanting to do it. Every time I run into you for the rest of our lives, I'll ask you to make a game with me. There's some groove in my brain that insists it *is* a good idea."

"Isn't that the definition of insanity? Doing the same thing over and over but expecting a different result."

"That's a game character's life, too," Sam said. "The world of infinite restarts. Start again at the beginning, this time you might win. And it's not as if all our results were bad. I love the things we made. We were a great team."

Sam offered Sadie his hand, and she shook it. She pulled him into her, and she kissed Sam on the cheek. "I love you, Sadie," Sam said.

"I know, Sam. I love you, too."

Sadie returned to the line. She was nearly to the front for the second time when she looked over her shoulder. "Sam," she said, "you still game, right?" Her voice was light, and her eyes were playful, and Sam recognized the invitation that was being extended, as clearly as if it were the title screen of a video game.

"Of course," Sam replied quickly and with too much enthusiasm. "You know I do."

She unzipped the outer pocket of her laptop bag, and she took out a small drive. She reached over the rope that separated them, and she placed the drive into his hands. "Have a look at this for me, if you have the time. I've barely started, and it's not good. Not yet, at least. Maybe you'll know what to do with it?"

Sadie closed her bag, and she handed her boarding pass to the gate agent.

"What's the best way to contact you?" Sam asked.

"Send me a text. Or an email. Or stop by my office, if you're ever in Cambridge. I keep office hours. Tuesdays and Fridays, from two to four."

"No problem," Sam said. "It's a quick six-hour flight from Los Angeles. Less time than it takes to get from Venice to Echo Park."

"If you come, I have a *Donkey Kong* machine in my office. Old friends play free."

Sam watched Sadie disappear into the connecting tunnel and then he looked down at the drive: the game was called *Ludo Sextus*. Sadie had handwritten the title. He would know her handwriting anywhere.

NOTES AND ACKNOWLEDGMENTS

There are no secret highways. None that I know of, at least. But if you find the right rideshare driver or go to a party with someone who has lived in L.A. a long time, you might hear a story about one.

Like Sam, I once lived in a house up a hill from the Happy Foot Sad Foot sign. The Happy Foot Sad Foot sign was taken down in 2019, but I am told you can still find its remains in a gift shop somewhere in Silver Lake. Across town, *Clownerina*, created by Jonathan Borofsky, was restored some years ago and now kicks for several hours a day, though I have not seen it in action.

The Necco Wafer Factory has not been in Cambridge for many years, but the water tower is still painted in pastels.

As far as I know, there was never a Christmas advertisement for Cheri Smith and Tom Baccei's Magic Eye series in Harvard Square's T station. On a related note, for many years I did not think Magic Eye illusions worked for me and now they do.

The book about consciousness that Sadie mentions when she is talking about the brain having an AI version of deceased loved ones is *I Am a Strange Loop*, by Doug Hofstadter, a source suggested to me by Hans Canosa.

The detail of Macbeth throwing dinner rolls at Banquo's empty chair comes from the Royal Shakespeare Company's 2018 production of *Macbeth*, directed by Polly Findlay and starring Christopher Eccleston in the title role.

The Tamer of Horses in Friendship recites from Alfred John Church's 1895 translation of *The Iliad*.

Although my parents both worked in computers and I am a lifelong gamer, these sources were particularly helpful to my thinking about and understanding of 1990s- and 2000s-era game culture and designers: *Blood, Sweat, and Pixels: The Triumphant, Turbulent Stories Behind How Video Games Are Made,* by Jason Schreier; *Masters of Doom: How Two Guys Created an Empire and Transformed Pop Culture,* by David Kushner; *Hackers: Heroes of the Computer Revolution* (specifically the section on Sierra On-Line), by Steven Levy; *A Mind Forever Voyaging: A History of Storytelling in Video Games,* by Dylan Holmes; *Extra Lives: Why Video Games Matter,* by Tom Bissell; *All Your Base Are Belong to Us: How Fifty Years of Video Games Conquered Pop Culture,* by Harold Goldberg; and the documentaries *Indie Game: The Movie,* directed by James Swirsky and Lisanne Pajot, and *GTFO,* directed by Shannon Sun-Higginson. I read *Indie Games* by Bounthavy Suvilay after I finished writing, and it's a beautiful book for those looking to see how artful games can be.

Despite its meme status, the phrase "You have died of dysentery" never appears in the 1985 version of *The Oregon Trail,* which is the one Sam and Sadie would have played and the one I played as a child. What they (and I) would have seen in the 1980s is "You have dysentery" and then, assuming they did not recover from dysentery, "You have died." This, and other facts about *The Oregon Trail,* can be found in *You Have Died of Dysentery: The Creation of the Oregon Trail—the Iconic Educational Game of the 1980s,* by R. Philip Bouchard, who was the lead designer for the 1985 version. I would also like to acknowledge the many games that inspired *Pioneers,* including *The Oregon Trail,* developed by Don Rawitsch, Bill Heinemann, and Paul Dillenberger; *Stardew Valley,* designed by Eric Barone; *Animal Crossing,* designed by Katsuya Eguchi, Hisashi Nogami, Shigeru Miyamoto, and Takashi Tesuka; *Harvest Moon,* designed by Yasuhiro Wada; *The Sims,* created by Will Wright; and *EverQuest,* designed by Brad McQuaid, John Smedley, Bill Trost, and Steve Clover. For the most part, I have credited the designers, but as readers of this book will know, it is difficult to say who is responsible for any game or game element unless you were there. What is certain: in my life, I have slaughtered more than a few virtual bison and rid much land of the scourge of pixelated rocks.

It is unlikely that Dov would have received a beta copy of *Metal Gear Solid* in January 1996, or that Sadie would have played *King's Quest IV: The Perils of Rosella* in August 1988. Throughout the book, I chose the games that made the most sense for the story, even when the dates were slightly wrong. *King's Quest IV,* for example, is one of the few prominent games of that era with a female protagonist and, not coincidentally, one of the first games I loved.

Tomorrow, and Tomorrow, and Tomorrow is a novel about work, and I would be remiss if I did not thank my colleagues, whose ideas, skills, questions, observations, provocations, encouragements, witticisms, letters, phone calls, Zooms, texts, PowerPoint presentations, and occasional course corrections have improved this book enormously. Thank you especially to my American editor, Jenny Jackson, and to my literary agent, Douglas Stewart. Thanks also to Stuart Gelwarg, Dana Spector, Becky Hardie, Lara Hinchberger, Bradley Garrett, Danielle Bukowski, Szilvia Molnar, Maria Bell, Caspian Dennis, Nicole Winstanley, Reagan Arthur, Maris Dyer, Louise Collazo, Nora Reichard, Katrina Northern, Emily Reardon, Julianne Clancy, Wyck Godfrey, Isaac Klausner, Avital Siegel, Bryan Oh, Daria Cercek, Ellie Walker, Kathy Pories, Tayari Jones, Rebecca Serle, and Jennifer Wolfe.

Tomorrow, and Tomorrow, and Tomorrow is equally about love. Thank you to Hans Canosa, my favorite human and person to play games with, even when he is a bad sport. I thank my parents every time, but why not? I have excellent ones. Their names are Richard and AeRan Zevin.

My books can be divided into dog eras. *Tomorrow, and Tomorrow, and Tomorrow* was begun in the era of Edie and Frank and completed in the era of Leia and Frank. Good dogs, all.

Gabrielle Zevin is the *New York Times* and internationally best-selling author of several critically acclaimed novels, including *The Storied Life of A. J. Fikry*, which won the Southern California Independent Booksellers Award and the Japan Booksellers' Award, among other honors, and *Young Jane Young*, which won the Southern Book Prize. The film version of *The Storied Life of A. J. Fikry*, for which Zevin wrote the adaptation, will be released at the end of 2022. Her novels have been translated into thirty-nine languages. She has also written books for young readers, including the award-winning *Elsewhere*. She lives in Los Angeles.

A NOTE ON THE TYPE

This book was set in a modern adaptation of a type designed by the first William Caslon (1692–1766). The Caslon face, an artistic, easily read type, has enjoyed more than two centuries of popularity in our own country. It is of interest to note that the first copies of the Declaration of Independence and the first paper currency distributed to the citizens of the newborn nation were printed in this typeface.

Composed by North Market Street Graphics,
Lancaster, Pennsylvania

Printed and bound by Berryville Graphics

Designed by Soonyoung Kwon